Saga of the
Dead Men Walking

Insanity's Reckoning
Book III of the Auramancer's Exorcism

Joshua E. B. Smith

DEDICATION

Three down, one to go.

As I write this, at this stage in my career, I have developed a small but absolutely ferocious fan-base. They (you!) are wonderful people. Amazing people. Kind people.

You've taken time out of your life to read, edit,
pick apart, share, fund, comment, or buy extra for your friends.

I know many authors that are vastly better at writing than I am, vastly better at marketing, and vastly better at the business as a whole.

But I know few that have fans like I do.

I do this because of you.
You are a very large part of what keeps me going.

Thank you.

Now let's kill some people.
(And there's a lot of people to kill.)

~Josh

CONTENTS

ACKNOWLEDGMENTS

The concept of an 'acknowledgment' page confuses me sometimes. I'm not going to lie about that. Most of the time, it's the part of the book I skip over because I want to read what I bought the book to read, which (probably) isn't the author giving a shout-out to his mom. But…

Hi mom! I love you!

It's also really, really hard to write. I'm much happier – and I have a much easier time – writing the murder/torture you'll see later in this book than I do this page. I almost skipped writing it this time. Maybe it's just me. Maybe not. I don't know. I don't have a problem filling my Facebook page with the stuff that's supposed to fit here. So why is it so hard to do when I write a novel?

I guess the ultimate thing is that there are so many people who go into helping me prepare a book – my ARC readers, my editor, my technical readers, my random_internet_experts_01, my ad school people, webinar hosts, virtual conventions, and so on that it's impossible to sit down and go, "Here's a list!" even though they all really deserve it.

At a certain point, it starts reading like a Marvel end-credits scene.

I wrote the first draft of Reckoning over the course of two and a half months. If I owe a debt of thanks to anyone, it's Craig Martel in the 20booksto50k Facebook group. Craig doesn't know me, will likely never see this, but he put on a contest at the start of the year that looked for authors who wanted to win some gnarly prizes, but he had some terms and conditions.

I didn't win, and I didn't meet the terms – one of which was to hit a certain daily word count.

Losing the first round did inspire me to write more, work harder, and push myself faster. Because of that, you get Reckoning a lot sooner than I had anticipated. Requiem a lot faster than that.

I sincerely do hope you enjoy. Because I absolutely did.

PROLOGUE

I suppose, in hindsight, disaster was a given.
Hindsight, of course, gives suggestion
that any sight was had at all.
How can I say that there was?

Basion City had grown complacent.
Who would dare strike the Kingdom
in a city that was neigh-on impenetrable?

Port Cableture had grown complacent.
What man would strike at the seat
of the Navy's second-largest fleet?

Lady Ridora Medias had grown complacent.
Who would seek to harass the mad,
when they are bereft of use even unto themselves?

Maiden-Templar Prostil had grown complacent.
Who would dare raid the vaults
when none knew the secrets buried within?

It was the dead.

The dead care not for walls.
Not for fleets. Not for the mad.
Not for secrets.

No living man would dare.

It took a man destined to die, and die, and die again,
to see how the damned would rise.

Sir Steelhom
Office of Oversight
New Civa

The Month of Deepfrost, 512 QR

The Q. R. W. *Hullbreaker*. A *legata* class cruiser, she had a crew component of forty-two men, eight less than the maximum of a ship her size. Used mostly for shuttling small military envoys or for hunting smaller pirate ships off the coast, they had a reputation for being the backbone of the Queen's Navy. Today, however, the *Hullbreaker* was accomplishing none of those typical tasks – and of the crew? Half of them were laying below-deck with fevers, chills, and worse.

"Captain, we *have* to go ashore," the quartermaster argued for the third time in the last hour, "and we have to do it now. We can get word to one of the temples as soon as we land or to a garrison or *something*. This isn't the typical sea-rot!"

Captain Taes, for what it's worth, didn't disagree. In what may have been a first time in his forty-year life, he didn't have a sneer on his face a cocky comeback on his lips. What he had were orders and a horrible feeling in his stomach. "We can't," he lamented between coughing spasms. "Our orders are to -"

"Our orders don't make sense," the gray-haired officer snapped back. "When we left port, you said they were for us to haul a shipment of sylverine to the capital for inspection. Then when we got underway, I looked. They loaded us with *coal*."

"I told you -"

"Respectfully, I don't *care* what you told me, Captain. What *exactly* are we doing out in the middle of the Alenic? We are *days* away from the coastline *at best* and right now we aren't at our best!"

Captain Taes turned away from the window in his cabin and wiped his sweaty face dry. "One month, that was our orders. Stay out, one month, and then head to the capital."

"But *why*?"

The captain sagged against the wall. "Queen's Intelligence. Said that they had heard whispers of a Civan spy," he answered with a tired wheeze. "Wanted to have a big shipment of sylverine get hijacked; embarrass the Crown."

"So, bait we are? Adrift on the high seas, waiting for an attack? And you didn't see fit to let us know?" the other man accused.

"My orders were to sail us out at a distance and keep my mouth shut. From Gonta to the Island Port of Bonchin, then straight to the Naval Yard at the Capital. The hope," he said before he was interrupted with another hacking cough, "was to get them on us. We've got some boys at Bonchin that are... were... gonna go back the way we came. The *Queen's Cut*. You know her. That big *Crownship* behemoth. Put the privateers the Civ's hired... put them down. Sink 'em."

"But why not tell the crew?"

"Her Majesty's agent warned that there may be a defector on board who might signal them away if they knew the truth."

The older sailor narrowed his eyes and drummed his fingers on the doorframe. "This have anything to do with the *Orboria* getting sunk in Gonta?"

"Don't know, Kespin." Taes admitted, "but there... was a warning right before we left."

"The battlemage that you had thrown off the deck? One of the midshipmen said he was spouting something crazy."

Taes nodded. "Said that someone planned on poisoning the crew. That's why I had you throw the provisions off; why we stopped at Oldek for fresh. Against orders, but felt the safest."

Kespin pursed his lips and looked at the flagon sitting proudly on the captain's table. "Except for your personal stores."

"It was a gift. I know the man that gave it to me. He courted my daughter once."

"And you've been letting the crew rot since," the quartermaster accused. "Why not say something? Why are we still out here?"

"Couldn't know if it was part of the plan."

The quartermaster clenched his fists. "You mean you planned to sacrifice the men. There's hardly a soul on this ship able to fight! We'd be dead."

Wordlessly, the captain picked up the flagon from his table and slowly poured the contents onto his desk. What should've been ale – what Kespin *expected* to be ale – landed on the wood with a disgusting plop. The gelatinous substance quivered and emitted a foul smell that hit the quartermaster like a punch to the gut. "We've no choice."

"For the Grace of Melia," Kespin choked out as he covered his mouth with his hand, "what kind of abomination is that?"

"The kind we can't take ashore, and the kind that my rations have reduced themselves to," the captain answered with a tired sigh. "Let the Civans come and take us. I will not compound the curse on the souls of our men by allowing them to spread this to the Queen's people."

"Captain, I insist. We can get to Alrediah in less than a week of -" Taes shook his head and silently pulled his tunic up. The words died in the quartermaster's throat as he stared, aghast, at his captain's chest. "Goddess..."

Taes pulled his shirt back down and looked at the rotten oily mass on his table. "That mage? Claimed that it was demon blood and corpse ash. I should've listened. Should've thrown it all off. Shouldn't have trusted that bastard Ralafon."

The silvery-haired sailor turned and looked out the cabin door at the remaining crewmen still standing on the deck and watched as one fell to his knees, clutching at his chest. Two men rushed over to help him; the rest made holy gestures in the air and moved as far away as they could. "But why didn't you take us back to port when it first started...? I'm no priest, but captain, surely...?"

"Was only a day after this started," Taes said as he waved at his stomach, "that Deltin was sick. And before night, three more."

"You thought it was too late. What did you think would happen? That it would pass?"

"Was my prayer," the captain agreed with another cough. "Didn't get answered. This is the only choice I have. For the good of the Kingdom. The only choice."

Kespin shook his head quickly. "No, it's not," he charged. "We sail to Alrediah, or we turn and rush back to Bonchin. We get these men the help they need."

"The wind is against us."

"The wind doesn't matter. We set the rest of the men to the oars and we push ourselves there by force if we must!"

The captain dipped a corner of one of his maps against a small candle and then placed the burning paper against the oily gunk on his desk. The pile of goo hissed as if it was in pain and the quartermaster went pale as it started to crawl away. "This plague dies here," the captain intoned tiredly. "We're already too late to get to safety. We just... have to hope we... we take the Civs with us. That's... that's all. Or if... if this gets much worse this week... I'll put the boys on their way."

The quartermaster's objections melted on his tongue. "Set them on their way? You don't mean..."

"It dies *here*. The Graveyard calls for my sailin' soul already, Kespin. I'll not drag my men with me to it. Not knowin' the what, not knowin' the how? *Can't* risk it getting on dry land. Civs get it?" he asked with a throaty chuckle, "they won't make it to coast either. We win either way."

"*Nobody* is gonna win with this, Captain! What if you don't make it 'till they get here?"

"Then I'm countin' on you to do it for me," Taes replied solemnly. "I need your word to it, Kesp. We're a ghost ship. Just the men don't know it yet."

The older sailor looked at his captain – no, his *friend* – and watched as he pulled his tunic up again. The black mass was roiling under his skin, and for a moment, he would've sworn he saw a face peek at him. "It's that bad? For truth?"

"For truth," Taes answered. "Be honest with you? I'm cold. So cold. I just want *warmth*."

The Month of Hearthbreak, 513 QR

The *Hullbreaker* was lost months before anyone knew — except for one woman. A dead woman. A wraith of fire and nightmares that watched it for weeks. In the days to come, she would show a priest of love what he had missed. What he hadn't seen. How his fear that a toxic, malignant, infection wraith might spread through the Kingdom had come true.

Just not where he expected it.

She'd show him as the demonic abomination that had tormented him for so long had found a way to survive. To thrive. To spread. How it had taken over the *Hullbreaker*. How it had managed to exist even though he was certain he had sent the beast screaming into the World Between the Worlds – and beyond.

She forced him to watch as the crew fought to save their lives, lost they already were. She forced him to bear witness to the way the wraith ripped their bodies to shreds. How it tore down the mast. How it harvested the bodies that had fallen into the water.

How it claimed what it could. He would cry broken tears.

Tears that were echoed in the past as Captain Taes died.

Tears that changed to screams when he rose from death.

Lithdis, the 18th of Riverswell, 513 QR

Silence had reigned for weeks. Birds had tried, at first, to come near her upper deck. They had been attracted by the stench of rotting carrion and festering gore. An errant seagull had made an attempt to land, and as if its fate had been seen by the entire ocean, nothing else in the sky had come close ever since. The seagull had died in vain, too, because with its core fractured, the wraith aboard the *Hullbreaker* couldn't muster the energy to reanimate it properly. It simply flopped around on the deck for a few days before the *arin-goliath* gave up trying to animate it.

It liked animals. A holdover from the mind of the original core. Except now, it didn't remember why. It raged at itself when it couldn't take the gull and move into it. It liked animals. It wanted to be one with them.

It had better luck with a few of the sailors. Yet as the days passed and the power that had been released when their souls were crushed and absorbed into the writhing nightmare slowly dissipated, they too began to slow. As the sun above beat down on the dead, they lost their strength.

Eventually, they shambled into the darkness below.

A merchant's boat approached it once. The barrelman atop her crow's nest warned her captain of the blood and wrecked weapons laying about haphazardly once they were close. The captain decided to do the wise thing – he had them turn sail to a different direction. A fishing trawler saw it among the waves a few days later, though neither the *Hullbreaker* nor the trawler came close to each other.

The wraith felt them. It felt the delicious warmth so close, yet so far. It felt their souls quivering, felt their energies, felt their ripples in the ether. They were what it needed. Not what it wanted. Needed.

It wanted what it couldn't have.

It remembered.

It remembered the man that had hurt it. The one it had swallowed. The one that had set it on fire on the inside. The one that had sent blistering pain through its tendrils. The one that had silenced so many of the voices it had in its core.

It *remembered* and it *wanted* because it *needed*.

That man had taken its core. He had taken its heart. He taken it and made it go away. It could still feel the pull of the voices that used to be inside. Felt the ones calling for the rest of the spirit to ascend to the heavens where some of it belonged. Felt the pull of others calling for help, calling for revenge, calling for damnation. Felt them pull and tug it to the below.

But it couldn't go. Wouldn't go. Didn't want to go. The souls within were too entangled to go their own ways. So it waited. It formed a new core, directionless, angry, lost. It didn't have the focus it used to. It had too many voices. Too many names. It was still Daringol.

The *Hullbreaker*'s captain tried to find a voice. But he was just one voice of many. He couldn't control it. It thrashed and screamed in the ether. It felt screams and thrashes from two more pieces of itself. They were far away. They weren't in the water. They were elsewhere. Close, but not close enough.

One piece was weak. It was overwhelmed. It had a hold on a soul that was as stained and dark as the wraith itself. The willpower possessed by the soul? It was charged. Strong. Violent. It kept the wraith at bay. It refused to submit. It refused to listen to the calls and the cries. So the wraith reacted. It burned him. It cut at him from the inside. It tried to weaken him.

It must have worked. It must have. The man left where he was. He traveled. He traveled towards the other piece. The *stronger* piece. Stronger but muted. Stronger but trapped in a prison of ice.

The wraith hated ice. *Hated* ice. It was so cold. So painful. It wanted warmth. It needed warmth. It needed the warmth hidden in the ice. It needed the warmth in *that* ice because *that* warmth was the man it remembered and it *wanted*.

But it couldn't get to him.

It couldn't go to him.

It couldn't move. The waves moved it. The waves would continue to move it. Storms would, though the wraith had little understanding of what those were. It knew, in a space of quiet buried in the cacophonous voices screaming over and over again, it knew that one day – maybe soon, maybe not – that the waves would wash over the top of the ship.

It knew that there was a watery grave waiting for it. It knew that in time, that another soul would come and claim it. Take it. Enslave it. It knew, because that was the fate of souls lost at sea. One of the newest voices in it kept screaming that. Shouting that.

"*The Admiral comes! The Graveyard awaits!*" was the scream it repeated. Again, and again, and again. It went unheeded.

It went unheeded until a man arrived.

The voice thought it was the Admiral. The one that claimed the souls of the lost in the waves. The one with a fleet of otherworldly ships that traveled the seas between the realms of those alive and dead. The one rumored as myth, the one rumored as legend.

It wasn't. It wasn't a myth. It wasn't the Admiral.

It was another man. One that trafficked in souls. One that traded the damned as much as one of his minions traded in secrets. One that had a name, though few knew it. One that had a cloak of red and a cane of onyx.

The man heard it screaming. The man silenced those cries with a wave of his hand. The ether was stilled, except for a steady throb beneath the decks. He preferred the quiet. The quiet was peaceful. The quiet allowed for plans to work without interruption.

Yet that's what he needed: an interruption. The wraith would do, he decided. It was a simple choice; bend it to his will or sink the *Hullbreaker* to the Abyss. Either would be easy enough. Both would rid the world of it – the abomination wasn't of this world, it didn't deserve this world, and it shouldn't be in this world.

One way or another, it had to be removed.

But he could put it to use before it was.

Enslaving the wraith was a matter of a few spoken words and a gestured spell. Except it wasn't true slavery. The wraith was given a choice. It could suffer, or it go get what it wanted. He could tell where it wanted to go. It was easy enough to send it on its way.

Except a ship needed a captain – and maybe a crew. A few broken shells to man the oars. A figurehead to warn away the interested. So, he worked. The shattered husks inside the belly of the boat gave him no concern. Bones lasted longer than flesh, soggy as some were. There was little else to salvage; the meat had gone rancid. Nothing to save.

He gave passing interest to the coal in her hold, and decided it had one purpose. The wraith watched with a multitude of eyes as he placed a pair of glowing gems in the center of the pile and smiled. "Resist, and this burns. If it burns, you do as well."

It wanted warmth. Warmth, but not fire.

A few hours later, and he had his crew. Seven men with more rot than muscle stood slumped, held up only by the force of will behind the wraith – and the force of necrosia the Man in Red gifted the misbegotten cretins. Seven men; six to man the oars, and one to steer the wheel. So crudely was his stitch-work completed that you couldn't tell who was who, or who had been what in life.

It didn't matter.

He gave it another gift, too. He taught it how to grow again – with constraints. The growth would have to stay near the hull. It couldn't seek out creatures or creations away from the path he had chosen for it. That, the wraith decided, was okay.

Then he reminded it how to like animals again.

A kindness, of a sort.

Lithdis, the 4th of Firstgrow, 513 QR

She came to them at night. It felt her pass between the worlds each night and day, until five days ago. As a storm battered the sides of the hull, she quit. The *arin* felt the link between them sever. It felt the piece of itself locked behind the prison of ice be forced out. Felt it destroyed.

Heard another voice silenced. Silenced by the man that had hurt it so much, so bad, so often. When it felt her, *saw* her watching, it was shocked – as much as it could feel such a feeling.

She saw it for what it was for the first time. She saw it with eyes not blinded by suffering, eyes not strengthened by thoughts of control and domination. She saw it for the twisted, devastated mound of souls it was. She realized in that one instant, that there had never been any hope in controlling it for herself.

And the soul of a spy long lost saw the terror that the Man in Red had unleashed upon the waves. She had been sent on a mission of mercy; a step on her path of penitence. An instruction from a woman who represented the Goddess of the realm that bridged the domain of Dusk to light of Dawn. Her task had been simple: find the ship, if it still sailed, and aid the passage of those few souls aboard to the next realm, if she could.

Upon her arrival, Rmaci knew that she couldn't.

She knew the ship would travel unbidden. She knew that it would arrive sooner than anyone would wish. She knew that the people that would believe her story were numbered less than the fingers on one of her maimed hands.

The spy-turned-wraith-turned-spy retreated as quickly as she could. There wasn't anything to be done for that ship of the damned. Not by her, at least. Of the five that would believe her, there was only one that could stop it. If he believed her. If he could make others believe him.

And as she returned to her new Mistress, that man was busy.

Busy spitting up blood, at that.

I. A MURDEROUS SAVIOR
Lithdis, the 2ⁿᵈ to Staddis, the 4ᵗʰ of Firstgrow, 513 QR

Late Evening, Staddis, 4ᵗʰ of Firstgrow

Blood splashed against the cobblestone streets as Akaran went down –
hard – for the second time in as many minutes. The fight was going on
longer than his assailant wanted, and to be fair, longer than what the
blonde-haired priest wanted to suffer through too. Still, despite a grievous
gash on his right leg that *still* hadn't healed, he was giving as good as he
got.

He had to. The cargo he carried depended on it.

It wasn't one of the special packages that Celestine 'Cel' Navarshi –
owner of the *Drunken Imperial* and councilwoman of the Basion City
Fleetfinger's Guild had enticed him to carry in recent days. Nor was it the
promised shipment of cocasa he had been counting on to dull the pain in
his leg. Instead, it was something both a bit more important and a bit
worse, depending on who you talked to.

As an axe with a sinew-wrapped wooden handle descended on his face,
the discussion about it popped into mind.

Late Evening, Lithdis, 2ⁿᵈ of Firstgrow

"I believe I found a way to restore your magic, should you be interested
still," Telburn had told him. He looked younger (a lot younger) than he was
(by a distressing amount), which made it easier to think less of him. That
was a perk that the mage appreciated, and one he capitalized on with
disturbing frequency. It was one of many personal attributes that made
dealing with the Headmaster-Adept of the Basion City Granalchi Annex a
headache, at best.

Still, some headaches found ways to be worth their while. Telburn was one of them. Even from his sickbed, Akaran had to admit that much. Even if it wasn't his own bed. "I want. What do I have to do?"

The mage looked around the simple, yet nice, dwelling and pondered its contents a little more intently than the owner of the abode would like — even as she served him a piping hot cup of tea. "He wants. What does he have to do so I can get him out of here?" a very disheveled, very tired, very *irritated* young woman added.

"I decided to research not just the fragment of the stone you gave me," he said, referencing the *other* bane of the young priest's existence, "though the coldstone shard is so remarkable that it is a shame that... what was it you said his name was? Yoizc? ...that he had to die to create it."

"He didn't die creating it," Akaran muttered as he swung his feet off of the edge of the hay-stuffed mattress and winced as a jolt of pain shot up his leg and into his thigh. "He died after. His name is Usaic, and presumably, he's roasting in the pit — so save your apologies for the man. I met him."

"You met him?" Telburn asked. "How? When?"

The crippled exorcist gave him a withering look and simply gestured at himself in response. The Headmaster cringed as the younger man cut him off. "What do I have to do?"

"I'm getting to that, oh Priest of Impatience," the other scolded. "As I said, I began to research more than just the stone. You claimed that the creature that severed your connection to all things magical was an *episturine*, if I remember the name correctly?"

"Yes, then one of your men — Lolron? — said that it was more that my magic was... bottled up? That I absorbed too much of it that isn't from *here* and it can't filter out naturally, or... something," he answered. "I don't understand it very well."

"Well, I would daresay that you have had ample time to learn," the Adept scolded as he took a drink from his tea. He grimaced and then very quietly whispered a spell that made the edge of the cup frost over. "Either way, yes, that is a succinct enough description of the problem. Your aura has been filled with magic not native to this plane of existence. As such, magic that would interact with your essence in a normal fashion cannot even gain hold of you, and you cannot correctly expel what is within."

Seline glanced at the frozen cup and growled in the back of her throat. Akaran thought he heard her mutter a promise to cut his scalp off if the clay so much as cracked. "Didn't you describe it like a jar filled with oil thrown into a lake? The bad magic is oil, the world is the lake and..."

"...and I'm the jar?" he finished. "That's right."

"An interesting way to describe it, and one quite right," Telburn agreed. "In order for such a thing to have occurred, four distinct things must have happened: one, you must have established a connection to another plane."

"I did that when I was taken to Tundrala," the priest interrupted. "Don't recommend the trip, do recommend the location," he said as he remembered the fields of flowing snow, the mountains seemingly taller than the world, and the glaciers flying through the sky – impossibly dancing and singing, but dancing and singing nonetheless.

The Headmaster blanched. "That part remains under investigation, you must understand, though I am willing to suspend disbelief to a certain extent. But, that was only step one. The second step would require that you were somehow completely drained of all of the mana in your aura; to be true, that alone should have killed you. All life, no, all *things* in this world are steeped with the ether of our plane, much as life in the *other* planes is steeped in energies of *their* homes.

Seline glanced between them. "I'm not sure that I just understood that correctly. Are you… claiming… there are worlds with life other than… ours? How… how is such a thing possible?"

"Because the Gods have Their own homes. They decided we'd be better off living on this one instead of setting up in Their yards," Akaran grumbled under his breath.

Telburn nodded in silent agreement. "Yes. Think of this world – Kora, the mortal realm, the Home of Humanity however you wish to proclaim it – as a… giant stew-pot. The universe decided to stick bits of everything from everywhere else into this plane and… well. We don't know the *why* but it *did* and this is what we're stuck with."

"Other… realms. And we're…"

"One giant buffet of bullshit," the exorcist finished.

The Adept cleared his throat. "Bullshit steeped in ether, as it turns out. To be without it is a death sentence in very short order. When you feel drained from exerting yourself from spellwork, you are drained because you have used up a significant amount of your personal store; while it can and does regenerate over time… well."

"Overuse will kill you, yeah, I know," Akaran agreed. "What's your point?"

"The point is that once you were drained, you then had to be filled. Forcefully, I would wager, as the fact that you were unable to *discharge* the ether in your aura must mean that you are unable to *absorb* the ether through merely being exposed to it."

"You can't just throw a jar in a barrel of oil and expect it to fill up, you gotta uncork it first," the blonde-haired healer replied. "That about right?"

"Yes it is! Very good, Missus Valdin," Telburn returned. "Daresay, have you ever had your aptitude tested in the Academy? You catch on quickly.

Faster than some I know."

Akaran ducked the insult and frowned. "What's the fourth? End the exposure?"

The mage nodded in agreement. "Yes. The entire experience is effectively a closed series of systematic of events, though I don't expect you to understand that meaning. A start, an action, an end, and no other outside or undue influence upon you."

"So the ether I'm supposed to have was pushed out and the magic I'm *not* was shoved up my ass with so much force I can't get rid of it."

"Crude, but… yes," Telburn finally agreed after a few more drinks of a now comfortably-chilled tea. "I realize that doesn't grant you a lot of hope to explain it as such, but the delight of such a closed series of systematic events is that if done correctly, it can be replicated."

The younger man pulled at the bloody bandage around his leg and hissed in pain. "Tell me, exactly, why you think that's a good thing? Is the Academy trying to learn how to mute former members so they can't cause this kind of shit again? Do they really want to turn this city into the land of the deaf and dumb?"

"Oh, no," he demurred, "we already have methods for that. I believe you've missed the point – if you've been voided then stuffed with ether *once*, we can do it again," he said as he pulled a glistening turquoise stone from his garish rainbow-colored robes.

Seline crossed her arms and stared down at both of them. "If I remember correctly, Lolron tried that already. The stone he used cost Ridora a pretty crown to replace."

"And nearly set my hair on fire," Akaran groused as he reached back and straightened out his ponytail.

"Ah, but that was then, and this is not a stone of absorption."

"What is it?" the priest asked.

"A cure."

Late Evening, Staddis, 4th of Lastgrow, 513 QR

The axe missed, barely. Chunks of stone bounced off of the street and sliced at his stubble-covered cheek. The son of a bitch had cut his cane in half in the first few minutes of the fight, though enough of it remained to let the one-eyed priest it as a blunted wooden sword. Akaran countered with a jab from below that forced his assailant to take a few steps back.

There wasn't a lot he could do from the ground. In the Order, the rule was – if you fall, use magic until you can get back up. There wasn't much training offered to account for falling and *not* using magic until you could get back up. That, he decided, deserved a sternly written letter sent their way later.

If (and that was a big if) he survived the next few minutes. From the hateful look on the dusky face of his assailant, and the wisps of dark energy appearing around his left fist, *later* wasn't a guarantee.

Late Evening, Lithdis, 2nd of Firstgrow

"I can't say you'll particularly like the method," Telburn warned.

"But will it work?"

"If I didn't believe so, I wouldn't be here."

Seline's shoulders sagged in relief. "That's wonderful. How fast can we get it done?"

Akaran glanced over at her and raised an eyebrow. "Didn't know you were so keen on letting me be able to cast spells again."

She crossed her arms and glared in his general direction. "You're reckless, impulsive, irresponsible, and curse like you belong with the navy. So no, I don't think you should be rushed into being able to do all of that with magic," she shot back. "I also think I'd like to be able to sleep in my own bed again."

"It's only been three days!"

"All of which I've had to deal with your snoring, incessant whimpering, and the smell of your –"

Telburn coughed into his hand. "Ah yes, I remember these days. All of which aside, yes, it should work. It will take some effort, I should warn."

"You understand the absolute *last* thing I want to do is go on some long quest to slay a dragon or ride a unicorn or anything like that, right? I know the type of stories men like you tell little children and I don't want to be the next tale some bard sings about."

"Oh, nothing of the sort," the mage assured him.

"Thank the Goddess," Akaran breathed with a sigh of relief. When the healer gave him a bemused glance out of the corner of her sweet-brown eyes, he shrugged his shoulders. "What? Unicorns are bloody scary."

"Although," Telburn cautioned, "you are going to have to enlist the aid of a few gentlemen, and they may take some convincing."

Akaran looked at the mage and considered, for a very long and drawn-out minute, if he could smother him to death in his flamboyant robe or not. "Dammit, I just said –"

"I can make arrangements to obtain the physical items we'll need," the Adept interrupted, and I'll ensure that I have all of the assistants that the invocation will require. Though, there are two people you have to speak to yourself. One, I think you'll get along with very well. The other..."

"What about the other?" the priest asked.

Late Evening, Staddis, 4th of Firstgrow

Errant torchlight finally gave Akaran a glimpse of his attacker. It wasn't anyone he recognized, but that didn't mean much. He was a Sycian, a little shorter than the priest and a bit lighter. Then again, after several months of hardly any physical training at all, the exorcist had put on a few pounds more than he wanted to admit.

None of which mattered when his attacker manifested a dart of magic with swirling royal-purple eddies fluctuating in the air around it. The spell drew the shadows away from his face, and revealed angular cheekbones and gray-green eyes that had been otherwise hidden under his hooded brown cloak. The assassin stepped back until he was concealed by the shadows along the street again, though the dart of magic stayed aimed at the priest's face.

The exorcist flung his broken stick at his attacker and was rewarded with a clean miss and the sound of broken glass when it shattered a nearby window. The crash drew the attention of whatever poor sod was trying to sleep on the other side of the wall – and earned a few choice words shouted from within. "You fisking shits!"

Which did nothing to distract the man with murder on his mind.

Either of them.

Pridis, 3rd of Firstgrow

"Lord Obermesc?" Akaran asked as he approached the old, slovenly, and wool-wrapped man as he approached the city's Shrine of the Under on the northern wall of the city. The shrine was carved into the rock-face, nearly an hour's walk east of Orshia's Fall (and longer when you had to approach it with a damnable limp). Everything around it was carved from stone in one way or another, with amazingly beautiful amethysts and sapphires glistening on every corner and raised pillar. The good news was that he was outside, and not sitting in his chambers much deeper into the mountain.

The bad news was that he still had guardsmen, and they didn't care that the man interrupting Obermesc's homage to the God of the Undertunnels had a cane or not. All they saw was someone accosting their leader – and a moment later, all the exorcist saw were two spears leveled at his face as two other bodyguards defended the Oldstone with a pair of overlapping tower-shields. The reception might have been a little less chilly if he'd been wearing his silver-coin sigil of rank.

Sadly, Maiden-Templar Prostil had yet felt inclined to give it back.

Lord Obermesc muttered something under his breath that enticed his soldiers to thrust the glistening steel tips of their spears even closer to

Akaran's throat, and for one brief fleeting minute, he debated trying to bluff his way through. Telburn had advised against it, so he did all he could, even if not all he should.

He shifted his weight to his left foot, grabbed the closest spear with his left hand, and used his cane to batter the other one away. The guard on the right recoiled in surprise, while the one on the left stumbled forward as he lost his balance. The exorcist pulled even harder, and staggered enough in the process to put the first guard between his chest and the second's spear. "Oldstone! I'm not here to fight!"

"Then you're failing," the old man spat, "because that's not how a man of peace acts."

"I'm not a man of peace," Akaran countered, "I just said I wasn't here to fight."

Lord Altund Obermesc, the Oldstone of Basion City, the speaker for the Order of the Unders, and one of the biggest bigots in the city where it came to matters of the Order of Love, pushed the two huge shields aside and projected *distaste* so fiercely that the exorcist could almost smell it. "You aren't a man at all," he spat. Then, to the guard Akaran had use as a makeshift shield, he added a blunt: "You've been compromised by a cripple. Leave my service and leave the city at once."

He tried to protest, and for a heartbeat, the younger priest felt a moment's pity. A very short heartbeat, and a very small amount of pity. "You need better men."

"I need to be left alone. We have no business," he shot back as he brushed his men away and started to make headway into the shrine.

"No, we do," Akaran interrupted as he pushed himself away from Obermesc's bodyguard. "I... I need your help."

The Oldstone stopped walking and turned back around to face him. "A Lover? Asking for help from the Unders? Now that's an absurdity I haven't heard in a long time."

"How'd you know I'm from the Order...?"

The old man snorted. "You're the Cripple-Priest of the Harlot, aren't you? The boy with his magical balls cut off? Please. You'd have sooner luck not being known if you cloaked yourself in the sun and ran naked down the streets."

"Okay, ouch," he muttered under his breath. "Yeah, that's me. Though I object to the 'balls' remark."

"Object as much as you want, magic-less gelding. Doesn't change what you are."

Akaran cringed and tried to salvage his dignity. "What I am is in pain, and what I need is help, and I need it from you. I have an offer, if you'll hear me out."

Altund's lip curled. "Did they take your brain when they cut your sack, boy? I know who you are, I know where you're from, and I know your Lady *isn't* giving Her permission for you to come to me. In fact, I bet that the cunt that beds down in the Repository would love to know you came here to pester an old man."

"That *cunt*, as you call her, could kill every one of us without breaking into a sweat," the exorcist shot back, "not that she needs to know that I'm here."

"Bargaining for silence and bargaining for help in the same breath. Aren't you just a cocksure twat yourself," the Oldstone scoffed. "Out with it then, less you plan to embarrass my men further."

With a vaguely-cautious glance at the remaining guardsmen – who, despite the earlier exchange, didn't look like the gaggle of fools he first thought they were – Akaran stepped back and leaned against a nearby wall to catch his breath. "I need a blessing of Stilamatheric," he replied. "Specifically, I need to have grounds consecrated in His name."

The priest of the Stonehewn didn't laugh, didn't snarl, and didn't give any of the responses that his guards expected (or hoped for). He bit his tongue and then strummed his fingers on his hip as he sized the Lover up a second time. "They only took your *magic* balls, I see."

"With respect, Oldstone, the ones I have left are still magical."

His retort caught the older priest off-guard and it resulted in a short little laugh and a lecherous sneer. "No. Now leave."

Akaran took a couple of quick steps closer before an errant spear thrust out in front of his chest to hold him back. "Oldstone, please. The Order of Love has worked with the Order of the Unders in the past. Stilamatheric doesn't like it when things that get buried get up and walk again and neither do we."

"Oh, that's right. And what has that gotten us? Gotten us here?" Altund charged. "A hole in the ground, filled with all manner of rot and *wrong* that festers in the mountainside."

"Filling graves sometimes means re-burying what was emptied out of them," the exorcist retorted. "There's plenty of *awful* that the Unders have claimed in their time. The Dwarves, the Damians, what's left of the orc tribes, the goblins of the midlands and –"

The slovenly, almost obscenely-sized man with jowls so deep you could get lost in them shook his head. "The Unders claim awful, there's no lie to be said there. But we give unto the Stonehewn what *belongs* to the Stonehewn. What your Harlot does is shove things that belong to neither realm into the dirt and leaves it there to poison the ground!"

"It's a testament to the Stonehewn's power that She feels safe to entomb the dark in His embrace. The ground deserves to have what should stay in the ground."

"You only care about what lurks over top of the world. Your kind has *never* cared about what is beneath. It's only when threats are made against *your* holdings that you care about *ours*," Altund snapped. "You've wasted enough of my time. See yourself gone."

Akaran pushed back on the spear and called out for him to stop. "*Wait*, Oldstone. I have something you might want," he said, "and maybe even that you *do* want buried."

"Are you daft, boy? I made it perfectly damn clear that whatever you have that you want in the ground can stay over it."

The exorcist stopped struggling against the guards and pushed his hand down into his pocket. "Heard you might know a man named Donta," he replied smugly, "and that you gave him a blessing, too."

That name made Altund come to a complete stop and he turned back around once more to give the younger priest a sly look out of his amber eyes. "Blessings don't get traded like a whore at a bar, boy. There are only so many to go around, you know."

"So you know him?"

"I know many people. He is not one I think highly of."

"I'd say not," Akaran agreed, "nor does he think much of you. Neither does his boss, from what I hear."

The glare from the Oldstone was ill-befitting of a man of his stature. "Both can go find a dragon's cock to suck. If you have dealings with either, I may have my men enhance the nature of your title, *cripple*."

The chainmail-clad guard adjusted his spear and angled it higher up and aimed the tip back at Akaran's throat. "You misunderstand, Oldstone. I'm dealing with them, that's true. Likely at the end of a noose," he replied, with a quiet thought of, *Not that I expect one to work*, before he added, "and they won't be the only ones. Consorting with the dead is a crime, after all."

"Consorting…? What are you getting at?"

"You know what I am, and you know what men like me do. I know that Anais made a deal with you and you were promptly screwed out of it when the Aquallan refugees flooded the city looking for places to stay. The Overseer reneged on his part of the arrangement that she worked up, right? But her mercenary made you hold up your end of their deal?"

Altund chewed on his lip. "What would a boy like you care about deals of rock and gold, hm? Some things are a matter of public record, but not the names of the deal-makers. Why do you care? What do you want? I grow weary."

The exorcist placed his hand on the shaft of the spear and pushed it down as torchlight reflected off of the cool, copper-colored walls of the shrine. "Told you what I want, but I care because consorting with the dead is a crime, Oldstone. You got played. I don't know why you cared about her offer, or what you thought you were getting from it, but you dealt with a woman with a walking corpse for a minion. I'm trying to untangle one trice-damned mess after another, but I need help to do it. I need yours."

He pushed past his guards and lumbered closer to the exorcist to speak in hushed, angry tones. "Are you suggesting that I worked with... a necromancer? Are you suggesting that I knowingly aided someone with a dead man for a pet?"

Akaran shook his head quickly. "No, nothing of the sort. You have a reputation in some circles, but nothing like that. To tell the truth, if I thought that *half* the people that had dealings with her knew what kind of power she seems to wield, Henderschott would have to build three extra gallows. Though if you didn't notice, they've made a mockery of you twice over."

"Made a... why are you confronting me? Eager to have your other leg shattered?"

"This isn't a confrontation," the younger priest argued, "this is information. One given out of respect. You're a holy man, and your reputation speaks volumes about what you feel is *right* and *wrong*. I *am* dealing with them and I *do* have help, but I need more than what I have to sort out their bullshit," Akaran admitted. "And to deal with another problem."

"So. You think you can bribe me with promises of revenge over a simple deal? Is that what this is? Do you think me so feeble-minded that I would bend over for such an offer?"

The exorcist reached back and tightened the strap around his ponytail before he gave the Oldstone an understanding smile. "Feeble, no; bend over? Really hope you don't. But," he added with a bit of a smirk, "I hear that Donta knocked you on your ass. Thought you'd like to help me do something about that."

Altund glared at him for the longest time, but he slowly started to rub his hands together. "If he is as you say, he does need to be consigned back to the ground."

"He is. And he does."

More silence reigned for a few long moments before the Oldstone extended a hand in Akaran's direction. "To a burial, then. Is the ground you need consecrated for his disposal or other...?"

Late Evening, Staddis, 4th of Firstgrow

The dart of magic hovered over Akaran's prone body for another heartbeat, and then suddenly sped for his face. At the very last second, he rolled over to his side and screamed as the move wrenched his bloody knee. The spell exploded against the stones and a cold rush of wicked flames scoured the back of his shoulders and set a length of his hair alight.

The assassin growled from the dark and sent another dart at him before Akaran could dodge. The impact hit him square in the chest and promptly put the exorcist's curse to the test. Instead of blasting his chest to pieces, the spell detonated, and burnt clear through his tunic. The blast of void-fire elicited a scream from him as the heat scorched flesh and incinerated hair and clothes alike — but a thin sheet of etheric ice blinked in-and-out of existence over his flesh and kept the blast from going any deeper.

For the first time in the fight, his attacker let up as his pale-pink eyes widened. "What... what are you?" he whispered.

Akaran patted the black fires away with a series of profane curses. Raw, seething *anger* welled up in him as an unfortunately familiar cold *chill* blossomed in his empty eye. It was soon followed by a pale blue glow that radiated from around his eyepatch as frozen crystals started to appear on his hand. "I'm the wrong man to try to mug, you sand-crusted Sycian asshole," he spat as he forced himself to a kneeling position on the street.

Early Afternoon of Staddis, 4th of Firstgrow

Tracking down Tidesinger Quinchecco was a task that was easier said than done. You wouldn't think that in a city surrounded on all sides by stone cliffs that there would be that many places that the high priest of Aqualla would wander off to. You — and Akaran — would be wrong.

Touring the city hunting for him took the exorcist on a trip to all the major waterfronts, plus a couple he didn't know existed. The first leg of his trip took him north to Avagerona's Rest at the base of the Orshia-Avagerona Falls since it was closest to Seline's apartment in Upper Naradol. When the only thing he found there were a bunch of fishermen and a gaggle of Aquallan followers at the Lord of Ocean's edifice, he followed their recommendation and headed south along the southern split of the two rivers.

The trip along the Avagerona's shoreline was quiet, pleasant, and a bit more enjoyable than the last time he'd been close to it. The shore offered an uninterrupted view of the Everburning Pyre and the hill where he'd operated on his leg. It also gave him a few glimpses at a handful of happy maidens frolicking around some of the shallower waters. It made for a wonderful spot to sit down and chew on a bit of cocasa as he watched less-happy maidens work and wash linen sheets and worse in the clear waters under the warm spring sun.

What wasn't so wonderful were the reminders of what he'd been through. The local fishermen had a *thing*, apparently, for a type of saltwater squid that absolutely *infested* the waters past Cableture. They called them 'yeshal,' and they swore it's meat had the best flavor to be found outside of the Fel'achir Forest – and that it was better than any of the crab down in Lower Naradol, too.

Every time he saw someone peddling one or waving a flag with squid all over it? He kept flashing back to the damn arin-goliath and Rmaci's warning that it wasn't done with him yet. *Every* single time he saw it, he remembered when that beast wrapped its tentacles around him, and the way it cheered in ecstatic glee as it tried to swallow him whole.

Which brought him to another problem on his mind – as if he had time to worry about a ship of the damned that *might* be floating off-shore somewhere. Granted, he had even less time to ogle the local "ladies" along the shore, but. You had to pick your priorities in life carefully.

Pleasant sights excluded, it didn't turn up the former leader of the Hall of Sea's Song in Vahail. *Or the leader of the former Hall*, he mused, *depending on how you look at it*. It did turn up an opportunity to overhear an argument between a war-maiden of Odinal and some sell-sword from Akkador East over who had the bigger blade.

That discussion promptly ended when she proved her point.

In more ways than one.

Even still. The brief skirmish (and ensuing cries for a healer) didn't provide more than a brief, amusing distraction. He did, however, take the time to send a measure of thanks to the God of Luck about the time he followed the river to the Hannock Bridge. The stone edifice arced over the Avagerona and served as the last line of defense for the city to stop anyone that made it through the other imposing and entirely unnecessary lines-of-defense that stood between the mouth of Yittl Canyon (which was a day's walk to the south) and the giant portcullis that guarded the main gate.

It was also named after the Overseers family, which he was *sure* was some kind of *coincidence* more than it was the Overseer stroking his cock for anyone entering the city. Which, thankfully, was not what he caught the Tidesinger doing. Instead, the priest was busy offering blessings to a group of refugees loaded in a caravan making their way out of Basion.

Tonhas Quinchecco was known to be a kind, benevolent man at his worst. What Akaran wasn't ready for, or expecting, was that the man was a hugger. He barely managed to get a greeting past his lips before the

Tidesinger had wrapped him in a tight embrace followed by a kiss on top of the exorcist's forehead. "Ah! Hello there, good sirrah," he shouted with a booming voice more at home at a battlefield than a bustling bridge.

Once the immediate shock wore off, Akaran managed to get out a stunned, "Uh, yeah, hi. Tidesinger, I am sorry if you are busy but –"

"Nonsense!" he boomed. "There is no man who should ever be so busy on a city street to give alms to those that need," he said with a smile across his bright pink lips that lit up his rosy red cheeks, "even if the man that needs alms is not one accustomed to giving them."

"I mean I agree, but..."

"...but it is not what you do, yes. I know of you. How may I serve, oh child of Love?"

Akaran checked his surprise and looked over at the caravan of formerly-flooded souls as they began their journey to parts unknown, and parts he could honestly care less about. "I need help, Tidesinger. There's a foulness in this city and I'm trying to uproot it. I've got an idea how to get rid of it, but I need a few things first."

Like damn-near everyone else he'd met, Quinchecco was a hair shorter than him – although he lacked the frame of a fighter. What he did have, and what kept waggling whenever he spoke, were his oddly pointed ears. "There's worse than foulness in the city, good man. There's foulness in the water."

"Shit. It's close enough to feel?"

"Feel? No, not feel. Hear, yes," he corrected. "Come. There are words to be had that are best not had where all can listen."

The exorcist gave him a quick nod in agreement, and the pair quickly (or as quickly as Akaran could) worked their way off of the bridge – and then under it. The stairs that trailed down were rough chunks of granite and covered in moss that absolutely didn't care for his cane. By the time he made it down, his leg was screaming and his head was pounding from the effort. "I really am sorry to bother you, Tidesinger –"

"It's no bother, I assure you. In truth, it is a grace of the waves that there are those on land that seek to wash corruption, rather than ignore it," Quinchecco replied.

"Not a fan of the Guard either, I see."

He smiled from ear to pointy ear. "Nor the others that profess an interest in the void yet do little to cleanse. I daresay that may be a curse of age – we are not so far apart that I do not remember the desire to change the unchangeable."

"Funny you'd mention the unchangeable," Akaran. "I've got a problem caused by a group of people that think they're eternal."

"In my travels in this world, short as they may be, I have encountered many that think they are – but few whom have lived long enough to attain to the title," the priest remarked as he adjusted his dark green tunic. The color matched his leggings, but they had been sewn from some kind of odd reed-like material the exorcist couldn't recognize.

The Lover snorted. "I've been getting that feeling as of late," he agreed with a grunt. "No, but in truth – I ran afoul of the Order of Ice. I'm trying to *un-foul* my... okay, I'd be lying if I said I thought I made a mistake, but..."

"I would assume they do not find your transgressions to be without fault?"

"Do you want the long explanation or the short one?"

"Neither," the Tidesinger replied. "The fact that you sought me out at all is proof of your honesty. Except, as you said, there is a darkness rising. And, a darkness floating."

Akaran nodded tiredly and looked down into the muddy river and watched a duck float by, oblivious to the discussion. "That's right. I don't know how far it is but I –"

"Close," Quinchecco interrupted. "Quite close."

"Dammit. Then I need your help *faster*."

The priest answered with a nod and reached back to stroke one of his pointed ears. "Tell me first – why is it you ask me? If you need aid with the dark, surely your own Order would be where one would turn. I wouldn't ask followers of Aqualla to seek out aid from, say, the Oldstone."

The remark set the other priest back a hair. "Desperate times, desperate measures. I've run afoul of more than Ice."

"How do I know you won't run afoul of me?"

That wasn't the question he was expecting, and he lingered for a minute as he tried to figure out a good answer. "You don't," he finally admitted. "Just... I don't usually intend to offend. Sometimes it just happens that way."

"A retort as honest as a man with as much blood on his hands as in his veins," Quinchecco replied. "I am intrigued; though I will admit, I will need to know what was done to anger the frozen. The realm of Istalla and that of the Lord of the Ocean of Souls are grander kin than few others things in all the worlds combined. They are... well, as you said. They fancy Themselves immortal, but They are merely a state of being, as are we all."

Akaran bit his lip and looked down at the river again. "You believe that water washes away sins, right?"

"I do," the Tidesinger answered. "Water can do many an amazing thing. It can wash, it can cleanse; it can extinguish flame and care for the parched. It can harm, too, as we have seen as of late."

"And it's said that the waves serve to claim the ills of man, isn't it?"

Quinchecco shook his head. "No; that is a folly of men. The water claims trespassers that do not belong, that is true. Many a soul have thought to conquer the crests of Aqualla's waves, yet paid no heed and no honor to the beast they claim to tame. The depths merely return the favor."

"But what about corruption? Water washes and cleanses, and takes it away."

"A bog is full of rot, and shallows may find themselves full of detritus," the priest replied, "even slag – though I believe you know as much yourself, don't you?" Before Akaran could reply, he continued by adding, "It is easy enough to assume that water claims the foul and controls it in the depths. It merely aids it to disperse, and slowly yet surely, reduces it to a form that is too weak to harm."

"No offense, good man, but I think I like our way better. We take it out of the water and simply get rid of it."

"Yet it still moves elsewhere, you see. Out of sight, out of way, out of hazard, perhaps, but the corruption still remains. I am not surprised – yet you haven't answered my question, which implies that I may not enjoy the response."

Chastised, the exorcist felt his shoulders slump. "My experience with Ice is that it keeps what it covers. I needed something kept. The ice didn't want it but it was too dangerous to let loose."

Quinchecco's eyes narrowed. "So you mean to suggest that you bent the Frozen to your will, and used It against Its own consent."

"I had consent," he hastily pointed out, "just not… Istalla's."

"You are aware that gaining consent from a princess to piss on the royal carpet is not a promise that the Queen won't be annoyed with you, yes? There are some actions that require a confirmation from those in the highest seat of power before they are undertaken."

"I was in a really big hurry."

"But did you even ask?"

Akaran cringed and shook his head sheepishly. "I'm going to assume this means that you won't help me."

The Tidesinger gave him a faint little smile, and then gestured at the river with a swirl of his fingers. At his beckoning, a small waterspout lifted up from the stream and began to spin errantly about. "I didn't say that I wouldn't. I only asked if you yourself *had* asked, and now that I know you didn't, I recognize that now must be a different time. You need, yet instead of doing, you come to plead – not threaten or attempt to force me act on against my own wishes."

"I don't think I can force you to do much of anything you don't want to do," the exorcist pointed out, "or specifically, what I want you to do."

"Oh, you could. Men are just men. They can be forced, given the right application of water – or the withholding of it. I do sense that if you felt you had no choice but to convert me to your cause by the blade, you would, just as much as I sense that the end of my help will result in you taking up steel against another. Am I wrong?"

He shifted back and forth on his heels while using the cane to keep his balance, tenuous as it was. "For what it's worth, the steel will be used on people that deserve it."

Quinchecco raised his eyebrows at the Lover and tilted his head. "Ah, you claim it is a form of divine punishment then, do you? Have you been instructed by the Gods to meet out such a task, or is it merely a man deciding the fate of other men?"

"I'm not going to decide the fate of men at all," Akaran retorted, "just going to try to save a few."

"Save a few by killing another."

"I'm not killing men."

The Tidesinger pursed his lips as his waterspout pranced back into the river. "Then what are you hunting, praytell? Is the darkness on the waves not man-made? Is the culling of souls in this city not done by human hands?"

Akaran shook his head and sighed. "Foulness. And no, and another no, and you won't believe me until I can prove it."

"A man of faith asking for a man of faith to act on faith," the Aquallan replied after a moment's pause. "Yet you've given me no reason to think that your faith is worth following in this case. How am I not to know that the ill I sense is not ill of your making?"

"Do I look like someone capable of making ill?" he shot back.

"Yes," Quinchecco replied without hesitation, "though not one to knowingly or intentionally do ill against the Light, given knowledge enough of what your actions may result in. You are insistent that the need is great, even if the trust you ask is as fragile as a reflection?"

"I am," the priest replied earnestly. "When I drag it into the light, I promise, you won't regret this."

With a haunting little smile, the Tidesinger bowed his head. "Water knows no regrets; it merely flows. What happens, happens, and may happen again, yet never in ways the same," he answered slowly, "though at times the waves may be choppier than others. What is it you ask of me?" As Akaran told him, the priest's ears began to twitch. When he finished, a true rarity happened:

The singer lost his voice.

Late Evening, Staddis, 4th of Firstgrow

A jagged gauntlet of ice materialized around his left hand before the assassin could get off a third dart. Each shot came with a matching glow from some kind of amulet dangling from his neck, which was both helpful – and utterly pointless – for the exorcist to care about right now.

What was more important was finding a way to get the asshole to stop kicking. Every time the priest started to stand up (a trying, difficult process at best), the bastard would deliver another kick at his head or hands. The third strike in half as many heartbeats split his lip and sent another wad of blood onto the stone street.

It was the last kick he managed to deliver. Akaran's assailant swung his axe down in a hard over-handed swing that would've done the head of the Woodmason's Guild proud, and it almost caved in the exorcist's skull. He managed to catch it at the last instant with his frost-covered fist before it could do any damage – but that wasn't to say there wasn't damage done.

The blade cracked the ice around his fist, but the power of the coldstone shard buried in his face pulsed through Akaran's body. The magic of the stone mixed with the foreign magic in his aura, and the ice around his hand mixed with the steel on the blade. The result was just as the Headmaster-Adept had warned.

Late Evening, Lithdis, 2nd of Firstgrow

"Now, there is some bad news," Telburn warned. As the words left his mouth, you could see the dismay blossom in Seline's eyes, but she kept her mouth shut. "I know you have taken a distinct distaste for all things cold, yes?"

The priest grunted and rolled his neck. "That's not a strong enough word."

"It will have to do," the Adept said dismissively. "The truth of the matter is that until you die and the ether of the world claims or rejects you and the energies around you do whatever it is that energies around you will do, you're going to be tainted with this other ether."

"I thought you said you were going to purge it from me?"

"I did, and I will," the mage replied. "But much the same as someone used madder-root to dye her dress pink," he said as he gestured at the plain, but pretty, thin cotton dress Seline was wearing, "the energies of the other have forever dyed your aura. I daresay that your possession of the coldstone shard may only make it worse."

"What... what are you saying, Telburn?" Akaran asked as he leaned forward on the bed and held his head in his hands. "I'll be able to use magic again but I'm going to be pissing snowflakes?"

The Headmaster cracked a smile and stifled a laugh. "No, no, nothing of the sort. Or at least, I would hope not. If you do..." he began to reply before a miserable glare from the priest cut him off. "As it stands now – or, before the now, I should say – those that draw upon the magic and spells of the Divine do so with the permission and strength of the God or Goddess you choose to serve. In reality, it's a bit more complex than that but that is the extent that most of the colleges of Divine studies tell you, yes?"

"More or less. A lot less, but I know that."

"Yes, well. What you may not know is that the magic you receive is filtered through your own aura and your own aptitude. It's how you'll never find a priest of flame using magic of water; the two aren't simply opposed to each other, there is a question of attunement."

Akaran's face went pale as he jumped ahead a few ideas and had an ugly one stare him in the face. "Please don't tell me you expect me to swear allegiance to Istalla from this point forward. What I do doesn't work that way. I can't –"

"Actually, it does," Telburn deftly pointed out. "We both know that members of your Order can cast spells and call upon the other Gods. I've seen some of the magic that your compatriots use, and they call upon Lumina, Pristi, and Isamiael alike."

"Ridora routinely calls upon Solinal to aid in calming minds," Seline added. "She gave up on his."

The exorcist ignored her barb and sighed in frustration. "So, what? I get that not everyone is able to channel magic. I also understand that there are people who wish they could channel Love but can't. The Order is full of them – people that claim allegiance to Her but couldn't cast a ward if their lives depended on it. You call it 'attunement.' The Brothers call it being 'touched' or 'chosen.' That's just the way it is."

"Well, religions always find ways to make themselves sound superior to the layfolk," the mage remarked dismissively, "but the point still remains. Ponder the question that those that try to channel Love cannot, maybe they have aptitude with channeling another. Or the elemental aspect of what God represents what."

"The 'Gods aren't real, people only claim they are to represent forces of the physical world,' argument? Now? Really?"

"Not making the argument – merely pointing out the likely change in your personal condition. When this works, that is."

"You still haven't explained what that's going to be."

Telburn blinked and looked bewildered for a moment. "I didn't? I thought that was clear by now."

"No, you haven't," Seline sighed. "And please be quick. I promised Ridora I would be in an hour ago. She's already very suspicious about all the time I've been spending at home lately and being later than I am is not going to help that."

"Oh, then I apologize," the Headmaster offered honestly. "Then let me be succinct."

Akaran glanced up and snorted. "That'd be a first."

The mage let the jab slide and cleared his throat. "I don't claim to understand what relationship you have with your Goddess, or the forces you claim that She manifests, as I've never seen them in action. However, I would assume that from this point forward, you may find things a touch... colder."

"A touch colder?"

"Your aura – soul, ether, energy, your personal jar that you store oil in, however you wish to consider it – will likely be *adjusted* to exhibit instances of elemental ice when you attempt to channel magic." Akaran's jaw dropped in slow horror as he realized what Telburn was trying to say. "I'd also wager that the longer you stay in contact with the coldstone shard, the easier you'll be able to call upon frozen magic as well. Didn't you tell me you were able to clad your fist in ice once already?"

He thought back to the fight with Annix several days back and how his hand had turned into a block of jagged ice. "Yeah but I thought was just the stone... I don't know... doing... stone things?"

Telburn nodded in agreement. "It was. As much as we are having problems with magic of this plane interacting with your aura, you are positively filled to the brim of ether that stone was made from. You may be able to use magic even before we attempt to purge – if you can learn to use the right kind."

"Tel... Headmaster. I've seen what elemental ice can do if it's not controlled. I don't want that. I don't want that power," he replied seriously as he felt his hands start to shake. "I'm... I think I'm good at what I do but I'm... I'm not the right person for that."

"As a man of faith, I would think that you – of all people – would understand that sometimes we are not granted a choice. Sometimes it is luck, sometimes it is fate, sometimes it is fluke. You are talented; I can feel it brimming. You wouldn't need the skill to be returned if you weren't."

"What's that supposed to mean?"

The Headmaster smiled and reached over to shake Akaran's good knee. "A painter with no ink will find a way to make some if he truly needs, or will change his medium. A bard with no instrument will use his voice – or one with no voice will use an instrument. Arts, talent, ability; they find a way to manifest. You've been pushing back against anyone that's told you no; it's not just youth being cocky, it's talent looking for an excuse."

"And here I thought he was a bored ox trying to find a pottery shop," Seline muttered under her breath as she rummaged through a chest in the back of the room.

"I should warn, of course, that until you undergo proper training, you're little more than an Instabilisist with quite literally *unnatural* potential. I would avoid using it until you have a few months with us at the Annex."

Akaran's face fell like a rock. "I... me. At... at the Annex?"

Telburn smiled from ear to ear. "Well, it isn't something we have to worry about right this moment, of course. We have to fix you first."

The exorcist ignored that particular criticism. "So what now? I'll go talk to the others and try to win them over. What happens after I get them?"

"Well," Telburn began, "it won't take long to gather what I need to do the work. There *is* a matter of being compensated, though this experience alone will cover the more material costs."

"Excuse me?"

"You didn't think this was for *free*, did you?"

Late Evening, Staddis, 4th of Firstgrow

The ice around his hand swirled like a maelstrom. The blade never broke through his gauntlet, and the axe froze in his grip. The mugger only barely managed to let go before the entire weapon froze over. Akaran clenched down and the glow behind his eyepatch flared even brighter.

The axe shattered.

Explosively.

Shards peppered his face, but the blast pushed the exorcist's attacker back. Akaran whipped his hand around and a jagged arc of ice ripped off of his hand and sliced through the air. The crescent slice cut through the air and struck his assassin square in the chest. When it hit, it didn't just draw blood; it shattered the amulet dangling from his neck.

A bolt of purple mana hanging in the air vanished the second the amulet cracked into pieces. The Sycian grabbed his chest and screamed in pain. That scream was matched by the exorcist – when the ice flung off his hand, it did more than just cut the mugger. It ripped his glove, his sleeve, and chunks of skin off with it.

His attacker kicked at him again, and even though the priest blocked it, it did enough damage to Akaran's already bloodied arm to cause the exorcist to roll over to protect it. A shout from down the street stopped his attacker from doing anything else, and the mugger ran off before the new arrivals could do anything to stop him.

Not that one of the new arrivals didn't have a lot to say. Or at least, a lot to accuse. "My understanding was that you were simply sent to go collect the aid of one of those unstable Aquallans," he scolded, "not to pick a fight with random gutter trash."

Akaran bit back a curse as he surveyed the somewhat extensive damage to his left hand and bit back fresh tears. "Wasn't… wasn't my fault."

"Many things in this city do not seem to be your fault," his savior scolded, "yet I hear you often end up in the middle of most of them."

"Coming from you that's a compliment."

Lord Riorik Dallidon, Guildboss of the Fleetfinger's Guild from Gonta (and newly apparent heir of the same title in Basion City), just looked down and smiled. "One professional admiring the work of another," he said as he gestured to the walking wall of muscle beside him to help the battered priest stand up.

"How'd you manage to find me?" he groaned.

Another voice chimed out of the shadows. As she appeared, Austilin – Riorik's hired muscle – warded himself with a (worthless) gesture and stepped away. "*Because I'm still bound to you, you jackass,*" the half-burnt/half-frozen woman retorted as she stepped into view. Horrific as ever, the wraith crossed a blistered arm and one covered in scabs and crystals over her equally-wrecked chest. "*And this thief is still touched by the wraith, almost as deeply as you were. Quite pissed I missed it. You're lucky we were so close.*"

Akaran cradled his ruined arm and bit back a groan of pain. "Lucky. Right."

"Did you at least get it?" Riorik asked.

"Quin's material for Telburn? Yeah."

The thief let out a sigh of relief. "Good. I'll have Austilin run it over to the Annex. The sooner the mages can get to work on it, the better for us all."

"You're that worried about me?"

Riorik touched a writhing black blotch on his cheek and gave the priest a thin smile. "Given the state of the local region, I'm quite worried about us all."

Late Evening, Lithdis, 2nd of Firstgrow

"I mean I had hoped it was free," the exorcist muttered.

"As a *certain woman* expressed to me recently, *hope* is a sad thing, and is only fun when you see it dashed," Telburn replied. "Though I have a feeling I should be grateful that I cannot put a face to that voice – I've found that those that spend so much effort to hide in the shadows have reason."

Akaran grunted in annoyance. "Cracked voice or sultry one?"

"Cracked."

"She has a good reason and yeah, you should be," he agreed. "I don't have anything to give you. You know that, right? Did you come here to taunt me with solutions then walk out with them in hand or...?"

The mage blanched and gave him a look like he'd been offered spoiled milk. "My dear boy, what kind of people have you been cavorting with as of late? Do you really think I would do that?"

Seline looked up from rummaging around in her closet and gave the Headmaster a roll of her eyes. "Yes. He does. And yes, he's been around people that would. My house has turned into a thoroughfare of unwashed and unwanted."

"Riorik would be offended by that," Akaran grunted.

"Riorik can be offended by anything he damn well pleases," she snapped, "but it doesn't change the truth."

"I keep forgetting what your profession has you do..." Telburn muttered under his breath. "That aside: you do have one thing I need. Two, actually."

He put his hand up over his eyepatch defensively. "The coldstone shard stays with me. You had your chance to play with it."

"I did," he agreed, "and got what I needed from it. How versed are you in the arrangements of the Academy and the Hunter's Guild?"

"Other than you're married to the local Huntsmatron? Not very."

"If but all of us were," Telburn sighed in annoyance. "It should go without saying that at times, the Academy needs... shall we say... assistance... in either traveling to and from places of etheric significance or in requisitioning harder-to-find objects that exist in nature."

Seline settled down with a piece of charcoal and an old piece of parchment. "Everyone knows that mages need bodyguards. What of it?"

The mage shifted in his seat. "Well. These dalliances are not often cheap. Worse, the Guild has recently begun to realize that and their costs have been growing... excessive. It would, to put it kindly, be useful to have someone on retainer, as it were, to aid with a few projects that I hear that the Dean-Adept plans to involve the Academy in."

"Are you asking me to come work for the Academy?" the priest asked, utterly flabbergasted by the suggestion. "We're not even sure this will save my ass!"

"I am confident that it will be an unpleasant experience. I am equally confident that by the time that we finish, you will have some measure of ability back. Either way, should you not be able to cast spells, you have training and insight into extra-planar events that may prove useful, given the correct situation."

"He's asking you to go work for them," the healer interjected.

"Not on a permanent basis," Telburn hastily added before the priest could offer up a complaint. "Simply that you sign a waiver that the Academy can refer tasks to you that might otherwise prove difficult without."

Akaran bit back a curse. "I already owe favors to the Fleetfinger's Guild. Now you want me to owe favors to the Granalchi?"

The Headmaster nodded in agreement. "Succinctly, yes. Three, to be precise. Or, we can negotiate a price in crowns – though the services may be both more exciting and more affordable."

"How many?"

"Three, as I said."

"I meant how many crowns."

"Oh," Telburn answered with a blink. "Five diandra."

Seline dropped her stack of papers with a curse as Akaran nearly choked on his own tongue. "*FIVE THOUSAND CROWNS*?! Are you *fisking* mad? I don't get that kind of stipend! I'll *never* get that kind of stipend!"

"I imagine you certainly won't if you don't regain the ability to channel the nature of your Goddess, correct?" Telburn pointed out.

"This is extortion."

"But it *is* funny," Seline chortled. "You have to admit that."

"No, I don't," the priest snapped as he gave her a foul glare. "Since when did you become so spiteful?"

She flicked her blonde trusses back over her shoulder. "Since you started sleeping in my bed, since you started using my kitchen as a meeting place for all manner of horrible people – no offense, Headmaster – and since your poor choices have required me to bandage you up more times than I want to remember," she shot back. "*That's* since when."

Properly scolded, the exorcist sighed and tried to figure out a way around this new mess. "I... I don't like not having choices."

"Few people do," the mage agreed.

"Two services owed, with the caveats: if I am on Order business, then I am unavailable *and* I will not run counter to my duties to the Goddess," he countered. "If your people call me and I run into some shit that needs to be excised, I'm excising it, regardless of if you're using it as a research subject."

"I wouldn't expect less than the second, given your attitude. The first? Would depend on the need. We will, of course, negotiate a temporary leave with your superiors, should the need arise."

"What makes you confident enough that they'll grant it?"

The Headmaster gave him what was supposed to be a reassuring smile.

It wasn't. "The Academy and the Lovers occasionally share assets. One of my Adepts is a liaison to the Repository, even now, for example. This type of arrangement isn't too uncommon, though it has been a while since the last one. That said – this is a *personal* arrangement, and you will be held and bound to it under Queen's Law of Contract."

"You may as well accept it," Seline chimed in. "Nobody else has figured out what to do with you. It's either this or keep working as a courier for Cel."

Before Akaran could decide, Telburn cut him off. "There is one more thing – if we do this, you *will* take some time with us to understand how you will respond to magic, going forward. This is not just my request, it –"

"– it's a matter of Queen's Law, I know," the exorcist sighed. "She doesn't like people running around using magic they don't understand."

"Exactly. Given the Kingdom's history of magically-inspired historical events, can you blame her?"

"I know, I know," Akaran sighed for a second time. "Two?"

Telburn pursed his lips. "Two, with your considerations understood, given one more request. A personal one. It won't enter the contract; it'll only be matched by your word."

"What is it?"

"Adept Odern was a dear friend of mine," the Headmaster replied. "I am not one for violence, yet I know the fate to befall murderers. I am at war with myself to request any other than my wife to take the task of hunting him down, but, the city feels more dangerous by the day. Danger, sadly, is a blade that oft cuts both ways – those that suffer the effect and those that create cause are both at risk."

Akaran nodded in understanding. "Headmaster, I promise. If you restore my magic, I'm going to execute the bastard that killed him. I swear upon my soul."

The mage flinched at the ferocity behind his voice. "I want to see him brought to justice. If the law demands his or her head, then I won't speak otherwise. Justice, not vengeance."

"I serve the Queen and the Goddess," the younger man replied, "which means I offer both. It also means I get to pick."

While Telburn tried to digest that statement, Seline started to snicker. "One moment? You're shocked that he is eager to kill the cretins that have taken over our city?"

"Taken over is a bit of an exaggeration, isn't it?"

"No," they both replied.

"Oh," the mage replied with a defeated sigh. "Then I implore you: justice over vengeance. Please. I recognize that the Lovers have a reputation for being forceful when the time comes to express it, but I'd prefer it if you not burn the city down behind you."

Akaran smirked. "I won't," he promised. "From what you said, I'll freeze it."

The healer stood back and gave a thoughtful stare at both of them before she broke down into a fit of giggles. "Oh. Oh my goodness. This is… this is utterly hilarious!"

"Funny…?" Akaran growled. "What possible part of this is funny?"

"Well, I mean," the blonde-haired healer tried to explain through another fit of giggles, "you're an exorcist of Love. But you… now you've got a heart of ice," she said with a snicker.

II. MURDERESS
Late Evening of Staddis, the 4th of Firstgrow, 513 QR

When her Meister moved, he did so quietly. He kept to the shadows, he stalked at night. Annix was a cold, calculating, and cruel creation of the dark. He was a man, or at least, had been. Once. It was hard to say how old he was; old enough, the battlemage presumed, that he had developed reason to strike as quietly he did.

Sherril wasn't him.

The two dead men laid out at her feet – in full public view – was enough to express that. They both wore long green capes with a gold crown embossed on the back. It was a declaration that their employer was some kind of royalty, which was true – though not as royal as he would presume to brag. A third man rushed out of a side room as she casually strolled through the fortress without a care in the world.

Like the first two, he hardly had time to swing his short blade before she flicked her wrist at him and sent an arc of electricity from her fingertips into his helmet. He crumpled with smoke wafting out from the holes in his visor, and his body twitched as the electrical shock ruined his nervous system. As she stepped over him, she extended her fingers and sent a second, stronger burst into his chest.

It stopped his heart, and did little else. She knew how much it took to cook a man, and men wearing steel were easier to fry than men without. Every bit of mana saved was mana she could use later.

And there would be a later.

Specialist-Major Sherril Inyadine strolled through Fort Massadine without a care in the world – which was a lie. She had many cares, although not all of them were of *this* world. Executing members of the Advensi of Massadine was only a bonus, and not even her actual task. Her mission was more or less a simple one.

It was literally the type of task he'd made her to do.

He moved silently in the shadows. He struck in subtle ways and only left a mess when it suited his goals. He preferred to hunt and torment in quiet. He did, at times, call on her to disrupt a hunting party that might be sniffing around his hunting grounds. When he called, she answered. The hold he had on her soul made it impossible to do otherwise.

As Sherril walked past an old wooden door, a young woman halfway out of her dress poked her head out from the room and screamed in terror. Sherril's left hand snaked out and impaled her eyes with sharpened fingernails. The girl's scream changed pitch as she fell back in a bloody, mostly-naked sprawl. The old naked bastard tied to the bed inside shouted curses and worse as the battlemage strode past without slowing down.

Finding her target in this pathetic excuse for a fortification wasn't hard. The Tessamirch family prided itself on knowing no expense they couldn't afford. That, she decided, was an outright lie. Or perhaps the Massadine's leadership decided that musty and moldy lodgings were enough to motivate the troops to take as many jobs as they could.

For mercenaries, they were putting on a poor showing. Their training lacked much, she mused, as she finally found the stairs a stable-boy had told her would take her all the way up to the top of the keep. He'd coughed that up just before coughing up part of his throat. There were a few disloyal pigs enjoying an unexpected meal outside – thanks to his reluctance to talk.

Of course, he'd have died either way. The other way would've hurt less. She was up the stairs in mere seconds with the bloodbath behind her a rapidly fading memory. They were gone, and she was too busy to eat. They'd be missed by someone.

That, of course, was part of the point.

The cries of alarm from below had the leader of the company already armed and armored, with a squire-like assistant cowering behind him in his bedroom. It wasn't perfect; leather straps dangled loosely and his mail hung poorly off of his shoulders. It wouldn't have mattered either way. Sherril approached him with a smile, her red and gold cloak trailing behind her like a waterfall.

She almost thought his attempt to have someone dress him was cute.

In life, she'd been a Specialist-Major from the Dawnfire army, and she'd never seen the necessity in changing outfits since her change in loyalties. It made life easier. It made things more exciting and surprising. Or at least, it was for the people she encountered. In death, she was more.

In death, she retained her abilities.

In death, she'd gained new ones.

Kee Tessamirch was one of the city's elite. He was the brother to the most talked-about woman in the province, and the leader of the Advensi of Massadine, *and* an all-around jackass. The glorious look of shock on his face was a wonder to behold. The fear in her eyes as she flashed a pair of fangs at him. The way he changed his stance and held his sword in front of his chest. The way he subconsciously glanced to his sides to find a way out when she smiled.

Annix had given her a direct instruction, one designed to inflict fear into the people of Basion City. One to spread chaos, one to disrupt the delicate balance of life in the safest place in the Kingdom. The Wedding of Dusk and Dawn was the biggest event the city had seen in years.

The wedding of Hylene Tessamirch, the Golden Baronessa, to Malik Odinal, of Clan Odinal, from the midland wastes. Marriages between houses was from an uncommon event, though a marriage from nobility in Dawnfire to one of those savage mountain-born barbarians from beyond the Queen's borders? They had to get special dispensation from the Crown itself for the wedding to even be talked about in more than hushed whispers.

There was a very large argument to be had that the city would be better off if it had *stayed* as just hushed whispers. It had taken a year to even negotiate the terms between the two families – and another year to prepare the city to receive the celebration. Two very trying, very difficult years as residents of Basion attempted to come to terms with the Baronessa's desire to marry outside of her... well, it wasn't just outside of her class or stature. It was simply outside of her everything to the people at large, and most of them were already disgusted with the concept.

A few disruptions to that would cause an explosion of anger between the city leadership, the Odinal delegation, and the family of the bride-to-be. The Crown wouldn't be blamed, but a disgruntled battlemage in the army would. Few people would bother to look past the cloak and the other clothes she wore, and those that did would have their voices drowned out by the screams of the Tessamirch family.

The Odinals would offer their sympathies. The remaining Tessamirches would demand justice, and would push the city guard away from their ranks. They'd hire more mercenaries, which would increase the chance of violent clashes – a given, considering the plans Annix had for the city in the future. More violence, more chaos, more confusion, more distractions.

Everything Annix wanted.

She lunged forward and shrugged off the slashing blow that crashed across her arm from Kee's sword. Much to her dismay, there were two caveats to her instructions: no feeding, and his face had to stay intact. That was unfortunate, but understandable. She took his second swing across her chest, and the most it did was slow her down. Annix didn't want doubt of Kee's death.

He wanted doubt of the nature of the killer.

Sherril was on top of the noble-born mercenary before he could get back into position for a third swing. Like his minions below, his armor didn't save him for long. A rune etched into his armor flashed briefly and dissipated the first blast she attempted to send into his ribs.

It didn't work after she punched it and crumpled the steel it had been etched on with supernatural strength that someone would later blame on a hammer. A wise man hid his defenses against magical arts, and Kee? Well, he was far from a wise man. The second blast of electricity from her right hand ravaged his plate mail and cooked him alive.

There would be three people happy to see the results of her effort. One would be delighted over the loss in competition – the Hunter's Guild didn't like upstart mercenary companies moving in on their contracts. The Advensi had been doing just that. The other would be Enth-Blade Parl, of the Odinal delegation – they'd had more than one argument, and the Enth-Blade had a very dim view of the man. The third had met him at the Danse Festistanis, and while he was busy having the swelling in his jaw cut and drained, Akaran wouldn't complain to see Kee sent to an early grave.

There would be, of course, all manner of wailing and gnashing of teeth from his sister. That was the point. Upsetting Hylene would tear the city apart. Murdering her brother? Openly slaughtering his men? The chaos would be incredible.

Kee's skin turned red and caught fire at the point of impact. Long streaks of energy left inflamed marks everywhere the electrical current spread. His muscles contracted and his shoulders dislocated. His fingers spasmed and clenched the hilt of his sword so hard that he couldn't have let his sword go if he had wanted.

He couldn't even scream. His mouth opened wide and blue sparks danced up and out of his teeth. His violet-laced eyes broiled in their sockets as she channeled a heavy, steady stream of constant electricity into his chest. It was more than she'd used to kill anyone else, but he deserved a heavier, harder treatment.

When it was done, she shoved his body back and onto his desk – some ornately carved family heirloom, she presumed. When he fell, it broke under his weight. She made a show of carefully sending a single spark into one of the Advensi banners hanging around his office; a single spark, dead center of one of the crowns. Just enough to burn a hole clear through.

As his squire cowered in horror, she calmly walked past him and jumped out of an open window. The story would be that she scaled the wall down, or had magical assistance to expedited her escape. In truth?

She merely jumped, and let her vampiric strength do the rest.

***

Sherril moved brazenly and violently. That was her calling card.

Annix took things in a different direction. Usually he worked by himself, but sometimes a new convert to his side could do things he couldn't. Or in this case, would be traced away from him – should the need arise. He didn't need his essence tracked; and with the increase in interest, that was a possibility should this go wrong.

The battlemage wasn't the only creation he claimed. There was another he had at his disposal. She'd been one of the first souls he had claimed after moving into Basion. She had her uses.

Serving as bait was one of them.

Much like the lanky, dirty man cowering in a stall, standing in horseshit. The reaction was natural. Who wouldn't run, who wouldn't try to hide? Who wouldn't cower in a corner drenched in piss and shit – even if it wasn't all his own?

He was nobody of interest. Annix had barely registered his name or even bothered to learn it. His helper had, and she called him out with a pleasant little purr to her voice. "Ettaquis... there's no need to hide. No reason to run."

"You're... you're not human!" he blubbered. "Neither of you!"

"Does it matter?" she whispered. "Many people in this world aren't human, but are just as capable of living. Or... existing. Or agreeing to a trade."

Ettaquis looked up at her with his eyes wide. She was more than half a foot shorter than him, and easily fifty pounds lighter. Yet she lorded over him like she was a Goddess – though that couldn't have been further from the truth. "I don't... n-n-no. Whatever you want, I don't have it. Please... please. I'm just her... her courier. She hasn't... hasn't had me carry or go... I just... I wait for her to tell me to..."

She reached over and ran the back of her hand over his cheek. "How do you know you don't without letting us ask? You ran at first sight, you poor thing. It's okay to be afraid," she added, "because fear is natural. It's normal. It's okay to be afraid of things you don't understand – but we want you to understand us very well."

Her voice was soothing, but all he could focus on was the dark look radiating from Annix's mismatched eyes. One had marbled over, and the other was a firm acorn-brown. The woman he didn't recognize, but the man behind her? He'd been well informed who he was. What he was. Anais had told him all about the vampire, what he could do, what he was, and what to watch out for if he thought he was being followed.

He wasn't smart enough to realize he'd been followed.

Until now, of course. The fangs she sprouted around her teeth only served to give cause to his terror. "It doesn't... doesn't matter what you want. I know who... who you are. If I give you... if I give you anything, she'll have my head. I can't. Please, I can't," he pleaded

"I'll have more than your head," her Meister promised from over her shoulder. "Choose your loyalties quickly. Understand their price."

As Anais's errand-boy quaked, the woman stepped closer. The shit on her shoes didn't matter. It'd be cleaned off soon enough, one way or another. "We want, we *need*, a name. Information. Grant that to us, and we will give you more than you can ever imagine."

"Or learn your *imagination* cannot prepare you for what's to come," Annix added.

She shook her head and her ashen hair fell off of the back of her neck. "Now, there's no need for that, Meister. He's confronting the unknown for the first time in his life. It's normal to be afraid, normal to shake. Normal to... well. Piss oneself, I suppose, though it isn't a sign of a solid man," she said with a dismissive sniff. "Yet you'd like to be a solid man, wouldn't you?"

"No, I... well yes but I..."

"Meister will make you a solid man, if that's all you need. You won't have reason to fear again. You'd be like me – fearless, vibrant," she promised. "You liked what I offered an hour ago, didn't you? You were eager to follow with promises of a change in your life – promises which I kept."

He paled even further in what little light the moons offered. "Not... not like this!" An hour ago? The promises offered had been given over rum with intent of companionship.

And *who* she was? Everyone in the city could recognize her. Her silver and ruby ring gave it away, even if her face didn't. She didn't come out of Hannock's Keep often, but nobody gave that any thought; she was a busy woman. Lady Sannah Hosheck – she was the Overseer's personal aide and what most people presumed was the source of the power that was behind what passed for his throne. Nobody crossed her, and nobody told her 'no' if they wanted to have a prosperous life.

That included subtle requests for attention. She'd earned a reputation for seeking out *interests* every so often. People gossiped, but that was the extent of it. Those that objected only did so once, and were given reasons to stay silent in the future. "If not like this, by other ways. You won't enjoy them as much," she promised.

The courier flattened himself back against the table wall. "What do you want? Just… just tell me!"

"Lovic," Annix spat from behind her. "She searches for us. We do the same."

"Give you… give you my Lady? You'll kill her!"

"What happens, happens," the woman replied with a dismissive wave. "She has done many things that have harmed others, so if you fear for her innocence – you shouldn't. You should know how much you've helped her to do those things."

Ettaquis swallowed nervously. "She's powerful. Powerful people do *things*. You… you know that! She saved me. Helped *me*. I can't just… I can't just turn on her. Not to you. Not… I mean because you are… you…"

"Because of these?" she asked as she flicked her tongue against her teeth. She pressed hard enough that a little droplet of old black blood swelled up on the tip. "We are open about what we are, she is not."

"You… you can't be open. If you were, you'd be hunted."

"As are you. Aren't you hunted by others? Or would be, if people knew what she did? What she *is*?"

He blinked and tried to look up into her eyes. "What she… what she is?"

Annix laughed coldly, quietly. "Sad little weak thing," he mocked. "Fear us because of what we are, and you don't even know what she is."

"I… I know she's a good woman! I know she's helped me, saved me from the gutter, done so much for me. If it wasn't for her…"

"If it wasn't for her, you wouldn't be in the middle of a pile of shit. She's not helping you now, is she? Or her murderer? There's risks of being left alone," the woman replied coolly, "which you won't be – if you decide to change your loyalties."

He shook his head violently. "Can't. Won't."

"That's a shame," she sighed. "She isn't worth it, you know. Worth the suffering."

"Suffering?" he asked as he clenched at the wall.

"Yours," Annix answered as the shadow he cast began to swell around him. The void he cast muffled the sounds they made as claws dug into the poor courier's flesh. You couldn't hear him on the street, outside of the spell. But in here? In the stables?

His screams were so harsh the horses struggled to escape their stalls.

***

It was a horrible night for screams.

Or maybe it was a wonderful one.

In the Office of Oceanic Divinations in Port Cableture, one of the last surviving members of the Basion City Fleetfinger's Guild wished for death. What he received instead was a broker of secrets – and as much as Annix was hunting *her*, she was busy hunting for one of her own. "Donta. Where is he?" she demanded.

Raes didn't answer – he couldn't. She'd blooded his mouth twice now, and had been kind enough to rip one of his sleeves off and stuffed it in his mouth. The argument had gone on for an hour now; she'd ask, he'd deny. She'd ask, he'd deny. The bickering had gone on for so long that she was starting to lose her grip on the glamour that protected her from outside eyes.

That was inconvenient. It meant there was going to be a mess, and a mess meant that she might be traced. It was going to be worse for him, of course – and she expressed her hope that he was in good standing with whatever God he offered tithes towards *if* he bothered to do anything of that nature. "I *promise you*, if you don't tell me where he is, I will do things to you that defy flesh," she spat.

Her eyes blazed with hateful fury. Or at least, one eye did. The other kept winking in and out of existence. There was an empty gash under the appearance of the other with a buried nerve that kept twitching as she paced back and forth. Raes finally, *finally* managed to spit out a variation on the same thing he'd said for the last hour. "Burning in the pit, I fisking hope!"

"No, there's no fire that awaits him," she spat back, "even if someone had killed him. They *haven't* because I would *know* and because I know he claimed ownership of your underhanded group of misbegotten bastards, then I must assume *you* know where he is."

"You fisking devil-spawned cunt, I have no idea! Nobody's heard from him in more than two days," the Thief-of-Mercenaries countered. "You can beat the damnation out of me all you want but I ain't gonna tell you none the different!"

Anais stepped back and sized him up again. He'd spent the last three-quarters of a candlemark dangling from the rafters with his hands over his head, and the experience had taken its toll. His breathing had turned shallow and sweat was freely pouring down his pale face. Much longer, and she wagered his lungs would give out entirely; though it was a miracle they hadn't yet.

A miracle she had no interest in waiting to fade.

"Please understand, good thief. I've no wish for blood on my hands. It isn't what I need. It isn't what I want. If I thought that I could offer you all the gold in the world to leave this city and never return, to put this Kingdom at your back and never speak of me again, I would," she morosely informed him as she walked to the other side of the tower's chamber and a large trunk sitting against the far wall. "Yet there is honor among thieves in this city, I have noticed, and between the ire that my man has earned from your delightful organization and the unpleasant conversation we've had, I doubt you would be willing to turn a blind eye so easily, would you?"

"You're a fisking little slitch, that's what you are," he wheezed. "Doesn't matter what... what you do to me. You're dead. The Fleet's are gonna find you, they're gonna string you up, and... and... make an *example* of you. We don't... whatever you are. We *protect* our city! Monsters aren't welcome here!"

She looked over her shoulder with her mouth open in surprise. "Good man! If you truly believe that your people do not allow for monsters in their midst you have had your eyes closed for far too long. This city is *managed* by monsters from the Overseer down. Him. His right-hand woman. The Guard. There are few souls in the mudpit you call home that *aren't* destined for locations far worse than even our little room here, you know."

"The Gods... the Gods will save us!"

"Ah, but you are wrong. Do you truly think that you can curry favor with the Divine when you wallow with the filth? Do you really think your half-assed attempts at power and personal gain will woo the Fallen?" she countered. "I am truly sad to let you in on one little secret: what you think matters does not, and what you hope for in life will not be granted in death."

He shouted a few more insults and curses in her direction, but the weight of her words shut him up very soon after. There seemed to be no chance the long-haired woman would get anything useful from the sputtering, wheezing, sad sack of a thief. Not as long as he drew breath, at least. The other avenues would take time, but if that's what it took, that's what it took.

The Merchant of Secrets, a woman formerly known to have formidable power among the rank and file nobility in Basion City, sighed in resignation and let her glamour fade entirely. There wasn't any point in putting on airs now; she needed the energy for her other pursuits.

As her ruddy-brown hair faded to a coal-gray and her skin lost all obvious pigment, the long-dead woman let her dress slide off of her shoulders. Her body was a mass of scars, stitches, and a crusty chunk of rot that spread from her thigh all the way to her heart. Raes screamed in terror and struggled against his bonds in a futile attempt to get free.

She cracked her neck, and a long scorpion tail began to unwind from the base of her head and from around her throat. By the time it unraveled, the only thing left that held her skull up was her old decrepit spinal column, a mass of shifting sand that slid up and down the bones, and pure necromancy that thrummed with a pale green light. The sight of the long, bulbous stinger lifting from her rapidly decaying flesh caused the thief to struggle and fight even harder.

Not that it did him any good at all. She stepped close and placed a hand on his cheek, a hand with skin so thin it was almost translucent. She stroked his damp beard softly and looked deeply into his eyes. "Raes? Answer honestly: do you know what I am?"

He didn't give an intelligible answer; only more screams. More struggles. More terror as the stinger circled the top of her head like it had a mind of its own.

"That's a shame," she sighed. "I don't either."

The tail-like appendage lanced out and pierced his tunic to punch right into his chest. The entire monstrous limb *pulsed* in an obscene manner as it injected far more poison directly into his heart than would ever be needed to kill a man. His body locked up in a seizure almost immediately as it coursed through his system. His head twitched back and forth like someone was pulling strings attached to his cheeks.

A pale pink froth bubbled out of his mouth as his tongue suffered bite after bite. An orange flush rushed up his throat and through the veins in his hands. He shit himself as a final indignity, and the loss of control was the last thing he'd remember of his life.

But not of his death.

The next hour went by excruciatingly slowly and yet, faster than she had given herself credit for. Raes' corpse was pulled down and his body was arranged spread eagle on the wooden floor. Empty sacks were placed under his head and ass to absorb any further fluid... discharges... his corpse might make either from his death or his temporary rebirth.

She'd rented this attic-turned-room for the fact that it offered a place to stay low. She imagined that any magic she used here would be noticed soon enough by the mages below if she wasn't careful. The spell would require finesse – more than usual.

However, her *benefactor* had made sure that she had all manner of masking spells and relics to use to cover her tracks *just in case* a situation like this might arise... plus a few she'd taken for other uses. She placed the Blessing of the Stonehewn she'd swindled out of the Oldstone down on the ground and activated it with a different spell; the effect would directly interfere with the hydromancy in the chambers below. She'd apologize for it later when they inevitability asked her what she had done.

That would serve to cover up her efforts. There were other spells she'd use to hide the smell. And the body. And the smoke. Those things would take time. Yet, they were doable, even if she hated to waste any more candlemarks than she *absolutely* had to.

Thick, brown, almost rancid candles were placed beside both his hands, his feet, his head, and one was nestled carefully in the foul wet spot between his thighs. All the while, the stinger dangling from the base of her skull snapped at the air like it was waiting for someone else to cross it. It had been the hardest thing she'd had to learn to manage. As useful as it was, it was also among the worst of her... abilities.

The spell took longer than anything else did. By the time she finished, all six candles were lit – though the one in the center burned black as coal. All of them emitted far more smoke than they would normally, and the hazy gray smoke soon blanketed the entire chamber. She placed a hand on the center of his chest and dug her fingers in deep on his naked skin. A soft hiss of pain slipped from his lips as energy crackled and a rush of heat welled up from his chest.

Raes' eyes flung open, but they had turned a dark black with flickering red embers dancing deep inside. Deeper than his eyes truly went, and deep into a place that Anais had no real desire to see ever again. He took a sharp breath that sounded hollow and empty – like he was trying to fill a true void, not just empty lungs. "*Damn you*," he whispered, though his voice was halted, raspy, and hard to hear.

"You are too late for that, although you know that by now," the broker replied. "Oh lost, oh dead, oh soul away from here; my request cannot be denied, my demand cannot be muted, my call cannot be ignored," Anais spoke as her voice boomed through the room. "I command and speak that you speak without command, that you speak with service, and that above all, you speak with truth. You are granted no permissions, no movement, no life, but what is needed to answer that which I ask."

His arms tried to move. His legs tried to kick. His head tried to roll back and forth. He tried to reach up with stiff fingers and wrap them around her neck. All he did, all he could do, was trash. After a few moments of the feeble attempts, he ceased and sank back against the floor. "*Dead woman. Damned woman. Ask now, before others hold your tongue.*"

"It will be a long time before my tongue is held, I promise, good thief. Now, while I do realize that you are not likely in a hurry to return to your not-rest, my earlier question still stands: Where is Donta, what has happened to him, and should you truly not know the answers to either, you will explain – with no detail spared – of what has recently transpired within your former circles of influence… regardless of how major or minor that may be."

The dead man twitched. Then he spoke. He spoke and she listened. He didn't have a choice. When the spell ended, the etheric window between his soul and his shell slammed shut. By the time he was done, she wished she could have brought him back in full.

Just so she could kill him twice.

Early Morning, Zundis, 5th of Firstgrow

As bodies piled up across the region, one was being rolled out of storage and delivered Lieutenant-Commander Henderschott's office. The L-Comm sat with his head in his hands and staring at a mug of frothy swill as two of his men delivered their protesting package. "I swear unto all that shits sunlight, I'm going to *cook* the pair of you in your boots if you don't get me out of these damned irons *right now!*" their captive roared.

It hadn't helped the first time he did it. He didn't expect it to work the seventh. "Let him go," Henderschott grumbled without even looking up. "Get the irons off, get him a uniform. Find him a sponge, too, with a bucket," he said before he looked up at their bedraggled prisoner with bloodshot eyes, "and don't you *dare* think of using it in *here.*"

"Oh, you've decided to give me a bucket, have you? Expect me to do more than shit in it? Though that'd be more than what you gave me downstairs, Henderschott."

"*Lieutenant-Commander* Henderschott to you, *Specialist-Major,*" he stressed with a growl from under his folded arms. "I can send you back down if you'd prefer. It's really up to you."

Their prisoner huffed in disgust as the other guards worked the iron cuffs fastened around his wrists loose. They'd left his arms a mess of red sores and a rash that was going to take a month to fade, the Specialist just *knew* it. "Just as damn happy you let me out when the sun ain't shining. Gods know what it'd do to my eyes at this point."

"Nothing good, but that's the theme tonight; haven't you heard?" the L-Comm grumbled as he slowly sat up straight. "Specialist-Major Badin Ouldsman, 13th Garrison. Known accomplice to the exorcist Akaran DeHawk. Arrived in Basion City on the 3rd of Greenbirth on a mission to escort said exorcist. Then you took a Grant of Leave from the 13th, decided to stay in Basion, and soon after became a known associate of the Mother Eclipsian, Erine Rrah."

"Yeah, that's me," the battlemage grumbled. "Long as you've had me locked up in the dungeon, am I supposed to be impressed you memorized all that...?"

"Arrested on the 18th of Riverswell and accused of murdering Upper Adjunct Lexcanna Jealions, who served as the High Priestess responsible for maintaining the Ellachurstine Chapel and overseeing the rest of the Order of Stara in Basion City."

"And I didn't have a damn thing to do with it, either," Badin spat.

Henderschott sized him up slowly as he drummed his fingers on his desk. "I know," he replied, "and that's why you're being let out. Well – part of why."

"What's the other part?" the mage asked as his eyes narrowed into cold slits.

"I don't have access to the full garrison reports for anything outside of Basion City," the bedraggled guard began, "but my boss – Admiral Theodin Maddon – does. This is important, because by my counting, and his efforts in dealing with the augers in Mulvette – a conversation had by way of Granalchi crystals, which was done at *very extensive and great cost to the army* – there are no more than thirty-seven battlemages currently serving the Queen between Kettering, Lowmarsh, and Waschali."

Badin frowned and slowly sat down across from the Lieutenant. "So you've gone and spent a chunk of the Crown's purse to count. Why?"

The other man's cheek twitched in annoyance. "Of those thirty-seven, nineteen prefer to use fire magics, another ten require extensive invocations to use most of their craft, and the other eight use what can only be described as bolts of raw lightning. Sparkcasters, I believe, the rank and file call them."

The mage flicked a finger and watched as a faint glow blossomed on his fingertips. The urge to just them up and burn the stubble off of Henderschott's face was so strong he could taste it. "We get the job done. What of it?"

"There are five battlemages spread between here and Cableture, present company included. Admiral Maddon has one in his port-side office, and there's a seventh currently serving on the Q. R. W. *Allohoc.* Three of the five staying here – S.M.'s Pryhum, Cellac, and Ki'stail – cannot use anything other than fire. S.M. Onngal *is* a sparkcaster, but he has an unshakable alibi. We also have you."

"Alibi?" Badin asked as the tone in the Lieutenant-Commander's voice changed for the angrier.

"Onngal and Maddon's mage – Orulf – have spent the last nine days violently ill, a fact that can be attested to by no less than three different locurats and healers in Cableture. Ran afoul of a bad batch of yeshal. As far as magical affinity, both of them require extended time to prepare before an action. The Admiral doesn't like to have 'loose cannons' on his decks." Henderschott paused and pursed his lips. "Neither directly use fire, nor lightning. Something about the 'elements not mixing with the oceans' or things of that nature."

"Shame, because it works. Spoils the water, don't you know?"

The Lieutenant-Commander looked up from the rough stack of papers and gave Badin a dirty look through bloodshot eyes. "There are a lot of very unhappy sailors in Gonta with your name on their lips, Major. It is a *miracle* that nobody died when you blasted the mast off of the... what was it? The *Orboria*? Reasons be damned, you aren't thought warmly of in the navy."

"Lot of unhappy women too, if you want me to be honest."

"Do you want back in chains?"

"I want to know why you're reciting the Queen's Rolls at me," the mage shot back just as bluntly. "Unless you think one of them was responsible for Lexcanna and not me, I –"

"They weren't. You weren't," Henderschott replied tiredly, "but."

Badin pressed his back against his chair. "Oh no. No no no. I have spent too much time around a certain exorcist to know when someone says, 'but' that I need to pack my shit and get gone."

The guard nodded in pained understanding and slid a small bottle across the desk. "I understand exactly what you mean."

He took the drink and sniffed it cautiously. It wasn't anything special, just rum. Rum at two marks before dawn rarely meant well when not done between friends, or at least, innkeepers. "But?"

"But someone dressed like a Specialist-Major, someone who slings magic like a sparkcaster? She just murdered nine people – five mercenaries, a stable-boy, a whore, and two of my own men – and roasted Kee Tessamirch alive in his armor."

Badin's eyes went wide and he took a very, very long draw on the offered rum and rolled it over his tongue. "You're very specific about numbers."

"I like them. They don't lie," Henderschott retorted as he drew a knife from his hip and let it fall onto the desk with a dull thud. "Neither did you. So. You're out of the cell. Conditionally."

"Conditionally?"

"Not even a 'thank you' first?"

"Depends on the conditions," the mage grunted.

The other man pursed his lips and sighed in defeat. "Nobody has seen or heard from that damned exorcist for days, and I've got even *more* bodies stacking up than just the Tessamirch's. Someone's been busy dumping *unmentionable* people in the gutters and they're showing up without feet.

I'm busy, as you can imagine, but it makes me *very nervous* with Akaran hobbling around out there without eyes on him that I can trust to –"

"Without feet?" Badin interrupted. "Uh. Are you… positive… about that?"

"I assure you, Specialist-Major, despite what some people think of me I am still perfectly capable of telling *hands* from *feet*. Will you take my word on that or must I count my fingers for you?" he asked as he extended a single middle finger towards the mage.

The drunkard laughed slowly, without a single hint of humor in his voice. "Then I've got good news, and I've got bad news."

Henderschott narrowed his eyes and leaned in. "I have had as much bad news as I can possibly stomach. Make it *actionable* news."

"That's the good news," the mage quipped, "you won't have to do much. Just take my advice."

"What?"

"There's a lot of people interested in him, from what I've heard from the sods getting pulled into the cells next to mine, but only one that likes feet. My advice, Lieutenant-Commander? If someone in an orange jacket that you've never seen around here before asks you to be his new friend, accept."

The guard ground his teeth together slowly. "And why is that?"

"Because I don't have a feeling you're all that jealous of Akaran's cane."

Later Morning, Zundis, 5th of Firstgrow

While Badin received his marching orders, the priest of Henderschott's concern was doubled over behind Seline's house with blood coming out of his mouth – and much to the healer's disappointment, that wasn't everything. "I swear to the Goddess, if you end up staining the wall, I am going to drag you back out here in the morning and replace the damn stones yourself."

"I thought you were nicer back… back in the Manor," he groaned through clenched teeth.

"In the Manor you didn't vomit all over my bed at three marks after midnight," she snapped. She looked almost as disheveled as he did; her hair was mussed up every which way, and she was wearing a simple strap of fabric across her top and an old tattered skirt covering her lower half. Any other day, any other time, he might have appreciated the glimpse of her midriff.

Right now was not any other time.

Right now, his body was rejecting the attempt he'd made to drink the pain in his face into submission. The mugging he'd gone through earlier had left him reeling, and *somebody* had decided that she'd continue the ban on cocasa that her boss had put him under.

Before her boss had summarily thrown him from the aforementioned Manor, at least. "Maybe you should've invited me to it," he grumbled before he realized exactly what he was saying.

"Invited you to it? Hardly. If I wanted disappointment I'd go find Henderschott. I'm *letting* you stay in it because I have a soft spot for the insane and I'm not convinced that you wouldn't harm people if I let you go, considering how you *have a man held captive* in the sewers."

"You could only," he started before another round of dry heaves wracked through him, "trade up. *Fisk* this was easier to tolerate when Rmaci was with me," he groaned. "And for the record, whatever that bastard is down in the tunnels? He's *not* a man. Whatever he is, he *isn't* human."

"Oh we still need to talk about *that*, too," Seline snapped. "You were walking around with a dead woman for months and didn't tell anyone? Don't you understand how dangerous that was?"

He looked up from the pile of gunk at his feet and clutched at the stone wall with a bloodshot, halfway-swollen eye. "You didn't believe me when I said she was in my dreams. You weren't going to believe me if I told you she was standing beside me in the loo."

"Certainly wouldn't have stood beside you if I knew she was."

"You *didn't* stand by me," Akaran retorted as he tried, and failed, to straighten up. "You let me go about my merry way a thousand different ways of fisked up and gave me shit in the process."

She flung her hands up in the air and then lunged forward to catch him before he could fall face-first into his mess. "Yeah well. That was the only thing that made sense to do at the time," she sighed. "Still about the only thing that does."

He grimaced as she helped him limp back into her tiny little *dormosul* — a small dwelling in a larger building called a *dormasil* with another fifteen such quarters — on the back end of Upper Naradol. "It won't get any easier from here," he promised with a wince. "In fact, I'd say it's going to get worse."

"Oh, you're very right with that," a different voice intoned. "I would say to get a room, but you have such a quaint place here."

Seline's eyes went to the corner and she nearly dropped the exorcist to the corner. "I don't care who you are, you *ask permission* before entering my house."

"Good healer," Riorik replied with a droll chuckle, "that goes counter to everything my business offers. You insult my craft."

"I'm going to insult more than your craft if you broke the latch on that door," she grumbled back as she looked over at the seemingly, and surprisingly, undisturbed door on the other side of the room.

Akaran half-limped and half-drug himself over to her bed with a tired groan. "I thought you were gone for the night."

"And I thought you were sleeping. It's my good luck that you weren't."

"I don't like it when your good luck depends on if I'm awake or not," he muttered as Seline handed him an old wet (and used) rag to clean up with. "What's wrong?"

"What isn't?" the Hobbler replied with a shrug. "I expect that you two have been too busy to hear, but I will warn you that the entire city will be abuzz before dawn breaks."

The healer cleared her throat and tapped her fingers on a counter-top. "*I* was sleeping. *He* was staining the alley. That is the *only* busy we're in the middle of, and I *trust* you'll remember that."

After he tossed the washcloth back into the bucket Seline had dug it out of, he turned his attention back to the newly-crowned Guildboss of Basion City. Or at least, crowned as far as the Fleetfinger's Guild was concerned. From what he'd gathered, it had been a rather short nomination and coronation period. "Is it anything that's going to kill me right now?"

"I don't know," Riorik replied without delay, which made his next remark all the worse. "I've made arrangements that you are to be protected for the rest of your stay in the city."

"Excuse me? What?"

"Does that mean he's going to get to sleep somewhere else?"

The Hobbler chuckled at Seline's hope-tinged outburst before he answered the less-thrilled noises coming from the priest. "Kee Tessamirch is dead. All indications are that it's a battlemage that did it – and I do recall you saying that the man behind most of the recent murders may have one in his employ."

"Hylene's brother?" the healer marveled as her eyes went as wide as saucers. "Someone murdered *him*? *How*?"

"Violently," he remarked, "and with ample witnesses."

"Oh Goddess," she exhaled, "that's... the wedding. Please tell me that he was mugged or got kicked by a horse or..."

Riorik shook his head. "I am afraid not. This was far more than a simple assassination. Someone wished to cause a great deal of damage, and they have. They've also seemingly decided that some actions are no longer necessary to do in the dark."

"Ugh. More like it was 'yes' to dark, 'no' to in the shadows," Akaran grumbled. "They're trying to destabilize the city."

"They may have succeeded with just this one murder."

"No, they won't stop at one. This thing *likes* killing. It likes it a *lot*."

Seline had to nod in unhappy agreement. "What's going on out there? I'm guessing Hender is losing his shit."

The master-thief nodded his head. "Oh, that's an understatement. Were the Tessamirch's wishes filled, he'd lose more than that. Officially, the family has stated their full faith in the ability of the Grand Army of the Dawn to find the killer, with understanding that it *couldn't possibly* be a current member of the army."

"And unofficially?" Akaran asked with an anticipatory cringe.

Riorik gave him a faint little smirk. "Unofficially, Clan Odinal has taken control of security of the Tessamirch Estate. They have armed men all over the outside of the grounds, and the groom has threatened the Overseer that if anything happens to his bride-to-be, it will *not* merely be viewed as a massive diplomatic incident. I think the phrase, 'an act of war,' might have been used."

"Oh, shit," the exorcist hissed. "It's not going to take a big step to think that the already-pissed locals are going to think that the Odinals are holding Hylene hostage even more than they already do."

"I almost feel bad for him," Seline remarked after a moment. "Almost. Akaran, you have to tell them what you know. You can't wait any longer."

"She may have a point," Riorik agreed, "but as much as we've already had the argument over suspension of disbelief..."

The healer lifted a finger as she leaned against the counter. "You don't have to tell them the what, just the who. Maybe that will help."

"Elsith was already supposed to turn over the dagger we found at the Landing. If Hender can't put these two developments together, he's dumber than I gave him credit for," Akaran argued. "But... I don't know. Maybe someone can recommend that he have the aura checked. If this mage had it in her possession long enough, there might be an imprint on it."

"That would be ill-advised, Akaran," Riorik countered. "Remember, if our prey thinks that it's been marked, we have no idea what it will do – and the only ones I trust not to screw this up, I daresay, happen to be the people you work for."

"Worked."

The thief shrugged his shoulders. "Either-or."

Seline steepled her fingers in front of her mouth and exhaled nervously. "So now we just wait and let more people die until this idiot can convince his boss what's going on? We can try talking to the Guild, maybe? Or the mages?"

"Who would be even *less* likely to find the truth in his words. The Granalchi may simply decide his mind is too damaged to try to heal him — and given that the Headmaster's wife is the Huntsmatron, neither can be trusted with this until proof is offered. I've seen much in my life and I wouldn't have believed it if you didn't have that walking affront to life stored safely away in Erine's basement."

"But people are *dying*," she protested.

"People are *always* dying, my dear. Some by these monsters, others? By people I may or may not personally employ. I thought I made that clear when you requested my help in purging the city of unwelcome influences."

"*I* didn't ask for *anything* of that sort," she countered. "*He* did."

"I didn't give you permission to murder at whim, Riorik," the idiot remarked with a sigh. "I said to bring them to justice."

"I have," the thief replied with a smile. "Not all justice belongs to the Queen. There is honor among thieves, and some thieves have lately been found without enough."

Akaran rubbed his temples and groaned as all of the implications of *that* statement ran through him like a herd of oxen. "Did anyone die that wouldn't have been met with the gallows if you'd handed them over to the Guard?"

The thief gave that a moment's worth of thought before he answered as honestly as could be hoped. "What I can assure you is two-fold: the first, that I did tell you that your crusade would result in people finding residence in other realms than this one."

"And the other fold?"

Riorik gave the poor priest another shrug of his shoulders. "There has been justice taken that would not have necessarily earned a man a hanging, that's true." Before bloodied exorcist could reply, he added a quick qualifier: "But, since the Queen's justice has always been blind to things such as station and purse? I promise, my good man, the actions I have taken have resulted in a brighter future for the region, regardless of what laws may or may not have been broken. Or that could have been proved to have been."

"You know, I'd believe that a lot more if you hadn't already expressed your concerns about the grief that your people will go through if this idiot's threat of a purge wasn't hanging over your head," Seline grumbled. "Don't you *dare* say another word about it, either, not under *my* roof. I don't want to know *anything* about it."

"Are you so lofty in the Manor above that you don't wish to dirty your feet with the muck the rest of us stand in?"

She shook her head. "I don't want to be put in the dungeon if anyone thinks I had a hand in it. I provide aid and assistance to those that need it. I do not provide a place to store contraband or a field to bury bodies."

Riorik chuckled and looked over at the priest. "She is adorable. Assuming I'd do something as benign as *bury* my bodies. A corpse is a messenger in and of itself, you know."

"I don't want to hear it," she repeated with a snap, "and you can have your meetings on how to undermine the city *elsewhere* if you want to keep running your mouth."

"She's got a point," Akaran muttered. "I don't suppose you'd be willing to answer if you'd be clearing out the city if I hadn't asked you to take a look into the shadows or not?"

"You mean, would I be as invested in purging those less-than-desirable to even my own underhanded interests were I not at risk of having club-wielding thugs storming through every alley and sewer?" the thief asked with a grin. "Perhaps. Perhaps not. Perhaps you merely expedited such a cleansing. Not every monster is welcome in the dark, you know, and recent revelations wouldn't have necessarily stayed hidden for long even without your help."

Akaran groaned and laid back on the bed. "Now you're sounding like the Mother Eclipsian."

"Yes, well, the woman makes a good point," Riorik countered. "Speaking of, she contacted me. She has something for you," he said as he began to fish something out of his jacket.

"Oh, *good*. Because the woman who's now keeping the ghost of a burned murder victim as her self-proclaimed *pet* is the woman I want inspiring the Guildboss of the Fleetfinger's Guild *and* the same woman I want giving gifts to my charge. How *lovely*," Seline hissed.

The thief gave her an askance look. "You know, you have been nothing but irritable since we started this little arrangement."

"Cut her some slack, Riorik. She's not used to dealing with this kind of shit," Akaran interrupted. "Not sure any of us are."

"I'd like to add that you threatened to murder me if I didn't help," she pointed out. "Or did you forget that part?"

"My dear, that wasn't a threat. That was merely a statement to motivate you into performing a service that was, and still is, desperately needed," he countered. "Would you be happier if I hadn't, knowing what you know now?"

"*Much*," she shot back. "I would love nothing more than to *not know* any of this, to *not* have him throwing up behind my house or bleeding in my bed, to *not* be a party to an underworld purge, and to *not* know that there are vampires killing people at whim."

"Those are all good points. I'd like to state that I'd be happier if I didn't know any of those things either," Akaran grumbled. "You don't have to make me go throw up outside, the chamberpot is —"

"*Mine*, you foul-smelling ass. The chamberpot is *mine* and *no*."

Riorik gave them both a warm, inviting smile and opened his arms wide. "Ah, but think of the things you'll learn from this experience."

The healer gave a quick glance at some of her belongings in the little hut and frowned. "I'm learning how much it's going to cost to pack these things and move to another province."

"No need for that," the older man countered, "because by the time that our works are done, this truly will be the safest city in the Kingdom."

"I'd believe that if you didn't have a moving blog of shadow shifting on your cheek," Seline snapped as she pointed at the blotch he'd tried to cover with shoddy makeup. "We are not even going to *discuss* how nervous that makes me."

"You never did tell us much about how you came into contact with it," Akaran added. "I keep meaning to ask but…"

"But you trust that as I've kept it under control for so long, you're happier not knowing?"

The priest gave a silent nod as he forced himself back upright.

"Take this and let me explain," Riorik replied as he tossed a small, corked glass vial with a yellowish powder inside over at him. "Direct from the Eclipsian. She has been made aware of your restorative efforts, and seems to think that this will help remove the lingering effects of the cocasa."

"Is he going to throw up more?"

"Yeah, am I?"

The thief answered them both with a chuckle. "She didn't say, but I would assume that there will be a period of discomfort. Erine told me you'd need three days after ingesting it before you'd be useful for much."

"Does he have three days to spare?" Seline asked.

Akaran rolled the vial up and down as he stared at the glistening yellow dust. "I'm not useful for much else right now," he admitted. "Telburn wants to put me through whatever torture he has designed, quote, 'When the sun reaches its peak,' on the seventh."

The healer frowned. "That's barely two days from now, not three. Did you forget how to count?"

He sighed and plucked the cork from the bottle. "Then I'm going to have to get through this faster than she suggested. I don't suppose the Manor would be willing to let you take a couple of days away…?"

"Ridora has already threatened to have my hide if I don't start showing up on time, so no."

"Oh, that's not a concern," Riorik interrupted. "I'll be sure that Austilin is on hand for anything you may need whenever your assistant isn't."

She whipped her head around and gave the thief a cold, hateful stare. "I am *not* his *anything*, let alone his *assistant*."

"You are assisting him, yes? Therefor, my dear, you are his assistant."

Seline clenched her fists as the priest popped the cork and poured the contents of the vial into his mouth with a shudder and a retching noise. "Goddess above, I hate you both."

The thief ignored her and covered his mouth with his hand. "Oh. Oh, dear, Akaran, she mentioned you were to mix that in wine! Not drink it straight!"

All the priest responded with was another pained gagging noise as he clasped a hand over his lips and another over his throat. Tears streamed freely down his cheeks as the powder somehow simultaneously managed to dry out his mouth *and* made him foam up around his lips. He started to thrash on the bed before Seline took pity and marched over with a flask of maybe-wine in her hand.

He took it gratefully as the thief cleared his throat. "As I don't know how long you'll have before you lose consciousness, I will explain my current situation as quickly as I can."

And he did.

His involvement in 'current affairs,' as he put it, started months ago — even before Akaran had banished Daringol the first time. "Rmaci had a handler in Gonta, a man named Ralafon. I know you had a brief interaction with him, but, he was not who he seemed to be. By and large, he served to shuffle stories Rmaci could gather back and forth to her masters in the Blazing Empire of Civa, limited as it was."

"Does that mean that the Civans know about the Coldstone?"

"That means that the Civans know less than what our Queen does, as Usaic was intentionally obtuse about his efforts. I imagine she had ways to discern some aspects of his work, though *how* or *what* I don't claim to know. I've had numerous dealings with Rala, though once he wore out his welcome, well. One cannot abide by a guest staying unwanted."

When pressed to explain exactly what he meant by that, the thief refused to answer directly. Instead, he simply reached down and petted the knife on his belt with a wistful little smile. "Regardless. At a certain point of our conversation, he decided that I would be best insulted by way of having a vial of foul... fluid... flung at me. I was insulted, though I came to discover later to what extent."

As he went on with his explanation, the crux of the matter ended up being the contents of the vial. Given his recent dealings with assorted priests of one stripe or another, Riorik decided to have the goo investigated. The results, he was told, were poorly at best: the mixture was a mix between *shiriak* blood and corpse-ash.

"*Shiriak*?" Seline asked cautiously, despite secretly *not* wanting to know.

"Demons," the exorcist replied. "Small ones. Scavengers, mostly. Yellow little cretins, smell likes the inside of a goat's asshole."

"And someone harvested their... blood?"

"It wouldn't be the first time," he admitted. "Demon blood is a prized commodity in certain circles. Prized, and contraband. I'm within rights to burn someone's shop down if I find out they're selling it."

Riorik shifted uncomfortably in his seat. "With or without the vendor still inside? I ask only out of... professional curiosity."

Akaran took another long drink and shrugged. "Honestly? After what happened to Rmaci, I'm fine never seeing another burned body again."

"That didn't answer my question."

"I know."

Slightly deterred by the verbal dodge, the thief continued on. While the leftover residue was promptly confiscated and disposed of, nothing else was said of it. The Civan spymaster was never mentioned again, and for the next few weeks, he didn't experience much in the way of symptoms. A rash, at first, a cough. A few restless nights. Nothing that wasn't unheard of for someone to suffer in the back alleys of the City of Mud, though trips to local healers and alchemists did nothing to ease the symptoms of either.

It wasn't until Akaran return to the city – albeit in relatively short passing – that things started to take a turn for the worse. "I meant to stop by and see you while you spent time at the surgeon's *practionia*, but while you were there, I was feeling... discomfort."

Discomfort was a small word for it. Over the ensuing two weeks, the master-thief suffered from intense nightmares, a "discomfort in my lower digestion," a worsening rash, and more. "The symptoms faded at the same time you left, though I must admit I was far more grateful that I quit feeling so dreadful that I didn't think to understand how the two were related. It wasn't until another month later that I realized what was going on."

That realization came when the wraith had manifested – albeit briefly – in the middle of a meeting with some of his men. A blotch appeared on his stomach, and as they watched, it crawled up his chest, sprouted a shadow-laced arm, and tried to rip his face off. He didn't explain why he was shirtless, and nobody felt that they would be better off to ask.

"We had a guest arrive from the local Stara shrine. She immediately attempted some form of exorcism or banishment, but it didn't complete the task – as you've noticed. She claimed she 'sealed it away,' though as it would turn out, 'away' was another word for –"

"She sealed it in you," Akaran interrupted, "which is half the job. The other half is to purify the soul."

"Ah, is that what happened? She mentioned something about an 'act of penitence,' and 'time to be spent purifying my soul from the grip of darkness,' but as I am somewhat adverse to a stranger 'purifying' my 'anything,' I politely declined."

The exorcist pursed his lips as his stomach started to burn and his skin started to feel... funky. "Stara, you said? Locurat or other?"

Riorik frowned. "An Undlajunct, I believe. Whatever it is they name the third-in-command of such a shrine."

"She should've known better," he grunted. "You should've been marched directly to the shrine and held over until a Lover could've come to collect or correct you."

"None of which sounds like a way someone like I would have been eager to spend my time, if we are to be honest, so I politely declined. It wasn't until after the nightmares returned that I decided that I needed to take steps to come here."

Steps that were helped by sudden distrust aimed his way from the members of the Fleetfinger's Guild in Gonta. They seemed to think that working for a man that might randomly sprout an extra arm that may try to kill them was a greater danger than simply working for a man known as 'The Hobbler.' "I came to an agreement that I would allow my interests in the city to be bought out under amicable terms with the understanding that I would find a way to seek treatment."

The healer and priest gave each other looks that silently screamed, 'He was chased out of town' to each other. As Riorik went on a brief tangent about the terms and conditions, Seline quietly mouthed to the exorcist, "They didn't want to deal with him either."

All Akaran could do was nod.

That was partly because it was impossible to get a word in edgewise, and partly because the powder the thief had given him had made his tongue begin to swell. It was also making his hands shake and his vision start to swim along the edges.

If Riorik noticed, he didn't care. He continued on otherwise unabated. "The dreams told me where to go. Really, it didn't leave much of a choice. This thing... whatever it is. It wants you, Akaran. It wants you dead. I get the feeling that it's... hmm. How best to say this. I feel that it is almost grateful that it knows how to get to you."

"Were the dreams of that... that woman...?" Seline asked.

He shuddered at the thought. "No. No, for that I will say no."

"How were you… how have you been able to keep it from…" the exorcist tried to ask before he gave up and gestured wildly with his hands in the air.

"Able to keep from succumbing to it like you've seen others do?" the thief asked. When Akaran nodded, he explained as best as he could. "I assume that it's because of the concentration – or lack thereof. Aside from that? When it first began to speak to me I made sure that it understood that the only way it could claim me was if I was dead. Granted, it was soon after that it tried to claw my face off but I presume that it took the warning to heart."

"You bullied it into silence," Seline marveled. "I'm… I'm impressed. But it didn't show you that woman…?"

"No, again for which I am thankful. When we met her a few days ago, I will admit that I felt a feeling of… familiarity… with her, for no other better word. I suspect, if what he's said is accurate, that there's reason enough for that."

"If," she replied with a tired sigh. "If."

"You doubt?"

"I want to," the healer admitted. "I want him to be wrong, I want him to have made all of this up, I want him to be wrong about what he swears is coming and what he swears is already here."

"Ship included?" Akaran mumbled as he drifted to sleep. "Because ship *especially*," he slurred.

Riorik looked over at the poor, bloody, and now blissfully-unconscious young man and nodded in respectful understanding. "Yet it's hard to assume he's wrong when he's shown us both the miserable ways he's been right."

She nodded and rubbed her temples with her fingertips. "Can I be honest with you, Lord Hobbler? Or is it Master Hobbler? Or Dalli…?"

"Please; not Dallidon. Hobbler itself is fine, if you need to leave me titled. As far as honesty? I would ask nothing less."

Seline took a deep breath and leaned back against the counter with her palms flat on the stone surface. "I've spent the last six years of my life in the Manor. I know that the people there have seen things. Done things. I care for them because they couldn't cope with the things they saw. Or did."

He nodded in understanding and spoke up before she could continue. "Yet you assumed it was a safe place, one that wouldn't draw the ire of such monsters that left men there to rot."

"I've started carrying a knife," she admitted. "I don't know what to do with it. Stab people, I suppose. I don't know if I'd be good at it. Never had to find out. Don't know if it'd do anything to protect me from this… vampire… or whatever it may actually be. Piss it off? Chase it away? I can't tell anyone that I'm scared of it because if I do, then I'm going to be planted in a bed right next to Bistra and the others."

"Have you asked him what to do?"

"Didn't have to. He gave me a long list of things I'm supposed to carry with me all the time. Silver. An icon from the Repository that I managed to swipe out of an Order waystation – after he told me how to get in and out without being noticed. I've taken to weaving a sprig of buckthorn in my hair whenever I leave the *dorma*. Doesn't feel like… enough."

The thief smiled sagely. "I'll admit that all of this – wraiths, nightmares, demon blood, vampires – is not in my personal purview. Is my interest in the sins and vices of men? Absolutely; as long as they are alive. That, and aiding their departure from the world of the living, at times. The after?" He shook his head and sighed. "It's no secret that there are things in the dark that, occasionally, have taken a kind eye towards men such as myself, and less of a secret that we share the shadows with true evil that walks the world. Now and again, that evil likes to take advantage of those of us in the dark that it finds, sometimes to exploit, sometimes merely to hunt. It's the nature of our business."

It was Seline's turn to shudder again. "I never gave it any thought. Suppose I should've. Afraid that if I start jumping at every shadow I see, I'll never stop."

"He raised something of a rabble back in Gonta. All at once, the city *knew* demons existed. Most people didn't take it well. I assume that's how you're feeling now?"

"But I *did* know. I just didn't think they'd ever come *here*."

"Well. We can't change what they've done. We can only change that they're here – and how soon we can make them leave," he replied with a faint razor-thin smile. "Though, I'll say this, if it helps. I have taken some effort to track down a few holy men that are friendly towards my new employees. I was going to politely ask that they *find* some kind of protective relics. I'll ensure that you're given one."

"You'd do that for me? Why?"

"Because we're friends," Riorik answered smoothly, "and I keep my friends near and dear."

Even after he left, she wasn't sure if that was a threat or not.

III. A GATHERING OF HEADACHES
Pre-noon of Londis, the 7th of Firstgrow

The outright horrific concoction that Riorik had provided had done a wonderful job in clearing the cocasa out of Akaran's system. It had done a far worse job on the street, the gutter, Seline's dorma (both *-sil* and *-sul*), his clothes, his borrowed clothes, and donated clothes that one of Riorik's men had dropped off the next day. Two days of the violent purge later, and it was time for Headmaster-Adept Telburn's so-called wonderful idea to finally restore the priest's ability to use magic.

Those days couldn't come fast enough for anyone involved. Despite Seline's desire to get the exorcist out of her hair, the bigger problem was the deterioration of society outside. The city was one sneeze away from riots erupting from the base of the Falls all the way to the gate, and everyone from Henderschott to Elsith had their hands full making sure every faction in town stayed *calm* – and didn't try to take advantage of things.

As far as Riorik was concerned, it was heaven.

For everyone else, it felt like the dress-rehearsal for the apocalypse.

None of which Akaran could bother to care about right now. Then again, he had good reason. The cocasa purge left him with just enough strength to put one foot in front of the other. That weakness, his bloodshot eyes, and the traces of vomit on his breath did him no favors when he arrived at what he could only describe (now, and forever) as a gathering of headaches.

The gathering at the Granalchi Summoning Grounds – situated in a far corner of the Annex compound, well away from the towers and walled off with bricks and wards to avoid any cases of *accidental* citizen entanglement – would have been an impressive show of force any other day. There were a handful of mages that Akaran couldn't recognize (though their insignia marked them all as either Mattanics and Elementalists), which wasn't unexpected. However, even though they had promised to help, he was a bit surprised to see the Tidesinger and his opposite, the Oldstone present.

He was even more surprised (and much more dismayed) to see a paunchy, short, balding man who went by the name Alverach standing next to the Tidesinger. *Wait, no, that's wrong*, Akaran caught himself. *Elverich. That's his name. Sire Elverich, a... watersculpt? Whatever that is.*

I'm sure I'm going to find out.

He was. But not before he caught sight of Telburn and Adept Ishtva, and had to deal with many shouts of "Greetings!" and "Welcome!" that were accompanied by as many indifferent looks from the others. None of which he felt like matching. All of which he did, because in a few minutes these nice people were either going to kill him or help restore him.

That was also going to be delayed, albeit briefly. Karaj appeared out of nowhere in a hooded white robe and spoke so firmly and quickly that not only did the priest not realize they were *there* at first, but even who it was. Which, he had to admit, was how Maiden-Templar Prostil's assistant seemed to like it.

"You decided to take action without consultation of the Order?"

Akaran gave the hooded figure a dirty look that you could've seen a mile away even if it *wasn't* a bright and shiny day. "You kicked me out of it."

"Your actions did," her aide retorted quickly and firmly, "and you undertake more actions that go against your instructions."

"My instructions were to stay quiet and don't start anything," the exorcist quipped back.

Karaj looked at the open field and slowly ground their teeth back and forth. The Annex's Summoning Grounds could have been used to hold a festival, a jousting tourney, or even a dance in the summer fields. It was a flat field with flags outlining a square that was buttressed by the curved wall that ringed the Granalchi's enclave. There was absolutely nothing special about it – except for his arrival. Everyone had questions, and they were quick to arrive.

Quicker than he wanted, for sure, quicker than he could deal with, maybe, and quicker than he could make sense of them – well, that was a distinct possibility. "AH! There you are," Telburn began, "I was wondering if you'd ever find your way here."

"I was stopped by the Guard three times on my way here. Didn't realize Henderschott was looking for me." That was a lie, though an easy one. Both Riorik and Seline had already passed word his way that the Lieutenant was after him, though nobody really knew why.

Plus, it gave him an excuse to cover up the fact that he'd spent almost an hour two blocks from here trying to keep get his hands to stop shaking. Whatever was about to happen was necessary, but nerve-wracking (even before the threat of summary execution). "Ah. Yes, he is. I didn't think you wanted me to let him know where you were – just to be safe."

"You don't think he has good intentions?" Akaran asked with his eyebrows lifting in surprise. "I can't imagine you'd want to harbor a fugitive..."

"Nothing of the sort," the mage replied with a soothing tone to his voice. "He wants to know what you know, and you've made it clear that you won't say what you know until you can prove it, and I, in all honesty, neither want to get in the middle of it – or risk that he'll have you held until you talk."

"Ah," the younger man replied with a little sigh of resignation. "You're worried you'll lose your toy."

Telburn gave him a wide smile and draped his arm over the exorcist's shoulders. "Education waits for no man, and there's only so much we can learn in a given lifetime. I'd hate to wait longer than I must."

Oh, I'd hate for you to miss this chance. It's not like it's my life we're playing with, the priest groused to himself. "So... uh. I assume this means you found everything you needed."

"Found, prepared, and documented. This is groundbreaking research, and I had to even send a missive to the Office of the Dean-Adept in Ogibus to advise them of our efforts. Your name is circulating through some very interesting halls of power."

"It is?"

"It is! No reason to sound so concerned, my boy; you are a man of historical intellectual importance now. Elementalists and para-psiphonics will be studying the results of today's experiment for *decades* if not longer," the Headmaster replied with far, *far* more excitement than he should've been allowed to have.

Akaran swallowed nervously and looked at the field full of assembled mages, priests, and the not-insignificant number of aides that each had brought with them. While the gathering consisted only of a handful of principal agents, it looked like each one had brought five more people with them. At a minimum. "So, let's talk about what's going to happen here. Exactly. I want details."

"And details you will have, young blood," Telburn replied as he ushered the priest forward with a wave of his left arm (and a firm push with his right). "Everyone! I think you all know the man of the hour. It's time we begin this little endeavor."

"I do," a sullen voice intoned. "You'll give me a moment with him, Headmaster." The mage turned his head to the interloper and suddenly shut up as Karaj stepped between them. "Does this look like you're staying quiet?"

"It's quiet right now, isn't it?" Akaran asked with a futile shrug.

The Lover shifted on their heels and clenched their fists between deep breaths. "We were notified of this endeavor. I am here to provide assistance in a very specific way."

Akaran took a moment to take a deep breath of his own as he looked a little closer. When he saw the outline of the sword on Karaj's hip, he had all the answers he needed. "Before or after?"

"During, if I must."

The exorcist swallowed hard as his stomach twisted itself into a knot. "The Order isn't offering any leeway with this one, are they?"

"No."

"Can I at least ask that you make it quick?"

"If I decide the need arises, I give word, it will be done before anyone can stop me," Catherine's assistant calmly intoned. "As of this moment, you are under an Inquiry of Order. This is resolved today, come one way or another – unless you leave these grounds now, and under your own power."

The knot in his stomach turned into a lead weight that threatened to leave a crater where Akaran stood. "So this is do or die, huh?"

The Lover nodded their head slowly. "The life we have is Hers to decide how it is used. My blade moves with Her wishes, and I do as I do to honor the Lady of Love. I would prefer that this is more 'do' than 'die,' as you've said it – but there are very many questions for what comes after."

Akaran closed his eye and bowed his head for a moment and steeled himself. "Karaj, with respect, if this doesn't end well – I have a journal in a dormosul; Seline Valdin's. She works at the Manor. Consider everything in it to be my last words, and the request inside treated as such."

"Matters of Order business?"

"If you won't believe me when I'm alive, maybe you'll believe me if I die trying to prove the point," the exorcist spat back. "Everyone thinks I'm mad."

Karaj paused and tilted their head to the side before they placed a hand on the exorcist's shoulder. "Child? It doesn't matter what I think. Or what the others of authority think. Only one thing does."

"What's that?"

Catherine's assistant smiled under their cloak and stepped away as the Headmaster appeared almost out of thin air at Akaran's side. "That we haven't been instructed to stop you from On High."

Akaran blinked and mouthed a nervous, "Oh," as he braced himself for the little endeavor.

Little was not the right word for it. As they approached the first set of flags, the younger man caught sight of what had been cut into the grass at their feet – and in some cases, milled into the dirt. Someone had spent *hours* etching wardmarks and what appeared to be a thin unbroken trench from corner to corner. It wasn't much wider than an inch at most, but it was deep, and filled with an odd glittering red powder.

The assembled throng of mages, priests, and their aides more or less turned to him all at once, and the murmurers from the entire lot immediately made the hair on Akaran's arms stand up. While everyone gave an additional round of, "Hellos," and "Welcomes," and, "Good to see you," there were a few that gave him a dirty look – the Oldstone, for one, and Elverich, for another – and another that was too busy with the setup to even look in his direction.

That was Ishtva, and the mage was busy installing a pair of hip-high metal poles on the ground. They were silvery and both had been shined to a mirror finish. Whatever they were made of absolutely boggled Akaran's mind, and it didn't help when the Adept slapped the second pillar and an arc of lightning bounced between them. "Telburn, I don't know how comfortable I am having this many people..."

"Swallow your discomfort boy, it's only going to get worse," the older mage retorted bluntly out of the corner of his mouth. Before the Lover could ask what in the pit *that* was supposed to mean, Telburn cleared his throat and addressed the crowd. "Assembled Masters, Adepts, seekers of knowledge, and Be-titled Individuals, welcome once again to the Summoning Grounds. It is time for the grandest mystical undertaking the city has seen in half a century. I present to you a man some of you know, and one some of you have only heard of – the exorcist bereft of magic."

"I'm not some damned show-pony," the aforementioned exorcist muttered under his breath.

"In my show, you are as presented," the Headmaster whispered rudely, "so prepare to prance, pony-boy. There's much on the line here, so mind your tongue. I do not have time to be concerned over manners or feelings."

Akaran bristled but before he could snarl something vile at the mage, a small procession of knife-wielding Adepts in dark blue robes broke off from the main cluster and marched their way. Telburn stepped away and let the four surround the priest. "Hey, what are –" he managed to get out before they quickly turned and flanked him protectively.

The march started quickly, and when he began to lag behind, a very firm hand from one of the mages at his back pressed him forward even as Telburn continued on. "As is standard practice, you've all been advised of what your tasks are and what is to be done. However, due to the *living* and *unique* nature of our experiment, I will explain things in full as the boy is made ready."

"Made ready...?" the priest asked in alarm, even as he overheard one of the mages in the crowd say something about him being a 'unique asshole,' or some such. *Thanks, Elverich, missed you too.*

"Of course, I should probably also warn the object of our interest of what's to be done, in entirely."

"You didn't tell him?" Ishtva asked as he stood up from the metal columns.

"He understands the concept, if not the execution."

"He's also not an object," Akaran muttered under his breath as his escorts turned and directed him to a doorway in the rear wall. "This is not making me feel comfortable."

Telburn smiled and nodded his head at the crowd before he turned and addressed the exorcist in a voice just above a whisper. "If comfort is what you seek, there are many a whores in Lower Naradol that would help. You asked for a miracle of magic – it doesn't come without cost." Then, as if he hadn't said anything at all, he cleared his throat and turned back to the assembled throng. "As you all know by now, the crux of this man's condition isn't by such trivial magic of divine curse or restrictive invocation. He has done a task most ill-advised: and simultaneously drained and allowed his aura to be filled with ether not of this realm."

Altund grumbled something about, 'not believing it was possible,' and a few of the other, unnamed Adepts matched his concerns with their own. It was Ishtva who finally spoke up to calm down the crowd, and he did it in a delightfully offensive way they cut the wind out of Akaran's sails in a hurry. "The Academy has often warned of the dangers posed by those not trained as an Adept to dabble in forces not of this world, and what is before you is the finest example of what happens when one thinks he knows more than what the All-Encompassing World itself controls."

He wasn't *wrong*, but it still hurt.

As Telburn continued on with his description of the events that were about to unfold, using such terms as, 'advanced para-psiphonic manipulations of trans-dimensional etheric substrates,' and, 'elemental transference through a shunt of manually-displaced astral super-consciousness,' Akaran... well.

Once his escorts had him to a door into the outer wall (which turned out to be more of an 'outer hall' than just a 'wall') while the Headmaster opined in the field, the gravity of what was about to fall on his shoulders made him sag against the doorway. His escorts didn't do anything to stop him or help him up as he stood there shaking. All he could do was pray – and he did.

After the first few words, he wasn't even sure what he was praying for. Guidance? Help? Peace? Patience? Possibly to find a way to salvage his reputation when this was finished? *All* he knew to do was to pray.

So he did. He didn't stop until the Headmaster came into the room behind him and expressed his dismay that he wasn't ready yet. "I gave you four strict instructions that —" he started before the priest cut him off.

"Give them a break, Telburn. I can't stop shaking, so whatever it is, just… a moment. Please."

"Trembles? I was lead to believe by that girl from the Manor that you had been sufficiently weaned off of the effects of cocasa, and the misery that follows extended use of it."

"I am," Akaran admitted, "which is a shitty absence in its own right. It's not that, I'm just… I don't know what I was expecting but it wasn't…"

The Adept smiled and nodded his head reassuringly. "You have fears over the experiment."

He took a deep breath and tried to put himself at ease. "It's not that I'm concerned that you're experimenting, it's that you're referring to me as an object. I'm not a 'thing,' Headmaster, I'm a 'person.' I'm *only* a person. I'm the only person *like* me. I can't even ask what will happen if this goes wrong because I don't think you know what'll happen if this goes *right*." He looked up from his shaking hands and frowned. "Actually, let me take that back. I *am* concerned that you're experimenting, but that much I understand."

"Ah," Telburn said after a moment's thought. "I think I understand the concern. We have to distance ourselves at times, and place room between us from our works. I am a man that channels the ether, that works with it. I am never the subject of the event, as much as my will and intellect is. The work may move through me, it may channel through my aura, it may interact with objects I have or possess, but *I* am not the experiment. My *work* is. If we don't take that distinction in our field, we begin to inject our sense of self into it. Doing so removes any objectivity we may have when it comes to our studies."

"Which is the exact opposite of what we do in the Order," the exorcist retorted with a little sigh. "Because it's our faith, it's our will, it's our understanding, and it's our vision of right and wrong that we based our calls to the Goddess on. If we don't center the magic in ourselves and understand that it will manifest because of who we are, then…"

"I do understand. Perhaps though, it might be easier to discuss it in these terms: we are attempting to work on the block that has prevented you from being complete. It isn't *you* that our focus is on, rather the etheric mass *inside* you. As such, we will strive to be as careful as we can be with the rest of your body."

Akaran swallowed nervously. "I'm not sure that's as reassuring as you had hoped it would be."

"Perhaps it was, perhaps it wasn't," the Headmaster admitted. "Either way, time is running out. Manipulations of the ether involve careful understanding of all the physics of the world – and that includes the position of the star that shines bright upon the surface of this ball of mud and dirt we live on."

"Oh. Right, sorry," Akaran sighed in resignation. "So what do you need me to do?"

"Not just you, but them," he said as he gestured at the armed escorts. "You will need to be shorn of more than just your clothes."

"Excuse me, what?"

"Naked, my boy. You'll need to be naked, and cut clean of as much hair as we can."

Akaran blushed a shade of crimson he didn't know existed. "Excuse me, *what*? You expect that I'm going to... do whatever... whatever it is out there *naked*?"

"And shorn, do not forget the shorn," the mage replied.

The blush dropped deeper down his chest. "BUT WHY?"

"We are about to call upon three different elemental states. The first, magic of geology, will likely result in your clothes being ruined. As you've recently alluded to being poor, I doubt you'd wish to lose even one outfit if you have no say in the matter."

"Well no," Akaran started to admit before the Headmaster cut him off again.

"Second, we'll be summoning elemental aspects of water. Not as dangerous or disastrous to your clothing, but it will likely leave you utterly drenched. That will be an issue when they invoke the magic of the elemental aspects of ice," the mage finished. "I will advise, again, that you be well and truly cut to the skin – less you wish to risk your hair to be frozen completely solid."

"But... but it would thaw..."

Telburn gave him a wicked little grin. "It might, yes. Though if we have to use elemental aspects of flame to hasten such a result, I've no stomach for the scent of burnt beard. I've done it enough to know."

The priest tried to work his mouth in a way that would form words, and only managed to get out pained noises instead. "I can't... you..."

"Poor boy, you act as if this is the first time you've ever gone through such a thing."

"It's *not*," Akaran whined, "and that's why I know I didn't like it."

"Your safety is my paramount concern," the mage replied, "so do understand that my reasons are quite valid. I've no desire to see all you have to offer the world, so this decision is not one being made for any lustful reasons – I assure you."

That he even needed to point that out didn't help, but the exorcist finally gave in and took one of the knives the other mages were offering him. "Fine just... tell me what you're planning to do?"

As he began to strip, Telburn was gracious enough to block the doorway so people couldn't peak in early. Not that it was about to matter, but the gesture was nice. "Ah, yes. I saw the other priests scratching their heads as I talked, so let me explain it in a way that might make more sense."

To his credit, he tried.

He really, really tried.

To the best that Akaran could understand it, the 'experiment' (and he *hated* that word) was going to unfold in five stages. First, four different Adepts – geomancers and conjurers alike – would create a hip-high mineral wall around the exorcist. "The measurements are exact. The wall will be no less than twenty feet from where you stand to any given side. Longer, from where you stand to the corners, though the numbers are not important for your understanding."

Those Adepts would be joined by the Oldstone actively invoking a spell (or more, there was some confusion on that point) to bless their efforts. Or bless the wall. Or possibly just the dirt. Again, there was confusion on that. That blessing was critical to the effort, though he didn't explain why at first.

Further, the next step would be to create a 'singularly-thick sphere of hydrologically-charged ether absent of typical movement,' which Akaran finally determined that he meant that they'd make a ball of water. When he challenged the mage on that assumption, the retort was a simple: "Well, yes, but it will be more like a shell. We won't simply create a ball and drown you in it. Ishtva will be responsible for that step."

That made him feel *slightly* better, but not much.

As Telburn continued, the third step would be to have a 'bridge' created that would serve to divert magic away from the priest and into the mud box. "This step is critical," he warned, "as it will serve as the shunt for the ether you have stored inside. We will introduce it into the sphere – which will serve as both a conduit and a shield – and then siphon it into a neutral field through the bridge."

To put emphasis on the 'critical' part of the spell, he made it clear that he'd handle the channeling efforts to create it and deal with channeling the offending magic through it. "I'll be joined by the Tidesinger. His essence in the mix may even be more critical than that of Altund's, given the situation. Oh, and the watersculpt. He'll be responsible for creating the bridge and merging it with Ishtva's sphere."

"Is that your way of admitting that I pissed off the minion of a Goddess on Her home turf?"

"It is merely an acknowledgment that there are beings that hold sway in realms other than this one, and that your claims of intervention of less-than-Divine mandates would suggest additional precautions are taken," the mage replied with an easy shrug. "Far be it from me to claim I know everything."

It was hard to believe that he *didn't* think he knew everything, but it was a statement that Akaran was willing to let go. For now. Either way, the final step wouldn't be as exhausting.

The ether that they were going siphon would be allowed to dissipate into the world once it was removed from his system. "An exercise that will occur naturally as it pools in the boundaries of the wall," the Headmaster explained. "To expedite the effect, we will have wards placed along the barrier to serve as a shield, one powered by the magic bleeding off from you. Much the same way that Usaic hid his own efforts in creating the coldstone."

He did leave out the part that Akaran felt was the most important – the how. The very big, very pointed, "How?"

"How? How what? There's many methods we'll be using to bleed –"

"How will you get it out of me? What's step four?"

The Headmaster blanched, then finally began to explain that facet of the encounter as the last of Akaran's hair was sliced off of his scalp and the aides helped him pull his tunic off. Before he could, he caught sight of something he hadn't expected to see – intricate scars etched into his skin in the shape of magical runes. "My boy...? What are those?" he asked as he gestured at the marks.

"My Words," Akaran replied simply, as if that explained everything.

Telburn cautiously reached over and let his fingers hover over the etchings on the priest's upper arm. "I have a very sneaking suspicion that were magic be your friend at the moment, these would radiate power. I don't quite recognize the language – or I should say that I recognize the language, just not the spelling."

Akaran brushed his hand away and shifted nervously as he undid the tie holding the swath of fabric covering his hips. "You're going to make me talk about them, aren't you?"

"I'm about to operate on your ether. If you have anything on you that may have an unexpected reaction, I'd like to know about it now instead of when we have to find a bucket and a shovel to clean you up off of the grass."

The priest made a noncommittal grunt. "Fine. It's ritual work. Those are my Words."

"I think you mentioned that already, though you didn't give much of a clarification..."

"Sometimes, we like to have the Words of the Goddess etched on our skin. It lets us channel them easier, and with greater force when we need to call on Her. I have five," he explained before he pointed at his arm, the side of his head, the top of his scalp, and then the back of his neck in order. "Bonds, kormatpat, luminoso, and purify."

"That's only four?"

He sighed and crossed his arms in an 'x' over his chest. Two long marks that Telburn had assumed were sparring scars turned out to be something else entirely. "*Eberandia*."

"I don't think I know what that means? Or... kormatpat, for that matter. Purify is straightforward, and I have seen many a priest of your order use luminoso to light their way. The other two? They are not spells I am familiar with."

"Good," Akaran grumbled as he uncrossed his arms and let his hands fall loose to his sides. "Now that I'm naked, do you think we can continue the question-and-answer session at a different time?"

The Headmaster nodded and took a brief moment to take note of his other scars. While most were minor, there was a giant one down his stomach that was speckled with deep craters and an angry red discoloration. "Of course. I'm merely... well. I assumed your knee had been your worst injury."

"It only makes me *wish* I was dead," the priest remarked snidely as he faced the door and took a deep breath. "Right then. Anything else I need to know? Aside from the part you decided not to tell me?"

"The part I...? Oh, yes. Here, take this, read it, and memorize it quickly. This is all you have to do. The rest of the efforts will be handled by my people, and the others."

All of that happened over the next few minutes. As soon as he stepped outside – fully naked, fully on display, and entirely *done* with this crap – time seemed to move in a blur. The assembled Granalchi, priests, and gawkers present took the time to look him over as he marched along the field. Most, thankfully, were polite and kept their stares to a minimum. A couple of younger boys snickered, and he thought he heard someone gasp when they saw the scar across his stomach.

He *knew* he heard the Tidesinger utter a startled curse when he saw the mess that was the side of Akaran's knee. For that matter, he distinctly thought he heard Karaj muttered something under their breath, too, and while he couldn't make it out, it sounded like some kind of profanity-laced spell. Why, he didn't know, but he swore he felt the stitches in his leg twitch.

Getting situated at the center of the grounds only took a few moments. He stumbled more than once in the cold, wet grass, and while his first escort vanished sometime after he left the preparation area, a new one appeared by his side before he could finish figuring out where, exactly, he should stand. That kindness was offered by Ishtva, who offered a few sage words of wisdom to the naked exorcist.

"I know our last encounter didn't exactly go well," the Adept admitted, "but I didn't think it would come to this. I don't know what Telburn told you, but he moved a *lot* of pieces around to get you here."

"I know something he doesn't, and I think that pisses him off," Akaran countered.

"Oh, it's more than that. He isn't a man that likes to consider the thought of miracles, divine influence, or other. And here you are, the object of just that. He's determined to show the world that there's nothing that can't be solved with applications of magical effort. *Man-made* magical effort," the mage stressed.

The exorcist just grunted and read over the instructions one last time before he handed them to the Adept. "So he's relying on a man of the Gods to prove that the Gods didn't do something?"

As he talked, the mage knelt down and carefully fastened shackles to his ankles. "Don't worry about these. We just don't want to risk you getting washed away somewhere," Ishtva replied before answering, "and no. He wants to prove that man can overcome whatever the Gods put in our way."

"With the help of spokesmen from two different Gods?"

"Magic is magic, my friend. You stay at this school long enough and you'll begin to wonder if any of this makes sense," he replied as he fastened the last leather shackle tight. "Now. You want your magic back and I want to see if this works. Come out the other side safely, priest; there's plenty of people that can't wait to see how this is done."

That wasn't exactly the vote of confidence he was looking for, but he took it anyway. In short order, the mages and priests all stood at their assigned places. The Oldstone was flanked by four Adepts in dark brown, muddy cloaks. Sire Elverich preened right beside Tidesinger Quinchecco and Telburn both. Of the two, Elverich looked like he belonged there.

Actually, no, the way that the paunchy, balding twit stood with his hands on his hips and his back as straight as it could be? He looked like he *owned* the yard. *Arrogant little cocksniffer probably thinks he's the most important person here.*

If he did, that wasn't far from the truth.

Still, with everyone present, there wasn't anything left to do but begin. A short speech from Telburn later – done, Akaran assumed, because he *loved* to hear himself speak – and one of the most painful decisions he'd ever made began to unfold.

The four summoner-type Adepts marched along the edges of the square they had carved into the ground and began to chant rhythmically under their breath. Two traveled along the south-west face towards the north, and the other two traveled along the south-east. When they reached the corner, two of them stopped and began a steady walk back to the origin point. The other two continued along the side of the square and reached the northernmost point where the Oldstone was waiting.

Nothing happened that the priest could see on the first pass. On their second segmented lap, the red dust they had sprinkled in the crack began to sparkle and shoot out of the ground like burning embers. On the third lap, the embers blossomed even higher until the ground began to give way.

A thick rolling wall of dirt and rock pushed out from the square-shaped crack. It slowly split the ground open like a tooth inexorably pushing through a swollen set of grass-covered gums. It was a horrible analogy, but it was the only thought that jumped to Akaran's mind.

Once it had fully egressed, Altund put his hands into the dirt and merely pushed it aside like it was nothing more than a cloud of smoke. *His* invocation was louder and clearer than what the Adepts had used, and for a moment, the exorcist thought he could feel the weight of the spell it in his feet. "*Invicitum, Invictium, ena'tur, rosad; Ena'tur Manastond, Heknas eh Therond, hesuv tia lodam ches vich kor-kall prothal! Hesuv tia lodam!*"

The invocation was a little more forceful than he'd expected, and managed to call on the God of the Unders with a pair of titles he'd never heard Stilamatheric called before. It was in purgalaito, and Akaran was reasonably proud of himself that he'd been able to make it out. "*Invincible, Invincible, eternal soul; Eternal Stone of Power, Inverse of Ether, secure and bury that which has wandered far. Secure and bury!*"

While he marveled at that, Ishtva went to work with his part of the spell. The hazel-eyed mage raised his hands and spoke forcefully and plainly. "Essence of Water! Ether born of pregnant clouds and the expanse off-of shores! I summon, I call, I demand! Set thyself into a form I can touch, set yourself into the shell I demand!" he shouted before he bent down and picked up a bucket of water.

With a solid heave, he pitched the water (and the bucket) over the dirt wall right at the priest. Akaran lurched back and nearly stumbled when the shackles caught him up to avoid it, but instead of soaking him head to toe, the water splashed around his face like he had blocked it with a shield. As Ishtva chanted a few more words and *demanded* that the elements adhere to his commands, the water spread out around the priest and formed a bubble almost nine feet wide around him.

It was a breathtaking, beautiful sight. The water spread around him and flowed in the air. It was like he was diving below the surface of the southern ocean without having to get wet. He stood with his mouth open and simply marveled at the sight all around him even as the sunlight reflected through the growing shell of water. There was more around him than there ever could've been in the bucket, and as he watched, dew and trickles of moisture lifted up from the ground. Grass withered and died as everything at his feet dried out completely.

Still, the death of Telburn's yard didn't stop him from whispering a semi-silent, "Wow," in pure awe. *Maybe, maybe I've been wrong about the Granalchi*, he allowed himself to think.

That thought was dashed a heartbeat later when he remembered all the reasons he *didn't* trust the Granalchi, not the least of which was that they felt that they had the *right* to tell the elements to do anything. Their hubris would be their eventual downfall. He could only hope that their downfall wouldn't be today.

His hopeful wish was made all the more imperative when Elverich joined hands with Tidesinger Quinchecco and the Headmaster. The sound of the water rushing all around him drowned out what they were saying, and he had a hard time even seeing through the translucent shield. What he *felt* was the dried-out, dusty ground at his feet *lurch* in a way that nearly knocked him down, and he had to grab hold of the two metal posts to keep steady.

On the outside of the shell, Elverich went to work and began to show that he could live up to the pretentious airs he put on. The self-proclaimed watersculpt (Akaran *still* had no idea what that was supposed to mean) pulled out a small flute inlaid with something pink and shiny that glistened in the light. He lifted it to his lips and began to play.

The tune was quiet and simple, with only a few notes touched. Life itself moved from his lips, and the essence of water in the shell reacted to its siren call. One note begat another and another. In short order, his melody enticed the shell to disgorge four different vortexes that arced over Akaran's head and touched the ground a yard away – each one aligned to run parallel with each corner of the Oldstone's mud wall.

The vortexes wouldn't settle to be miniature waterspouts, however. No. For all his faults, Elverich was very good at his craft. The Headmaster had wanted bridges, so bridges he would get. As he worked his magic on the flute, each high note gave way to a new arc. Each flat created a pylon. Each sharp created a new beam. By the time he completed his tune, the vortexes had become literal bridges made of swirling trickles of shifting water ever steadily shrinking in size until the ends dangled precariously off of the ground.

When the Tidesinger joined his voice to the song, the bridges doubled in width and began to glow. From inside the shell, Akaran watched as the water lost any dirt that had gotten kicked into the bottom edges, and the sphere sang with an etheric chime. When Telburn added his own reinforcement to it, the bridges gained definition to match their volume.

It was a sight that nobody was going to ever forget. Not for it's beauty, as awesome as it was. No, they wouldn't forget this demonstration of magical art because it failed to warn them of the blood about to flow.

With all the pieces in place, there was one last thing to do. When the two silvery pillars flashed twice – the Headmaster's signal – the priest did exactly what he'd been instructed. It wasn't hard, really. It should have been as simple as putting his hand in the shell. His hand, with the coldstone tight in his grip.

That was all he had to do.

Put his hand in the shell of water. That was it. That, and merely *think* and *imagine* a stream of ice forming that would be washed away in the rush to be carried through the shell, over and through the bridges, and into the box where it would safely melt away into the ether. He would do that, and hold it for a period not to last longer than a quarter candlemark until the magic safely left his system and the ether of the human world would naturally fill him in equal parts and slowly enough to prevent a catastrophic failure.

In his defense, that was all he did.

Nobody was going to believe him, but in his defense, that *is* all he did.

Or at least, that was all he did until everything went wrong.

When he put his hand in the water shell, the resistance he met was firm but nothing he couldn't counter. The outside of the shell bulged out and refused to let his hand through, and he felt the etheric charge to it tingle over his skin. When he opened his fingers slightly, the water rushed to the coldstone and he felt an immediate jolt, like he'd been punched in the palm of his hand.

Then, he did as instructed. Unlike the last two times, the ice didn't manifest immediately. It... struggled. He felt the stone *want* to open up, he felt it *want* to unleash, but unlike the two fights he'd been in, it didn't have quite the same drive to it.

So, he pushed. Akaran stared intently at his fist and the water coursing over and around it, and very intently, very firmly, expressed his feelings from the bottom of his heart. The blast of directed profanity made the frozen rock twitch in his fingers. The heat behind his words, the anger behind his simple, "Damn you, *WORK*," coursed through his being.

The coldstone shard pulsed once, twice, and then, just as suddenly, the water around his hand froze solid. He felt the frozen charge blast into the shell and felt the shell forcefully try to respond against him. The streams quit buffeting his hand gently; they hit the ice like the waves in a typhoon.

He thought it was the magic working like it was supposed to. He kept thinking that until a humanoid form took shape in the parchment-thick wall of the watery shield and the waves quit buffeting his hand – they gripped it. The water *clutched* his hand like a vice, and ice erupted down the length of his forearm. He saw the face form in the waves, and heard a voice call out his name with the sound of a thousand sheets of ice cracking all at once.

"**DEAD MAN**," it called out as the priest lost all color in his face.

Oh shit. Oh no. No…

Outside the shell, the Oldstone felt the disturbance first. He felt the dirt recoil against a force as it rushed out of the edges of the sphere. The conjurers around him followed suit, and two of them stumbled. Elverich took the hit next, as the watery bridges lost their cohesion and threatened to collapse as something that *wasn't* the pure ice they'd expected rushed through and down the fluid pylons.

Telburn took the biggest burst of feedback. The spike of unfamiliar and unexpected energy rocked through the shell and briefly made it double in size. The blast doubled him over and stole the breath away from Quinchecco standing next to him.

"**RED STAIN!**" the voice thundered as a figure all-too-familiar to the priest manifested in the water.

There wasn't a damn thing Akaran could do about it, either. He couldn't get his hand free; he couldn't kick his feet free of the shackles. The vice-like grip on his hand tightened around his wrist and he had a terrifying flashback from the last time that happened. He wrenched and pulled back as hard as he could and felt a brief moment of relief as his hand broke free.

He lost that relief when an all-too-familiar skeleton manifested in the shell. The front of the empty-eyed, haunting skull pushed through the water as two impossibly long arms peeled away from the inside of the shield before they collapsed onto the ground.

Makolichi.

The demon that had created Daringol.

The one he'd left stranded in Tundrala.

The act he'd taken that had infuriated the Goddess of Ice so many months ago. The creature lunged forward and hovered inches away from his face. Then the skull and the ice around it fell to the ground a moment later. It left a hole inside the watery shell – but it didn't stay open for long.

The hole gave way to a different face from his nightmares.

It was obviously a 'she,' or at least, it liked to appear as one. It wasn't human, and the priest sincerely doubted it had ever been. That knowledge, in and of itself, was a bit of a relief. Not enough of one, and not much of one, but a little bit of a relief.

What she was, however, was angry. The last time he'd seen her, she had been a shifting pile of pale pink, sparkling blue, and shimmering green ice. This time, she appeared much the same – though the vibrant hues were gone, and replaced with streaked cracks of angry red that seemingly bled drops of gold ice. She was otherworldly, she was beautiful, and she was the one constant that he had cursed about every single day since he fought Makolichi in the elemental plane of Tundrala.

He didn't know her name (or even if she had one), but he knew exactly *what* she was, and as she pushed herself out of the shell to stand in front of him, he cursed her very being to her face. "Oh you fisking *bitch*," Akaran snarled. "Found a new way to make my life miserable? Brought back Makolichi to taunt me?"

Her otherworldly voice boomed in his mind as her face continually shifted in a slurry of ice shards and snowflakes that kept billowing through her body. Her mouth – when she had one – didn't move, but her eyes did. Her calculating, multi-faceted eyes darted around her face independently of each other before they settled down to stare into his. *"Taunt? No. Condemn. Yes. Death would not be condemnation enough against you,"* the creature spat. *"Death and preservation in ice for eternity."*

Akaran flinched and bit back a curse as a sharp stab radiated through his knee and another one blossomed under the scar on his stomach. "You condemned me for being in your home once. Now you show up in mine? I don't need any more shit from you, *episturine*!"

"What you want and what you need matters nothing," the guardian of Tundrala retorted firmly and harshly enough in his skull that it nearly knocked him to his knees. Her hand closed around his fist and pried the coldstone out from under his fingers. *"That you seek to undo the Judgment of the Heavens is why I am here."*

"Heaven's judgment – or yours?" the naked priest snarled.

"They are one and the same."

Akaran twisted his leg and fought the chains at his feet as another sharp pain radiated from flesh to bone through the bloody wound. "If that was true then those men out there wouldn't be able to do all of *this*," he said as he gestured up at the shell and out beyond. "They can, so it isn't the Heavens."

The episturine melded back into the shell for a moment and reappeared beside him with a cold hand pressed against the back of his neck – a press that quickly turned into a rough grab. *"What care do you think that Ice gives dirt? That Ice gives water? One is impure. The other is of no significance to That Which Matters."*

"What care...? Ice *is* water!"

"Water that has not been made solid, made perfect," the otherworldly woman countered.

Akaran twisted his head out from her grip and tried to punch her, but she melted back into the shell before he could do more than swing into the empty air. *"You* aren't solid. Look at you – you're a blizzard with extra steps."

"I am as I was made," she chimed, *"Yet a man as flawed as you? What excuse do you have for your failures?"* A fresh stab of pain made him turn his head and look down at his leg. She reached down and sliced the gash open with her fingers with such speed that he almost missed it. As he watched, a trio of claws punched through the skin as he screamed in pain. *"You claim to serve the Pantheon. Yet you? Full of darkness. Full of shadow. Full of death."*

He bit back another curse but couldn't stop a cry as three fingers were joined by two more, and the faint outline of a small face that pushed against his bloody skin. "Full of your shit!" Akaran screamed. "*You* did this, *you* filled me!"

The episturine laughed with a musical cheer. *"You sinned against Ice. I removed your ability to do so again. Yet here you are. Filled with darkness. Filled with agents of shadow. Filled with foulness. Filled with the befouled, and yet you seek to purge yourself of the Pure."*

"Purge myself of the...?!" the exorcist thundered as more of the *thing* in his knee started to push itself out from under his skin. "You took the Goddess away from me!"

"I put you closer than you ever been," she chided. *"You chose to be deaf."*

He reached down and clutched at the mass in his knee as he doubled over in pain again. Crystals of ice erupted along the length of the wound, and more erupted across his stomach. The monster inside clawed bloody furrows in the top of his hands as he struggled to keep his leg together, and the episturine thrust her hand across his stomach and laid open his flesh with a razor-thin claw. "I CHOSE TO FIGHT!"

"Fight – or cower?" she demanded. *"Wallow in pity – or live to your name?"*

"There was plenty of time for... FISK... there was plenty of time for both!"

"Only Ice can say what there is time for, or not," the guardian construct replied tartly, *"and you have failed. In all ways, in all things. Fail to even know your blood as it hides locked in a vault made of your own mind."*

Akaran fell down onto the grass and screamed as a long, snake-like creature with a human face slithered out of his leg. The coldstone shard glittered on the ground a few feet away, and the monster slithered over to it. "You took magic from me! You took my Goddess from me! Not yours, *mine*," he argued as the episturine stepped between the monstrosity and the glimmering rock. "You took Her voice and left me with... with *that*," he screamed as the last of it disgorged itself from his bloody leg.

She looked down at the worthless remnant of Daringol and snarled in disgust. *"You had it in you before I arrived – and failed to purge it."*

"I tried! I did what I could!"

"You did what you thought *you could, and gave no heed to what you* actually *could,"* she scolded. *"With every prayer you made. Every voice you called. You granted none to Ice. You granted no respect to Mother. You grant no adoration or consternation and yet you seem confused why your suffering continues?"*

The exorcist tried to move his leg and bit back another howl of pain. While he struggled, more ice erupted along his stomach and ran up his arms. "What was I supposed to do?! You cursed me," he hissed, "and took Love from me. You punished me and threatened me that if I ever –"

The elemental being pulled his face around to hers and gave him a piercing look into his eye. *"Yet you never sought forgiveness or mercy. The same demand you ask of the dead, you do not offer yourself. You claim to be a man. You claim to deliver righteousness. To offer a path from perdition. Yet like the dead you seek, you do all* **except** *seek the Light. You seek aid from your fellows, not forgiveness from the Mount."*

"You threatened me that if I ever uttered Istalla's name again that you'd have my head," he snapped back with an icy froth appearing on the edges of his lips. The frost on his skin continued to spread around his stomach and to his throat.

"Sinners are damned," the episturine retorted, *"yet even those in the Abyss cry for mercy."*

"I've been crying since you did this to me."

"But not for forgiveness. Only for reversal of your punishment."

Akaran twisted in her grip and watched as the last bit of Daringol's essence made a lunge for the coldstone. The divine guardian kicked it away and quickly spread her arms wide – and summoned a line of floating, pink crystal daggers between her hands. "Then you may as well kill me," he snarled, "because I *can't* ask you to forgive me."

The episturine paused and tilted her head in sudden confusion. *"I stand before you, the instrument of your punishment, and you refuse to do the one thing that would ease your suffering? Are... are you mad?"*

He lunged up on one leg and grabbed one of the daggers floating in the air. She spun away and twisted her arms to block the blow she expected, but he didn't take a swing at her. Knife in hand, he turned around and drove it into the wraith's tail. His knee buckled again and tore open even deeper, but he slammed the knife into the spirit again and again until he effectively nailed the squealing monster into the dirt. "Because I did what I had to do to save lives. *You* were better equipped to deal with that demon than I was – and I *can't* apologize for doing it because I'd do it again if I had to!"

"You would re-enter eternity, knowing what awaits you, if you felt you

must?"

"I would. Makolichi was a threat that had to be stopped. *Had to be.* I couldn't. Eos'eno couldn't. Steelhom couldn't. *Nobody there could have* and there wasn't time to get help from the Order," he growled as he climbed over the wraith as it struggled to pull itself free.

The episturine flung a trio of her daggers around the ground in front of it as it struggled to reach the shell of water and ice. *"You invaded my home – and you'd do again? You brought corruption to the Heavens, not knowing what would result, and yet, you'd repeat? Why?"*

"Who better to purge the damned than an essence of purity? I knew you would. I knew Ice would because Eos'eno repeated it again and again: Ice *preserves* and ice *protects.* If Istalla couldn't stop it, we were all dead anyway."

The frozen woman circled him slowly and placed a foot on the back of the damned creature. *"You knew you would be punished, didn't you?"*

"Assumed," he admitted. "Had to hope it was worth it."

"Was it?"

Akaran looked down at the vile blob under him and looked back at his bleeding, twisted knee. "Goddess above, I hope so. But I'm not done. This *thing* still exists. There's worse than this that exists. There's worse than this that exists *here,*" he replied. "Please. Let me fight it. It's all I know to do."

She walked over to the coldstone shard and picked it up in her hand as she silently judged him. Outside the shell, Karaj had their sword drawn, and faint flickers of pale white ether flickered down the edges of the blade. Telburn struggled to keep the sphere intact even as the watersculpt beside him began to shake and sweat profusely even in the face of the cold wind that whipped around the shell.

The stone started to crackle in her hands as she held it over his body. Long wisps of freezing ether started to radiate off of his skin up towards the rock. *"You fight because it is your nature, not because it is of your choice?"*

"I... I don't... I don't know," he groaned as he watched her work. "It's... it's what I know to do. Please, it's how I know to help."

"Help by violence. A human perspective only, you should know."

"Really?" he challenged. "The Divine send souls to violence all the time."

She paused again and for a moment, the icy shift stopped. *"Only those that are impure. Though that argument has merit. Nature? A drive to do because it is what you do? This... this I understand."*

"Then understand how desperate I am to get back to it."

"Understand, I do – but violence is impure. It is the nature of death to rot, yet it too is of darkness. Why should purity seek to aid corruption? I gave you punishment, yes, to prevent your violence – and you still found ways to express it."

Akaran looked up at her with tears flowing freely down his eye as he struggled to keep a tight, ice-covered grip on the shuddering monstrosity below him. "Because things like *this* don't respond to anything *but* violence. Please, episturine, let me do what I'm supposed to do."

She pressed the stone against his back and leaned in hard. The rock shuddered as frost surged across his naked skin. "*You are a man with pain on his breath. Are you willing to admit your judgment may be wrong? Will you learn that much?*"

"Will you?" he demanded through the pain, "or is Ice as unchanging as you say?"

"*Ice preserves,*" she replied, "*yet it does shift and reform. I am not wrong about you, human. You are a danger. You are a failure. You are flawed.*"

"I'm *human,*" he answered with a choked sob as the frost sprouted fresh crystals across his back, "we *are* flawed. The Gods *made* us flawed."

"*You admit how far from perfection you are,*" the episturine agreed. "*Ask yourself now: are you willing to pay the price? Ice leaves a hole when it melts, and scars may last a lifetime.*"

Akaran reached back and broke a crystal knife free before he turned and slammed it into the head of the squirming beast under him. "Add it... add it to the others," he snarled.

She reached down and lifted the squirming wraith up high over her head and her crystalline voice reverberated in disgust. With a single thought, she willed twisted spires of ice to erupt down the length of her arm and through her hand. Daringol's essence evaporated under the assault and faded to nothing. "*You have shown willingness to sacrifice yourself before. I accept the sacrifice now. It does not change that you are punished – only the form that it will take. Offer contrition, and it will be less.*"

The exorcist rolled onto his back the best he could and stared up at her with tears down his face. He was covered in muddy dirt and blood, and the frost across his skin had begun to leave red welts on his flesh. "My life to the Goddess. Lead by example, one way or another. I offer that."

"*Oh, an example will be made,*" she promised.

"Then make sure they see it."

The episturine tilted her head again. "*Ice is clear. You are not.*"

He gestured at the shell and took a deep, ragged breath. "If you want to make an example of me, make sure they see it. Neither of us want to give those idiots out there the idea that pissing around in Istalla's home is a good idea. Whatever you're going to do – let 'em watch."

She stood in silence as he bled onto the grass. Finally, she gave him a failed attempt at a human nod. "*Ah. Lead by example; as you wish. Understand, human. Should you trespass against Mother again, this will be but a plucked hair in comparison to the suffering you shall endure."*

The priest grabbed one of the metal pillars and pulled himself upright. It took a couple of tries – the episturine didn't offer help, and his blood-slick hands didn't offer any kind of purchase. "As long as I can call on the Goddess again, I'll do it. I'll do my best to avoid pissing off your Mother. As a child of Niasmis, I swear it on my soul."

She floated up into the air and a long spiral of frozen daggers spun up from the ground at Akaran's feet with a gesture of her snowy hand. *"Do better than your best,"* she cautioned.

With the second wave of her hand, the shell lost the opacity that had obscured their argument. An audible gasp went up from the crowd outside and around as they saw him – bloody, dirty, and soaked in grime – and saw her – pristine, perfect, and inhuman. Elverich's music faltered as some of the lesser Adepts lost track of their chants. The Tidesinger bowed his head in respectful reverence, while Altund stepped back and made a warding sigil in the air with his hand. Telburn's eyes went wide, but he didn't let his spellcasting waver in the slightest, which was a testament to both his skills and his nerves.

The Maiden-Templar's assistant, however, did none of the above. They stepped forward and calmly walked over the barrier with their sword drawn. The blade flashed violently as they quickly marched up to the sphere – and only stopped when Akaran raised a hand and two fingers to wave them back. Karaj noted the wordless order and thankfully backed away.

"Do better than your best," the episturine repeated, *"or discover how Ice can feel when it preserves,"* she promised. Before he could reply, a new wall of crystal knives appeared in the air – and the first one shot forward like an arrow. The blade stabbed into his thigh and sunk in so deep it might have gone out the other side if it had been bound to the rules of nature. He screamed as blood spurted from the wound.

And screamed again when the next knife sunk home.

And the next.

And the next.

The pain was blinding; the agony was unreal. As the knives sunk into his leg, and then his hips, and then across his ribs and up his chest in a long spiral, he lost his voice from his cries of raw pain and cold anguish. The last blade split his skin somewhere just below his jaw, and blood froze as it touched the frost on his skin.

She peered down into his weeping eye, frozen open from the otherworldly torment, and asked him a simple question. *"Shall I undo what has been done – or can you see through to the thaw of the ice in your soul and master this gift of pain?"*

He worked out a raspy, tortured, "Ju... just... get... get it... done! DO IT!"

The episturine was almost happy to oblige.

She flung her fingers back and the knives ripped away from his skin and crashed against the shield. For a few long moments, the water lost all clarity, and the bridges that Elverich had made turned bright red with his blood. When the crowd could see inside again, they saw her standing behind him with her arm wrapped around his ribs...

...and her hand buried under his sternum, with a bulge pressed up in his chest around his heart. He couldn't scream. His lungs couldn't expand enough to breathe. Blood splattered out from his lips as he arched up. For a moment, he thought he was dying.

A moment later, and he was certain he was. She *clutched* at a cord deep inside his body and *ripped* it free. He spun like a top to the extent the shackles at his feet would let him as she unwound a brilliant, glittering rope made of jagged ice that spilled out from him. Fiercely glowing blue and white light poured from the wound with a frigid blast of air behind it as she whipped the strand free and vanished from sight as it froze everything it touched.

The gash sealed itself shut as he collapsed in a heap between the pillars. The world swam around him as a brilliant display of colors he would never be able to describe rushed into his sight. He felt warm, he felt cold, he felt like he was embraced by agony and held by perfection all at once. The sensations were more than he could bear.

Akaran held on long enough for Karaj to shatter the frozen shell into nothingness with a barked Word that undid all of Telburn's magic before the Headmaster could stop them. The exorcist looked up at the Lover and quietly, painfully croaked, "I... I can hear... I can hear eternity..." moments before he passed out.

IV. FUNDAMENTAL FRACTURES
Late Afternoon of Londis, the 7ᵗʰ of Firstgrow, 513 QR

It didn't take long for Seline to decide she was completely out of her depth with her new (and utterly desperate) idea. By the time the guards at the second gate decided that the guards at the first gate weren't daft to let her climb up the side of the mountain, she was ready to give up and quit. Still, perseverance was a virtue, and in a palace of the righteous, it had to pay off. Or at least, that's what she told her shaking hands.

The Repository was as grand on the inside as it was on the outside. For all her time in the city, and for all the years spent working at the Manor, she'd never made it past the first gate. Getting past the upper doors and being able to stand in the main hall was impressive enough, and she could only imagine the splendor that awaited deeper into the Order's outpost. It was beyond anything she could've imagined, and she counted herself lucky for even making it this far.

What was more expected, though not as welcome, was the tepid response she received from the staff. To those on the outside looking in, it was often a surprise to realize that when it came to worship, the Lovers rarely had shrines devoted specifically to that. Yes, there was the Grand Temple of Love in Mulvette, but given the typically unfriendly attitude the world had to the Order, most of Niasmis's worshippers kept to themselves and celebrated in their homes.

With that tidbit in mind, the *other* aspect of the Repository was also on candid display: for all of the gold, all of the greenery, for all of the splendor, this was a military base. Just a very shiny one filled with shiny armor. With shiny swords. And shiny arrows that ached to be pointed at soft places.

Very shiny swords and arrows held by very dull and gloomy people that seemed to be very insulted that they wouldn't have reason to use any of them today. The healer made the most of every opportunity she had to demonstrate that she wasn't a threat, and that she was here on business. She also stressed that she respected those that answered the more militant call of the Order, and that she had no plans to cause harm to anyone or anything inside.

Even still, they treated her like a goblin in a pretty tan dress until the Maiden-Templar agreed to see her. Even then, the general aura only shifted from, 'Ready to murder her,' to, 'still ready, but at least with a promise of a quick death.' *If this is how the Lovers act among their own, it's no wonder the Repository is given a wide berth*, she mused to herself.

"I have to admit, it's not like Ridora to send one of her minions to these cherished halls," Catherine said by way of greeting once they settled into an office marked with a sign that read, 'Receiving Room.' Simply named, but impressively built – gold trim ran along the edges of the room, and the back wall had a trio of alcoves with statues of Niasmis's Three.

"Lady Medias didn't," Seline admitted, "though I am here with her permission. She didn't expect that I would make it past the front door... I imagine she's wondering if I've been chopped up and dumped into the Orshia Overflow by now."

"Come now. I may have my differences with that irritating old bat, but I'd never go to those lengths."

"That's a bit of a relief," the healer sighed as her shoulders sagged. "I was under the impression that I wasn't welc–"

Catherine lifted her finger and leaned back in her chair. "Not when Avagerona's Rest is at least an hour's walk closer. Now, what is it I can do for you today – Seline Valdin, healer of Medias Manor, and known assistant to one of our currently disgraced priests?"

She bristled slightly and squared her shoulders back. "I am not his 'assistant,' Maiden-Templar."

"Co-conspirator?"

Seline blanched at the accusation, halfway true as it may be. "Nor that."

"Then what, exactly, are you – and why are you here on his behest?"

Seline laid the small pile of books and scrolls she carried down on her lap and settled in against the aged oak chair. "With all respect, Maiden-Templar, I am not that either. I'm here of my own accord, for my own reasons. I promise; I haven't been asked to come by anyone but my own curiosity." *And desperation*, she sighed to herself.

The Repository's overseer raised her eyebrow and leaned her head into her hand. "Reasons which you haven't given. If I have to ask again, you can answer from the door."

"Yes, well, then, I, ah," the younger woman stammered as the weight of the threat pinned her to her seat. "I'm here because of one of the Manor's residents: Bistra Enil."

The mention of her name made Catherine cringe inwardly, but bristle on the edges. "I know her. The man you say you're not here for has been involving himself in her care lately, hasn't he?"

"So I've been told," Seline muttered darkly, "but I so promise: I'm not here because of him. I'm here because since Livstra's passing, I've had to take over her care – and lately she's said a pair of names that I have heard in other circles."

"I imagine the circles that a healer with your inexperience travels in are very small. This isn't helping your claims of working on your own accord."

"It might not, but it's still the truth," she retorted. "As you know, the requirements and oaths that those that serve in the Manor require obedience to the Queen's Law and Niasmis's Three. We hear things that... honestly, Maiden? Things I wish I didn't know and I'm not sure anyone else should, either. She suffers, and unlike Akaran, I think I can help her nightmares."

"Is he still afflicted with them? I had hoped that they would be under control before he was removed from the Manor."

Seline blinked. "What would make you think that? The boy is broken. When he's not rambling about some kind of hidden conspiracy in the streets, he's staring at the shadows like he expects them to lunge out at him. He can't walk past a rack of hung squid without breaking into a cold sweat. He almost ran away from a squirrel the other day for reasons I do *not* want to comprehend, thank you."

"But... nightmares? I cannot fathom what they are like now, but the Order listens to those. They can often be portents."

"Aside from his rants about being tortured in his sleep by a woman he watched die? There's been more than a few about being swallowed alive by a monster of hands, faces, and pitch-black shadows. Or what about the one he made me *promise* to run away from?"

"What would that be?"

Seline shook her head as she answered. "Some ship. He claims Daringol – the wraith that he destroyed? That it took one over. He thinks it's hunting him."

The Templar curled the corner of her mouth up into half a smile. "Hunting him? A ship hunting a man in a landlocked city? Does he think it's small enough to float in the Overflow, or that it plans to fly down the Falls?"

She let out a breath she didn't know she was holding. "I don't know. He didn't tell me either way. Maiden, I have tried, very hard, to help him. I promise I have. Until he unravels whatever mystery he thinks he's found, he's going to find no respite for his insanity."

She pointedly left out the part that some of his mystery was indeed fact. Or if not fact, a shared delusion among a handful of very powerful figures.

Herself… reluctantly… included.

Catherine nodded in measured understanding. "It is a shame this world contains darkness that can warp the mind, but the choice is simple: confront that fear or run from it. He and Bistra both made their choices. I respect them for that, right or wrong, however it plays out or has played out. I do. However, the Manor should have everything about her that you need to know."

The healer fished the first of three leather-bound journals out of the pile on her lap and handed it over unbidden. "*About* her, yes. She was born back in 476, and went right to Niasmis. She trained at the Grand Temple until 494, when she graduated. She had no lineage of note, with her father being a minor functionary and her mother less notable than even that."

"So you've shown you can read a scroll and memorize a few things," the Templar idly taunted. "Since you have her journals, you know the things she fought in the Goddess's service. That's the extent of what you *should* know," Catherine added pointedly.

"I know the parts that weren't redacted," the blonde-haired woman retorted, "and I read around the parts that were made-up bullshit, if you'll forgive my language, Maiden."

"Secrets do no good if they're put out in the open. Certain things have to be massaged to make them more palatable. But, the Order is at war with the very things you wish you didn't know about, and wartime requires careful words said and even more care given to words written."

Seline weighed that for about as long as she felt she had to, then dismissed it entirely. "That would be acceptable if I was the woman washing her laundry, but as the woman who has taken on her case with care, I can't be expected to champion for my patient without knowing more about what happened to her."

"I have no doubt that you read some of the scrolls that Akaran stole from the vault," the older woman accused, "and I'm sure you asked him first. What makes you think that you'll learn more if you asked me?"

"Because he spoke exceptionally well of you, even after you threw him out," Seline admitted, "and because while I may not have many years serving for Ridora, I have seen how the Order treats their fallen. I want to help, but I need to know more before I can. Specifically," she added before the Templar could interrupt again, "about a man named Annix – and a woman named Zilyph."

"Annix and Zilyph?" the outpost's ranking officer repeated. "I can't say I'm familiar with either."

"Bistra is," Seline replied, "as is written in one of her reports that Akaran came into possession of."

"That is a fancy way of saying 'stole,' you know," the Templar warned.

"Though it doesn't surprise me. An exorcism is a very personal thing, Missus Valdin. When we place our lives into the hands of the Goddess to condemn those that should never see the light of day, we hunt, and as we must, kill. As names have power, we seek to know them – to imbalance power into our favor. I know the name of every demon I banished; I'm sure you've heard a few other names of the things in the dark slip from lips that would otherwise stay silent, if not for fits of madness."

The younger woman nodded as she tried not to think deeply on the myriad titles and names she'd heard in the last few scant years, but then countered with a simple, "Except she isn't saying the names of the others. Just these two – and Annix the most often. It would help if I knew what it was, if the Order knew."

Catherine steepled her fingers together under her chin. "What exactly do you hope to learn from discovering more than a name? A dead monster is a dead monster. Once condemned to the fires of perdition, they do not return. Those merely sealed, yes, they can; but she is an exorcist. Her seals last only as long as it takes her to judge and destroy."

"Except for the Burned Woman," Seline muttered under her breath.

"The Burned Who?" the Maiden asked as her eyebrow popped up.

She shunted the memory of seeing Akaran's personal nightmare aside and deftly danced back to the first question. "Her mind is broken. If she endured a physical assault, perhaps more comforts of luxury could ease some of her pain. A strike of dreams? Maybe deeper sleep could help her mend. Magic? Another look by the Granalchi may make inroads," she said with a simple shrug of her shoulders. "In truth, I won't know until I know."

The Templar pursed her lips and flicked her fingers through the journal on her desk. "Except the fact that the Order found need to bury those secrets means that you shouldn't know."

"I suppose that means that someone decided that the Order should just turn a blind eye to one of ours in distress," Seline countered, "rather than risk exposing a truth. Is that the way that those who bring the Gauntleted Fist to bear act to treat the ones that need the Velvet Hand?"

The way she twisted one of the Order's oldest slogans hit the Maiden like an unexpected punch in the gut. "You have spent too much time with Akaran, I see."

"Believe me, Maiden, I will not argue with you on that."

Catherine chuckled softly. "Well. I have been in positions myself where foreknowledge might well have saved me a forearm," she replied as she flashed the healer a disgusting scar along her wrist and arm. "If you truly feel that there could be worth in risking retribution to even come here and ask, I will go look."

"You, yourself?" Seline asked as her eyes widened slightly. "I didn't mean to drag you away from more pertinent matters at hand, I only –"

"Bistra was once one of our most promising. That she ended up so broken is a loss that some of us in the Order have not fully forgiven ourselves for, and that she is so close but I cannot help her myself? Well. The last few months of disquiet in this city have been an insult to all that is right and righteous, so if I can see that a few old wounds are given new salve, then I will."

Seline relaxed into the chair and sighed in appreciation. "Then I offer you thanks, Maiden. I'll return to the Manor and await word for what you find."

"Oh you will?" Catherine asked with half a smile. "Little blonde kitten, you have wandered into the lair of a lioness. With a request for *me* to do a favor for you, a trade must be made. You'll stay here until I'm done."

"Oh," the healer quietly responded. "Well, okay, I'll stay right here and –"

"Here, as in the Repository, girl," the Maiden replied with a wolfish grin. "I do hope you don't mind putting in a day's worth of hard work."

She did. It didn't matter. And the Burned Woman had an issue of her own, and one nearly as nasty as the work that Seline was about to find herself elbow-deep in.

***

Basion City, despite itself being *in* a basin already, had no shortage of underground catacombs, walkways, tunnels, or manner of underground storage areas. It was as if someone had decided that while it would be perfectly acceptable to build up, building *down* might be even easier. That person must *not* have been placed personally in charge of moving the sheer volume of dirt and rock from underneath the city to places somewhere beyond the edge of the pit itself for the vast number of tunnels present. Or, if they were, it was far more likely that they were in charge of the whip rather than the wheelbarrow.

Either way, it suited many of the lower-status citizens just fine (now that the hard work was done). Who was going to argue with a few tunnels to discretely move a few things from one shop to another – or storage for all manner of wines and worse?

Well, aside from the worse. The worse had plenty of reason to argue, and the two women standing in the dim tunnel had spent the last hour attempting to answer some very poignant questions about their captive. Namely, what exactly Donta *was*, and who exactly had resurrected him from the grave.

"*I like very little about the state I'm in,*" Rmaci complained – mostly to herself, though with an edge towards the woman that currently held her metaphysical leash, *"but I like the fact that we're holding that man captive even less."*

"Oh?" the Mother Eclipsian remarked from behind her floating, spectral body. "Of all the things that currently occupy your mind, heart, and your very literal soul, it's that we have a prisoner that concerns you?"

The shade looked down at her equally-frozen-and-burnt hands and made an exaggerated sighing noise. *"Of my current issues, it's the one I can control."*

"Is it?" the dusky-voiced woman asked as she approached the doorway – and the assassin stored safely on the other side. "Do you think that your voice in his fate has any more bearing than your wish on yours?"

Rmaci bit down on her lip and gave the priestess a very literally smoldering glare. *"Speaking of voices. I find yours far more irritating than I ever did that boy-priest."*

"That boy-priest is not currently much of one, and little of the other," Erine replied, "all of his myriad other faults aside. I am not at all surprised you'd rather have his company than mine, but it isn't so bad, is it? Compared, shall I suggest, to other aspects of your life? 'Un-' as it may be?"

"At least when he reminded me of my absence of a heartbeat, it didn't sound so damnably condescending," she countered.

"You are of the damned dead, my dear, and as such, are not afforded the same respect as the living. Nor of the divinely-departed." The priestess tapped the wooden door and smiled as the sound echoed down the underground hallway. "Much as him."

"I still can't believe you convinced the boy to let you keep him. Me? Holding me is foul enough, though I understand why he'd want to be rid of me. But that thing? I've been inside Akaran's head – I can only imagine how desperately he must have wanted to march that beast into the Temple with a flag buried firmly in his ass."

Erine chuckled as her flowing black hair fell down around her shoulders. "Our conversation about the man went along those very same lines," she admitted. "His concern was that this cretin might get loose in transport, and mine was that his Order wouldn't attempt to have me put in irons at the same time."

The spy gave a faint nod and pushed herself deeper into the shadows of the underway. She hadn't been a fan of her body before it had undergone its most recent metaphysical metamorphosis – and now that she was covered in equal parts frost *and* flame, she'd decided she wanted to see it as rarely as possible. *"His people have a flair for that."*

"That they do. Not that either one of us have much to say over that, I am dreadfully afraid."

"My bonds aren't as flimsy as iron, it would seem."

"No, my dear spy, that they are not. Yet they are bonds of your own choosing; don't forget that."

Rmaci huffed quietly in the shadows. *"As if I could, with the desire you have to remind me every chance your mouth opens."*

Basion City's resident priestess of the Goddess of Night quietly chuckled as she ducked her head inside the makeshift prison she'd constructed to check on her unwanted guest. "You are a damned spirit seeking redemption. You don't belong in this world any more than he does," she said as she gestured in at their captive. "Less, if anything, as you are between worlds more than you are simply visiting."

"So I'm worth less than that thing in there? Is that the point you attempt to make at my expense?" she groused.

"Yes, and no. I'd wager the blood on his hands – well, *hand* – weighs on his soul heavier than yours, if only by volume. Quantity has moments where it rivals quality."

The wraith grumbled noncommittally. *"You still haven't told me what you intend to do with me."*

Once she was content that Donta hadn't slipped his binds, Erine turned her full attention back towards the specter. "That is a question you'll have to answer on your own. That answer, and your actions, are yours and only yours to decide."

"How can I answer the question of your intent? I'm dead – not a mind reader."

"And it is the first of those things that provides the problem. You are dead. Very dead, very damned, and very lost."

Rmaci shuddered in the darkness and bits of glowing embers bounced out of the cracks on her skin before they disappeared on the floor. *"Damned? But Akaran said that I... if I could... if I would... pledge to his Goddess that I wouldn't... so I did and..."*

Erine nodded and leaned against the wall of the old brick tunnel and crossed her arms. "And you became lost. Not of the lower world, not yet of the upper – and may never be. Of course, that is why you gravitated to me; because of what you are, because of what I am."

"Because he did something magic with that damn rock you've got in your purse and I seem to be stuck to it," the dead woman shot back. *"None of which I claim to understand. How he captured me in my realm; or how you control me now."*

"Control you? Do you truly think that I have control over you, dear wraith?" the priestess retorted. "I only possess your anchor. You have free agency to do as you wish, if you knew what that would be."

A twisted and cold smile flickered across Rmaci's blistered and chapped lips. *"If I could do all as I wish, you wouldn't have that stone,"* she countered, *"because as long as you have it, you can end my stay in this world, can't you?"*

The Mother Eclipsian nodded slightly. "I could, but then your attempt for redemption would come to an end before you'd like it, I would wager. Unless you ask me to do so, of course."

"If you control my life by holding a rock, don't you have control over me?"

"As much control as you exerted over others in your life, prior to your fall. I expect that seems like much to you, but I cannot pull your strings nor direct you. Your choices are your own; consider the binding stone merely a way for you to be reminded of the consequences before you decide to make an act."

Rmaci tried to come up with a counter. Any counter. Anything at all. All she could do was float quietly and stare at the woman with long black hair, a flowing black dress, and deep brown eyes in defeat. *"I don't know what to do."*

"None of us do, in the long run," the Eclipsian replied after a moment's thought. "I also suppose that some respect can be given to your personal plight. How rare it is for a body to die, yet the soul to remain. Rarer still for it to buck against the fate that befell it, and so much the near-incomprehensible that it would work to find a way back into the light."

"All of which are statements and conditions you feel comfortable with seeing me in," the dead woman pointed out. *"You speak to me as if you have seen a dozen damned souls such as myself in these halls beneath the streets."*

"How do you know I haven't?" Erine pointedly asked. "I speak for the True Woman, the One Who Bridges the Realms. Is it so hard to believe that I have seen many such as you?"

"Yes."

The directness of Rmaci's retort caught the older woman off-balance for the first time since they'd met, and it made the priestess chuckle. "Then you'd be right. What I have seen are glimpses; twists and visions in the night of things that were, things that weren't, and things that might be – or might not."

A single glowing, ember-covered finger slid out of the darkness to point at the supposedly holy woman accusingly. *"You told the boy that you could help me. That to cross into the light, I'd have to – what was it? To go from the dark to the light, I'd have to go live in the realm of the dusk until the dawn?"*

"To pass through the Dark to the Light, you must first trek through the realm of Dusk to the Dawn," Erine replied. "I did, yes. Except that Her realm is not *this* realm. You still stay in places you do not belong instead of seeking the paths in the gloom that lead out of the shadows."

"I suppose it would be too much of a kindness to assume you'd tell me how to do such a thing, wouldn't it?" the spy charged. *"How am I supposed to move on without knowing how to go?"* she demanded before she added, *"By the by – has anyone mentioned how ironic it is that the wedding that everyone is on about is named the same as Lethandria's realm?"*

Erine crossed her hands behind her back and smiled faintly. "How are any of us to know what it is we are to do, except to use our best judgment when things change against us?" she asked before she looked into the shadows behind the wraith and frowned. "Sometimes changes happen before we're ready, as well. It is on our own souls to act... much as I might have when the Overseer pressed his attendants for a name to give to the current celebrations," the priestess replied slyly and smugly.

The wraith glanced in the same direction and for a moment, she thought she saw a spindly figure that was darker than the rest of the shadows. It vanished as soon as she started to focus on it, and left her with an even worse feeling of impending doom than what she already had. *"I am in no hurry to act if it means that I may return to damnation,"* she muttered under her non-existent breath.

"There are more worlds than that of either great peace or great perdition. You have already taken the first few steps to find your way to the light; are you so willing to let your fear of the other slow your pace?"

She wanted to retort with a simple, honest, and easy, 'yes,' but Rmaci thought better of it. *"I always assumed that when you died, you would travel to one place or another... and stay there. This experience is... more than I could have imagined. I am truly lost in it."*

"Truly lost, or truly blessed?" Erine asked as she glanced at a different spot in the darkness – and a sharp clatter that echoed down the tunnel. "Or are you willingly confusing yourself, rather than face the future?"

"I don't know," she admitted.

"As I said, you are a rarity," the priestess repeated, "though we may both have fewer days left to us than behind us if we don't leave. Now."

Rmaci bristled and stepped back into range of the torchlight. The shadows around her melted away as she forced herself to become more translucent, and the ice on her side glistened and sparked like streamers of quicksilver. *"You say it in a way that implies that we leave our prisoner behind. Akaran was quite clear – he's never to be left alone for more than a few moments at most, though if you want to break your promise to him, I won't argue. The headache he'll have from it will be worth it. Though whatever it is that has you spooked can wait a few minutes more for more of the thief's men to arrive, can it not?"*

The Mother Eclipsian looked down one branch of the old brick tunnel and nodded sharply. "Leave him behind or risk our fates if we stay with him. There's worse than either of us coming – and it is coming quickly."

"*But that cretin...?*"

"Yes, well. I imagine Akaran would be angrier at us for losing our heads than he would if we merely lost our charge, wouldn't he?"

The spy had to think on it for a moment and even then, wasn't able to come up with a suitable answer either way. "*Only if he didn't decide to do it himself after the fact was brought to his attention. What is it you hear?*"

"More than you, I fear," the Eclipsian said with a frustrated sigh. "Come quick or stay behind. We've no other options."

"*We should be rid of him before we do,*" Rmaci quickly replied.

Erine shook her head and lifted the end of her dress slightly as she turned to leave. "I've neither the knowledge to take his head in a meaningful fashion nor the desire to spill his blood, regardless of how much the ground cries to have it."

"*It's more sand than blood,*" the spy remarked dryly, "*though I can understand your hesitance, given the retribution I endured for much the same.*"

When the Eclipsian made it halfway to the next bend, she stopped and quickly turned back to the wraith. "Are you not coming?"

The wraith smiled and faded back to nearly full transparency. "*I have to choose, you said – action or other. If we have to abandon our prize, I'd like to see who it is that came to claim it from us.*"

She didn't have to wait long for the answer. The last time that Rmaci had seen the so-called Lady Anais Lovic, she had presented herself as nothing but as the pinnacle of proper. Now, however, she had a grip on her humanity as thin and flimsy as the other shadows in the tunnels. Her pristine, perky skin had lost most of its color and gained more wrinkles than an old crone, and her hair had lost what little it used to have.

How the woman had found their lair was one important question to answer, but one that would have to wait until later. Of equal importance was the question of *Where are the other guards?* that she wondered to herself.

Specifically, the ones Riorik had left behind, but Rmaci assumed the answer was directly related to the snapping appendage that casually coiled and uncoiled itself from around her throat. The spy hadn't liked her when she'd first seen her, and the realization that the Lady was either subhuman – or, worse yet, an otherworldly magical *inhuman* – only served to justify her initial opinion. *Didn't like her then, do believe I like her less now.*

When Anais shattered the door's old iron handle with a quick twist of her wrist, the wraith finally felt happy she wasn't human herself anymore.

The next few moments were little more than the sounds of rope and chains being pulled on and a few carefully uttered spells that finally undid the binding on Donta's tongue, if nothing else. "Anais," he croaked, "you shouldn't –"

"As if I had a choice," she seethed. "For all we've done, how close we are – you let yourself get *caught*? Do you have any idea how much risk you've put me in?"

"Put you...?" he asked through dry, split lips. The last four days of captivity hadn't done her bodyguard any favors, and his jailers weren't concerned for the comfort of a dead man. Rmaci had done the bulk of the interrogation, and since Akaran had helped her break free of his mind, she'd developed a few beneficial *traits.* Donta gave his boss a look of disgust from around his bruised, broken eyes and tried to free his arm. "My risk was worse."

She sneered down at him and only gave his wounds a passing glance. While Akaran and Erine had both used assorted 'Divine and Damnation' arguments with him to try to get him to open up, Rmaci and Riorik had been granted permission to use more direct methods that had burned off most of his clothes, and flayed his waxy skin to shreds in other places.

The spy had her fun with his mind. Unfortunately, it didn't take long to realize that he had seen as much of the Abyss as she had. Much as she was able to make him suffer, the effort did little else. *Once you've been through the rigorous of the Abyss, there is little suffering that does not become bland over time*, she had pointed out to the others.

"Torments are passing," she retorted. "Don't whine as if you don't have prior experience with it. You *knew* what would be at risk if you were ever caught! For you and me both! Now look at you – I can only assume they discovered your lack of humanity."

That was a truth that had been revealed before he'd even been caught. Though it was the exorcist's ideas on how to keep him secure had shocked almost everyone in the room at the time. His argument of, "He's a pitborn monster," was enough to (eventually) win over those with means to work towards his ends, much to the assassin's regret.

As such, there was little Donta could do to move, and few chains he could even struggle against. While the Guildboss had made sure that there was plenty of rope to tie his arms up with, Akaran had personally overseen the placement of the iron bar across his chest and his thighs. The iron bar with a pair of holes in the middle – holes that were quickly spiked with a pair of old rusty rivets as thick as the assassin's forearm and improperly driven through the back of his chair.

They'd only tied his legs up because the thief was outvoted on how comical it would have otherwise been to watch him try to get away if they hadn't. "I'm not dead," he grunted as he looked down at the spikes in his chest, "so they know."

"For the sake of the Fallen, how could you have been so *stupid*?" she seethed as she looked for the *other* bonds that had to be holding him in place – because it was a given there were *other* bonds. Once much more magical that had been crafted by Erine herself.

"Was that… Eclipsian. And the Fleets," he groused. His voice cracked with every other word he spoke and oily sand trickled down his chest each time he started to move. "I got attacked. They had a mage. Heavy one. Overwhelmed me. Brought me here."

His Lady frowned and sized up his other wounds. They'd dissected him extensively, and hadn't gone to great pains to patch him back up. He was covered in burns that had left little glassy patches on his chest, and the stump of his left arm had only been bandaged up with a few rough straps of burlap. "So it was the Fleets? They're the ones that left you like this?" *That would explain a lot*, his handler assumed, though there was a tinge of *other* hanging in the air that she couldn't put her finger on.

"Not… not just. The priest. The cripple," he croaked.

Anais stopped searching and blinked in surprise. "Akaran? You lost a fight to a man with one eye and half a leg?"

The assassin shook his head carefully and inadvertently showed off the one thing she was searching for. "No. He… he came later. Rishnobia was right. He's a son… son of a bitch. Haven't seen him since. Glad I had… had him killed."

"Had him killed?" she asked as she peered close at the runemark someone had carved into his skin. *Lythrivol*, she mused to herself. *Know the damned; know thy writhing; know they move. That exorcist wrote this, but if he's magic-less, then why go to the effort…? Unless he expects to get his powers back somehow.*

"Ye… yeah," Donta croaked. "Before I got caught. Decided… too much. Too risky. He felt… dangerous. Guess I… I was right. Haven't seen him since… second night."

She looked into his murky, yellowed eyes and scoffed in his face. "Oh. You mean you're glad you had someone *attempt* to *mug* him, but failed to do more than knock him into the dirt? If his death was your intent, then you failed quite spectacularly at that, too."

He snarled and wrenched hard at his bonds, and only settled because she placed a hand on his chest to force him back down. "He's alive? Dammit. Don't get near him. Leave him to me. You can't risk him."

Anais brushed the warning off like it was nothing. "Unlike you, Donta, I am perfectly capable of handling a cripple on my own. He is a magic-impotent, stick-wielding *child* that wouldn't know what to do if he saw a woman's teat. I have managed far brighter and far more resilient souls in my time."

"That's... the problem. Not just him. He has a wraith."

"He has a what now?"

Still carefully hidden and intentionally silent, Rmaci chuckled inwardly to herself. *Oh! I love it when people talk about me.*

He cast his gaze up to the far corners of the room and shuddered like he expected her to come barreling out of the walls at any moment. The mix of revulsion and horror that flickered in his otherwise dead eyes gave her a brief moment of joy in her burnt, ravaged heart. "A wraith. Some burning cunt. Pitborn."

Anais didn't even bother to hide her disbelief as she stepped away and crossed her arms. "A pitborn wraith? Are you delirious? Did they find some way to poison your senses? And if they did, do you know how? That would prove useful."

"No. No. She's with him," he groused. "She's the bitch that..." he started to explain before he let the words die on his tongue and tried to move his legs and arm around to draw attention to the myriad burns across his body. "Don't... don't know who she aligns with. Charnac. Maybe. Emberforge. Helped... helped show them. Ways to burn."

Out in the hall, the spy grimaced at the misaimed accusation. *Suppose I can't blame him for that assumption. The Brineblood isn't known to freeze the souls in His ocean, but Charnac... if this whole thing with the boy doesn't work out, I wonder if I can find allegiance with Him...*

Utterly blissful to her thoughts and presence, Anais spoke back up. "He's aligned himself with a minion of the God of Ashes? That's decidedly worrisome, given where we found Moira. Had to have the mace stolen from an old Illiyan temple desecrated in His name. Surely the two can't be related?"

"Doesn't matter," her minion croaked. "Will kill him once I'm out. Myself. Pay him back for this. Then give her to... *him,*" he added with a throaty chuckle. "Teach... teach her what pain is."

Oh I sincerely doubt that, Rmaci snarled. If her thoughts could've cut his flesh, he'd have suddenly understood why Akaran had to walk with a stick.

Anais waved her hand dismissively and pulled a twisted, blackened, pit-metal knife from inside her faded-pink robe. "While you worry on that, I don't suppose you'd care to tell me what all you may have told them...? Do they know about me, or about our benefactor?"

"You, yes," he admitted. "Nastavol, no."

The name sent a sudden pang of fear in the back of Rmaci's mind, for no reason she could understand. She'd heard it before. She *knew* she had. Heard it, and blocked it out – or the Abyss was working Its will on her again to keep her from remembering. Either way, in life it wasn't often that a simple name would make her flinch in fear. In death it was all the less. *Nastavol... the Red... something*, she thought to herself before she glanced down at her burned and frozen hands. *Why... why am I shaking?*

The Merchant of Secrets hissed sharply and quickly struck his cheek with an open-handed slap that echoed down the tunnels. "You *know* damn well not to say that name!" she scolded sharply before she froze up and her gray eyes went wide. "You... you sold me out? Traded me for comfort? What did you tell them, exactly?"

He shook his head and immediately tried to downplay his failure. "Didn't... have to. They assumed. They think you are my summoner," he grumbled in disgust. "That you hold my leash. They don't know about your... condition."

Anais pursed her lips and carefully reached in to start cutting at the mark on his neck. He hissed and growled in pain, but she quieted him with a sharp rebuke. "Well I suppose that's a tad better and I'm willing to let them entertain that idea. If they merely suspect me of necromancy, that's only an increased price for my head. Still cheaper than the truth. Do they know why we are here?"

"The priest guessed. Pieced together about Miral," he grunted through the sharp jolts of pain her knife inflicted. "Knows you want something there. Doesn't understand Moira."

She hooked her fingernails under the flap of skin she cut loose and quickly ripped it off without care for his discomfort. "But he doesn't know *what* I'm after, does he? *Think*, you fool. This is *important*."

"No, I... he doesn't," he croaked as she flung the wardmarked strip of flesh to the ground. "Told him more.... More about Annix. They want him. More than you."

"For the sake of my resurrection, I did not expect to be thankful for the interference of a bloodsucker," she muttered under her breath. "I shall assume that even without these runes, they took enough of you to find you in the future?"

"My arm," he growled. "Vampire's whore. She blasted it off. They said they have it."

Anais sighed in irritation. "So it's merely a matter of time that they figure out how to track you down. And," she went on with a defeated little grumble, "a matter of candlemarks before they discover *what* you are, if they haven't already."

"Get me out," he replied as he pushed against the iron bar across his chest. "They don't know everything."

"They know enough. *Dammit* Donta. You have wrecked *everything*. The only reason we've had any success is through *my* actions, not yours!"

He looked up at her and bared his chipped teeth. "Did what you told. Carried out your orders. Not you trapped in here. Get me out. Get what he needs."

"What makes you think I don't already have it?" she scolded as Rmaci watched the tail along her throat slowly unravel and dance in the air. "Our work here is effectively *done*, or would have been if you hadn't gotten caught! We should be days away from here by now – leagues even!"

Her assassin huffed his chest and pushed against the iron bar hard enough to make the stone creak behind him. "Then let me out. I'll kill them. Then we can go."

"Our benefactor made it *very* clear that we weren't to interfere further. *Find it* and *report it* then let him do as he sees fit."

"Listening now? You sang differently before."

"*Before* I didn't have the Orders of Light, the Hunter's Guild, the city Guard, and the Fleets after my scalp! Or, apparently, the ire of the Mother Eclipsian *and a fisking vampire*. You have stuffed your withered cock in this so hard that it is nearly impossible to see daylight around it!"

Donta snarled and rocked violently in his chair. "Arguing here won't help! They'll be back soon. Get me loose!"

"Between your arm and your essence," she ranted, "they have enough to find you – and through you, *me* – if they put knowledge to thought. I don't know what possessed them to leave you in a hole like this one, but it's surely a blessing of the Lowers that they did. I cannot fathom what our benefactor's wrath would be if they had marched you into the Repository and stuffed you in a box beside the Urn *he* wants so badly!"

"I'll clean up. Fix my mess. You can run. Hide like a bitch."

"Oh, so I can be blamed if you get caught a second time? I think *not*," she thundered. "It's bad enough they have parts of you. Should they figure out what you are, what *I* am, there will be more to pay than what my flesh can give."

"What are you…?" her thug asked as his eyes narrowed into cold slits as her tail twitched.

Anais relaxed her shoulders, and what was left of her glamour faded. The scorpion-like stinger swelled up and hardened as she let the illusion go. Before Donta could object again, she flicked her head forward – and the tail followed.

The end of the appendage shot into his stomach with a meaty thunk, and punched upwards under his ribs. A blast of bloody, oily sand erupted from his mouth and sprayed all over her desiccated face. She twisted and tugged inside his chest so violently that it dislodged the metal bar and knocked the nails loose.

When she finished rooting around inside his ribs, the inhuman monstrosity pulled her tail free – and pulled out something so foul that the wraith wished she could vomit. Charred black and coated in a slick oily mass of clotted blood, it was a rotted, compressed skull. One that was the size of which could only have been found in the discarded early birth of a failed child.

Anais handled the pile of bone and gore carefully as she slid the tip of her stinger free. She didn't seem affected by the pure sense of *wrongness* and *foulness* that radiated off of every inch of the abominable relic. In the hallway, however, Rmaci couldn't do more than quake. *That… no. That should not exist in this world. That… that should not exist in the next. Should not exist. Should not never ever exist hat are these things… who are they?*

"I've no desire to be an example used by our benefactor to remind his other minions to stay in line, nor do I have any faith in that I can trust your tongue. You will have to do as an example, and I am *sure* we will talk more soon," the merchant – the *monster* – promised as she carefully tucked the putrid skull into her dress.

When she left, Rmaci did the only thing she could do.

Since the mere mention of the name of that woman's benefactor sent a cold chill down what was left of her shattered spine, the spy resorted to her old nature: she followed. It was the last thing she *wanted* to do, but there were limits to what she could tolerate in this world, even as a dead woman. More importantly, if a name alone terrified her, she was damnably interested in finding out *why*.

Besides, she told herself as she remembered Erine's earlier words, *my actions are my own. I just…* the spy thought to herself before she shuddered in disgust. *I just pray that I don't find one of the other realms of perdition she mentioned.* She drew to a sudden stop and looked down at her blistered, burnt, and frozen form. *Oh. You'd think someone would've told me Who I'm supposed to pray to NOW, wouldn't they?*

Dammit.

***

Five hours later, and the laundry room in the Repository was as clean as it ever had been. The same could not be said for Seline's dress – nor the words that had fallen from her mouth in a progressively fouler and darker cascade all day long. It had gotten to a point where the normal aides assigned to the room had taken to calling her 'Wash-Commander Valdin' when they thought that she couldn't hear them.

She, in turn, made it a point to hide the lye.

And spit in it, for good measure.

"I don't think I like you," Catherine intoned from the door of the washroom.

Seline turned to her and frowned at the stack of papers in the Maiden-Templar's hands. "I'm not sure I care for your cleaning staff. I recognize that they are warriors of the Divine but cleanliness is –"

"– the least of my problems," the other woman intoned darkly. "I truly, *truly* do not think I like you."

The healer's indignant bravado crumbled under her withering stare. "Maiden, I'm not sure what I did to earn your ire...?"

"You're about to," she grumbled. "My office. Now."

Dutifully, Seline followed through a shortcut that took her down several more gilded halls and alcoves that could be used for silent prayer and reflection. Or used for stationing guards and priests. Or used for people like her when they wanted to hide from people like the Maiden – a desire that grew with every single step.

When they arrived back in her office, the Templar slammed the doors shut and dropped the stack of papers on her desk with a 'thud' that was heavier than it deserved to be. "I am not sure where I am going to begin with this, other than I am *dead* certain you've spent too long with Akaran."

"As I said earlier, you're not going to get any disagreement from me there – but I don't understand. What's wrong?"

"What's wrong is that I can't tell you," Catherine replied miserably, "not without having your name, first."

"Having my name?"

The older woman gave her a curt nod and pulled out a small scroll from her desk. A quill dipped in ink and a handful of short, almost violent scribbles later, and she passed it over to the healer. "You have two options. Accept that what you've been told before today is all the truth you need, and we don't speak of this again."

That really, *truly* felt like the best path forward, but she hesitantly asked, "Or?" with a voice that quivered in naked nervousness.

"Or," Catherine replied, "you mark this paper here, here, and *here*. Doing so promotes you into the Order, with a proper stated rank of *Medicianna*. If you do, I can tell you what I found. On the usual penalties, of course."

"Usual... penalties?"

"Oh, you know," the Templar replied sardonically. "Failure to Hold an Oath, Diverging Secrets of the Crown, Bearing False Witness to the Goddess of Love, and I think there will probably be a request from the army to hang your corpse after your first execution for treason and espionage."

Seline's jaw dropped and she shrunk deep into the chair's cushions, which no longer felt as relaxing as they had a few hours ago. "I... I don't like those penalties."

"Nor do I blame you. If I may suggest – don't sign. Don't sign, go back to the Manor, forget that today happened. And *when* you see Akaran again, you direct him to see me. Immediately. *If* I haven't already found him – and he isn't dead from whatever metaphysical jaunt in the park that Telburn plans to put him through."

The healer sighed to herself at the mention of his name, and carefully took the quill and began to jot as much of her name down as she could. "If that's the case, then I'll take the rank because I think I already know what you're going to say," she replied as she wrote. "Annix… Zilyph. They're vampires, aren't they?"

Catherine's eyes darkened even deeper. "One is a pile of ash. The other isn't. Not to the best of the knowledge of the Order, and the Order's knowledge in such things is among the best."

"Oh. Well. Well, damn."

"Well damn indeed. I don't know what you've been told, or how much of your interest in Bistra comes from Akaran, but you've just picked open a very big sore. Bistra was sent to go find out why a village in Lowmarsh had gone quiet, and found a massacre the likes of which few of us have ever seen. She lost all of the men sent with her, but managed to cull the monster responsible. Yes, a vampire. One named of Zilyph. *Just* one."

Seline swallowed and looked down at her fingers. "Just the one?"

"Just the one. She spent the next year working through Lowmarsh to find one of the soldiers that had went missing in the investigation – a woman by the name of Sherril. A battlemage. This is where my headaches begin."

"Headaches? Why?"

"Because a rogue battlemage that matches her description just butchered her way through the Advensi of Massadine," Catherine groused, though her lips narrowed into a pale white slit as she realized that the healer hadn't moved. "And I think you knew that, didn't you?"

"There… were ideas. And… and a suggestion that it was a battlemage that destroyed the Landing, too."

The Templar sucked in air and drummed her fingers on the desk. "Suggestions were made, were they? I'm. Sure."

Seline cleared her throat and carefully adjusted her hair and took another breath. "Akaran's ramblings aside, ever since Bistra was admitted to the Manor, she's been afraid of her own shadow. The dark terrifies her, and she's always talking about 'fangs' and 'claws.' We always thought it was some kind of demon, but… if she's been right all this time…?"

"Then with luck, what I just told you will help her find some peace. Except that I think there's something you're holding back from *me* about the other name. Why do *you* think that it's also a vampire?"

"Why do you?"

Catherine stopped herself from retorting and flicked her tongue against her teeth in mild surprise. "You're quick. I like that," she quipped back before adding, "but your signature says that you answer questions when I ask them now, so. Answer."

The healer-turned-mediciannia blanched slightly and carefully handed over another journal. "Because Akaran does. He came back from that mess at the Landing with his leg cut to shreds. Blasted idiot earned himself a fever for that. Between his ramblings and his other *friends*, he's got it in his head that this Annix... creature... is alive and well." Before the Templar could ask, she put her hands up in self-defense. "Please don't ask. They scare me more than you do."

"Then you don't know me well enough," the Templar muttered before she lifted her hand with her palm facing the younger girl. "Speak truth and be judged," she intoned – and invoked. "Why do you think that there's a vampire in this city?" As she spoke, a small golden shimmer erupted along a faint scar along the underside of her jaw Seline had barely noticed before.

She tried to ask what it was, but a sudden *force* gripped her deep in her mind and she started to answer the rest of Catherine's questions before she knew what she was doing. "Because it's not just Akaran," she blurted. "He's been working with Erine Rrah, a thief named Riorik from Gonta, and a dead woman. He's also made deals with the Granalchi and the Hunters. I... I believe that Riorik is *the* thief from Gonta, and has taken Basion as his territory."

Catherine couldn't keep the shock off of her face. "The Eclipsian, the Granalchi, and the Guild? Presumably the Fleets, if I understand correctly? And what do you mean by a dead woman? He didn't kill someone... did he?"

"Not recently," Seline replied earnestly. "Though he's out for blood."

"I'm not sure if I should be impressed or angry," the Maiden muttered. "He was given instructions to rest and recover, not... not whatever fool's errand he's on now. How in the world did he convince...?"

The healer blanched slightly. "He's also got a... prisoner. Or at least, Erine does. I don't know what. It looks human. It isn't. I don't want to know what it is. They kept using the word 'construct' and 'animate.' That pet wraith of his, too, it just..."

"He has a prisoner? How does a man without a home have a prisoner? It isn't in your dormasil, is it?"

"Ah, no, no," the younger girl hastily denied, "Erine does. I don't know where. It's underground. She won't let him have it."

"I am beginning to feel that your question about Bistra was understated in importance. Don't think I didn't hear you say, 'pet wraith,' either, but I can't imagine you'd be able to describe that in a way that would satisfy my curiosity."

Seline sunk into the chair, utterly defeated. "Maiden, please don't ask me to make sense of any of this. It doesn't. It doesn't, and I'm scared, and I just want to help my patient. *Patients*, apparently."

"Scared seems like a reasonable state of mind. You know – if Kee hadn't just been assassinated, this wouldn't make much sense. Even *with* that massacre, it doesn't. I am going to have a *lot* of questions for that fool."

"Maiden, with respect, I'm not sure we *all* haven't lost our damned minds. All I know is that I've got a mad woman that says that the shadows are tearing her soul into pieces, that a creature named Annix is torturing her, and that she can't scream because screaming isn't safe," Seline offered with a sigh of frustration. "And then there's a man limping along outside right now that says there's a vampire in the city that's gained access to the Manor and I don't want to believe *either* of them but when someone knocks on your door often enough you can only pretend it's the wind for so long."

The older Lover opened her mouth to lodge a rebuke against the healer, but after a moment, she calmed herself and reconsidered. "Bistra... she had a knack. She was... special."

"A knack?"

"Her ability to read the auras of the world – and the other world's influences – is a rarity. If the Order hadn't gotten her, the Guild would've, and if not the Guild, then the Granalchi. She could see not only the traces of the ether, but the moods that were left behind. Even more importantly: what she could see, she could track. In truth, she may have been the best tracker we've ever had. Not the best fighter – but we have a rule: you can't kill something until you can *find* something."

"Okay..."

"We have a... unique... seat in the Queen's Court," Catherine explained slowly as she delicately picked her words. "This world is... broken, fundamentally. That's what we believe, at least. That with the rise of Archduke Belizal, and his armies in Agromah, Kora itself is at risk of imminent cataclysm."

Seline's hands started to shake again and she felt her eyes go wide. "How imminent?"

The Maiden stood up and walked around the desk to take the poor girl's shaking hands in her own. "Imminent in that one day, something may happen that we cannot control that would force the Heavens to unleash True Perfection on this world."

"Maiden, with all the grief I have seen in the Manor, I am not sure that the Heavens unleashing 'perfection' would be such a horrible thing, would it?"

"Maybe, maybe not. Even if it would be as wondrous as it sounds, and even if the world may be better after it is over, there is no question of the suffering that the Abyss would unleash in response. There are many a theological thought to be had about the nature of the end of the world, yet, there are those who aren't so keen on the idea. The Queen is one of them."

Her new medicannia tried to digest some of the implications that Catherine was suggesting, but to her credit, she worked to stay on topic. "What does that have to do with Bistra?"

Catherine picked up the contract and dangled it in front of Seline. "I'd like to remind you this exists before I continue." After the healer swallowed nervously and meekly nodded, she went on. "By charter, we are forbidden from operating outside the borders of the Kingdom unless we are specifically asked or invited by way of envoy to or from the Crown. However, it is rare that the Abyss cares about 'borders,' and there are those that actively act in ways to undermine our own efforts. The Luminary of the Missian League is one such of those."

"I'm not sure I understand what you mean, Maiden? The world is at risk of ending and you're accusing the Luminary of having a hand in it...?"

"Not in so many words, no. What I mean is that the gates of the Abyss have opened once before and spat out a Daemon Lord. If it happens again, there is a deep fear that the Heavens will not allow it to stand – yet there are those that still seek power at any cost. Our Order exists, in part, to help mitigate the efforts of the desperate when they bargain with the other side."

Seline blinked. "Oh but... wouldn't that mean that you have to do things outside of the Kingdom? I mean there are surely people all over the world that...?"

"I'm going to say the quiet part out loud. Our charter is a very *fluid* document, as far as our Holy General is concerned, and sealing cracks between the world is more important than simple border squabbles. It makes our lives *a great deal easier* if we have someone that is able to track the damned with skill when such *fluidity* is necessary."

The light, dim as it was, flickered to life in Seline's mind. "Oh. So, Bistra was being sent to do things that the Crown didn't want to admit to."

"And a few the Crown probably doesn't even know about," the Templar added. "Which is where this becomes a concern. Did Akaran happen to tell you why the Order takes accusations of vampires so seriously?"

"No," Seline replied honestly. "Though he rambled on about how you'd never believe him without any kind of proof so there wasn't any point in telling you."

Catherine tried to hide the smirk that appeared on the edge of her lips.

"Oh, I still don't believe that we have a vampire in Basion. I happen to think that there is some very unpleasant correlation with an old excisement, but I am not willing to go that far. Since he didn't tell you let me say simply that of all of the undead we are tasked to return to their graves, abominations such as Zilyph are near to the top of the list; and to the very bottom of the things we discuss in public."

"Duly noted," the healer eked out.

"Bistra caught Zilyph – who, I will agree, was a vampire – in the border town of Squistal. The border with the League, I should clarify. In the process, she lost her men, as I mentioned; but then she decided to search for an extended period of time to find one that disappeared seemingly into thin air."

"That would be this Sherril thing... woman?"

She nodded in affirmation. "A Specialist-Major in the 5th. She was never able to find her, but she did find evidence that a vampire had slowly been working its way along the Lowmarsh border. For how long, she couldn't say; years, maybe more. There was never – and there still isn't – evidence that Zilyph ever spawned more of her broods."

Seline frowned and shifted uncomfortably in her seat. "But the stories? They all say that vampires are a curse in the night, that they kill and resurrect their victims?"

The Maiden-Templar pursed her lips. "Which is how they often do. Over the centuries, at least, we have been lucky; only a few dens have ever been discovered north of Ogibus. This Zilyph, for whatever her reason, must have learned that leaving a brood behind is the fastest way to gain unwanted attention." Catherine paused and grimaced. "In complete truth? It's likely if Bistra hadn't found her when she did, we would have assumed the destruction at Squistal was a raid from a Missian bandit-king and never looked twice."

"If you will forgive me, I will say that I wish she hadn't, given where it took her," the medicannia replied after a few silent moments.

"There may be some fairness in that wish," Catherine agreed. "Except Bistra became *obsessed* with the idea that there was more than one, or that the mage she had lost in Squistal wasn't still alive and well. In her zealousness, she found... a development... that warranted immediate attention in a town called Stovannahsburg."

"Stovannahsburg? I can't say I know where that is?"

"For good reason – it's beyond the border. Days beyond. It's firmly in the middle of the Luminary's territories, and she wasn't invited."

Seline made a quiet, 'ah' sound. "The liquidity of the charter?"

"More-so than even water," the Templar replied with a smirk. "It went... poorly."

"This is the mission that led Lady Ridora to admit Bistra to the Manor, isn't it?"

"Eventually," Catherine clarified, "with a few unpleasant stops along the way. I'm sure you're aware of them."

Seline shuddered. "Handed off from convent to convent, rejected by the militant minds in the Lovers and treated like a monster by the army? Yes, I'm disgustedly familiar with her treatment."

"That may be revisited in the future," the outpost's commander replied with an unpleasant grumble. "I'm going to review how she was handled later. She should have been sent to the Manor immediately, instead of sent to languish elsewhere."

"Thank you," the younger girl replied with a relieved sigh. "Except, horrible as that is, it doesn't explain who or what Annix is?"

The Maiden walked back around her desk and flicked open one of the scrolls. "When our recovery team found her, she was in... a poor state. Aside from the horrors she had inflicted upon her own flesh, she had scrawled the word, 'Annix' across the walls. We assumed it was the name of the... well, that doesn't matter. We assumed it was a name of a creature that was later disposed of."

"I think what it was you sent her to kill matters a great deal," Seline protested. "I can't treat her if I don't —"

"It doesn't matter," Catherine repeated firmly. "What it was is not something that could be in Basion, now, nor ever," she repeated before she picked up another scroll and let it fall to the top of her desk with a sigh. "Either way, what she was sent to destroy is quite dead — because the Order took special care in making sure her work was complete."

Seline looked at the scroll and then back up at the Maiden. "I sense that there's something that you aren't saying."

"There's a lot I'm not saying."

The healer nodded, but then flicked her eyes back to the scroll. "You're also not saying why you look like you want to set that on fire."

"Because I do," Catherine admitted. "We killed it. And we got its name. Some things prefer to live life under a falsehood, so more than one name is not terribly uncommon on the lips of certain damned. Only one name is true, however."

Seline blanched and braced for what she expected the older woman to say next. "Its true name wasn't Annix, is it?"

"No," she sighed, "it wasn't. Which leads me to a very sincere problem."

"Why is a battlemage that was killed by a vampire suddenly walking around in our city, and why is the name of the *thing* that is terrorizing Bistra's dreams not the name of the thing that brought her to ruin?"

"And why is the name of the thing that brought her to ruin not the name of the thing that the Order executed, quartered, and then buried across Ameressa, Sycio, the Midlands, *and* Matheia?" the Templar asked. "With, of course, the obvious issue of the ramblings of your other patient. These questions will take a great deal of time to answer, yet they're going to have to be."

"We may not have that long to wait," Karaj said as they slipped into the room so quietly that Seline thought the white-robed figure had materialized out of thin air. "It seems that events are transpiring against us even as we speak."

As she cursed and tried to slow her racing heart, the Maiden looked up from her records and scowled. "Another attack?"

"No. Word from the Sisters."

"The Sisters...? Urgent word or other?"

Her aid smiled slightly. "Do they send any other kind?"

"Do I need to send her away?"

Seline looked up and cringed at the aura of simmering anger that radiated off of the Maiden's assistant. "She may need to send word of her own."

Catherine rolled her tongue over her teeth as her scowl deepened. "Karaj, that's not comforting. What's going on?"

"The Order has been placed on high alert – orders from the General. The Sisters threw a fit an hour ago, with a, and I quote, 'Vague yet concerning prophecy,' end quote," her aide replied. "Johasta feels that an *event* of some kind is about to unfold in due course," Karaj added, with a stressor on the word 'event' that was more for the healer's ears than Catherine's.

"I'm sorry, forgive me for interrupting, but the Sisters? *The* Sisters? The ones that sit in the Grand...?"

"Yes, those Sisters," the Maiden replied.

"They just interpret the Word of the Goddess, don't they? Why would they... throw a fit?"

"Because the Order does more than what the Order lets people know," Karaj responded. "If you don't have need, you don't know."

Catherine nodded but didn't entirely agree. "With the revelation this girl just delivered, it won't hurt to tell her," she replied as her assistant frowned. "We are blessed that the Goddess has seen fit to grant us a measure of foreshadowing through Her seers. They listen for Her whispers on the wind, and disseminate Her wishes to us." She paused and strummed her fingers nervously on her desk. "The old texts from the First Exorcist claim that it is to prevent another ascension of the damned as what befell Agromah."

Seline formed her lips into an, 'Oh' shape without responding, but then after she thought better of it, went on and asked an innocent (yet damning) question. "So if they're having a temper-tantrum, it's bad?"

"Quite," the Maiden tersely retorted. "This... this is troubling. What did they say? Any clues as to what's coming?"

Karaj cleared their throat and quietly pulled the office door closed the rest of the way. "It's an odd message. Nothing as vague as, 'cast your eyes to the east,' or whatnot. They said, and again I quote from the General's emissary, 'In the Realm of the Deep, in the Land of the Be-muddled and Deaf, the Kings of One Eye shall decide Fate of Shadows in the aftermath of a Ship of the Enshrouded.' The General seems to think that it means a battle is brewing either near Sycio or a new threat arising from the Cursed Continent."

The Maiden viably relaxed. "If it's something to the west, it's nothing we have to worry about. Less, if it's in Agromah. I'll have the scribes prepare the reliquar–" she started to say before Seline cringed and meekly said something under her breath. "What was that, girl?"

"What if it's here?"

Karaj tensed up as Catherine leaned in close and spoke with deathly malice in her tone. "What would cause you to say such a thing, *medicannia*?"

She took a deep breath and looked up at the suddenly very menacing, very *deadly* woman sitting across from her. "Akaran called this the city of the deaf and dumb a couple of days ago," she offered, and he's got one eye and..." she said as she gestured at one of the reports on Catherine's table. "Well... and his nightmares? More than a few have been about a ship full of the dead."

"The girl has a point," her aide added slowly. "Spoken that way, it does sound more of a rebuke than a vague destination. And he does have one eye."

Karaj lingered on the thought. "Didn't he say he was in a fight with a man with a cloudy eye a few days back? Claimed it was some kind of inhuman...?"

Catherine made a face like she'd just swallowed a live rat whole. "But he is no king."

"For which I think we should all be grateful," the cloaked priest added.

The Maiden didn't say a word as she and her assistant looked back and forth at each other for the longest moment in Seline's short life. "Did he survive the Granalchi? What's his status?"

"Left in the care of the Headmaster-Adept. He has not roused since the event."

"Is he okay?" Seline interrupted.

Karaj wavered on the answer before they found a way to phrase it for the poor girl's ears. "He's either going to return to your Lady's Manor, or go to the grave. Which, I cannot say. As his other status goes, Maiden, he was purged of the otherworldly aura."

"Was anyone harmed?"

"Only himself – but grievously. A few stomachs without constitution did not survive the experience in comfort."

Catherine pursed her lips. "Karaj..."

"I know, Maiden," the Lover replied, "you detest being at the center of Divine Ordainment."

"There's much to be said about chronicling events historic to the Order; there's much less to be said about living in one."

The Maiden-Templar sighed in frustration and stood up suddenly. "Well, young Medicianna Valdin, I suggest you take me to the Manor. I think I may need to speak to your patient – regardless of how Ridora feels about it."

Seline didn't even bother to argue. There wasn't a point, and it wouldn't have mattered anyway. The Kings of One Eye would wage war even if she did. A war that was coming sooner than they could've ever expected.

It was only going to take an awakening...

V. UNSTABLE MAGICS
Early Evening of Londis, the 7ᵗʰ of Firstgrow, 513 QR

The beach was nice. It always was. It always would be. That was its nature. Soft waves crested in the distance. Foam washed ashore. An errant piece of seaweed that brushed against his leg. A starfish that seemed to shimmer in the sand. A log that fit the curve of his naked back – one that was smooth and comfortable and it fit him like it was made for him to lay against.

For all he knew, it was. That was the nature of the beach. It was perfect. It was probably different for someone else. Instead of a starfish, it might have been a conch. Instead of foam, it might be roses. Instead of a warm sun, it might be a cool dusk.

It was peaceful. It was kind. It was joy. It was more than that.

It was Love.

"She's going to kick your ass so damn hard you're going to lose teeth," the little girl beside him pointed out. She hadn't said a word since he'd arrived, and after she spoke, he realized he liked her better that way. "I don't wanna hear any of your bitching when you go find someone to help you put 'em back in, either."

She was also Love. It was hard to say what *aspect* of Love she was, but the little girl *was* Love. Or at least, that's what he kept telling himself. She should have him angry enough to go punch something, but he just didn't have it in him. The beach was too perfect. The foam was too warm. The sand didn't stick to his skin.

So he sat there and he listened to the waves wash against the shore. "Can't I stay?"

"Stay?" the child retorted with a nasally, high-pitched voice. "Oh wah, you went and got your leg broken and now you just wanna take your toys and go home, is that it?"

"Close," Akaran admitted. "I take it that means no?"

"That means no," the little girl repeated. She flicked a long braid at his arm like a whip and smirked. "If you did, She'd stomp your head into the sand so hard you'd think you were downing in the Lowers."

"That happens up here?" he mused sadly. "Didn't think the Heavens would let there be pain in the Upper realms."

The girl flicked her braid at his arm again. "Eh. They don't. Defeats the purpose of purity, I guess. Just means She walks you out past the edge, slaps you around, then drags you back over. The virtuous ain't perfect, an' even the holiest need to be told they screwed things up," she retorted. "Some of you more than others," she added with a decidedly *icy* tinge to her voice that sent a brief chill through his heart.

A chill that was decidedly unwelcome. "If I go back, I'm gonna break some shit," he warned. "Can't promise I'm gonna make friends."

The little brown-haired girl chuckled gently. "You know, you're the first person in a couple hundred of your years that's ever sworn on this beach. Usually, the lot of you are either really grateful or terribly sad – well, sad at first, anyway, before they understand where they made it to. You? No wonder She's taken a shine to you."

"You didn't answer my question."

"You didn't ask one," she deftly returned. "You think She doesn't know you're gonna go heavy-handed? You think She hasn't already made that clear that you're *supposed* to?" the girl scolded. "She's *Love*, you idiot. She knows what's in your heart better than *you* do."

He took a breath and looked down at his hands. There was blood on them. Blood that hadn't gone away when he'd tried to wash them off in the in the surge. "Then why can't I get my hands clean?"

"Because they aren't clean," the child said after a long moment. "You've made mistakes. You can't take those mistakes back just by getting dead on occasion. You skipped the sands past the Veil, so you brought sin with you. Not the first time, either. Pristi does *not* approve of your behavior; I'd be careful about crossing Her people anytime soon."

"I don't remember getting them dirty. Not... not like this."

"That's part of the problem," she intoned. "I'm not gonna tell you everything you got wrong. That's not my job, and that ain't how it works. You're gonna have to figure that out, make your amends. If you can. If you can't, then you're gonna have to work to make up for it." She paused and lingered on the thought for a moment. "Then again, the fact that you've screwed up but still plan to go try to set things right... well."

"Well what?"

The girl stood up and put her hands on his shoulders as she leaned in to whisper in his ear. "Maybe that's another reason why She likes ya. And, maybe..."

"Maybe...?"

She pointed past him at a distant spot on the horizon. It was a little blue and green dot in the sky, and it seemed to grow bigger the longer he looked at it. "This place ain't that place. That place ain't perfect. That place ain't Love. That place is a mess. Sometimes, you need someone with dirty hands to do dirty things in a dirty place."

Akaran looked down at his leg and the steady flow of ice that had been seeping from the gash ever since he'd arrived. Each little chunk of frozen rock bounced into the sand and melted away into the ocean. "I just need to know that I'm doing the right thing."

"We all need to know that. None of us find out until after we do it. Not even She does. There's *one* Being in all of creation that does, and It just sits back and watches. Or sleeps. I've got coin on sleeping."

"There's money?"

"It's the Mount," she answered with a shrug. "There's everything. Doesn't do a whole lot because when you already have everything, you don't need coin. Still we have it. Coins you've seen; coins that haven't been minted yet. We've got everything, even when nothing matters."

The exorcist took a deep breath. "So I gotta go?"

She pointed at the ball on the horizon. It was rapidly approaching, and he was starting to feel a painful pull towards it. "Don't be in a hurry to come back here. You've got work to do, and She's been screaming Her head off about it. You've had your ears so full of ice that you've been practically deaf. Gonna warn you now – when you start to *hear* Her, She's gonna *speak* in some really *fun* ways. Remember who you're supposed to be."

"A messenger?" he asked, but she didn't answer. Finally, he shrugged and added an extra thought. "I thought I heard something on the wind."

"You should try sitting next to Her," the girl muttered. "It's like spending time in a gale."

Akaran tried to turn to look at her, but the rule prohibiting him from doing anything other than looking straight ahead was still, apparently, in effect. "I hurt. Am I going to hurt when I wake up?"

"Oh, you poor, sad fool," she said as he began to fade from view – and the giant ball in the sky along with him. "Not only are you gonna hurt, you're gonna find ways to spread that hurt around... because you're wrong. You ain't the messenger." She looked at the fading ball of dirt, water, and humanity and let loose a sigh that could be felt all over the plane.

A different voice intoned behind her with a very smug, threatening crackle in the air. The little girl tensed up as she felt the presence appear. The sea roiled away as the waves grew choppy and rough.

"[He's the Message.]"

***

"He's moving," a muffled voice called out.

Except it wasn't the voice that was muffled, Akaran slowly realized. There was something around his ears. *Bandages*? he quietly wondered as he slowly started to wake up and feel more of them. He was covered in cloth strips that were wrapped around his face, his right arm, and his torso felt absolutely covered.

Not just covered, but pained. A long strip of cutting pain radiated into his bones from his neck all the way down to the gash on his knee – which itself was bound so tightly he could barely move it. Someone came over and offered him a small pewter cup, which he eagerly started to sip at. It was water, but at this point, he'd have been happy if it was piss – just as long as it was wet. Liquid was optional.

He was exhausted. Every inch of his body felt like it had been dropped off of a cliff. His *bones* felt tired, and a throbbing *noise* in the back of his skull started to draw his attention. It felt... it felt like someone was *knocking* on his head from the inside.

"Ow..."

"Ow, hm?" he heard Telburn say from off to the side. "In all my years of life and study, I'm not sure truer words have ever been spoken. Boy? Can you hear me?"

The exorcist tried to nod his head but that lasted all of about five seconds. "I... ow. I'm here. I'm awake. I can't see."

"Well, your face is wrapped up in cotton, so I'm not at all surprised by that," the older man said dismissively. "How do you feel? What do you feel?"

"Pain," he groaned. "Lots of pain. Did I die again?"

Ishtva looked over at the Headmaster and mouthed a silent, "Again?" at his boss.

"There's debate over that," the mage admitted, "but since you seem to show signs of life now, it's a moot point. I've been assured that you are currently breathing and that your heart is beating, so I assume you are alive and not, to the best of our knowledge, you're not simply being used as a vessel for something that is other than native to our world."

"Oh," Akaran croaked. After a few long moments, he spoke up and asked the obvious question. "Did it work?"

"Well, you destroyed the yard, so if that was a goal of yours, it succeeded," Telburn replied slowly, "and I daresay that I lost a few students."

"Did *they* die?"

The mage shook his head. "No. They quit. Decided that what you went through was a bit much for them. As I've heard it said from your Order: there is *knowledge* and then there is *knowing*. A few of my less-promising students now fall into the latter category, and they didn't appear to enjoy the trip."

He laid in silence as the pounding in his head grew louder. Larger. "That's... good. Bad. I don't know. Glad they didn't die."

"Be glad for a multitude of things," Telburn suggested. "I honestly see no reason that you should still be among the living, yet, we are often surprised by the unknown and things that defy understanding. The extent of which, I can say, that of all the things I expected during the dissolution of your etheric malformation, the arrival of an extra-planar entity was not one of them."

"I didn't imagine that?" the exorcist mumbled as vivid images of the spell started to drift into the forefront of his mind. The episturine. The daggers. The wraith. The blood. So much blood. *Bandages*, he groaned. *I'm never going to be able to walk again, am I?*

The pounding in his head ceased for a heartbeat, and he faintly thought her heard a voice mutter a disapproving, *[Not with that attitude]* before the throbbing resumed.

"Unfortunately not. Was that... I daresay to even utter the name to give credence to your claims, but the female form that appeared in the sphere? Was that the episturine? The dark... *thing* that I saw you wrestle with – do I dare even ask?"

"Yes, and no," Akaran replied. "That was the bitch. The no was... no."

Telburn looked over at Ishtva and nodded. The other Adept quickly scooted to the other side of the room and started to make hurried notes in an open journal on an old oak desk. "Intriguing. Witnessing such a creature. Had it not been so violent with you, I'd have interest in trying to summon it again to see what I could lea..." he started to exclaim before the thought died on his tongue. "You didn't *encourage* it to be violent, did you? To *dissuade* anyone from wanting to replicate this experiment?"

"Did it work?" the priest repeated.

There was an extended moment of silence as Akaran slowly, *painfully*, worked himself into a sitting position before Telburn finally answered. "Investing in you was either one of my best ideas or one of my worst," he finally answered. "As far as your state: there *is* ether about you and you are regaining a concentration of ether native that is native to this plane. There is a measure of... disruption... in your aura. It is turbulent."

"What's that supposed to mean?"

"I'm not sure," the mage replied with a shrug. "Either it worked or it didn't, and until you are faced with any opportunity to put it to test, we won't know if it did. I can say that your aura is tainted with cryomantic residue, and I daresay that you'll always either have an aversion to or a blessing from the cold. Again, I can't say which – but I'd ask that you'd send a letter next Deepfrost so I can make note of it."

Akaran started to work the bandages free from his eye and tried to take stock of the room he was in. He looked bad enough that he could've been sent to the Pyre if someone looked at him in just the right way. It wasn't a difficult chore to trace the episturine's work in a spiral down his body just by the trail of blood across his wrappings. "Right," he muttered as he realized he was in someone's very prim, very proper bedroom, complete with not only fairly ornate furnishings, but also a crystal chandelier that emitted light from a flame-less source of some kind. "Where am I?"

"I wasn't entirely sure that you should be left in the care of my underlings," Telburn replied without directly answering, "and I have recently been threatened by my doting bride about spending too much time at the office."

"I'm at your house?"

"My estate," the Headmaster corrected. "A guest room. I would ask that you not wander. My daughter is staying with friends tonight but I dare not risk you scaring the staff."

From the other side of the room, Ishtva coughed into his sleeve. "Any more than you already have," he added. "Myself included."

"Sorry," Akaran muttered tiredly. "Shit. What time is it? How long have I been out?"

Telburn looked at a dimly glowing lamp on the wall and frowned. "I didn't think it was much after lower evening, but it's later than that. It's near moonrise."

The exorcist cursed under his breath and struggled to loosen some of the wraps around his neck. "All day, huh?"

"All day, I'm afraid. Though to be fair, it's a miracle that you're able to speak now as it is."

"Well, shit."

"Shit, indeed," the Headmaster agreed. "Ishtva? Could you please go see if my wife has made it home yet? She's late, and I don't want her running afoul of our other guest until I have a chance to explain myself."

Akaran looked up from his bandages and frowned. "Other guest?"

As soon as the Adept was out of the room, Telburn turned his attention back to the priest. "I didn't want to say anything until you had more of a chance to rouse up, but the wick is low on the candle. A man arrived a pair of hours ago, demanded to speak to you. Claimed it was excessively urgent. When I explained the situation you're in, he opted to wait in my foyer – and reiterated how important it was that I make sure you heard a message once you woke up. That, and his very *insistent* desire to wait here until your condition improved."

"Karaj or other?"

"The swordsperson at your purging? No. Whomever it is, my staff refused to see him out and advised that I not push the issue. I don't know what exactly to think of that, other than not fondly."

Akaran winced, though from the comment or the way he was tugging at his bandages, Telburn wasn't so sure. "Riorik. Great."

"I must ask you an important question: he made an intimation that you may somehow have someone held prisoner. I couldn't imagine that was the case, given you are without *legal authority* but I was also left with the opinion that this man didn't particularly care what it is the Crown would authorize either way."

"Yeah. Riorik," Akaran groaned. "Before I answer, how badly do you want to know?"

Telburn pursed his lips and pondered the question for longer than the priest felt entirely comfortable with. "I suppose that would depend on the nature of the person that has been found detained... or why."

Akaran carefully untied the bandages covering his left hand and slowly flexed his bloody fingers once they were free. The pounding in his head was getting worse by the moment, but for the first time in what felt like years, his knee didn't hurt at all. "Remember the arm you found?"

"I imagine that unless old age robs me of my senses, I will never be able to forget," the mage replied.

"I have the rest of him."

The surprise at the revelation only lasted a moment before the mage lifted a finger. "Had, apparently."

"Had?"

"Had," Telburn replied slowly. "He didn't give specifics, but he was rather agitated about it. Did you discover the nature of the owner?"

The exorcist shook his head and immediately regretted it. "Part of it. You won't like it. Shit. Did he say if anyone got hurt?"

It was the Headmaster's turn to shake his head. "No. Nor do I wish to know, if you have accomplices. Given the fact that the fellow is presumed to be inhuman, I don't *have* to bring this to Elsith's attention but at the same time, I do recall that she has a writ against him. She might be at odds with me if I didn't tell her."

"Trying to get me to pay you off?" the exorcist grunted.

"Nothing of the sort," Telburn countered. "Just suggesting that you may want to encourage this Riorik fellow to return to whence he came before she gets home. For *all* of our sakes."

Akaran took the warning in the helpful nature that it had been intended, though before he was able to get a single word out of his mouth, another voice interrupted him. As the mage quickly ran his hands through his hair and smoothed out his robe, the source was soon to follow. "Telburn? Love, I'm home. Sorry I'm late. Finally found B'tril. Said he got attacked a few days ago. He's been hiding in some shitty hovel to heal up. Brought him here for safety, just in case. Who's that ugly looking sod out by the doo... oh, another guest," Elsith remarked before she realized who he was and how badly he was hurt. "What are *you* doing here?"

"He's recovering," the mage quickly interjected. "Our experiment was earlier today."

If she was phased by that explanation, she didn't show it. In fact, what she was showing was an entirely different side to her than the priest had ever seen. She wasn't dressed to kill, she wasn't angry, she didn't look like she was ready to murder someone on a whim. The Huntsmatron was dressed like any other woman of the city, with her short-cut golden-blonde hair down and a pretty yellow dress on that accented her silver-and-gold-flaked eyes. "Doesn't look like it went well."

"That's still to be decided," Telburn hastily replied. "While we hope for the best, it's understood that this too will take time."

"Hopefully not much...?" she asked with a raised eyebrow.

Akaran coughed as he felt a surge of *anger* boil up inside his chest. It wasn't *his* anger, it was just *anger*. "I won't," he started to say before a coughing fit doubled him over and split open cuts all over his ribs. Blood started to seep back through the bandages before the fit subsided. "I won't stay long. I'm sorry to abuse your hospitality," he croaked.

She blinked in surprise and then carefully placed her hand against his forehead. He flinched but she kept the contact even as her eyes deepened into a frown. "You're fevered."

He groaned and took another raspy breath. "Then I'll stay for less."

"You'll stay until I say you can go," she declared. "Telburn? Husband? Why isn't he with a medicannia or surgeon?"

"Given the reaction that he had at the summoning grounds, I wasn't sure how wise of a thought that was," he admitted. "Or how wise it would be to let him be out of sight."

Another wave of foreign, unexpected, and unreasonable rage ripped through the exorcist and he started to shake. Elsith must have thought it was a shudder from the fever, and she moved to drag a blanket up over his shoulders before he pushed her away. "No, don't. I think I... I think I need to leave."

"Leave? In your condition? Are you in a hurry to die in a gutter?" she snapped back. "I know we haven't gotten along but I don't want to be responsible for —"

"It's not you," he interrupted as his hands started to clench on empty air. His teeth started to grind and when he looked back up at her, his eye had turned bloodshot. "Something's wrong. I don't… I don't know what."

"Wrong? Wrong how?" Telburn asked as he carefully pushed his wife back.

Akaran shook his head as the pounding in his skull took on a furious roar that threatened to shake his skin off. "I don't know," he replied through gritted teeth. "I feel like… like… I'm about to…"

Telburn quickly drew a glowing orange octagon in the air with his fingertips, with a flair leading away from each point. A web of crackling ether appeared as the shape filled with smaller lines of magic like a net. The mage waved his hand and directed the semi-translucent shield over the younger man and hissed as it made contact with a shimmering, roiling mass of energy that he hadn't been able to see before.

The exorcist made a snarling noise of his own as the netting buckled and frayed around the edges. "Telburn…"

"I warned you that there was a turbulence around you. I didn't expect it to be… this…" the mage halfway marveled even as he pushed himself between the priest and his wife. "You need to calm yourself; breathe. Slowly. But quickly. Please."

Elsith watched the exchange and wisely scooted over to the door. "Akaran, don't you dare get blood all over my house," she warned. "Or I swear… B'tril! Come here quickly!"

Her husband looked over his shoulder. "B'tril? You brought a Hunter home?"

"I said I did. He was attacked a few days ago. Given all of the other grief in the city, I thought it best to keep him close until we found the man that went after him. It's my night to offer him room and board."

"Oh, I see, but right now is not ideal —"

"I didn't know you were conducting experiments in the house again," she countered.

Before her husband could say another word, B'tril stepped into the guest bedroom. "Huntsmatron? My blade is yours."

Except it wasn't *just* hers. Except his loyalty wasn't *just* to the Guild. Except that the Sycian, who still bore numerous scratches and scrapes across his hands and cheeks, took one look at the priest and his pale pink eyes went wide.

Telburn's net shattered as the air went perfectly still. B'tril's lips curled up in surprise as the world seemingly shrank to the size of a head of a pin. Akaran looked at the slightly-ragged mercenary and slowly smiled. Against all odds, against all sanity, the exorcist stared over at the intruder and uttered a single, simple word that had the weight of the world behind it.

"You."

B'tril's jaw dropped as a wave of unbridled fury radiated out from the priest. "I... I do not know you!"

That lie wasn't believed by a single soul in the room. Akaran lifted his right arm off of the bed and straightened it out, palm forward. A sudden gust of energy billowed through his bandages and made them puff out menacingly before every scar, every rune, and every scratch on his body erupted in a brief and brilliant gold-and-lavender sheen. Some retained the glow, some faded, and a series of etchings that went from the underside of his left wrist to his shoulder began to take on a furious red glow.

A bolt of nearly-solid blue ether shot out of his palm before the Headmaster or the Huntsmatron could do anything about it. It was partially encased in ice, but in the time brief it took to speed across the room, most of it had melted.

Most, but not all.

The impact struck the Sycian in his upper chest and dropped him to the ground in a heap of pain. He struggled to breathe as Elsith stepped between them and drew a blade almost out of thin air. *"What do you think you're doing*?!"

Beside her, her husband had a briefly different response. "He's demonstrating that my efforts worked, I would say," he interjected before he looked down at the recipient of the spellcast. "Except the why strikes me as somewhat important, I concur."

Akaran swung his legs out and tried – but failed – to stand up. When he toppled back, he unleashed a series of obscenities that actually made Telburn's wife blush (though she'd never admit it). He snarled and focused another burst of energy out, though this one was caught and blocked by the Headmaster and a small defensive shield that sprung to life between the priest and his victim. "Move. Now," the exorcist demanded through clenched teeth.

"STOP IT! THAT'S ENOUGH!" Elsith screamed.

"Not nearly."

For the first time since he'd met him, Telburn actually raised his voice right with her. "AKARAN! NOT IN MY HOME!"

Not that it seemed to matter. "Asshole. You. Whatever your name is. By the power granted to me by the Queen, I am ordering you under arrest for an assault on an agent of the crown and an Exorcist of Niasmis. You are in *such* deep shit."

B'tril groaned on the floor as Akaran tried to stand up a second time with just about as much luck. "Arrest?" the Huntsmatron repeated incredulously. "What the piss is going on? Tel?!"

"Don't look at me!" her husband answered hastily. "I just helped the maniac get his magic back. A decision I am quickly regretting. Explain yourself right now, exorcist, or there will be a debt earned you are not capable of covering."

Akaran caught his breath and *finally* managed to push himself up on wobbly legs. "Him. That's the one that attacked me."

"Attacked...? The mugging you...?"

"Him," he repeated firmly.

Elsith blinked and looked back and forth between her groaning subordinate and the cursing priest. "Mugging? What...?"

"Mustn't've been a mugging," the battered priest grumbled under his breath. "If he's Guild... oh. Weren't trying to rob me. Trying to *kill* me. Oh you are in *such* deep shit, asshole. Whatever your asshole name is."

"B'tril. Huntsman B'tril," she answered as she slowly lowered her dagger and crossed her arms. "I don't know what permissions you think you have, but the Guild operates outside of the Queen's law for all intents. As long as he holds that badge, he is answerable to *me*."

The exorcist looked down at his left arm and the glowing runes on it with a snarl – though it was hard to say if it was from pain or for other reasons. "Fine. Then *you* can arrest him and *we* can sort it out later. Either way, he stands up again, and I'm putting a foot in his mouth. Maybe his."

"What exactly are you claiming he did?"

"Few days ago. Got attacked. Thought it was a mugging. *Asshole* there jumped me, beat the living shit out of me," he explained. "Barely managed to fight him off, the prick."

Telburn cleared his throat and moved a few feet away from the downed Hunter as he sensed what was to come. He was only partially wrong on his fear, though the move was a wise one. "He did get attacked, Elsith."

"How can you tell?"

"One of mine saw him after the fact, and he had word sent to the Annex about it. Not all of those wounds were inflicted by my hand."

Akaran growled down at the disabled huntsman. "Bastard nearly shattered my knee all over again."

Elsith nodded and looked down at the heap of a Huntsman below. "You so swear that he is the one that attacked you then?"

Akaran nodded and ground his teeth. The rage, the fury boiling in him, was almost more than he could bear. It felt *familiar* but not, it felt *wonderful* but *terrible*, and it all-but muted all of the other thoughts in his head. "I do."

"I see. It would be exceedingly illegal for one of us to accept a writ against one of the Queen's exorcists," she mused to herself as she lifted B'tril's head up with the point of her boot. "Such a writ would have to come directly from me, unless..."

"Unless?"

"Unless he didn't take a writ from me," she said as the corner of her mouth stretched into a cruel, deadly smile. "Did you? Did you happen to take a writ from someone else?"

"Matron, admitting... admitting... would remove me... from service."

"*Lying* gets you removed *faster*, and after the executioner gets to play with your stomach a bit," she warned as she slid the edge of her blade across her fingertips.

B'tril looked up at her and rubbed a gloved hand across the dark plum bruise forming across his chest. "Then, aye, yes, Matron, I did."

"You did," she stated flatly. "What kind of contract?"

"Fi... find him. Take... his head. Or... at least. His heart."

"Writ of Execution. How quaint," she snapped. "The boy is right – you have truly found yourself in a pile of shit."

Akaran choked back something vile on the tip of his tongue (words or vomit, he wasn't sure which) and challenged his would-be assassin. "Who? That other sand-prick? Ocsimmer?"

"N... no. But your... your treatment of him. That is... this is why I accepted," the dusky-skinned mercenary retorted. "I... I do not know his name."

"You took his coin but not his name? I am fairly sure that I had taught the men in my employ better. The odd side job is one thing, but certain standards can often save your life," Elsith scolded. "So you admit it?"

The Sycian nodded his head as he pushed himself into a sitting position against the doorframe. "Aye, Matron, I did. Justice for Se'daulif. A strike against... the Lovers. A joy, both. Send me to the Maestar. Let him judge if these hands are weighted with blood."

"Why would I do that?" she asked as her eyes narrowed into very dark, very cold slits. "The Maestar only handles members of the Guild. You aren't."

B'tril blinked and shook his head as Akaran slid (with no small degree of difficulty) into a pair of hastily-offered pantaloons and an ill-fitting white and brown tunic that ended up bloodstained almost as soon as the exorcist put them on. "My Matron? My hand has been to contract for years ten?"

"Contracts end," she pointed out as she stepped away from him and slid the dagger back into her dress and out of sight. "Exorcist? If you can walk, he's a private citizen now."

"Is he?" he asked as a cold glint flashed in the corner of his eye.

"He is," she repeated before she leveled a finger at him. "DON'T stain my carpets."

The exorcist smiled and brushed past her, limping – but for the first time in months, without the need of a cane. He looked down at the former Hunter and slowly looked him over. "Hi there."

That look alone was enough to make the mercenary panic. "ELSITH!"

Akaran placed his right foot on B'tril's collarbone and pressed down. "I said, hi there."

The shorter man cursed and grabbed at his foot to try and push him away. Try, and fail. "AGH FISK! STOP IT!"

"Who hired you?"

"This, I do not know, as I said!" That didn't work. At all. All the priest did was push down harder even as he started to lose his balance. "I DON'T KNOW!"

Akaran stepped back and grabbed the wall before he could fall over. Not even a moment passed before a particularly cruel idea landed in his head. "This could've gone easier, just so you know."

"A man that jails another on charges false? Expect me to think that there would be ease?"

"Yes," the priest admitted without further thought.

"My boy, before you do anything, how do you feel? I have... very strong concerns about your current state," Telburn interrupted.

He looked down at his bloody, glowing arm. There were seven marks, each one a warning. Each one a rune – with a matching mark elsewhere in the city. "I don't know. Either... either something went badly wrong with the spell... or..."

"Or?" Elsith asked slowly.

Akaran held up his arm and showed them off. "Or remember when I said you were about to get a writ that you couldn't turn down?"

She nodded with a grim smile. "I'm not going to get to enjoy dinner tonight, am I?"

"I don't know. I could be dying again, so there's that," he offered before he looked down at B'tril – who, wisely, hadn't decided to try and get away. Or unwisely, depending on how you looked at it. "Tel... I feel... I feel like I'm about to explode. I can feel it under my skin," he gasped out. "It's not just... not just energy. It's just not just ether. There's..."

"That turbulence around you," the priest mused, "it has oft been said that the more militant mages in your order act in manners thought to be chaotic. Maybe there's a metaphysical truth to that, and not merely a component of psychology."

"Pretend I knew what you meant by that," the exorcist groaned as he reached down and pulled a familiar sigil off of the (former) Hunter's neck. "Quickly."

"Your vessel has been emptied of foreign ether, and now what we consider native magic is trying to rebuild your aura. If what you channel is volatile by nature, then it could... oh."

Elsith looked at her husband and took a very slow step back. "Tel, you know how much I hate it when you say 'oh' like that."

The Headmaster wet his lips and formed another shimmering etheric shield between her and the twitching priest. "Akaran? You cast one spell. May I suggest another? It might ease some of that pressure. You may have to allow some of the ether to flow *through* you rather than merely build up *in* you. Irrigate and drain your magical aqueduct, as it were."

Akaran looked at the shield, looked at B'tril, and shrugged painfully. He closed his eyes, visualized his goal, and whispered a word that had eluded him for months. "Bonds," he whispered under his breath.

At his command, silvery etheric chains manifested along his right arm from elbow to wrist. They glimmered in the room's dim light as a smile blossomed across his lips. For a moment, he looked like a child gifted a brand new toy, and a wave of relief washed off of him that the husband and wife duo felt flow across their own skin. He flicked his arm, and a length of the phantom chains spun free of his arm and wrapped themselves around his knee to form a makeshift brace.

Telburn watched with his eyes wide in absolute delight. "Brilliant! I wouldn't have expected an etheric conjuration, but...! Oh! Are those ice crystals? They *are*! Cryomancy from a Lover. My mind be gifted knowledge more than I ever expected!" he gushed. "How do you feel? The pressure — has it ebbed?"

"I... I can use magic again? That wasn't a fluke?"

"I would be careful, of course," the Headmaster cautioned. "We have no idea the extent of the damage that the episturine caused when it first poisoned your aura... or the damage it caused when it cleansed you."

"I promise," the priest lied as he started to laugh and cry at the same time. "I can do it again. I'm... I'm cured. I'm... whole. I'm..." he managed to croak out before a new wave of ether crashed into his back and nearly lifted him up from the force of the blow.

New. Different. *Charged*.

The Headmaster *saw* the ether ripple. The Huntsmatron *felt* it. They *all* heard it. Akaran? Akaran just stood there. His muscles clenched from head to toe. His wounds split open and started to bleed even more. His hands clutched at his thighs so hard his nails left furrows in his flesh.

It was different than anything else they'd felt from him.

And it was full of *rage*.

"I [*am*] so [*pissed*]," he said through clenched teeth. His voice wasn't solely his anymore. It was his and it was overlaid by a woman's. His face flickered from joy to Love to rage to grief to fury to happiness to unfiltered desire to raw *anger* in a scant few heartbeats. "I [*feel you*]," Akaran snarled as the chains on his arm shot out and wrapped around his would-be assassin. "I [*know you're*] here."

"Akaran! What happened?! Are you –?"

He was oblivious to Telburn's call, and he *wrenched* B'tril around so hard that the mercenary only managed to get a strangled cry out before his head hit the ground. Akaran's arm flexed and he twisted again as he stormed out of the room with the force of a hurricane – and the phantom chains pulled the mercenary along right behind him as if he weighed nothing.

Elsith's dagger was back in her hands before her husband saw her do it, and the low growl in her voice carried a threat that the mage took to heart. "If he makes a mess on my rugs, I swear I am cutting you off."

"In my defense, my love, you're the one that brought B'tril here."

She glowered at him as they followed the rampaging priest out of the room. "It's not like I knew he was taking outside contracts."

Telburn cleared his throat. "Your job to know, isn't it?"

"And *you* know that there is a strict *no-research in our house* rule, too," she snapped back as they followed him down the oaken-floored hallway. "Right, *my love*?"

"It wasn't research."

"Oh? Then what do you call it?"

He paused as Akaran kicked a door open. How he knew where he was going was a mystery, but it was obvious that he was headed to the foyer. "A good-natured favor turned mistake?"

Elsith sighed in disgust. "Whatever is about to happen…"

"…you don't think we want it spilled on the floor," the mage finished.

"Or the walls."

"Possibly the ceiling," he quietly quipped. "I swear, I don't know what's going on," he said as the priest made it into their receiving room. "Though I'm not entirely confident that he's alone in there."

She shook her head. "No. There was that other fisker in there. You never told me –"

"I don't mean in the room," he quickly interrupted. "I mean in *him*."

Before she could challenge him on what *that* was supposed to mean, a fresh exclamation drowned out her complaints. "Akaran! I heard screaming. I was starting to feel left out."

"I can fix that," the exorcist retorted as he finished pulling the struggling mercenary into the room behind him.

Riorik smiled up from the long, comfortably-padded couch he had taken it upon himself to claim for his own. The master-thief had seen better days; his face was covered in a red flush and his jacket had been stained with mud and other, less-identifiable concoctions. "Oh can you? I see you've gained some measure of your magic back; maybe today isn't entirely a loss."

"I can. Want me to owe you a favor?"

"Another one?" he asked as he straightened up. "You're living dangerously. With magic too, I see. A cause for celebration?"

Akaran flexed his hand and tugged on the chains. "Yes. And I brought you a toy. [*You brought*] me one [*too*], I see," he coolly seethed as the rage simmered back down.

The thief sized up the disgraced mercenary and chuckled to himself even as the shifting tone in the priest's voice set him back. "Oh did you? Is that for me?"

"I'm a gift for none!" his prisoner argued to absolutely no success or anyone's interest.

"You met this asshole before. He's the one that jumped me on Staddis. "I'd like to know who hired him. He says he doesn't know."

"You don't believe him."

"Would you? [*Because I don't.*]"

The Hobbler flicked his tongue against his teeth and chortled. "I believe it would be a cause for a conversation, yes."

Elsith interjected herself into the conversation with a firm cough and a deadly glare. "Care to tell me who your friend is and why he's here in my house?"

Akaran raised his hand and blocked the thief from replying. "If I told you, you'd try to arrest him," he hurriedly interjected. "He's a friend, and he's help, and he'll get answers. [*I promise.*]"

"I already have answers. You won't like them," Riorik warned. "Did the good Headmaster tell you why I was here?"

"He did. Is everyone okay?"

"No."

A shudder went down the priest's arms as another flash of anger boiled up in the back of his skull. "Is everyone I like okay?"

"The burn victim is missing, though her current handler believes she's as healthy as she can be," he replied. "Though we are now without a lead on your other issue."

"Shit," Akaran spat. "Goddess knows what that bastard is going to get to if he's gotten out. That's a headache we didn't need."

A smug grin danced across the thief's face. "Ah, no need to worry. He's no longer among the living. Or does that saying apply to one in his shape?"

The realization drew the exorcist up short. "I wasn't even sure how to kill him. What happened?"

Riorik walked around him and studied the mercenary still struggling against the metal chains. "While I can't speak for certain, it seems that someone removed his heart. Or what passed for it, at least – I found few other organs that should have been present. Yes, I looked, yes, I took care, and yes, he's as dead as one presumably can be."

"[*Damn.*] I guess we have two different suspects."

"One," the thief corrected while the mage and his wife watched in utter befuddlement. "My men caught sight of a woman leaving the tunnels. It matched the description of that vexing Anais bitch. I swear, I'll see her dead."

The exorcist grunted in disgust and held up his arm and pointed at one of the glowing runes on it. "I left a wardmark in Thesd Estate, where she used to stay. I think we've both already seen her dead, if my magic is working right."

"Anais?" Elsith interrupted. "What's your dealing with her?"

"Only a desire to put her out of business," the Hobbler earnestly replied. "She's made that difficult, but not impossible. I know of the writ you have on her and her associate, but the latter is no longer valid." He paused and looked at Akaran in utter disgust. "Did you just suggest that she's *also* an inhuman? You have gone a long way recently to keep me from having new toys for an extended period, you know that, yes?"

The Huntsmatron's jaw dropped as she attempted to glare a hole in Akaran's chest. "You have Donta captive?"

"Had," Riorik clarified, "much to my intense disgust."

"And mine," the exorcist grumbled. "I was looking forward to that. [*I really was.*]"

"I know," his friend replied with a sad sigh. "As was I. Before our hosts can object to your off-the-candle hobbies, how are you feeling? You look positively deathly ill, if I do say so myself. Deadly, too, though I'm not entirely sure why – although if your voice is going to continue to shift like that once you recover, may I suggest putting effort into *not*? It's... unsettling."

Akaran grunted and flexed his fists as the chains holding B'tril captive faded. "[*Be careful what you wish for.*] I'm willing to owe you a favor again."

"A third favor," the thief countered.

"Second."

"Third, my boy; do learn to count," Riorik chided. "I provided you with that cursed relic that demon owned when you were traipsing around the eastern part of the Kingdom. Then I helped purge Gonta of the Circle's influence – at significant cost to my own operations. Now you want me to have a discussion with this gentleman? This is your third."

"Come here, Riorik," Akaran replied flatly.

"Not even a please?"

"*Please* come here, Riorik," he asked with an annoyed little sigh.

Elsith frowned and started to repeat his name a few times over under her breath as it registered with her in the back of her mind. While she did that, her husband summoned a wisp of flame to envelop his fingers and aimed them at the former Hunter when the Sycian started to make a few too many movements. Warning given, B'tril settled down while the priest slowly studied Riorik's face and then closed his eye.

As if on cue, the black blotch on the thief's face pushed itself to the forefront of his skin, even as it made the rotund man squirm and curse quietly in pain. It had nearly doubled in size since the last time the priest had seen it, and its sudden presence drew immediate concern from the Gorosochs. The air around Akaran grew dark and almost damp with an oppressive chill as he approached and shut his eye.

The priest very slowly, very intently, let his fingers hover over the blot without touching it. "I see you."

"I don't see how, with your eye closed," Riorik quipped even as the mark on his face began to painfully burn. When the burn turned to a stabbing pain, he tried to pull away. The priest caught the other side of his face with his left hand and held him steady as the blotch shifted, moved, and long inky veins began to radiate down his throat.

"You know me," he whispered. "You know me, and you hate me. [*Don't you?*]"

"I'm finding myself a bit less fond —"

Akaran ignored him. For that matter, Akaran ignored everything else in the room except for the surge of rage that boiled back up in his throat. Anger, rage, fury, all of it. It came unbidden but not unwelcome. He grit his teeth so hard that they creaked, and his body tensed up so tight that a long trail of blood pulsed out of his wounds and immediately left a long, ribbon-shaped stain from his neck to the waist of his tunic.

He saw the rot in his mind's eye. Saw it shift. Saw it *twitch*. He felt etheric tendrils push free of Riorik's skin before the shadowy form even did it. He saw the face appear in the murky blackness. He saw it, he felt it, and it felt him.

Elsith grabbed her husband's arm even as Telburn tried to push her back away from the roiling mass of unstable ether that boiled out of Akaran's skin. "Goodness…" he whispered more to himself than anyone else.

"Tel…? What's going on? I can feel that… magic. No… it's… *anger*. I can feel that *anger*."

While Akaran pulled at the black morass with his mind, the mage took a very deep and nervous breath. "We need to keep him as a friend."

"Are you sure? Might be safer to kill him."

"Friend," he repeated, "we need to keep him as a *friend*."

The priest ignored them. He ignored B'tril as the mercenary scooted away across the wool and reed rug. He ignored the thief as he tried to get loose from his grip. "[*I see you,*] you sack of shit. Think I'd forget about you? Think I'd *ever* forget [*about you*?]"

Riorik reached up and grabbed both of his hands and tried to pull away as a sick chill ripped through his gut and a cold sweat blossomed across his face. "Ah... Akaran I... I don't feel so..."

"Condemned you. Banished you. Sent you screaming," the exorcist intoned with deathly malice coating each word. "Watched you get ripped to shreds. You know it. You weren't there but you [*know it,*] don't you..."

An anguished, high-pitched wail erupted in the room from everywhere and nowhere at once. It was sharp enough that it set the Huntsmatron's teeth on edge even as Telburn felt a distinctly *toxic* stench of magic radiate away from the thief. "Akaran! I recognize that I may have come to you for aid with this but *you're hurting me,*" the Guildboss managed to utter through tightly closed lips and clenched teeth.

His complaints didn't work. The wailing didn't work. Nothing worked, and nothing was going to stop Akaran. Not even when the wailing turned to words, and the words set a chill in everyone's souls. *"SEEKS WARMTH! JUST SEEKS WARMTH! SO QUIET SO QUIET NO OTHERS NOW JUST QUIET COLD AND QUIET!"*

"Let me [*fix that,*]" Akaran snarled as he dug his fingers into the Riorik's cheek and *twisted*. The black morass clung to his digits and tiny claws tried o scratch at his skin. He pulled his hand back and pulled the vile, twisting mass of malice and damnation away from the thief's face. The more he pulled, the more the shape solidified until he held a dripping mass of ethic shadows and oily goo that clutched desperately at the Guildboss's face and the exorcist's hand alike.

"JUST SEEK WARMTH!"

"**I CONDEMN**," Akaran thundered. His voice carried such weight that you could hear it outside of the estate – and inside the room, the call for judgment almost hammered the mass into oblivion on its own.

The wraith screamed and twisted away from Riorik. Tendrils and veins of shadows ripped away from his throat and neck as chunks of the creature's essence were pulled out of his body and forcibly hauled out of the aura around him. The thief screamed in pain and collapsed helplessly back onto the couch as the damned spirit fought against the exorcist's grip.

The Gorosochs didn't waste any time either. The moment that the spirit manifested in full, Telburn had a pair of burning smokeless fireballs in his hands, while his wife raked her left hand down her dagger and forced arcs of electricity to radiate off of the edges of the blade. B'tril, for his own credit, clutched a charm on his waist and began to summon a swarm of shadows of his own before the Huntsmatron kicked his wrist and broke the spell before he could finish invoking it.

"PLEASE JUST NEED HOME SEEKS WARMTH AND HOME!"

"Then go home," Akaran spat coldly as his voice changed again, as a woman's sultry tone overlaid his angry growl. "**EXPUNGE!**"

The Word ripped down his arm and the force of the spell caused an explosion of light in his palm. The magic barreled through the wraith and incinerated it from the inside out. Giant cracks appeared and blew outwards with streamers of lavender light and pulsing streamers of blue energy. Daringol's essence lasted for a heartbeat longer before the Divine edict boiled it away to nothing more than a greasy gray steam that filled the room.

When it faded, Riorik sagged on the couch in exhaustion, while Telburn knelt to the ground and placed his hands to his ears. Elsith moved behind him and put one hand on his shoulder while she aimed her knife right at the priest. "What did you do?"

Her husband matched the question with a shouted cry. "WHAT WAS THAT?"

"An exorcism," the priest seethed through clenched teeth. His voice slipped back to normal, but the angry throbbing in his head had only grown worse – and the glowing runes down his left arm were as furiously brilliant as ever.

"Boy, I have *seen* exorcisms before!" the mage exclaimed from the floor. "What was *that?!* Who did you channel?!"

"I'm in a foul mood," Akaran explained as if that answered everything. When the Headmaster gave him a renewed look of shock, he clarified slightly by saying, "Really foul mood."

"Are you NORMALLY like this?!" Telburn shouted as the black-haired mage pulled himself up off the ground. Elsith hadn't yet uttered a single word, but the crackling electricity that quietly arced down her blade said all she needed to.

"In a foul mood? Yes."

The mage swallowed hard and shook his head as his ears rang. "Do you normally... Gods above. I've never..."

"I've never heard you invoke the Gods before," his wife quietly whispered behind him as she helped him up the rest of the way.

"I'm going to evoke a lot of things in a minute," the Headmaster muttered under his breath. "Boy, *who are you?*"

Akaran watched as streamers of light steamed away from his arm and the obvious appearance of magic around him faded into the air. The chains around his knee faltered and fell apart into silent nothingness before they even hit the floor. The only magic that remained were the glowing scars on his left arm, but even those had dimmed to a muted emanation of light. "Pissed."

"That's a *what*, not a *who*," the mage retorted.

"I... I am sore. I don't know if anyone is interested, but I am sore," Riorik complained from the couch. He'd landed in a heap and the unpleasant red glow on his cheek was uncomfortable enough that he felt just fine taking a few moments to catch his breath, awkwardness be damned.

The Headmaster gave him a vexing, vaguely annoyed glance. "You. I want to study you now."

"Me? Why me?"

"Because I doubt he's going to let me," Telburn said as he pointed a shaky finger at the exorcist, "and quite frankly? I am afraid to ask him. I want to know what he just did to you."

"Got rid of a leftover," Akaran quipped. "Does anything else matter?"

Telburn and his wife both answered that question at the same time, and in the exact same way. "YES. YES IT MATTERS."

"Great. Listen, can... can I have some water? Suddenly tired."

"Don't even know how you're still standing," the mage admitted as he carefully walked into an adjoining room for a glass of water – or at least a glass of something. "By the Gods, that was..."

"Really getting uncomfortable here, my love," Elsith charged. "I'm fairly certain that not only did you break my rule on 'no research,' you also allowed for an etheric summoning..."

"Love is right," the mage muttered, "though since it was a *banishment* instead of a *summoning*, it seems like the rule of, 'no hunting monsters at the dinner table' may also need to be revisited."

"We're not at the dinner table," she pointed out as she seethed quietly and knelt down beside B'tril. "And I swear, priest, if you expect me to think that was necessary to do while steps away from my daughter's room..."

Akaran ignored the Huntsmatron's reprimand and focused on the master-thief. As he offered Riorik a hand to help the rotund Guildboss straighten up, the priest addressed his friend directly. "Now I owe you *one* favor. If you take care of *that* idiot, I'll owe you a second. Purging Basion doesn't count. You're protecting your new investments doing that."

The thief rubbed his cheek and sighed in relief. "I... yes. You've made the screaming in my head stop, so I'll accept that. One favor fulfilled, I suppose. What do you want to know?"

"Who hired him," Akaran started, "and if not who, where. When. Why. I want to know why someone wanted me dead. Annix isn't the type to hire assassins, so it's either Anais..."

"Or you've angered someone else."

"Never a possibility I can discount," he admitted. "I also want to know everything bout this," the priest added as he dangled the silver-chained necklace he'd taken from the former Huntsman. "It looks like it belongs to the Lethandrians, and I'm getting tired of picking up their toys."

Riorik slid his fingers over the moon-shaped icon and frowned. "Interesting little bauble. It will be done. Will he resist?"

"Probably."

Elsith rapped the hilt of her dagger on the wood flooring and continued to glare up at them as she continued to crouch down. "I've granted you permission to take him into custody, though I'm not sure if you have any kind of rank that lets me do so. I didn't give you permission to give him to someone else."

Akaran paused and tried to think through the pounding that radiated through his skull. "He's admitted to attempted murder. We can take him to Henderschott and wait for his idiots to find out nothing, or I give him to my friend here and you can find out if the Guild has been compromised by anyone else before the sun comes up. Up to you, I suppose."

"If you put it like that," she murmured, "then I'm going to have to clean a house either way. Or... possibly both ways."

"Afraid so," the priest admitted with a shrug. "Give him to Riorik."

"I know who he is, you know," Elsith countered. "I'm impressed, but."

The thief smiled from ear to ear. "But my dear Matron, the Crown has not yet accused me of doing anything in this Province that would require the Guild to take an interest in me. The things the Guild has my name on for in *other* Provinces won't apply until your co-workers in those regions ask the writ to be carried over across the regional borders – if my understanding of Guild law is correct."

"It... is," the Huntsmatron finally admitted. "Not that I think that excuse will hold for long."

"It won't, but it won't need to," the Hobbler replied as he firmly grabbed B'tril by his shoulder. "I'll have what answers our errant priest has requested in due time."

The former Hunter tried to argue the decision, but it went completely ignored and utterly unheeded. "I said as I said; what you ask, I do not know!"

"Boy, what of you?" Telburn asked. "You need more than water. You need rest. You're – well, quite simply, you're a danger to yourself and all those around you, I believe."

Akaran looked down at the glowing marks on his arm, and clenched his fist. When he looked back up at the Headmaster, there wasn't any doubt to his intent. "You gave me back my magic. I'm giving the Goddess another one of Her people back."

"How do you intend to do that, hm?" When he explained the way, and the how, and all of the other secrets he'd unearthed as he found shoes and an extra weapon of his own, the answer was clear.

With a harshly spoken Word.

VI. GIFT OF PAIN
Evening of Londis, the 7ᵗʰ of Firstgrow, 513 QR

Blissfully unaware of the impending chaos soon to land on the Manor's doorstep, Seline took a few moments to feel particularly proud of herself. She's been gone all day and the asylum hadn't fallen apart, all of the residents seemed to be oddly calm, and Saa Telpid hadn't given her any shit about being late getting back. Best of all, the two people that noticed she smuggled Catherine inside the Manor walls were amiable to having their silence bought with the promise of belian-berry tarts the next time a shipment was made available.

All in all, it hadn't been a bad day, the laundry-Repository aside.

What darkened it wasn't the aura of the impending doom that the Maiden-Templar was putting off. That, the healer had decided, was simply the way that the militant arm of the Order of Love expressed their feelings. Nor was it the realization that her new title of medicannia meant that she would now be expected to split a portion of her duties between the Manor and the Army – though Catherine had been kind enough to promise that she wouldn't have to answer to Henderschott.

Once had been enough of that, and that was the extent of the topic she was willing to think about. No, what started to turn her day sour was Bistra. Nothing, absolutely *nothing* she had done had been enough to convince the poor woman to leave her room. She'd tried food, she'd tried promising that there would be light every step of the way, she even caved and promised to spend the night in her room with her (a practice that was frowned upon by Lady Ridora, but sometimes one that worked to encourage good behavior for those afraid of the dark).

None of it worked. Still, the young healer continued to do her best, if not for the simple reason that she felt it would be a terrible idea to not meet Catherine's expectations (and because if Catherine stepped foot upstairs, there was no question that Ridora would find her). While she did everything she could to cajole the former exorcist into following her downstairs, the Maiden-Templar ended up in an odd conversation of her own.

As late as it was, the atrium was quiet and all-but abandoned for the day. A brazier lit in the center of the garden emitted a warm firelight that illuminated the three larger-than-mortal-life statues of Isamiael, Solinal, and Niasmis while no more than four other sconces hung on each of the east and west walls. The north side of the garden trailed uphill and out to the back garden of the U-shaped manorhouse, and it was back there – past the flowers, past stone benches, past a few thorn bushes placed to gently persuade the curious to stay within the confines of the grounds – that the Templar stumbled across one of the women that had taken Akaran's interest recently – even if the Templar didn't realize it yet.

Before she'd left the Repository, Catherine had taken it upon herself to don simple armor that ultimately, wasn't that simple. Nobody should (or would) see the platemail vest she wore under her white tabard with the gold and black colors of the Order of Love embossed on the front. Few would notice the steel hidden under her skirt to protect her thighs and shins. If you knew what to look for, you'd realize that the Templar hadn't armed dressed for a conversation – she'd armed herself for a war.

Yet for all the careful ways that the Order prepared themselves when they didn't want others to know they were prepared – a tucked piece of cloth here, an extra covering there – the woman she found by the rear gate immediately walked up to her and tugged at her sleeve until a glint of chainmail could be seen in the torchlight.

While the pale, waifish woman wouldn't actually talk, she communicated in a series of chirps and squeaks that were equal parts endearing and irritating. Still, the Maiden played along for a few minutes when she realized that the blue-eyed manor resident wouldn't (or couldn't) say more. While that was interesting (somewhat distressing), there was something about the waif that kept her attention longer than she had expected.

That 'something interesting' was less the cheerful, bubbly, otherworldly charm offered by the Manor's resident, and more from her doll. Dolls were as common as chamberpots, and while this one was about as average as average could be – it wasn't... pleasant. It had been hand-crafted from old scrap wood and cloth, with a dress partially stuffed with straw and weeds from the garden. It even had a goofy little face that had been carved into its wooden head.

The hair. That was what bothered her. It wasn't horse hair, or not any kind of horse she'd ever touched. It didn't feel like goat or sheep or other, though the Templar admittedly didn't have much experience with many of the above.

It was probably human, though there wasn't anything wrong with that. Except it didn't feel *right*. It was too greasy. Too oily, too slick. Almost sticky. Some of that could've been forgiven considering the person who carried it around, but there was more to it. It was if there was a sickness to it that made the hair feel fundamentally *wrong*.

She was halfway through a spell to examine it closer when a sharply disapproving voice cut through the air like a knife. "Every time you come near one of my residents, something ill transpires," Lady Medias intoned from across the garden.

"Oh. You're here."

"It's my house. You expected me elsewhere?"

"I don't know," Catherine muttered to herself. "Flying like a bat somewhere over the pits of infernal damnation sounds about right."

The waif beside her chirped in mild disapproval at the remark.

Ridora either didn't hear it or didn't deign to give it the response it deserved. "Dare I ask why you've decided to darken my halls this evening? Dare I ask even louder why you dared darken them without receipt of a proper invitation, per our outstanding agreements with each other — Templar Prostil?"

"*Maiden-Templar* Prostil," the Lover countered with a huff, "as you know, *Lady* Ridora."

"Yes well, my title came with lands. Yours with a leash, and I daresay that you've slipped it."

"My title extends to where I say it does, pursuant to Queen's Law. Law, which I may add, has dictated my arrival here. Contrary to your belief, I don't need permission to seek out wayward souls that have aligned themselves with my Order."

Ridora strode up the grassy hill, and her maroon dress practically floated across the tips of the scythe-trimmed blades of grass at her feet. The woman seemingly refused to even know what dirt was, let alone allow it to touch the hem of her clothes. "That poor girl has not. So, I ask again: why are you here? Why are you bothering my sweet little Appaidene?"

The Maiden glanced at the disheveled little woman and pursed her lips. The poor blue-eyed woman had gone back to playing with her doll and chirping at the gate rather than focus on the argument going on next to her. "So you're the one that Akaran been going on about, are you?" When the befuddled woman didn't respond, Catherine turned her attention back to Ridora. "The Order has been issued a warning from On High. I came to check on Bistra and a few of the others to make sure that they are under no risk."

"Oh? The Order has? Why haven't I been informed?"

"Because you opted against it?" Catherine groused, "Or maybe because you laid down your arms to care for these poor souls. Either way – you can consider this the official notice."

The Lady of the Manor frowned. "I never had arms to begin with. I had healing hands. 'A gauntleted fist, or –'"

"'– a velvet glove, know which I want you to be,'" the Maiden finished. "Yes, yes, we're all familiar with the edict. You do the Goddess's work here. I do it elsewhere. My work seems to be needed more than yours at this moment."

Ridora shook her head. "If that was true, you wouldn't have climbed out of your hole to visit my place on the wall," she countered. "I assure you. The residents here are as safe as they always have been, and there's no need for your presence. Even less need for you to be accosting one that has no ties to the Order."

"I'm waiting on another one. Bistra."

"Her? Whatever for? Did you send someone to get her?" the older woman asked as her eyes narrowed. "Do not tell me that you have one of your thugs running about disturbing my guests."

Catherine snorted. "Hardly. I've borrowed one of yours."

"Oh you have? Which of my aids is about to find herself charged with the chamberpots until the end of the year for not coming to me first?"

"One I directly ordered," the Lover retorted harshly. "Or did you forget that this *institution* is directly under the managed purview of the Order itself?"

"No, it isn't," Ridora snapped. "This institution is under my and only my governance. I have first, final, and *only* say in all matters relating to the souls under my care and the upkeep of these grounds."

"Grounds, souls, and care – all paid for by the Grand Temple."

Ridora shrugged and gave the Maiden a razor-thin smile. "My goal is to heal, not to profit. I'll leave that much to you and yours – as you sell what secrets the Order finds to the highest bidder, all in the name of 'peace' and 'progression.' I'll mend the souls that you break, just as I tried to mend yours."

The Templar looked down at her arm and felt the corner of her mouth curl up in disgust. "Just because you gave me use of my wrist back doesn't mean I'll forgive you for –"

"You expect that I'd ask *forgiveness* for what happened to Warnoff? It was a horrific occurrence. *Not* an accident. Had he been excised *properly*, he would still be alive, if not well."

Behind them, Appaidene had gone to the garden's center and had busied herself bouncing between the statues. She skipped and pranced with joy as the statue of Love began to emit a quiet little hum that went otherwise unnoticed by the arguing pair. It sang at her, so she sang right back. If you looked closely – like she did – the other two statues seemly were moving *back* in the yard away from Niasmis's bust.

"Oh, yes. How dare I forget. The man placed in *your* custody is *my* fault because *your* wards and *your* skills couldn't detect he had a *shell-shon* hitching along for a ride. It was literally *in his bones*," Catherine spat with hateful vehemence. "Thus it became *my* fault when it –"

"For the love of *all* of the Goddesses, would you two stop it?" Seline interrupted with a furious snarl of her own. "I could hear the two of you from *upstairs*. You're interrupting everyone's sleep!"

Ridora turned and affixed the young healer with a fiery glare. "Mind your tongue. You've no right to interrupt us."

"Someone needs to," the blonde-haired girl retorted as she gestured back at the three statues in the center of the garden. "You two are standing here pissing about like a pair of angry cocks and not paying attention to what's going on!"

It was a hard guess if she meant roosters or something else, but the desperate way she waved at the edifices made Catherine pause for a moment. "What exactly do you mean? And why isn't Bistra with you?"

"Bistra isn't with me because Bistra wouldn't come," the healer replied with a frustrated sigh. "Couldn't get her to get out of her room. She kept ranting that the, 'shadows are angry, shadows are angry,' and won't say another bloody thing," she explained before she pointed back at the statues. "Though I don't suppose either of you want to explain *that* to me if you're not too busy picking at old wounds? Perhaps, maybe?"

"Oh. You're the one doing this witch's bidding?" Ridora groused. "Not at all surprised, given your recent allegiance with that failed exorcist. I expect you'll have your room cleaned out before daybreak, yes? Or should I plan to see you fishing your belongings out of the pig's trough after breakfast?"

Seline took a step back and steadied herself for a long moment before she looked the Lady of the Manor right in her sky-blue eyes. "You know what? I will take my leave of this place. I care for the people, I care for the work, but I do not care for the attitudes espoused by certain staff *here* or *elsewhere*," she growled as she pointed first at Ridora and then at Catherine. "I have seen *too much* and heard *far* too much about the nature of this world and the goings on in this city to *ever* feel safe within its walls ever again."

"Oh please, child," Ridora retorted. "There is darkness everywhere. You think that by leaving a place of healing you'll find better ways to the light elsewhere?"

"There's a source of light right behind me that neither of you are paying a whit of attention to," she spat. "For a pair of women that express themselves as being able to sense and tell of the existence of magic, you've both failed at nigh-on every opportunity to notice it when it's right under your noses as of late."

"I sense magic of ill-intent just fine," the Maiden retorted. "You make it sound like I'm as dulled as that man-child you've been following around."

Seline crossed her arms and rolled her eyes at her. "Oh *I'm* sorry," she whined, "I forgot how perfectly natural it is for stone statues to *move their damn arms.*"

"What?" Ridora asked incredulously as Catherine looked behind the healer for the first time and realized that the edifice to Niasmis had done just that: her arms were spread wide, and the other two statues had indeed scooted back from it. The medicannia had the very brief realization that the groundskeeper was going to be utterly, completely, and totally *pissed.*

The Maiden rushed across the garden and cursed her every step as she approached. Appaidene continued to bounce between them and chirped a rhyming lyric of some kind out between happy little wordless shouts. Not only had the statue spread its arms wide, cracks had erupted across the words carved into the base. "I swear, I know you two don't like each other but I have never seen you two snap like this," Seline ranted as she followed. "And I am not entirely sure why but I have this intense desire to punch you both."

Her declaration made the Lady pause in her own haste. "You... you are right. I feel... *angry.* No; I am not angry. I am *livid.*"

"We... we are not alone in that," Catherine intoned with a shaky, suddenly nervous tilt to her voice. "While I still think you're a hateful bitch, I think... I think that I see the source of our mood."

"What? Out with it, you simple-minded gimp," Ridora groused.

The Maiden took another deep breath and pointed at the broken letters on the statue. "She's telling us something. 'Gah... tif... bee grah ann... ta dad... pae en bee ev an,' or... this is so butchered, I can't tell," she replied as she read out the broken letters.

Appaidene could.

Appaidene spoke.

For the first time since entering the manor, she *spoke.* All three turned to her at once as she lifted up her doll, and with brightly shining blue eyes, she said it out loud. The ground at their feet began to rumble as a man on the other side of the manor brushed past the Manor's wards.

The skin around his knee blackened. The scars on his arms began to steam. Saa Telpid tried to stop him, and he only ended up being punched in the face for his troubles. He kicked the doors to the Manor open with a curse, and Appaidene *spoke.*

"Gift be granted!" she cheered. "Pain be given!"
And eyes of Niasmis's statue began to glow.

***

Getting Akaran to the Manor took more effort than anyone had expected It was not, as Elsith had suggested, "Just a matter of getting Telburn to float him up there."

It was hard to say who objected to the idea more – the mage or the exorcist.

Aside from finding him shoes and, at his repeated request, a coat of mail, the next question was what to do with B'tril. The first part of that was easy – he was roughly Akaran's size, so while it was ill-fitting, his armor was forfeited to the cause. Why he felt that he needed armor was an *entirely* different discussion, and getting the would-be-assassin to surrender it was another bit of difficulty. That problem was solved when Riorik had Austilin join them in Telburn's estate.

Many decisions were made and problems solved when everyone involved came to the realization that maybe, just maybe, pissing off the wall of muscle he called 'a friend' would not be a good idea. When the thief's back was turned, the Huntsmatron put a bug in his ear about employment with the Guild, should his arrangement with Riorik fall through. However, it was to her slight distress that his arrival meant that B'tril would not be handed over to the Guard anytime in the immediate future.

Possibly not even intact.

Riorik's assertions that he would make it to Henderschott in one piece was neither trusted nor appreciated, but it would have to do. The Sycian objected to it the most, though nobody really cared. The only question was to ask 'when' the answers he supposedly held would be forthcoming.

Much to Akaran's surprise, that wasn't going to be in the next few hours. The Master-Thief made it quite clear that he intended to follow the priest back to the Manor. The why was harder to discern, but it ultimately boiled down to a simple, "Because, my friends, I want to."

So he did. B'tril was sent off along with Austilin, Elsith took the exorcist's suppositions about Anais and her unlife back to the Guild – and Riorik's proclamation of Donta's death along with it. When she realized how many crowns she'd lost by not getting to the assassin first, she fumed with every breath and step she took.

That was mitigated only by the promise from her husband that he would (and do so personally) clean up the mess the last two hours had left their house in. That, and a promise from Akaran that once he proved his case to his superiors, she'd have more than a small opportunity to make that much back and more. She wanted to disagree with him, wanted to argue him, and for that matter, she wanted to punch him in the jaw for ruining the bedding in her spare bedroom with bloodstains.

It was only at Telburn's insistence that she didn't.

Once all was said and done, a horse was requisitioned shortly – and Akaran arrived at the Manor after a trip up the front of the Orshia Falls (and a host of promises made to reimburse the wall-workers who had to hoist him up the side). Interestingly enough, nobody picked a fight with him on the way. Not the few Guardsman that saw him tearing through town on a horse, not the Wallmen, and not an orderly that saw him approach the grounds that he'd been banned from.

There were times when traveling with a purpose worked. There were also times when the sight of a crazed man on horseback was enough to make you reconsider your objections to his presence. Be it any or all of the above, not a soul challenged the pair of riders until they reached the front gate of the Manorhouse.

For that matter, not a soul challenged them until they'd cleared it. The gate itself had offered a moment of pain. For reasons that concerned Riorik greatly, Akaran faltered as they passed through a set of wards neither had been aware of. The priest didn't show his companion, but some of his scars started to steam as he tripped each piece of warding in turn. By the time he made it to the door, his knee had effectively been cauterized, though the burning char didn't matter as much to him as he would've expected.

He was too angry to feel the pain.

He was too angry to realize he wasn't the only one angry.

He was too angry to realize that his anger was Her anger, and She was already moving Heaven and dirt to make way for his arrival.

While She may have moved rock and more, She didn't bother to move the Saa from his gatehouse. Telpid, for a change, actually tried to do his job. He stumbled out of bed and warned the exorcist that if he took another step leading to the manor, he'd have more than a bad knee and a stick to live with.

A stick he didn't realize that Akaran *wasn't* using to walk with even after they had ditched their horses at the gate. A stick that he still carried. A stick that ended up planted under the Sargent-at-arm's jaw, and a stick that nearly broke the poor man's mouth. He made a promise to send a letter to Malik for his suggestions on the uses of such sticks, whenever time permitted to have a chat with the groom of the Wedding of Dawn to Dusk.

That time was not now.

With Telpid out of the way, that left the occasional orderly to stand between him and his goal. While they objected to his presence, they did little to stop him. Riorik helped with that here and there, because while a few of them felt it necessary to shout warnings and stir up assorted souls with assorted wooden clubs, the Master-Thief did a wonderful job of having his back.

A job made all the more impressive given that ever since the exorcism. Not only did he find himself light on his feet and slightly in a daze, but also because he felt strangely rejuvenated. Even *cleansed* in a way. He hadn't realized how *dirty* he felt – and even after the fact, he wasn't sure *how* or *why*.

The thief was certain that there would be time for introspection.

And much like the letter for Malik – that would be later.

For now, the first stop for Akaran was where his interests in the city's murders had first been stifled. The Auramancer would wait; his first goal was to return to the Gambling Mind's office – and the scene of Livstra's death. If Annix had killed her, as he suspected, there *must* have been a clue left behind that the others had missed. *How* or *why* were two good questions, but he'd settle for *what* the vampire could've left behind.

On his first visit to her room, he'd taken the time to carve a ward into the bookshelves and placed a matching one on his arm. Just in case, just in hope, that there would be a day when he'd be able to put it to use. When it started to glow in Telburn's estate, that told him all he needed to know.

He'd done the same in almost a ten other places, too. His room, of course. Livstra's office. There was one squirreled away at the Granalchi Annex, though that one had been hard to place. There was another etched in his room at the *Drunken Imperial*, and the one at Thesd Estate gave away Anais without even seeing her. He'd dropped one at the Ellachurstine Chapel and on a lark, beside a cocasa den he'd otherwise deny ever having been at.

The fact that the Chapel didn't light up on his arm was a relief. Neither did the den, or the *Imperial*. Everywhere else had. His room would be next, but that, he wagered, was because of whatever magic Annix had used to sneak into it and leave evidence to make Ridora think he was a thief.

Here though, right in the middle of Livstra's old office? The feeling from the spell on his arm was different. It was muted. Cold. Like someone had wrapped a shell of solid lead around it and pressed it tight.

The blood was finally gone. The floorboards looked like they'd been replaced, and the ceiling had been plastered over. Anywhere else it would've looked gaudy and out of place, but it was understandable that the Lady of the Manor would want to have all trace of the massacre wiped from memory.

Although... it didn't look like they had touched her bookcases, he realized as he stepped inside the shadowy room. When he crossed the threshold into her office, he *immediately* felt pressure that wrapped around his head. It was a dampening, darkening, soothing pressure. Except it wasn't soothing. It wasn't calming; it wasn't loving. It wasn't the embrace of someone being kind. It was a subtle *smothering* feeling that threatened to choke him.

If he hadn't been so damn angry, he wouldn't have felt it.

But he felt it, clear as day. He felt it cease when he took a step back into the hall. A quick back-and-forth made him realize that it was all around the room, but it only became prevalent when he stepped inside. The room itself was the source, and he struggled to think past the muddled memories he had of it.

He'd felt pressure when he was investigating Liv's death. It hadn't been this strong, but it was enough to give him a headache. In the aftermath of the explosion of magic in the atrium, he'd forgotten about it. He remembered Seline acted funny when she'd been in there with him, like she'd turned into an idiot for a few minutes.

"Riorik?"

The thief looked away from the trio of men flanking them at either side of the hall. Akaran had ignored their orders and shouts the entire time, and his friend had been all that was needed to convince them to stay away. "Ah, speaking to me now? I was beginning to think that —"

"I need to ask you a question," the exorcist interrupted. "Walk in there first, please?"

The Master-Thief haltingly peered past the doorframe and frowned at the shadows within. "If I ask you to step in first, would it matter?"

"No. Do you mind?"

He did, but he did it anyway. As he crossed the threshold, he looked around the darkened room and frowned. "You know, for as much as I assume the Crown pays to have this manor staffed, I would think that they could do more for the décor. It looks rather drab."

"I'm assuming it was nicer before your predecessor was slaughtered in it," Akaran countered as two of the orderlies advanced on him. He lifted his left hand and a crackle of white light danced between two outstretched fingertips, and the guardsmen backed down with hurried exclamations and wide eyes. "Here's my question, and I know you know this: how many provinces are in the Kingdom?"

Riorik frowned and gave the priest an absolutely befuddled look. "How many provic...? What kind of question is that? What bearing could that possibly have on... anything?"

"Just answer it," Akaran pressed. "How many provinces are in the Kingdom?"

"Well that's easy, there are... there are... well, there's this one, and

Waschali and..." he slowly answered — but the more he struggled, the harder it was to say. "There's also..." he tried to voice, but after a moment he clenched his eyes tight. "Whatever happened in this room? Did they bother to clean? I am getting such a splitting headache."

The priest pursed his lips and waved him out. "And now? How many provinces?"

"Kettering, Lowmarsh, Waschali, Mulvette, Imaii, Kralos, Ummasil, and Thatchell," he replied easily before he paused midway through the list, "and sometimes people spell 'W-a-s-c-h-a-l-i' as 'W-e-s-c-h-a-l-i. Some regional dialect between the east and west sides of the kingdom," he added as his face suddenly went blank. "I couldn't say that when I was in there. I couldn't *think* that while I was in there."

Akaran rubbed his hands together and smirked. "Oh, my oh my. Someone is an *inventive* son-of-a-bitch, isn't he..." he mused aloud as he stepped inside. *Not the floor, not the ceiling. The walls. Behind something. What did I figure out when I was here last?*

The window.

The cleaners hadn't touched the windowsill. There probably hadn't been any reason to. He pulled B'tril's sword out of its scabbard and approached it. Even as Riorik continued to demand answers from outside, the priest went to work with the edge of the blade and calmly popped part of the sill clean from the frame.

He missed catching the window when it fell, and the glass crashed into the yard outside. The wooden sill gave up an answer nobody thought to ask. Likely, he realized, because nobody could. It wasn't that they wouldn't have known to. It was that they *couldn't*. The nature of the problem itself would've stopped them from figuring it out.

No, that's incorrect, he mused. *It DID stop them.*

The argument he'd had with Seline that night popped right into his mind. "It's a shrine to Pita," he'd exclaimed. "The Madwoman."

She'd denied it. To her, it was a house of healing. To her, it was a place for all these woeful and misbegotten broken souls to find solace and help. She didn't see it the way he did. She never would. She'd never have to, if he did his job right.

It was going to take more than his word to make his point. While Riorik watched, he lifted the wooden sill away from the frame and let it hit the glass outside with a crash. That wasn't important. The claw marks under it were.

Where he found the words etched into the top of the board below the sill? That was important. That was the cause. It would've lost potency within hours anywhere else. Here? In this place of healing and care? Here, in this place where the auras of the souls within were as steeped in madness as his had been in ice and frost?

Here, where the chaotic energies of grief and confusion and insanity and loss and sadness and twisted minds filled the air with the very essence of the Goddess of Chaos and Insanity no matter how much Seline and the others denied her presence?

Here, an invocation to Pita would last for months. Maybe even years. You could use it to hide yourself. You could use it to hide just about *anything*. You could renew it with impunity. Renew it as needed. If Annix had a way to get past the outside wards, the spell engraved on the wood would let him return with none ever the wiser.

Or it would have, if the exorcist hadn't called upon Love – and then if he hadn't driven sword tip as it burned with holy light through the center of the carved inscription. The very phrase itself twisted on the wood and the words briefly lifted into the air. They crackled with silvery light and blood-red flickers of shadow and shade. The wood buckled and pulled away from the remainder of the wall.

He took a breath and roared at them, a scream of, "**DISENCHANT**," that brought the weight of his Goddess across them like a stable of warhorses that crushed the offending marks with ease. The spell faded, and the board dropped to his feet, split in half and rendered completely inert. The words – whatever they were, whatever language they were in – reverted to nothing more than lifeless scratches.

He thought about burning it – but decided not to.

It would do for evidence later, if it was needed.

Because he wasn't done yet.

He wasn't even close to being done yet. While Riorik held his head in the hallway, the orderlies stumbled and quit yelling at them. Akaran felt another spell in the room pulse and recoil at the effect his voice had brought forth, and this one didn't want to go away so easily.

As the oppressive befuddlement faded into memory, he felt a steady – yet oddly pleasant – tremor in the air from the bookcase. It was almost unnoticeable, but he had a feeling that it was undoubtedly placed after the befuddlement enchantment had been laid down.

A whispered Word left his lips, and an invocation of "Illuminate," made the entire room pulse with an etheric glow, but a second utterance of it next to the bookshelf caused a small glow to appear behind a row of books that only remained on the shelf for a heartbeat longer. Another tome had been hidden behind them – a small one, barely larger than a journal. In the room's dim light, he couldn't make the inked title stand out from the old leather wrap around it.

He didn't need to. "Unmask," left his lips next – and each Word he spoke served to make his skin crackle and the wardmarks on his flesh shine even brighter in the dim. The spell made a flicker of light pulse in the book's spine, and a hard shake later released a rolled-up scroll hidden away. He felt an immediate sense of calm when he laid his hands on it, and a quick glance told him that there was nothing written there that he'd be capable of understanding.

By the time he made it out to the hallway, the orderlies had multiplied by a factor of three with the Lady of the Manor at their head. Akaran shut her up before she could even get one screeched condemnation past her lips. "Take this, hold it, don't fisking lose it," he ordered, and then he added, "No, I don't know what it says, I can't read it, it's non-hostile magic, and it's important."

The implied instruction to shut up and follow wasn't lost on her either. Not that she did the former – as he grabbed Riorik and stormed down the hall in the other direction even as she demanded he halt and demanded to know why he was back when she'd banned him from the building. And what he was doing. Or how he was doing it. Or how he was *walking*.

He didn't give her the time of day, and the master-thief merely nodded his head and tipped his non-existent hat in her direction. An aide tried to stop him from his quiet rampage and much like the Saa outside, dropped to the ground as he clutched the bruise that was soon to form on his stomach. His assault didn't go unanswered though, and a wisp of magic spun through the air before it wrapped around his wrist.

If he'd been paying closer attention, he would've heard Catherine call for "Bonds!" before he blew past her and went straight for his next stop. The spell worked, and it froze him where he stood. Except it only worked for as long as it took him to look down at his arm and the tendril of lavender light that had wrapped around it.

Her chains weren't like his. They – be it from her or the rest of the Order – almost always manifested as ethereal rope. His? His appeared as course, cold, rough silvery links of metal. Nobody had figured out why there was a difference. There just was.

And for this one moment, he wasn't concerned by the difference.

Akaran looked at it, and then he looked back up at her. The growl that ripped out of his throat wasn't entirely human, and wasn't masculine at all. It wasn't *his* and the sound set *all* of them back.

The sound scared them. The hateful, furious red light briefly pulsed in his eye? That made bile rise up in her throat as she lost her grip on the spell as if she was trying to hold onto air with her bare hands. The bonds faded, and he continued his warpath – and his next stop should've been obvious to everyone.

It probably was. They just didn't know how to stop him. Seline tried, to give her credit. She was the last one to the party, yet she froze and her mouth flew open and eyes wide in shock when he bumped into her as he rounded the corner to the next hall. She stayed frozen even when he shouldered her to the side and left her in dust.

Catherine spun another spell in her hands and shouted at the uncontrollable priest, but her new medicannia suddenly moved to block her from launching it as he approached one of the resident's doors. Seline's eyes quickly grew cloudy, and a voice not her own slipped past her lips to shut all of their efforts down at once.

"[*Witness My anger,*]" she intoned with all of the force of the Pantheon behind her voice, "[*and behold My blade.*]" Her eyes snapped back to normal, and she drooped against the wall until the Maiden-Templar caught her and kept her from falling on her face.

The edict given, they fell in line.

They had to. Even if they didn't understand why.

Whatever sense of calm he'd forced on himself in Livstra's office died the second he stopped outside of Bistra's door. The feeling of *hate* returned. It boiled and raged in his skin. Maddening. Furious. It clawed at his heart and his throat felt like it was going to be crushed. Behind the wooden door, Bistra screamed in terror.

She screamed, and nobody would ever know if it was because of him, his anger, or the one that haunted her. She screamed, and a feeling of grief and loss and despair washed over him with such force that he answered with a choked cry of his own and a muted whisper in the wind that followed.

They *all* heard the three words that prefaced the end of her terror.

"[*I am sorry.*]"

Niasmis's whisper on the wind was followed by the whisper of leather on steel as Her weapon drew his blade. He snarled, just once, and brought it down against the door's handle so forcefully that it ripped the wood from its moors. The door itself hit the floor with a crash even as Seline called for him to stop.

Bistra looked up at him from her bed. She had her blankets clutched tight around her as her hair hung limp on her shoulders and soaked with sweat. Tears covered her face and her breath came out in muted choking sobs. She screamed again when she saw him and felt the rage projected across the room – and then she laughed. Just once. Just once, one tired, one joyful, one relieved laugh.

"T... told you," she whispered as the priest sized up her room and *looked* for the source of her pain. "To... told you... his shadows..." she squeaked out as he marched to her side, "they... *They. Don't. Like. You.*"

When she finished, he reached out and took her hand in his. "Would you like to come home now?"

Broken, beaten, and tortured in ways he hoped he'd never understand, the poor woman looked up at him and gave him a crooked, cracked smile. "You… you don't get… get to bring… bring me home," she lamented. "You bring… you bring…"

"I bring what, Auramancer?"

"Pun… punishment," she finished as she let go of his hand and scooted away from him.

Akaran nodded slowly, and for a moment, hung his head. "I can do that too."

The shadows in the room pulsed around him, seemingly in mocking laughter. They didn't laugh for long. Catherine, Ridora, and Seline crowded around the door in the hall outside and waited for him to do whatever he intended to do – though it was Riorik who was the calmest of the bunch. "Do be more careful with her than you were with me," he called out. "I'm still somewhat sore, not that I think anyone happens to give much of a care."

They didn't.

A fleeting smirk passed over the exorcist's lips, and he let the rage – it wasn't even *his* rage, or at least, not his alone – flow through him. It started at his feet and rushed up his legs. By the time it hit his heart, he already had a Word on his lips. By the time he spoke it, the Goddess was ready to answer, and answer She did.

The Goddess of Love answered with Hate and Fear.

"**LUMINOSO**!" he screamed, "**LUMINOSO – CO-VOTH!**"

He called to the Pit. He called to Covorn. He invoked Hovoth. He called for Love and She spoke with the essences of Hate, and of Fear, and of nothing but raw and true *damnation*.

In the heartbeat after the Words, three different reactions unfolded at once. Catherine and Ridora reacted first, almost in tandem. Luminoso called for light. It was a neophyte spell. That wasn't worth a mention.

Co-voth. To call upon them? The mere *suggestion* that an *exorcist* would call upon two of the absolute worst of the Fallen? Nobody had *ever* used the names of those demented Gods in action carried out by the Order, let alone to call upon Them in the same breath.

Hovoth. The Father of Torment. The true God of Elemental Fear.

Covorn. The Father of Sin. The God of Hatred.

Invoked with – and bolstered by – Love.

As they worked their own magic to defend themselves – either against Akaran or the shadow in the room, they honestly weren't sure – his did what he intended. A ball of brilliant red light erupted in the center of the chamber and spun to the ceiling. The spell permeated every inch of Bistra's room and blanketed both of the exorcists in a bloody shine.

The third, and final reaction didn't come from the broken woman on her bed. Or from the medicannia or the thief. It came from the shadows in the room. Most of them melted away, as shadows do in the presence of light, be it holy or natural – or craven and rage-fueled.

Others coalesced into the far corner. Those shadows quaked and trembled under the bright light. The Hate and Fear mixed into the essence of Love terrified the darkness into a shocked retreat. It fought and it strained against his spell and pushed back against his edict.

"Too little, too late," Akaran snarled as he brought his arms together with his fists clenched tight. When his forearms touched, he called out again. This time, the shade couldn't hide. This time, the shade was forced to give up its retreat. "I SAID – **LUMINOSO. EBERANDIA. UNMASK!**"

Eberandia and Unmask were the Words he needed.

And unmask it did.

The shadows didn't shatter, but they shrunk to the size of a man. They shrunk to reveal the creature of darkness that hung in the corner with phantom claws on its hands and feet digging into the wood. It wasn't Annix, as he'd hoped to find, but it was the next best thing. It was his shade – an old spell, a powerful one, one that let someone give life to their own shadow and use it as an avatar.

Either way – it was a gift Akaran was granted.

The chains appeared on his arms in the blink of an eye and they were in the air before he could even finish calling for them to manifest. They shot out and snarled themselves around Annix's shade and bit into its shadowy, phantom flesh. Brilliant white light exploded down the lengths of the phantom silver and scored the monstrosity with cruel ease.

A cold laugh went through the priest, and he wrenched the snarling, struggling beast to the floor like you would a rabid dog. Except you'd show a dog mercy and respect for its misery. Annix deserved none. Akaran gave even less.

The shade had more strength to him than Akaran knew he had in himself, even with the font of rage burning through every fiber of his being. Every ounce, every twinge, everything that screamed through him, he knew it was burning all of his control away. Catherine could've done it, easily, and if he'd been fully in control of himself, he could've... probably.

Except the Maiden-Templar was too busy warding herself and bracing the Manor from suffering the wrath of whatever had possessed the broken little exorcist. So he did the only thing he could think of – and cursed at them. "GET OUT OF MY DAMN WAY!"

To their credit, the assembled throng of terrified onlookers did just that. Akaran hauled the shade out of Bistra's room and forcibly drug it into the hallway. It screamed, cursed, shouted in inhuman rage. It made unintelligible cries that might've been words, or might've just been sounds of pain. The shade struggled and fought and made him work for every step he took.

Candles and sconces flickered as he went past. Starlight from the windows dimmed. Doors shut themselves tight against their own frames of their own accord. The Manor quaked as the air pushed back Annix's very presence. He was an abomination. Not to just to humanity. Not just to the Gods.

The essence of the Manor *itself* rejected the vampire.

The very *world* welcomed Akaran's rage.

Seline watched in raw horror as he battled the monster. Everything he'd said. Everything Bistra had said. Every cry about the shadows, every broken sob about the fangs being real. Every delirium-induced remark about vampires stalking the city. Every insane theory. Every suggestion that things weren't what they seemed. Every clue, every thought, every idea.

She watched it unfold in front of her eyes and something in the back of her soul snapped. She slumped to the floor with her head in her hands and closed her eyes. She wished, she prayed, she *begged* for it to stop for all of it to *stop* and for the world to make sense again.

It didn't, but a voice in her heart made her stand up and follow him no matter what she wanted to do. As he pulled the screaming monster along, she dutifully followed with the Lady and the Maiden behind him. He walked with the confidence of Eternity, and in his wake, the Goddess seemingly manifested as the Maiden, the Mother, and the Lover at his back for everyone watching. As She should be. As She wanted to be.

And damnation followed in his steps.

Damnation followed until he approached a window that overlooked the atrium. He cried out in agony and fury as he used the last of his might to fling his phantom chains and the monstrosity through the glass. "MY GODDESS," he screamed as the window shattered, "I HAVE SOMETHING FOR YOU!"

"Gift be granted!" Appaidene cheered from below as she saw the snarling, hateful beast fly into the air, wreathed in razor-sharp shards of glass that reflected not just his formless face — but the seething visage of Love herself. The waifish woman's cheer turned to a delighted laugh as the shade landed in the arms of Niasmis's statue.

The shade screeched and tried to crawl away. It never got the chance. Akaran slammed his arms in an 'x' across his chest with a heavy thud. The statue did the same, and pinned the shadow to Her marble body.

That same otherworldly voice spoke again — and this time it came from Seline's lips. "*[Pain be given]*," she intoned through clenched teeth as she watched through eyes that were clouded, glowing, almost inhuman eyes.

His chains faded. Annix's shade unleashed one more desperate cry that did no good. The exorcist ripped his arms down to his side. The statue did the same.

Annix's shadow was ripped asunder in flaming embers and blazing light.

Before the exorcist could say another word or do another miraculous act, Seline stepped between the Maiden and the Lady and placed her hand on the back of his head. "*[Rest now,]*" she whispered. "*[My Blade be sheathed.]*" She invoked a spell, a simple one, a calming one, and he slowly slumped forward against the shattered window's frame.

Nobody spoke in the hall for the longest time, even after the clouds left Seline's eyes or when the priest started to snore. The crazy, ecstatic woman in the garden danced and cheered and chirped approving noises at the statue, almost like she was trying to encourage it to do it again. It wasn't until Ridora walked over and put her hands over-top of Seline's – and even then, until the healer sagged down beside him in utter exhaustion – that anyone spoke.

"Henderschott was right. He is the most dangerous man in the city," she whispered more to herself than anyone else.

"Madam, if I must say, I am quite offended by that," Riorik replied with a tired smile of his own. He was the only one that didn't appear shaken, though in his defense, he'd already had a front-row seat at this particular show once already.

She looked over her shoulder at him with her mouth agape in disbelief. "After... after all that? Who... who are you to be offended?"

"Oh I'm one of his absolute best friends in the world," the Master-Thief, formerly of Gonta and now of Basion City, answered with a mirthful smile, "and this is a very fine Manor you have. Maybe we could be friends, too?"

VII. CONFESSIONS OF COUNTENANCE
Very Early Morning of Madis, the 8th[th] of Firstgrow, 513 QR

All she knew was that her Meister was in pain. The night had gone on for what felt like years, and he'd spent most of it writhing in agony. Blistering welts had appeared across his body in strips that covered him from shoulder to shin, and dents covered his ribs. He howled and screamed and writhed so much, so intently, that Sherril thought he was soon to join her blood-siblings as nothing more than dust.

It was almost more than she could bear listening to or dealing with. When he finally did calm, he begged – no, he ordered; Annix would never beg – the battlemage to find him fresh blood. He was desperate for it to the extent that he refused to explain what was wrong. He'd only say that his shadow was gone, which made next to no sense to her, but it seemed to matter the world to him.

His pain adjusted her timetable... or at least, adjusted her targets. There was blood to be spilled, chaos to be inflicted, and hapless souls to scatter across the cobblestone streets. She tasked their newest spawn with keeping him safe and with keeping him hidden (though the locals didn't concern themselves with a few screams in the dark; not in Lower Naradol).

Sherril had done more research and talking to the locals of this misbegotten pit than she'd wanted to. The list she'd developed of movers and shakers in Basion was by no means extensive, though a few names had stood out over others. Kee, for one, may his soul rot in perdition, and a half-assed Lieutenant-Commander that wouldn't have lasted a day in her old posting. There was the bride and groom of the overly-celebrated wedding that had gripped the dank hole in the ground, though she was going to save those for last.

A few priestesses here and there, heads of various merchantile guilds. The fools in the Fleetfinger's Guild; they were turning into an odd problem, though one she made a point to resolve soon. Yet, few would care if she executed a thief; and she'd already had her way with a priestess. Another wouldn't have the same impact.

Or maybe it would, but the heightened risk was without notable reward.

Instead, the next name on her list was an elderly fellow. He spoke softly, yet was the kind to carry a big stick. Or at least, he had two delightful women who carried around sticks for him – or maybe they helped him play with his. One, or the other, or some combination of all of it. Regardless of that, it wouldn't do just to leave the bride's family with tears in their eyes.

She waited until he left some unmentionable tavern on some downtrodden street. She'd staked him out for days now, and he'd always spent until near the break of dawn dealing with the unseemly and unsavory in Akkador East. She presumed – and almost entirely correctly so – that his mission was less the stability of the wedding and more an establishment of trade with the underworld.

The midlanders were men of very specific honor, yet when it came to cutting coin and arranging dealings, they were as vicious as the Blackstone Trading Company. As a nomad kingdom, it behooved them to recruit from wherever they could, and this so-titled 'Enth-Blade' was just the man to do that.

Parl was a bit of a proud figure in the Odinal delegation. A strong man accompanied by two warmaidens, he was a grizzled veteran of the conflicts of the midlands. He was also a shrewd negotiator, and recently – though Sherril didn't know it – had made friends with a certain exorcist after Akaran had saved him from being the target of a riot.

That part she knew. She knew that the head of the Woodmason's Guild had tried to kill him once. Kill, or at least put a beating on him. She knew that some idiot from the Order of Love had interfered and kept them from brutalizing each other (though she'd have put money on the Odinals more than the woodcutters). That made this so much easier; so much sweeter.

Whatever moron got involved would blame himself. Call himself a failure. It would do more than force more chaos and distrust between the two nations. It would embarrass the Lovers, which served as another goal her Meister had handed down.

One she decided to relish in.

The assassination was over before Parl knew what hit him. She didn't bother to keep his head intact. There were enough witnesses around to identify him later, and she left his sigil and ring and other objects of station on the corpse. She didn't feed, either. That was too risky. That would've given the game away, she assumed, and the murders themselves were damning enough in the public eye.

Even still, it wouldn't do any good to bury a strike of electricity in the back of his skull, as delightful as the ensuing fountain of gore would've been to watch. It simply wouldn't raise the stakes enough if someone thought that members of both families were being assassinated by the same person.

No. She saved the lightning for one of his two warmaidens. The dark-haired bodyguard never saw her coming, and she died when Sherril clamped her hand on the top of her head and discharged a bolt of energy directly into her brain. She didn't kill the second maiden at all, but she did deliver a charge into her chest that was enough to render her unconscious.

It was an art. Electricity could do many things; stun, disable, destroy, burn. But the axe she carried? That was a different story. Axes did one thing well; they cut. When stolen from a wood-mason that had earned a reputation for trying to kill midlanders scant days before? Well. That would be enough to push the city almost to riot, and in truth, Basion was almost there.

Parl fell with the axe buried perfectly in the center of his face. He managed to get out an exclamation of surprise, but it wasn't loud enough to draw attention at the pre-dawn hour. She pulled the axe out of his head and swung a few more times for good measure; it wouldn't do to make the murder look *too* clean. Lumberjacks weren't the most refined of men, and his death had to match.

The battlemage made a show of hacking the first war-maiden to bits as well, and punched her a few times for good measure. Her death would be more suspect, but that was a problem solved by dropping the torch she'd been carrying onto her hair. A few sparks later, and her skull had been set ablaze enough that the discharge of her magic was well-covered.

Nobody would bother to examine the corpse. There wasn't need to.

And his other bodyguard? Her purpose was simple: food for the Meister, and maybe a little snack on the way. Her disappearance was as equally important and much more chaotic.

The Odinals would assume she had been kidnapped, after all.

It wasn't wrong, but they'd incorrectly assume that the locals would have been at fault. They'd start to rip the city to shreds in an attempt to find her, and they would. Eventually. Likely with her severed head on a flagpole tomorrow night, unless Annix decided that he needed another broodling around.

She hoped for the former. She had grown tired of tripping over his spawn when she was the only one that he needed. That, and the truth was that before she'd met him, she had always enjoyed the rare interactions the 5th Garrison had with midlanders when they ventured into Lowmarsh. They had such pretty faces.

It would be shameful not to display it for the whole world to see.

If anything, that would make up for not being sent to Cableture with the rest of the brood earlier in the evening. She'd been to the port city once before, and hated the place. It would've been a joy to go back and redecorate.

Morning of Madis, the 8th of Firstgrow, 513 QR

You couldn't exactly call it 'morning,' but it wasn't quite 'noon' either. It was that time of day when people were expected to be out and about, when people were busy tending crops and churning butter or whatever it was that farmers did when farmers were of the mind to do. Even in a city, there was a great deal of such things that had to be done, and there were plenty of guildsmen – of every guild, including the Hunter's and the Fleet's – who were busy doing things that guildsmen did, too.

Things that included, but were not limited to, patrolling the grounds. And repairing a window. And repairing a garden. And repairing at least one door. There were also guildsmen of a sort who were busy pouring over a scroll that had been found in Livstra's office, and priests that were busy examining yet more spellwork on a broken sill.

There were healers tending to the wounded – and, blessed be her name, a scarred woman that ran a tavern with the *finest* beverages imaginable that could calm the senses had marched to the Manor and offered free drinks to anyone that needed them. Seline had availed herself in excess by this point, as sleep had not decided to grace her pounding head. She wasn't entirely sure if she'd been fired or not, so what harm could it do?

It seemed that everyone else was perfectly happy being turned into a cluster of nervous wrecks, and to tell the truth, she was tired of being left out. So, she contentedly chugged a bottle of wine in the atrium and kept Appaidene company – and they *both* made giggling, chirping noises at the burly men who tried to move the statues back in place (yet hopefully for entirely different reasons) while other work was undertaken and rest was not had by anyone.

Except for Akaran. Had the assorted guildsmen been a tad quieter, he would have continued to blissfully sleep back in his old room even while the other woman that kept watch over him couldn't decide to pray harder or punch him until he woke up. The thought to punch was about to win out when he opened a bloodshot, dry eye and croaked out an unintelligible curse.

Had it been less un- and more in-, the punch would've been assured. "Goddess above, you are lucky you are breathing," Catherine whispered under her breath.

"Am I?" he croaked. "I don't feel like it."

"You are, though in the more than thirty-five years I have spent serving the Order, I have never met nor heard of an exorcist as foolish or reckless as you," she uttered before she leaned back and crossed her arms. "Or as terrifying."

He groaned and slowly pushed himself up in bed and rubbed at the back of his neck. His body *hurt*. It ached like he'd been on a month-long bender, and he couldn't help but notice fresh burns across his fingers and palms. "Sure you have. They're the ones you don't talk to after they take a job and —"

The Templar pointed a long finger at him and gave him a smoldering glare. "Don't. Don't be witty, don't be snarky, don't be *you* right now," she warned. "I know you have absolutely no idea what you did last night, I can see it in your face, and even if you might *think* you did, I don't think you *know* what you did."

Akaran rolled his head around his shoulders and groaned in pain as he felt muscles he didn't know he had pull at the back of his skull to the back of his eye. "I broke things," he replied after a moment of twisting around, "and I exorcised things. That's the job, isn't it?"

"That's the job?" she asked incredulously. "That's the *job? That's* what you have to say for yourself?"

He looked around his room and then promptly dropped back down onto the straw and down-feather mattress. Down was good. Down was better than 'up,' and he had a distinct feeling he wasn't going to be allowed to enjoy it for much longer. "I'm thirsty?"

"Of course you are. Of course that's all you'd have to say," she muttered under her breath. "You didn't perform an exorcism last night, you damn dolt."

The priest looked up at the ceiling and counted the nails sticking through the floorboards. "No. No, I'm reasonably certain I did. There was the possession that had hold of Riorik and —"

"Would you please, please, just *stop?*" Catherine implored as she leaned forward in her chair. She hadn't changed out of her armor, and although he was wearing little more than bandages and a thin gown, she looked a lot more regal and a lot less ready for war than he did. "You didn't perform *an* exorcism last night, Akaran. You acted as an Avatar. You acted as one of the Three. Except *not* one of the Three."

"The Three? Niasmis's trio?" he asked as his face went blank. "What are you talking about?"

"Oh no, you *don't* get to play the fool. Last night, you bore the hallmarks of an *Avatar*, which *only* happens in our Order when we channel one of the three Archangels of Niasmis. *You know that,*" she accused. "And *when* that happens, *rare* as it is, that manifestation occurs in *very specific ways* that we have *very well documented*. You *didn't do that*."

He blinked and looked at her in utter confusion. "Maiden, I have no idea what you possibly mean. I just... I got angry. I got hot. I had to do something. I *needed* to do something."

"Oh you did *something*, that's for *damn* sure," Catherine seethed. "You acted like some kind of unknown *Fourth,* which is terrifying on it's own – made moreso because *YOU INVOKED TERROR AND HATE* in the process."

She might've been speaking in dwarven, for all the sense that made. "I banished the essence from Riorik, and then –" he began before she cut him off.

"*That* was an exorcism. Telburn and Elsith had a lot to say about it, and the new *Master-Thief of the City* filled in the blanks. Not mention the fact that you performed an exorcism on *the Master-Thief of the City*, whom you seem to be *close personal friends with*, which I *promise you* will be a discussion for *later*," she threatened through clenched teeth.

"Oh. Joy," he grumbled.

"He sends his regards, by the way. Mentioned that if – and I do need to stress that there were many of us concerned on the '*if*' of that statement – you were to wake up, that yes, you did indeed owe him one less favor. Then he said you owed him two more, the first for, 'carrying him to bed,' and another for 'answering what he knew of the day.' He stressed that I was to point both of those out and that I was not to hold it against you because, and I again quote, because he would 'take care of that concern directly.' Just so you know."

"Shit," he grunted before he paused and looked over at her. "You're holding it against me?"

Catherine let the question slide. "It's what you did *after*. The *after* is important. I'm going to make this as clear as I possibly can," she growled as she leaned in and spoke in a hushed whisper. "As far as anyone else is concerned – and Akaran, I do mean *anyone else* is concerned – the actions from last night were the result of unexpected magical anomalies as a result from the spell at the Annex. That's all. *Wild magic* made you act in a wild way."

The exorcist looked at his singed fingertips again and grunted. "Wild magic, huh?"

"Wild. Magic," she stressed. "If it was *anything else* then I'd have to request the Holy General and a Sister to be dispatched to the city. I do not think that you want to be under their scrutiny given your *other involvements* at this time."

"Are you covering my ass or yours?"

Catherine shrugged and settled back in her chair with her legs crossed. "Yes."

He laid in silence for several long moments as he listened to the sound his breath made, and took slow and careful stock of every wound he had – new and old. "Your ass I understand. Why mine?"

"Because you've managed to both expose the Order's failures and solve half of them in a single evening," she admitted. "Not to mention, you've released one of our own from a demon… and opened the doors to numerous inquisitions that will need to be addressed."

"That wasn't really what I intended to do."

"Oh? And what did you intend to do? Tell me," the Maiden demanded, "because I am genuinely curious. I am absolutely waiting with baited breath to understand the chain of decisions you made that resulted in your ability to *channel the Goddess Herself* through means unknown into a house of healing. A house that, I may add, you damn near flattened."

The way she phrased 'Goddess Herself' only made him groan louder. When he realized she wasn't going anywhere until he answered her questions, he sat up and started to explain himself. Which, he admitted later, was arguably harder than it should've been. "Karaj asked me to poke my nose around the Manor when I first got here. They were right; something felt off. Then you asked me to look into Livstra. I did."

"I also specifically told you to stop!"

"Yes, and I decided ignoring you was better than telling you to shove it," he grumbled before he added a quick, "with all due respect."

Catherine glared.

She just glared.

Without any further response incoming, he went on. "I couldn't get close enough to Bistra to do anything but I got close enough to her room when nobody was looking to runemark her wall. The same in Liv's office. Same in here, too, though… huh. I'm not glowing anymore," he realized as he checked over the marks on his arm. Three of them were gone completely, without even a scar to mark their passing.

For that matter, he was breathing a *lot* easier than he expected with the gash across his chest. *Hungry. Damn, I'm hungry. Why am I this hungry? I could eat an ox.*

"Glowing or bleeding," the Maiden pointed out. "You're welcome, by the way."

"What did you do…?"

"Check your knee."

His face went pale as the sheets he was under, and he quickly scrambled to get access to his leg. His leg that… was not bandaged. That wasn't bleeding. That he slowly flexed with only a faint tremor, and almost no pain at all. "It… what did you…"

"I am not the most accomplished healer in the Order, but I am a

Templar of Maiden rank," she explained as she gave him a slow, warm smile, "and despite her faults, Ridora is of equal strength. It was made easier with the leftover ether you had absorbed, though I am afraid it isn't perfect. With an injury as severe as that, for as long as you had it, *and* for the multitude of times you've torn it back open, you'll likely never gain full strength back in it. I wouldn't try to run anywhere – for many, many, reasons – but you shouldn't need your cane unless you over-exert yourself." She paused and gave him another dirty look. "Which I suppose means I should have someone make a sheath for it to hang off of your belt."

"But... but I can move it. I can... I can *move* it," he whispered as he flexed his leg several times in a row before he slowly started to stand up.

Catherine slammed the palm of her hand down on his ribs and dropped him back to the bed. "No. You are *not* getting up until I have *answers*. I imagine you're starving, so let that be a motivation for you to answer earnestly and honestly."

Akaran nodded as tears welled up in the corner of his eye – in pain from his ribs or from raw relief, he wasn't sure. "I can move it again. I can move my knee. I can move my knee and it doesn't *hurt* now. How... they swore that..."

"There is a discussion we can have about the nature of healing magic and chronomancy and nature and more – *later*," Catherine replied with a content smile all over her face. A smile that faded as she picked up his journal from his bedside table and tossed it on his pillow. "After you explain *this*."

He faltered and flinched at the soft 'thump' the book made when it landed. "Oh. Yeah. You uh... found it, huh?"

"Uh-huh. Missus Valdin handed it over while you let the Granalchi experiment on you."

"I had a plan to tell you all about it. Ease you into it."

"And another plan that said, 'shove it in her face and make her read it,' in case you didn't survive Telburn's experiment. Am I right?"

There was no way to lie around that one. "So you know what I'm going to say."

Her face darkened as she resisted the urge to unleash a torrent of impolite (yet apt) adjectives about him, his methodology, and his usage of certain individuals of questionable authority in the city. "There's rules for this sort of thing. You broke damn near all of them. You should have told me the minute you had suspicions."

"I told you when I thought it was an inhuman, and you blew me off," Akaran retorted, "and then you promptly proceeded to kick me out of service. I did what I had to do to try and lay the groundwork to if not catch it, help get eyes looking for it so someone else could. For that matter, I don't even know if what I did last night needs to be recorded under sigil or if you consider it a freelance job."

She ground her teeth together and drummed her fingers on her lap. "The exorcism of spirit of unkn… no," the Maiden corrected as he started to object, "no, it wasn't unknown. The exorcism of the Daringol remnant from Riorik will be recorded under sigil, and you will be recorded as the Executor of Judgment."

"Thank you," he breathed with a sigh of relief. "I earned that one." In addition to the rest of the reports the Order generated every time someone so much as spit in the direction of the damned, the annual listings of Executors was an honor. He'd been awarded a mark for defeating Daringol the first time, and one for the pair of hounds. Makolichi countered as a third.

It also meant that he was going to be due for a raise in the near future.

If she reinstated him in full.

"Cannot deny that," she admitted. "The shade you destroyed will be considered your fifth of the year. It would be impressive if it wasn't so abjectly *horrifying*."

"No," he countered, "it shouldn't. That didn't solve the problem. It solved a symptom."

Catherine blinked. "Accept it. You did good. I think."

"I didn't *complete* the good," the exorcist returned with a frustrated sigh. "Same could be said about Daringol. All I did was buy Bistra time. This isn't over and won't *be* over until Annix can be found."

"That leads me back to the issue at hand. How sure are you that this beast is a vampire? How certain?"

Akaran took a deep breath and tried to think of the best way to phrase it. "Enough that I've been working with a dead woman, the Fleetfingers, and an Eclipsian to find where it's hiding. As soon as you let me out of this bed? I'm going to catch it and shove it in a cage and drop it off on the Overseer's doorstep. Let the sun deal with it."

"How do you intend to do that?"

"It covered Liv's room in spellwork. Its shade has been living in Bistra's room. Unless its shadow could move physical objects, it's either had someone working for it here or it's had a way to get in and out – not to mention what it did to Livstra."

She nodded slowly. "That spellwork is… problematic. It's not in any language that the scribes can easily recognize. I've sent it to the Annex. It's steeped in chaos magic – *old* chaos magic. Whatever invoked it has access to very old teachings, and that rarely bodes well where Abyssians are concerned."

The exorcist grunted in an utter lack of surprise. "The chaos part doesn't shock me. The old part worries me. At least we can hunt it down by its essence now."

"Essence tracking? That isn't a lot to go on in a city this size. If it's as well hidden as your journal suggests, that won't be enough to find it. You and I both know it."

"No," Akaran agreed, "but it would provide enough proof to make you lock Basion down and march the Order through it until it turned up."

Words died on her lips as she realized what he was suggesting. "You planned to work without permission and force my hand once you had proof. You didn't expect to be reinstated just because you regained magic, did you?"

"Nope. Except now you know, and now I don't think you have a choice."

"I know what you *think* and damned if you haven't proven that there's a *problem* but if... but..." she tried to explain before she gave up and dropped her head. "Shit."

"Yeap."

Catherine looked up at him and almost pleaded with him with her eyes. "You understand that it isn't just my decision. I can proclaim an emergency but without more proof I won't be able to lock the city down. The Overseer *might* be amenable if it wasn't for the wedding, but with Maiden Esterveen's Betrothed calling the shots right now? There's simply no way. I'd have to have fangs in my hand to get them to let us act on that scale."

"So it's a good thing that you already have allies in the underworld working on it, isn't it?" he asked with a hopeful smile. "I did what I could with what I had. Now you need to let me do the rest."

"You have broken so many laws," she murmured as she ran her hands down her face, "and so many edicts of the Order. You found evidence of the damned walking the streets, and turned control of one of them – of *her* – not to us, but a priestess of one of the Fallen. You've aligned yourself with a man that I am fairly certain is a wanted murderer, and you've hidden an investigation from your superiors while people died."

Akaran raised his index finger and cut her off. "Yeah but you'd already told me you didn't believe me and you wanted me to piss off. So you can say that the investigation saved lives once we behead the bastard."

"If your excuse for breaking the laws of the Temple is that you were explicitly told *not* to break those laws, I would reconsider it," she warned, "regardless of Who or What you channeled last night."

"Except that I was right, and I *did* channel a Who last night."

"Results are not justified by the means!"

"Not always, but I think in this case you can make an exception."

She gave him a shocked stare. "Can I? Do you remember Who you invoked last night? It's no secret that we call upon other Gods to give us magic – Lumina and Pristi to manifest light. Isamiael and Kora'thi when we need to heal. Answer me: do you remember who *you* invoked?" she challenged.

"Well I remember that I summoned light, so I –" he started before she cut him off.

She gestured like she was about to wrap her hands around his throat. "You are a follower of *Love* and you invoked both the *Lord of Hate* and the *Lord of Fear*! You called on Hovoth and Covorn! You! An *exorcist of Love* invoked two of the grandest of the Fallen!" she exclaimed in a hushed, strangled voice. "Until you can explain *that*, I have absolutely *no* idea what I should do with you!"

"You healed my knee, so I think you –"

"We healed your knee because you gave peace to Bistra and secured this house of health," she countered, "and because in the event that I have to have you hung for heresy, it won't be as hard to march you up to the gallows!"

The conviction in her comment was matched only by the frustration in her voice, both of which he had more than ample experience with. "I don't know if this will convince you otherwise," he began slowly, "but I truly don't remember much of last night once I left Telburn's. What I can tell you was that I was full of so much anger that I felt like I could rip open the world. I felt... I remember feeling... I remember feeling like She wanted me to send a message. She didn't just want that shade destroyed, She wanted me to make a *point*."

Catherine mulled his statement over. "If that point was to terrify everyone that witnessed it, I'd say you did a spectacular job. Even without invoking *elemental fear*."

"One that isn't over."

"No. One that certainly isn't," she snapped. The Maiden sighed and tried to look through the cracks in his closed shutters. "Shall I assume then that short of having you chained and stuffed in a hole someplace far, far away from other people, you are going to continue to dig into this?"

"We aren't to quit when we know we're fighting for the right and the righteous," he replied with a shrug. "I would like to be official within the Order again, but I *felt* the aura that shadow had last night. It can't be allowed to survive. Rank or not, I *can't* let it go. I *have* to see this through."

"On that, we agree," Catherine finally had to admit. "You are then returned to your rank with privileges restored. *With conditions*," she added before he could thank her. "You will grant a full deposition to the scribes before you make one move more, and you will submit to a wellness session at the Repository within the next two days. I should order you to have one now but I don't think we have the time. Expect to live your foreseeable life under every eye that serves the Goddess under me. I want to know every time you get up to go piss, let alone deal with… *whomever* you've been dealing with as of late."

He didn't expect it to be that easy. Conditions had been expected. But full permissions? Without an argument? Either his luck was suddenly getting better, or…

"Thank you and… uh. Why don't we have the time?" he asked with a vague wince.

Not that the threatened tasks were going to be *enjoyable*. A 'wellness session' involved a few hours spent in mediation at the local Temple while others would be assembled to stand around him and pray until a ranking Lover was convinced his aura had been healed. It was boring beyond belief, and could take hours before it was completed.

Or days, given all of the other concerns.

"Because while you invoked Her wrath last night, Cableture was attacked. Because before you invoked Her wrath last night, the Order was given a warning from the Sisters. And because after you invoked her wrath last night, your friend the Master-Thief handed over the doorman to our custody."

Any one of those comments would have been reason enough. All of them combined? "Let's start small. The doorman? Telpid?"

"Telpid," she replied – and then she started to explain.

Soon after Seline put Akaran to sleep, the rest of the fun started. To say that the residents were stirred up by his cascading magic and the open warfare was an understatement. As the orderlies were overwhelmed, the Repository was contacted. Before long, the Manor was swarmed with medicannias, wardkeepers, and *kols* alike.

That, in turn, woke up the Guard, and presumably Henderschott.

Thankfully, nobody had heard from him. Yet.

While they did that, Riorik made a point to politely get Catherine's attention to the foyer – and then had Austilin less politely drop Telpid's unconscious body to the floor. It turned out that the Master-Thief had learned a great deal about certain people in Akaran's orbit, and the Saa's alliance with Livstra had been near the top of the list. However, his *other* alliance had fallen out of notice.

At first.

It did not take him a great deal of time to discover that the Sargent-at-arms of Medias Manor had an arrangement with Annix – and while the circumstances were vague and mostly consisted of a steady stream of threats against his health – the question of, 'Who at the Manor has been working with the vampire?' was soon answered.

"Once he woke up, we pried some tidbits out of him. Your assumption that Annix — and I should stress that I am *only* naming the creature that because of your assertions — is working with a battlemage are correct. Combined with your other evidence, and what I was able to find at the request of that healer girl, I have a name for her."

It went as he had vaguely sorted out on his own. Her name was Sherril Inyadine, formerly of the 5th Ray of Dawn. She had gone missing back in 510 at the same time Bistra had exterminated another vampire — a female bloodsucker that had called herself Zilyph. No body had ever been found, despite the Auramancer's efforts to find her.

"I have a strong feeling that after the golem in the Indexiary scours our records, there may be a few occurrences where someone by her description may have been seen. If not, a query will be sent to the Grand Army. Assuming it isn't too late."

"Going to need to do it anyways. Make sure she hasn't spawned anything in the last few years."

Catherine blanched at the suggestion. "Don't repeat that thought aloud again, please? You know the pressures the Order is under to make sure there *isn't* a repeat of the demise of the elves."

"Burying the problem only works when it won't crawl back out of the grave," he cautioned.

She refused to dignify that with a response, regardless of how correct he was. "So now we've tied a battlemage to this supposed vampire, and we believe she's the one that assassinated Kee. If you're right, this is also likely the one that massacred the Landing, too, as your journal accused."

"The bitch is stirring up a shitload of chaos, that's what she's doing."

"It seems so. He gave us a rough idea when she arrived, and that itself is problematic — it was right around when Lexcanna was murdered. By magestrikes, I point out."

Akaran blinked. "So you have proof I was right. It wasn't Badin."

She nodded and frowned. "It does seem so. I just heard less than a half-candlemark ago that Henderschott had him released after Kee was killed, so he's been set free of his arrest."

"That's... that's freaking wonderful," the exorcist exclaimed. "Any idea where he is? I want to get him involved. A battlemage versus a battlemage sounds like a wonderful way to even the odds in our favor."

"I don't know, but that is a good point. I'm sure he'll find you soon."

"If I don't find him first," Akaran replied with a sigh of relief. "I don't suppose Telpid explained *why* Sherril is out murdering people left and right, did he? It's gotta be more than just to put on a show?"

"No. He was very vehement about not having any idea. The Saa claimed he even cautioned her not to make too much of a fuss, for risk of discovery," she replied before she lowered her head and closed her eyes. "He did allege that Annix has been active in the city for a long time."

"How long?"

"At least two years."

"That's about how long people have been going missing."

Catherine ran her hands through her hair and sighed. "I know. The General is going to have a field day once she gets word…"

Akaran nodded and then pursed his lips. "Any chance she can wait on getting that word until after we're done?"

She gave him an askance look. "You assume she hasn't already had a missive sent after the mess you made last night."

"Great," he grumbled. "Wait. If Badin has been cleared, does that mean that Erine has too?"

"The Mother Eclipsian? It does seemingly absolve her of Lexcanna's murder, if Badin had no hand in it. But," she cautioned, "just because she's clear of that does not mean that she is innocent of all charges. She is currently consorting with the dead, as you yourself admitted, and has been named in a kidnapping."

Her subordinate frowned. "Technically it's not a kidnapping if the victim is a corpse — reanimated or otherwise. That makes *me* immune to that accusation, too."

"You, and a few others," she icily pointed out. "Yet it's still consorting, regardless, and if you truly wish to split hairs, hiding evidence of a murder."

"That only counts if you know how he first died. It could have been old age."

She growled at him and he decided it might be better to shut up. "Given the circumstances, the usual punishment will not be invoked for the unsanctioned detention."

"Given the circumstances, no punishments should be," Akaran countered as his mouth overrode his brain.

Catherine grunted under her breath at him. "That is going to entirely depend on what she does with that wraith while she's still bound to this plane," she argued. "A wraith that she is *going* to surrender to our custody should she wish to avoid a grave herself."

"Rmaci… that's… a complicated story," he sighed. "She helped. I offered her an Exorcist's Forgiveness. She accepted. I will swear to that."

"You won't have to once we have her," the Maiden retorted, "and given that you offered her the Forgiveness and she wasn't destroyed either means that you didn't channel the Will of Love correctly — which would not be a surprise, given your magical inhibitions at the time — *or* it means that she must begin the Otherworldly Walk."

"That Walk is about penance, and she's trying to give it."

She shook her head 'no.' "That is a claim that a neophyte exorcist has no call to make nor experience to declare. No, Akaran. The moment that she can be recovered for the Order, she must, and must be delivered to the Repository with all haste." After she made that clear, she further added, "Erine will… I will have to speak to her myself. *If* your sequences of events are true, then the Order will reach an agreement with her that will avoid strict… negotiation, given all circumstances."

That – unfortunately – was the best deal he was going to get for both of them, and he knew it. Though it wasn't as if he could blame Catherine for her reluctance to accept the situation without investigation. He wouldn't, and there was no reason to expect her to do the same.

Rmaci sure as all wouldn't like it, but that didn't matter. The Maiden was right: an inqury had to be carried out. There were rules to such things, and some of those rules were less immutable than others. There were rules to other things, too, and the dour look on her face suggested the next one to discuss was coming up. "Elsith beat us to the animate… former animate… that Erine had in her care. The body has been surrendered to the Repository, though we had to come to terms with agreements on how to study it. That's an entirely *different* issue and one that concerns me *greatly*."

That was an understatement. They argued back and forth about that particular monstrosity, and he agreed to take a sanction against his record for the way he handled him. "While I understand that giving him up would have put Erine and your other interests at risk… now we have a necromancer of unknown ability loose in the city."

She liked it a whole lot less when he told her how one of the warning runes he had set down in one of Anais's bases had also gone off. "I'm not convinced she's human, either," did not sit well with the Maiden in any way shape or form.

Catherine was happy to announce, at least, that his corpse was on its way to the Repository, if it wasn't already there by now. "Who – or what – he is or was will be determined before dark. The Huntsmatron seemed to think that I would offer her a writ 'the likes of which she had never seen' once she handed him over. You wouldn't know anything about that, would you?"

"That? No," he answered honestly. "*That* writ was what I had promised her when you realized we have vampires running amok," Akaran corrected. "I assume you're offering a writ on Anais anyways."

"I am, but I would prefer you not promise my name to future contracts with the Guild before speaking to me. Especially when you speak to someone when you yourself are without any rank," she warned with a pained sigh. "You have put a lot on the line with these assumptions. What would have happened if you were wrong?"

He pursed his lips and shrugged. By this point in the conversation, he'd found old clothes and finished off all the water they'd left in his room. "Chased out of the city or buried under it," he finally admitted. "So what happens next? You said something about an attack in Cableture?"

"In a moment. There's one more topic to address."

"What? We covered everything."

"The ship. The one you keep dreaming about. The one your wraith warned you is coming. Do you still...?"

Akaran winced. That was something he'd hoped she'd forgotten — at least for the moment. "Do I still think there's a ship of damned souls embarked on a mission to hunt me down and swarm over the city?"

The Maiden nodded without any expression to give her thoughts away.

"After Rmaci left my body, I haven't dreamed of it. But between Riorik's testimony and her warnings... I don't think that I can ignore that it's a possibility. I hope that I'm wrong, but I'm not going to lie to you about it. If it's close, I need to go deal with it. Somehow. Not that I'm not busy or anything."

"I do appreciate that you specify that you won't lie about *this*," Catherine deftly pointed out, "though... it is wrong to say that there isn't precedent. Nesting wraiths are very temperamental beings. They don't like to move out of the area they've infested, except to spread... unless the core or their anchor has been moved. If it has developed an anchor to you... or is at least approaching this general direction because of the other wraith..."

"...then it's entirely possible there's a ghost ship on the horizon."

"Well. At least it isn't in the city," she lamented. "I'll notify Admiral Maddon once I'm down there. I'm sure the military will be happy to have something to do."

He almost dropped his belt as he looked at her in surprise. "You're thinking of sending the navy after it? You should send me. It's after me."

Catherine raised an eyebrow at him. "You want to give up your search for this vampire to go on a sea-borne tour to hunt for a ship that might not even exist? Or do you think you can somehow do both at once?"

"Yeah but... the navy. *Our* navy," he stressed. "Let me go down-shore, east of Cableture. I'll try to set a trap, and excise it before it gets any closer. If it's as close as Rmaci warned, you should be terrified. You don't know it like I do. It'll infect the city in an afternoon if it's given a chance."

"Are you implying that the glorious Admiralty of the Dawn is somehow not up to the task of patrolling the world's waterways?" she asked with a sly smirk.

"Yes. Yes I am."

Unfortunately... "Once we have this Rmaci woman... wraith... in custody

– that is her name, yes? – then we can attempt to have one of our scryers get a better bead on it to see if it even exists. Right now, it is just a 'maybe' in a metaphorical ocean of madness. Compared to the vermin infesting the streets that we *know* are currently tormenting our charges, I must pick my battles carefully and assign my men accordingly."

Akaran cursed under his breath. "We better pray you're right," he grumbled, "because I know *I* am. Is Maddon a reasonable man or…?"

"Oh, no. He's Henderschott's boss. Make of that as you will."

"Shit."

"Correct," Catherine replied with a nod. "Faldine is already down at port. Once I get there, I'll have her establish a forward base. If this rumored ship of the dead does exist, and it *is* coming, there's only one way up Yittl."

He started to agree with the idea, then stopped and smirked at her. "You know, it'd be an utter delight if the Second Queen's paranoia to put a giant stone wall at the ass end of the canyon was paid off by defending against a ship of the dead."

The Maiden couldn't even hide the grim chuckle that welled up in her throat, but she was able to deflect the conversation. "You won't like what I'm going to tell you, though at this point I feel giving you foul news is appropriate retaliation."

"I'm about to ask you why you didn't start our conversation off with this, aren't I?"

"Yes, so let me save you the effort – debriefing you was, and is, of the greatest importance. We have agents of our own already dealing with whatever fallout that's come from the Lieutenant-Commander's concerns at the port."

Akaran tried to find a way to argue with her logic, but he couldn't. "So what happened?"

She stood up and cracked her knuckles with a loud 'pop.' "I don't know, exactly. All he said was that there as an attack at a taberna. Several dead. Magic involved."

"Sherril."

"Quite likely," Catherine agreed. "Though he didn't say that there was anyone of note deceased. That doesn't seem to fit her current motives. I'm afraid the city already had enough of that last night, even outside of your show."

"What's that supposed to mean?"

"I've been told that one of the Odinals was murdered, along with one of his bodyguards. Another has gone missing. Parl, an Enth-Blade. They're *incredibly* pissed."

The exorcist didn't bother to hold back the obscenities this time. "Of all the shit-eating goatsucks. Who… and… do they have any idea who did it? I *liked* Parl."

She shook her head. "I wasn't told if they did. I only heard about it because of one of Ridora's orderlies."

"Damn," he grumbled. "This city is a powderkeg."

"Truly is," the Maiden concurred. "Which is why everything we do from this point forward *must* be within the rules of the Order, and nothing more. Once we start digging, all eyes will be on us, and there will be those eager to capitalize on our mistakes."

"Speaking of," he added as they left his room, "what about Ridora? I can't imagine she's happy about... well. *About.*"

Catherine huffed in irritation. "She isn't. I doubt you'll see much of her for a few days – she's made it clear that she plans to rip this Manor to shreds. You embarrassed her in ways I didn't think were possible last night – so thank you for that, if nothing else. Not only did you heal yourself without her involvement, you showed her she had been wrong about her security, wrong about the methods she cares for her guests, and wrong about the need to have Order oversight," she explained. "To say the least, she is *irate.*"

"I'm not sorry."

"Nor should you be. You don't see tears in my eyes, do you?"

"So what happens next?"

The Maiden sighed – though if it was from frustration or exhaustion, he didn't know. Neither did she. "I should order you directly to the Repository, except I don't particularly want you out of sight of at least one person with greater rank than what you have."

He grunted in mild annoyance at that. "I'm not going to burn the city down or anything."

"I am not convinced of that," Catherine reprimanded. "Nor, now that we've connected a few threads, do I think that you'd stay here instead of heading to the port even if I told you to."

Akaran grunted again, this time in reluctant agreement. "Didn't think I was that transparent," he muttered. "But. I don't think I'm welcome to poke around here anymore, and I don't have much to go on with where to look around the city. Besides – if Sherril was involved with whatever happened in Cableture, I want her head. She murdered someone I had taken a liking to, and I'd like to return the favor."

"I'm also not convinced your bloodlust is appropriate. Or entirely *human*," she cautioned. "I think I forgot to add – should you feel that rage come over you again, you are to tell me."

"So you can put me to sleep again?"

"*Yes.* While it no doubt makes you *effective*, I don't think that it makes you *safe.*"

He exhaled a deep breath and tried to come up with an argument to counter her, but nothing came to mind that she'd believe or agree to. "What about Bistra? Is she at the Repository now?"

Catherine answered with a needle-thin smile. "No. Her magic, prior to madness, was to see the true nature of objects and people. I don't think that exposing her to a mountain full of demented and buried creations would be wise," she replied. "I have stationed Paladin-Commander Spidous at the Manor for now; as of last night, he has full control of this facility. The treatment of the residents is to remain with Ridora, but the rest? It's mine."

That wasn't ideal. But it was probably all he was going to get. They talked for a few minutes more as they left the grounds, and they agreed that he'd accompany her to Cableture. Once they investigated whatever had Henderschott worried, he would return to Basion and hand Rmaci over – and Erine, if he could find her.

At least it let him back into the field, for which he was grateful.

A feeling that expired the moment that they arrived at the *Narwhal's Spike.*

INTERLUDE

Water lapped at the sides of the Hullbreaker. A storm the night before had ravaged the decks, and a few of her decrepit men had been washed overboard. The Man of the Red Death had expected that. His magic effectively leashed her crew to a central anchor in the center of the vessel — the Captain. A weak point, to be sure, but an effective — and wonderfully ironic — method of control. As the shells of men long dead drifted into the depths, the wraiths that had inhabited them were pulled inexorably back to the core.

Except that wasn't all that was pulled to them.

The bodies floated into the currents of the Alenic. None of them floated high in the water; their armor was too heavy. Most simply sunk to the depths, much to the delight of scavengers on the ocean floor. The depths were deep. The depths were encompassing. The depths were hungry.

Except more than the depths themselves were hungry.

The Alenic was no stranger to shipwrecks. No stranger to warfare. No stranger to sailors that met a watery end. With the red-robed man's power, the wraith had learned once again how to reach into shells and spread.

As one storm-tossed sailor sank to the bottom, the wraith took note of an overturned ship. It had a hold full of men that had cowered for safety as their air slowly ran out years and years ago. It was impossible for the wraith to tell how long their souls had been gone. There was a ledger somewhere in Dawnfire that tracked the vessel as missing. There were family members that had mourned their passing.

Daringol didn't care. Daringol never cared. Daringol only cared that there were empty shells waiting to be used. The wraith struggled with the constraints placed on it. They kept it from working quickly. Yet it worked. It fought through the spell. It inhabited shell after shell, and its numbers swelled.

The corpses pulled themselves free of the wreckage and began an ascent to the surface. It would have made for a devastating attack on Cableture. If they had made it that far.

Except the depths weren't just hungry. The depths were jealous. The depths were greedy. The depths didn't like to part with what it had claimed. The dead in the water belonged to the water. Sailors that lost their lives to the waves were claimed by the unforgiving ocean floor, or the unforgiving Graveyard and the otherworldly Admiral Roschell that ruled over his flotilla of the damned.

Or they belonged to the monsters of the depths, great and small.

Just as it had been in the mountains around Toniki, Daringol was a blight. An abomination of nature. A cruelty of the Abyss. A construct of magic that had broken free of its chains. An aberration that didn't belong.

Daringol was an affront against nature on land.

It was an insult to the depths on the sea.

The depths would not tolerate such a transgression.

As the dead — long-rotted shells of little more than chunks of bone held together by strips of rotted clothes and rusty armor — began to rise from their muddy graves, the depths took notice. A creature of the depths took notice. A creature that had more in common with the wraith than one would have expected. A creature with bulbous eyes, a creature with an angular body, and a creature with a mouth that could crush even the strongest of boards and driest of bones.

Neither of which the Hullbreaker had.

The beast followed the trail of the empty corpses before it discovered the old bodies given new life. It scooped them up one after another. It ate; freely, eagerly, happily. It consumed the poisonous constructs without care or concern. It was a beast; it was *the* top of the food chain in this realm. These were snacks. They struggled, they moved, they stank of rot and decay. They were barely worth the effort.

As it digested the damned, it set its sights on the Hullbreaker.

The ship of the dead was food. Or so it thought. If her crew had been alive and well, it would have gone down easily. Their blood and bones and muscles and bits would have kept it fed for weeks. The remnants of the ship would have joined the other hulks nestled into the sandy floor below. If her crew had been alive.

Daringol wasn't. It was an aberration. It wasn't food.

The beast didn't know that.

Even as it pulled the Hullbreaker under the waves, it didn't know that it had just doomed itself. It didn't know it had doomed the lives of unwitting souls in Cableture. It didn't know.

The wraith twisted and fought on the deck of the ship. The wraiths that had inhabited the corpses it consumed waged war in its gut. The beast didn't know what horror its hunger had wrought.

But everyone was going to find out.

VIII. ONCE A SPY
Evening of Londis, the 7ᵗʰ of Firstgrow, 513 QR

Hours before Akaran and Catherine could arrive at Cableture by way of Granalchi portal, another series of events unfolded much to the chagrin of nearly all of the souls involved. It took a spy to suss them out, and a Merchant of Secrets to keep it hidden. All told? It was going to end in bloodshed, with the only question being:

Who's?

Despite declarations to the contrary, the purported safety of Basion City was decidedly lacking – and that was coming from a dead woman. Aside from the whole eternal torture and suffering in damnation side of the coin, being dead had a few perks. For one, the wraith *still* had no idea how she was supposed to earn her way to the Heavens,

Of course, there was always the Fields of Ash. When you fell to the pit, you – no matter who (or what) you were – took at a stop at the Precipice. It was the realm of the Warden, the Gatekeeper of the Pit. He'd judge you and send you on your way. If you could prove your worth, or prove that *maybe* you weren't worth the effort to condemn? You *might* get sent to the Field of Ash.

There was no hope there. No joy. No sound. Nothing but silence. Nothing but huts made of bits of bone and worse that fell from the clouds above damnation. It was the *only* avenue for escape from the Abyss, because even those that got free would eventually return... one way or another. If you couldn't be granted the Heavens, maybe, just *maybe*, you'd be granted ash.

On the other hand, there were apparently entities that were either jealous of her slight ascension or who were merely craven cretins with an appetite for spiritual flesh. The city itself wasn't so bad, but Yittl Canyon was a different beast entirely. Centuries of floods and drowned souls –

livestock, mostly, but not entirely – had turned the steep muddy walls into a funnel of all sorts of wailing soul and sulking monster.

It was probably a minor miracle, or maybe the presence of the Lover's outpost, that kept those monsters from slipping through the ether and into the mortal world. It was one of several observations she planned on turning over to the exorcist once she caught sight of him next. Maybe if she sold a few of the demonic-wannabes out, it might grease the gates of the Heavens.

Or it might not. Either way, it was worth a try.

If nothing else, it gave her a slight moment of delight to know that the ones that reached for her through the shifting currents of magic and the edge of the veil may pay for their attempted transgressions. Rmaci *also* had to admit that the little bit of joy she'd feel at their potential suffering wouldn't sit well with the Heavens. That is, if she was to be judged on thought as much as action.

Truthfully? It felt like she was going to lose either way. Still, as she dodged one wayward spirit and minor monster after the other (though really, there weren't as many as she seemed to think there were; her mind and her time in the pit were not doing her perceptions any kindness), she continued on with her self-imposed quest to learn more about the abomination that called herself 'Lady' Anais. A quest that, until they arrived at Port Cableture, was utterly boring.

Except for the aforementioned lost souls, of course.

However, by the time they arrived, not only had Rmaci's mood soured, but Anais – clad head to toe in scarves and wraps to hide her face from the locals – had taken on a darker aura than even when she'd murdered her associate. Part of that, the spy presumed, was due to the simmering rage and constant stream of curses she'd uttered with every step through the muddy canyon. The other part, she had to imagine, was the toxic ether that seeped out of the skull she'd absconded with.

That had been the better part of six or seven hours ago. Rmaci didn't realize it, but while she stalked Anais, Akaran was slowly regaining consciousness from a brief stay on Niasmis's beach – and despite a few ethereal tugs back to that direction, she had no idea what was about to unfold or the damage he was about to inflict. She thought she heard him scream at one point, and the frost-and-ice-covered half of her body had erupted in a shell of phantom crystals that took the better part of a candlemark to fade.

If he's getting killed, do I get pulled back into eternity with him? I hope not.

She made *sure* to cuss him out for that, too. She had no idea what he'd done, but she just *knew* he was at fault for her misery. Nothing new there, of course.

The impressive part of it was the speed of which Anais had ripped through the Canyon. For most people, it would've taken a solid day. This 'Lady' or whatever she was supposed to be? She'd cleared the entire length of it in a matter of hours without the benefit of a horse. She simply *moved* like she was made of a multitude of legs when she was forced to touch the ground; the rest of the trip she easily *floated* down the path. The only time she walked like anything *human* was when she saw other people nearby.

However, once the Lady arrived at her lair, things started to get a lot more interesting. Magic was not a skill that Rmaci had been born with, and she didn't inherit it after death. Did she turn into a haunting etheric being of embers, ice, and nightmares? Yes. Did she develop the ability to inflict torturous illusions that had some minor measure of sensory projection? Yes – but that power seemed to only work when she had direct contact with her victim as Donta had been briefly able to attest to.

Did that mean she felt comfortable getting close enough to Anais to touch her? Absolutely not – nor did it mean she understood the spell that the information broker spent an hour preparing once she was safely hidden away from prying eyes.

But you didn't have to be an Adept to understand the result.

Soon after she dumped a pile of herbs, rocks, and a vial of a blood-like substance in a plain clay bowl, Anais set fire to the whole mess and stepped back. It ignited with a sickly yellow flame that did little to improve her complexion. Rmaci's eyes went wide as a swirling, hazy portal appeared in the air that swallowed smoke and flames alike until a furry, multi-legged, multi-eyed monster popped out. He wasn't much bigger than her head and didn't look *ugly*, but the waves of *blackness* that radiated from him made her stomach churn.

"[Master grows impatient/News you have?]" it chittered. Its voice was sharp and grating; its laugh made the burns on her skin blister all over again.

Oh I'm not *going to like that thing*, Rmaci muttered to herself as she looked down at the fresh sores across her arm and chest. *True-born demon. Their very voices blacken a soul. Damned or otherwise.*

"My benefactor can grow a new arm at this point, for all I care. I am done here, Rishnobia," Anais groused as she pulled the disfigured head from her robes before she added, "and Donta is as well."

Rishnobia – if that was really its name – scooted over to the lump of bone and mottled flesh. "[He was to be removed from city/Not to be removed from this world.]"

She crossed her arms and curled her lip into a snarl. "He was to avoid being caught. And yet, here we are. He *was* caught, and I've been exposed."

"[Caught condemned or converted/or caught and dissected?]"

"Most of the above," the regal and refined woman retorted. "I couldn't rescue him. I did what I could to cover our benefactor's tracks. I had to leave the body."

Rishnobia chittered in irritated distress on the table and thumped one of its legs against the desktop. "[Rescued *chacos*/abandoned body. No victory/no joy.]"

Chacos? the spy wondered quietly from the ether above. *I... feel as if I should know that. Abyssian tongue, but what it means...*

"None of us are playing this game for joy," she retorted. "He can do what he wants with Donta's anchor. Bring him back, or leave him in the pit. There's no repairing the mess he made, or the exposure he's caused." She leaned in and placed her hands on the desk. "I need *out*, Rishnobia. I need to get *far* away from here. Ogibus. Matheia. Send me to Sycio for all I care, but if I have to stay in this city for much longer, it's not just going to be *his* anchor that Nastavol has to recover."

Nastavol, huh? Rmaci noted. *Has to be her benefactor... and an anchor? She mused before it hit her. Oh... that's what that is. The source of Donta's ensoulment. How vile.*

The mote of a demon edged backward and nearly knocked the clay bowl off the desk. "[Impossible to trace Master from a body/To trace you is a different concern. Rishnobia does understand/does not care. One more task/and then leave.]"

"Another task? *Another task?*" she seethed after a moment of fury ripped through her. "Are you *absolutely daft*? I have done *all* you two have asked and all I was to accomplish *and more* and now that my life is at risk, you want me to do something else? The whole city wants my neck in a noose! I have to leave!"

"[Another task/another job,]" it repeated. "[Successes may allow for exit of service/Failure is a risk of your own.]"

Anais blinked and stepped away from it as her jaw started to droop. "Exit... of service? He'll... release me?"

"[To your freedom if successful/to the Palace if not,]" it chittered. The way it said *palace* made the broker violently flinch and sent a shudder through Rmaci's entire essence. "[Choice is yours/as always is.]"

She stood in stony silence for the longest time. The only sound she made came from the way she ground her teeth against each other, and the almost inaudible noise her fingernails made as they raked against her dress. "You are a bastard," she finally hissed. "Damn you. *Both* of you."

"[I?/Bastard? Who knows/who cares? Ate mother/shit father,]" the demon mocked with a sickening laugh. "[Serve him/serve lower? Be free/be condemned? Decide now/or surrender.]"

"*Damn. You*," she hissed again. "What *impossible* task does that monster wish me to do? Capture the sun? Piss on the moons? What more could he want of me?"

Rishnobia kept laughing and then briefly vanished from the table only to reappear on the wall behind her. "[He wants a priest/a very specific one.]"

Anais snarled and twisted around to face the beast. "If you tell me you want that one-eyed one after you warned me away from him, so help me I —"

"[Not him/him avoid,]" it cautioned. "[Another/different. He holds the secrets/hidden in the waves. A man of song/a man of oceans. A Tidesinger/ he missed.]"

"A Tidesinger? There's… hmm. There's only one in the city… Quinchecco, I believe his name is," she remembered out-loud. "Is that why he destroyed Vahail?"

"[Destroyed for knowledge/was not there. Quinchecco has what he needs/or knows where to sing.]"

The merchant pursed her dead lips and glowered at the beast. "Alive or other?"

"[Alive is needed/soul otherwise ascendant,]" Rishnobia replied with what sounded like a sigh that passed through its spiny teeth. "[Aqualla would not be most willing/to let Master ask if after.]"

"No, no, I imagine not," Anais replied after a moment. "You so swear it — I detain this singer of the waves, and I presume remove him from the city — that once done, I'll be granted freedom? No more favors, no more service, no more command or control. I'll be allowed to *live*?"

"[Live no/exist yes,]" it answered. "[No better bargain/no other chance. So sworn I/and he too.]"

Anais rubbed her hands together and dropped her head. "Fine. Then as he has requested, it'll be done. Am I being allowed an assistant, or am I required to do this on my own?"

Rishnobia let loose with another horrific laugh, and Rmaci felt even more of her skin blister and slough off into the ether. "[As helpful as your last/would think want none now. No help/you alone. You will deliver not to Master/but to his woeful lost Hunter.]"

It should have been impossible for the self-named 'Merchant of Secrets' to lose any more color in her face. That last statement, however, did just that. "Mael… Maelphistiphan? He… is here? Or… in the city?" she asked as her hands started to tremble of their own apparent accord.

"[In city/outside of. Matters not/not now,]" the demon replied with a wave of his paw. "[Master not impressed/with your failures. You are under eyes/by more than mine.]"

"I... I see," she whispered softly. "Then ah... his will be done. Where am I to deliver the Tidesinger?"

"[To be said later/when you go acquire. Time is short/that be known. Your assistance of chaos/the ship of souls? Do not forget/soon be here. Master has seen to it/it is on its way.]"

This... cretin... knows about the Hullbreaker? Rmaci thought to herself as she just barely managed to keep herself from flickering into view. *It makes it sound like it's... it's been directed? How? WHO?*

Anais bit down on her lip. "A ship of the damned with the Man of Red directing the helm, his assassin watching my moves, the threat of being returned to the Palace, an offer of freedom, a demand for the Tidesinger, *and* no word of his plans for the Urn?" she asked with bile dripping from her words. "He certainly does know how to make a woman concerned for the future."

Rishnobia jumped in front of her face and flashed a row of silvery, saliva-coated teeth at her. "[Do as our Master commands/to ensure you have one.]"

Instructions and warning given, the beast vanished as quickly as it had appeared – and it took Donta's chacos with him. The broker stood in silence for several very long, very tired heartbeats before she looked up at the shadows in the ceiling. "Shall I assume you heard all of that?"

She can't be talking to me.

"Oh now, do come on dear. Yes, I am talking to you, yes, I know you're there, and yes, I know you've followed me since Basion. I considered that you might be a bored ghost at first, but I've felt your concern growing by the minute. I daresay it pales in comparison to mine, though I don't expect you to realize that."

What is it that asshole always says? Rmaci thought to herself as she slowly descended from the ceiling and allowed herself to appear at the far side of the room. "*Shit.*"

"Is that how you normally greet people?" Anais asked as she flipped one of her scarves loose from around her shoulders and into a heap on the floor. "Do tell me you're capable of saying more than that or I will be most disappointed."

The sheer frankness behind her voice stunned the wraith into near-silence before she frowned and answered her. "*I don't get to greet people much anymore,*" she lamented, "*and had not planned to greet you.*"

"Given your efforts to remain hidden, no, I do suppose not," the broker replied with a haughty lift of her chin as she studied the spirit. "You look quite the fright; your intent, or intent of others?"

"*Many others,*" Rmaci spit in disgust. "*You don't seem particularly concerned.*"

"About your presence? Of course not; I'm as dead as you are, and I suspect you have realized that already," she offered in reply. "Though given your… shall we call it, present condition? …I would say that I well may be more alive than you. Tell me: Who's cock did you end up suckling on to leave you so twisted? Charnac? Makaral?" she asked before she wrinkled her nose. "You didn't run afoul of Geshalda, did you? Giving you both fire and ice seems fitting for She Of Never Enough."

The spy stepped further into the light and crossed her arms as she hovered over the floor. "*Zell.*"

"The *fish*?" Anais asked with a gag. "Oh, you poor thing. I hadn't heard that flames were His interest but I suppose the nature of the Abyss is an ever-present twist of torments. Always experimenting, always playing, the Fallen are. I will say that it's a pleasure that you're not some bored and wayward creature – you seem to have much more of a mind than that."

"*You seem to have more problems than masters,*" Rmaci remarked after she admitted enjoyed the compliment. It was nice to speak to a peer, in a fashion. "*Along with associates as dead as us.*"

Anais made a disgusted noise from the back of her throat as she settled down and began to scan through a letter that had been left outside of her door. "Yech. One could only hope, but no. The mote has more life to it than my baited lack of breath, and I am none too sure if my benefactor is mortal or simply better at covering his true nature than I ever could," she explained before she looked up from the scroll and raised an eyebrow at the spirit. "I trust you understand that I have no desire to add either another master *nor* another associate *nor* another *problem* to my plate. As you've neither attempted to run or kill me, shall I assume that you are amenable to a conversation?"

"*That depends,*" the otherworldly woman asked. "*You asked me to appear. Do you intend to do to me that which you think I'm not here to do you?*"

The broker lifted a finger and twirled a tendril of cloudy, deep lavender magic in the air that dispersed almost as quick as she summoned it. "As you're mindful enough to hold a parley, I almost must assume you're spying on me for a reason – and I can think of few. It would indeed be easier if we spoke as friends, rather than spoke as other."

The threat of speaking as *other* immediately set the wraith on edge. One arm ignited as the other developed a shell of ice. "*I do nothing I do not wish.*"

"Then you are a freer woman than I fear I shall ever be; sworn promises and remarks from a mote aside and ignored for as worthless as they are," Anais answered wistfully. "So let us be down to it: you've been at my back since I helped my last associate leave the realm, which implies you are either allied with the fools in the Fleet – which is unlikely – or the Eclipsian that held him captive. The latter is possible, though with your alignment to Zell that places you in an interesting position," she continued before she lifted her eyebrow again and calmly stuffed the scroll into the folds of her dress. "Especially if you claim you are not enslaved. Attempting to negotiate your way out of perdition?"

Everything about this woman was off-putting, and her ability to break Rmaci down to a few short sentences did not help put the wraith at ease. *"As it seems you are the same. The Palace, hm? There are many. Which?"*

"One which needn't be named," the other woman answered, "though yes, you may be right. So now that we've established our mutual desires to avoid returning to the underside of the Grand Storm, why should I not expedite your trip there?"

Rmaci didn't have a doubt in her mind that the Merchant of Secrets could, or that she *would* at least try before the spy could get away even if she wanted. *"You broker in secrets, yet you just gave away many for free."*

The older, animated corpse merely nodded her head as she began to work a spell to bring the appearance of life back to her flesh. "Did I? Or did I offer them and spare your unlife for my own ends?"

"Both," the spy retorted just as quickly. *"Shall I assume that your position in this world is not as secure as you would like?"*

"We are dead women in the world of the living. Neither state – bereft of life and lack of ownership of cock – do us any favors when our fair sex is traded as cattle when we draw breath. In death, it is only our wits that allow us to attain that much, let alone reach for more. As such, neither of us have positions that the other should envy," Anais replied as the words drolly rolled off of her tongue. "Of course, you are right. I do not have a great deal of trust with the cretin you saw – and less, now knowing that his Master's assassin is nearby."

"Then you bargain with a spirit you don't know for what end? You don't even have a name to my face."

The broker leaned back in her chair and let a bemused smile flicker over her pale lips. "Why do I need a name when I know how you feel so close to me? I can invoke you on that alone, should I wish," she warned. "No; it's simple. If you've aligned with Erine you've likely somehow aligned with that crippled priest; I know she has an interest in him. Or, if you aren't, you can be – by way of the Eclipsian or by way of other. Am I right?"

"Even if you are, you would expect that a dead woman has power over a living man? An exorcist, at that?"

"I said nothing about him being an exorcist," Anais retorted, "though I do appreciate your candor. I would like you to deliver a message to him for me, and then you may be upon your merry way."

It was Rmaci's turn to smile. This so-called 'Lady' may think that she was twisting words or catching her in slips of the tongue, but dead or not – she was a Civan-trained spy. Even if past loyalties failed to be appropriately rewarded. *"I plan to take a very large message, regardless of your consent. What do you have to add?"* Despite what Anais thought, the wraith picked every word carefully and made note to how other woman reacted to each one.

The animated corpse stood up and began to make herself proper. "Much. My benefactor seeks an object his Order owns. If Akaran agrees to call the search for my head off, I'll make sure he knows what it is once I am well and clear from Basion."

"Before or after you hand Quinchecco over?"

"If I can *negotiate* with the Tidesinger, ideally I won't have to," Anais replied with a shrug. "I'm willing to throw in a vampire, to boot, if it'll give him something to do while I'm busy. He and I did agree to that much."

Rmaci fought the urge to rub her hands together. She also fought the urge to dive forward and fill the woman with such sights of terror that they'd make a mortal man die of fright, but... there was something about her candor and the way she had casually thrown around the names of the Fallen. *"Bargaining for freedom from a demon and negotiating terms with a man who converses with the Divine? You seem to think much of yourself."*

"As if you aren't doing the same," Anais scolded. "Glass houses, pits of burning snakes, and such as that. If he agrees, I'll know. If the Lovers don't retract their claws, I'll know, and I will deliver upon my promise to Rishnobia once I have my discussion with the Tidesinger. Don't waste time trying to find me; I'll take care that you can't," she added as she made her way to the door. "Now, as it turns out, I actually do have other business to attend to."

"Oh do you now? Whatever could that be?"

"Business I am sure you will attempt to discern as you follow me to it. I'm not so daft to think that you won't try – so don't deny that you intend to. That said, I didn't expect to have to entertain more than one messenger tonight, and I cannot leave my intended contact waiting. So do be a dear and make haste? You heard the warnings from Rishnobia as clearly as I did – there's darkness soon to land on the shores, and we'll *all* be too busy to wait around once it arrives."

With that, she left, and with that, Rmaci was left alone with her thoughts. Though, she didn't bother to dwell on them for long. *From spy to damned soul to tormentor to petitioner to the Pantheon, then once more spy and now reduced to a courier,* she lamented. *The mighty do indeed fall far.*

Early afternoon of Madis, the 8th of Firstgrow, 513 QR

It was bad. It was brazen, it was bloody, and it was worse than they expected. Henderschott had caught them as they prepared to leave the city, and he had an Adept in tow. "I just found who it was," he started, and then directed them to the Adept beside him. "I have an Adept that will get you delivered to the port. You'll need more men, too," he added. If that wasn't concern enough, he even offered to pay for it out of the Guard's coffers.

What's worse – he was right.

The *Narwhal's Spike* was the kind of taberna you went to when you needed to get your mouth or dick wet, and you had few concerns over the quality of either. It wasn't the type of place where you stuck around for hours on end; you showed up, you ordered a drink, you waited for someone to catch sight of your purse, and you left. It was exactly the kind of place where you went if you didn't want witnesses.

Whomever attacked it either wanted that thought kept in mind, or didn't care. The Lieutenant-Commander apologized before they were magically whisked away to Port Cableture, for how little it was worth now. "Fisking... *fisking* idiots. All they told me was that someone had attacked a bar, it was worse than a regular fight, and that I should ask someone to send some of your lot down there. You said you already had people there hunting for that Anais woman. I assumed they could handle it," he'd half-complained and half-explained.

Even though Spidous had failed to apprehend the broker a few days prior, Catherine had left Paladin Faldine behind to oversee the investigation of what Anais had been up to. Unlike the Knights of Love – or Kols for short – Order Paladins had magic to back up their swords. Their official title, Messengers of Love (or *Mols*), had more to do with the Order hierarchy and each branch's patronage to one of the three Archangels of Niasmis than it did anything else. Of course, when a paladin was sent to deal with a problem, there was usually a message of 'begone' attached.

Either way, you didn't ascend to the rank of paladin in the Order without being able to pull your weight in a fight. That explained some of the damage, but didn't excuse the result. It *did* explain why there were witnesses left behind, too, because it was obvious that witnesses weren't wanted.

Once they arrived, Catherine had an obvious and immediate concern to attend to, which left Akaran on his own to survey the damage and talk to what witnesses he could find. As she ordered a full report from an attending medicannia and a few healers that had been pressed into service before they arrived, he did his best to piece together what actually happened. *At least I don't have to ask the dead to help this time*, he groused to himself, *and it doesn't look like someone threw the corpses into a barrel of burn-dust before they set it off.*

All told, eight bodies had been recovered. The taberna's owner had been sitting upstairs at a table next to an upper-level internal balcony that gave him a vantage point to see what had transpired below. The owner had a habit of staying up late, he'd admitted, because that was when people usually started to get rowdy.

The attack had hit a couple of hours past midnight, and not long before the shop would've closed. The doorman outside didn't get killed outright, though one of the three attackers had cracked his skull. Nobody could say for sure if he'd recover, or if he did, if he'd be more than a drooling, vacant-eyed wretch for the rest of his life.

Not that he'd been a pillar of education and refinement to begin with.

The trio seemed to know exactly who they were looking for. The owner – a man named Ledel – described her easily. She happened to frequent the *Narwhal*, though normally with a pale-skinned companion. He was almost relieved to hear that her bodyguard had been killed before the attack, though he wondered if Donta had still been alive, if his cook would've lived through the night.

Anais had been at the *Narwhal* for an hour before she'd been joined by one of the Order's own – a Paladin that Akaran had heard of, but never met. The only assumption that he could make was that Faldine she was attempting to negotiate Anais's surrender, which meant that she was probably getting played. If he was right about the Merchant of Secrets and her otherworldly nature, well. Rmaci aside, dead women don't typically bargain their way into the Order's custody.

And he strongly, strongly doubted she was angling for a reprieve.

Ledel, naturally, made it a business to *not* know what people were up to at any given point in their lives, and very specifically, what they were up to when they met up *here*. So while he couldn't help with that, he was able to describe what happened next.

One of the three attackers parked himself by the door and refused to budge. Of the other two, one went straight for Anais while the other made a beeline right for the rear door of the dining area. They didn't talk, they didn't try to make demands, they didn't do any of that.

Faldine, Ledel commended, had spotted them as they barged in. "Something about 'em must've been off, 'cause she jumped to 'er feet and drew 'er sword. Blessed thing caught fire right as she pulled it. Ain't never seen anythin' like it before, and ain't got a care to see anythin' like it again," he explained.

She wouldn't have done that if they were just garden-variety assholes, Akaran decided. *More monsters wearing human skins. How freaking wonderful.*

The *Narwhal's* owner went on to explain the next few minutes. Faldine, for her credit, kept Anais from having her head ripped off. He specifically pointed that out, because that's what happened to his bartender. When the man behind the counter had pulled out a sword of his own, the raider closest to him had cut his neck open and then pulled until his skull was completely peeled off of his neck.

*Defiled **and** strong*, the exorcist cursed to himself. *Doesn't take a genius to see where this is going.*

As soon as the fight started – and right as the bartender's blood soaked the poor drunken sods waiting at the counter – the small crowd devolved into a reasonable, yet terrified, panic. The last thing that Ledel saw before people swarmed up the stairs were two of the three attackers as they literally tore through the handful of people in the dining area. They provided cover while Faldine and the third member of their group battled it out.

Another witness described what happened next. She was one of the last up the stairs, but she happened to turn around in time to see the paladin cut her opponent in half. "I can't've seen what I saw," the young, almost waifishly-thin woman explained as tears continued to stream down her face. "*Can't've.* People don't just... just... *burn up* and turn to *ash* when they get cut by a sword! Even if the damn thing is a burnin'! They don't *do* that! Not... not 'less your swords... they don't... If you cut me would I...?"

It took him a good five minutes to reassure her that no, if he cut her with his, she wouldn't die like that. Even if it was an accidental brush against his steel. *Especially* if it was an accidental brush. He didn't go into full detail about why her attacker had, but, it was better off for her sake.

She'd find out soon enough, anyway.

After Faldine destroyed the one that had gone after Anais, the other two got involved. Presumably, Donta's former employer managed to escape in the ensuing confusion. It didn't last very long, though her actions probably saved the lives of everyone else left in the taberna.

Except she couldn't save her own. That was one of the first sights that had greeted them once they had arrived at Cableture. Catherine didn't cry, she didn't swear, she just stood with her hands clenched and her eyes brimmed with fury. While Akaran worked with the witnesses, she worked with Faldine's corpse to prepare it for travel back to the Repository.

The exorcist didn't even have to examine the ashes in the middle of the room to know what they belonged to. The witnesses were enough. But it left another problem – the attack happened at near-dawn. Witnesses said the remaining two scattered into the city. Alarms went off and every gate and exit from the Port were either sealed off or staffed with your pick between the 4th Garrison or the 2nd Naval Armada. They might have made it out.

But they probably hadn't.

Which meant they had little more than eight hours to rip Cableture to shreds if they planned on catching them before nightfall. "Shit," he swore under his breath as he peered down at the shattered tables and bloody stains below.

"*Shit indeed,*" a voice whispered from just behind his head. "*That word truly expresses more than I'd ever given credit to it – or you – for, just so you know.*"

Akaran whipped around and saw Rmaci as she manifested just inside the closest room at his back. "Where've you been? I had started to think you'd taken your freedom and ran."

"*Living up to my reputation,*" the spy replied earnestly. "*We need to speak, urgently. You have more problems than you know what to do with.*"

"Yeah, we do," Akaran replied with a sigh. "I need to find Erine. Sooner than later. I also have to –"

Rmaci reached out of the shadowed room and tried (but failed) to pull him inside. He followed anyways just to humor her – and to keep people from noticing her arrival. "*Pay attention,*" the wraith warned with a fire in her eyes. "*You have to listen because I know who that bitch is working for. His name is Nastavol, and I cannot tell you why, but that name makes me want to slit my own wrists and that particular act lost any power over my existence a literal lifetime ago,*" By the time she finished explaining everything she'd heard, he was ready to throw up. "*And that demon with her? It... it smells. Etherically. I can honestly say that I do not know what pit that Rishnobia creature crawled out of, only that there is not enough dirt in the world to bury it with to hide its stench.*"

"Everything you've said is bad, you know that, right?" he asked as he rocked slowly in a chair that wasn't designed for it. "She was here. We have witnesses. She came *here* after she met with you."

"*I wouldn't say she met with me,*" the spy half-grumbled and half-purred. "*Merely that we had the opportunity to make each other's acquaintance.*"

"You're positive about this, right? She wasn't lying to you, wasn't trying to fill your head with bullshit to slow us down or...?"

The wraith nodded her head. "*Oh, she's full of lies, of that I don't doubt. Yet – when Donta first mentioned her 'benefactor's' name, she grew angry and distraught. When that disgusting ball of fur mentioned the name of the assassin, her tune changed completely. She is a creature in fear of her soul; a state, I should mention, I have some experience with.*"

"So Anais works for the man that murdered Galagrin back in Toniki, and the one who half-blinded Mariah. Plus he's the man who slaughtered some giant rot-demon, from what Brother Steelhom told me. He wants Anais to track down the Tidesinger, for reasons unknown, and he's responsible for the Hall of Sea's Song in Vahail getting destroyed?" he asked. "Is that what you're telling me?"

"*Don't forget about the* Hullbreaker," she cautioned. "*I found it. It's still days away but there is power in that wraith that it* didn't *have before. I can't tell you when it's coming, or even if. But Daringol is out there.*"

Akaran clenched his teeth. "Great. It found a way to get stronger. Just what I didn't want to hear. I'm going to have to set a trap and… shit. It's either the wraith or the vampires. How the pits am I supposed to deal with *that*? I can't be in two places at once!"

"*Plus the truth you've already come to fear: Anais is not human,*" the spy added. "*I don't know what she is, though she's different than that laughing little dust-ball. I assume she's more like Donta, and can be slain the same way when the time comes for it. There are a surprising number of walking corpses in this city, but you know that now, yes? It's taken away some of the uniqueness of my presence and situation and I have to admit that –*"

"Oh, yes. I'd hate for you to feel like you're not *special* to me anymore," he retorted with a snort. "So the next step is to brief Catherine, who isn't going to believe any of this and –"

"What won't I believe?" the Maiden asked as she poked her head into the bedroom, "and why are you hiding in here?"

Akaran started to stand up, then thought better of it and sat right back down. "Because she'd cause too much of a ruckus if I marched her outside," he replied as Catherine stepped into the room and realized he wasn't alone. Her hand immediately dropped to her sword as a spell sprang to life on her fingertips before he could step in-between them. "Maiden-Templar Catherine Prostil, I'd like you to meet the woman you said wasn't in my head. Rmaci, this is my boss," he said by way of introduction. "I'd humbly ask that you don't kill her, and you don't try to terrorize her. Deal?"

***

The meeting of minds didn't go well at first. Or at second, or at third. Catherine managed to keep a level (-ish) head, though once she demanded that the wraith submit to the Order for penance and was summarily rejected and rebuffed, the conversation turned to a more violent series of suggestions. However, with a surprisingly calm and caviler attitude about the entire experience, Akaran managed to play peacekeeper between the two vastly different women – which, he personally thought, he should be lauded for.

Neither of them agreed, but neither of them asked for his opinion.

"Right now, the truth is simple," he interrupted as they continued to exchange barbs back and forth. A few passersby had stopped to try to listen, but another Lover (a wardkeeper, at that) had escorted the Maiden upstairs, and he – showing substantial wisdom – pretended he couldn't hear anything and made a point keep people moving along.

Wardkeepers: the direct opposite of Order exorcists in both mannerisms, patience, and magic. Useful bodyguards, great guardians, and the bulk of the Repository's forces. They knew their place as a whole, and reveled in the fact that they didn't *have* to have conversations like the one going on behind him.

"That you can call any of this *simple* does not give me reason to think highly of your current state," the Maiden grumbled as she kept her back against the shut door and stood with her arms crossed.

"*Says the woman that'd be happy if I was dead and gone,*" Rmaci quipped.

Catherine huffed in annoyance. "I shouldn't be the only one."

"Shouldn't, but you are," the exorcist interrupted. "Listen. We're utterly fisked over a barrel right now and you both know it. We've got two bloodsuckers loose in the Port and the longer we argue the better the odds that they're going to get away. Right now they're serving Annix, but they botched their job. They could either retreat to his lair for different instructions, or decide that they should cut loose and go wild in the Kingdom."

"Even if they did, they'd be summoned back to his side eventually," the Maiden countered. "It's documented that sires of a brood can reach out to their children wherever in the world they may be."

"Before or after they add to their tallies?" Akaran retorted. "I know. You want to deal with her right now and I can't exactly blame you for that, but –"

The spy smiled over at him. "*He really can't. Despite his interest in saving my soul I know he'd be thrilled to know I've moved on. You do need to give him that much respect.*"

"– but," he continued through the interruption, "we have about seven hours, maybe eight, before the sun sets and they get loose. We're going to need her help to find them."

Catherine faltered and clutched at the handle of her sword for the umpteenth time in the last fifteen minutes. "Are you asking me to allow a true wraith, a *sentient* at that, to roam free in the harbor? Do I need to remind you of your duties, Exorcist? To help the souls that can be salvaged find peace; to release the souls that are cursed to walk of volition not of their own; and –"

"– and to condemn the ones that should never be allowed to see the light of day. I *know*. She's harmless. These two shitheads that've gone to ground *aren't*."

"*I think I rather object to being called harmless,*" the spy muttered to nobody in particular. "*Has anyone told you that your Order is the epitome of pretentious when it comes to sayings like that?*"

"Don't make this harder than it has to be, please?" Akaran pleaded. "Maiden, we have to purge the city and I don't think we have time enough to call for the entire Repository to get down here, do we?"

Catherine flattened her lips together in a grim, parchment-thin frown. "Even with the Granalchi assisting, we'd only have time to get a handful of fighters. I've already sent a message for additional aid, along with a request for the Guild. Admiral Maddon will pledge troops as well."

Akaran shook his head. "The Grand Navy of the Dawn can barely find water. I don't think they'll be much help blanketing the port."

"It is a start, at least."

"Well, yes," he agreed as Rmaci snickered in the corner. "If nothing else, we'll find the vamps when the sailors get eaten, so there's that. Rmaci, can you tell us anything about them?"

The wraith looked over at the Templar and met eyes with the woman. "*Yes, though it won't make* her *any happier with me.*"

The Templar just glared.

"*I opted to follow Anais here. I know she sensed me, but I didn't particularly care. She didn't arrive alone. Worse was that the paladin down there happened to sense me too. She worked some irritating spell – that light thing you do. Despite my recent pledge to your Matron Goddess... well, our Matron, I should suppose to say... I didn't feel it would be overtly wise to attempt a dialogue. Or see if her magic would do anything to me or not.*"

"So you took off running?" Catherine grunted with a dismissive smirk.

"*The fact that I am already dead does mean that I have a greater sense of self-preservation than others. I would hope you would expect and understand that,*" Rmaci retorted. "*Suffice it to say, I was unable to enter this establishment so I cannot tell you what business the two had. I can tell you that one of the vampires called for the dead bitch by name.*"

The Maiden took a menacing step forward and willed her left hand to glow with divine light. "That *dead bitch* was my friend. Faldine was a great woman, and better than any *Civan spy* piece of guttertrash," she seethed.

Rmaci flattened herself against the back wall. "*Not that woman,*" she clarified. "*The one that wanted to turn me into a go-between. A demotion worse than any I've had.*"

Akaran reached over and stopped Catherine from doing something rash. Reasonable, but rash. "Let her finish. Anything we can get on these would be helpful."

"*As I was attempting to say,*" Rmaci went on once she was satisfied with her safety for a few moments longer, "*it called for her by name. 'Lady Lovic! I am here with Ettaquis! He's injured!' It was a very banal attempt at getting attention. It worked, for which everyone involved should be embarrassed.*"

"Ettaquis? I don't know that name," the exorcist mused.

"*Nor I – though you know the name of one of the women with him.*"

"I do?"

"*A moment, and I'll say it,*" the spy replied. "*Anais stepped out of the taberna, took one look at the trio, and ran back inside. That's when they attacked. She recognized them for what they were, right away. The talker – some woman I don't know? She claimed they was there on behalf of their 'Meister,' which is a conceited title for a lord if I have ever heard one.*"

Akaran grunted in disgust. "Everything about this bastard has been cocky and conceited. Did you see Anais leave?"

The dead woman nodded her head. "*Yes, though, as I said, I could not linger. When the guard arrived, they brought a battlemage, and, again, to speak truth...*"

"Didn't want to be destroyed. I get it," he noted. "You said I know one of the others?"

"*Yes,*" she admitted and tilted her head in his direction. "*Though not well. I met her through you, specifically when I was along for the ride. I am afraid I found the woman that your blonde healer was concerned over.*"

He sat straight up and covered his mouth with his hand. "Oh, dammit. No. Erine was right about her?"

"*I am afraid so.*"

"Well, shit. This is going to break Seline's heart," he sighed. "Maiden, add another name to the list – Raechil Lamar, formerly a healer and aide attached to Medias Manor. Sister to Kiasta Lamar, the Mother Eclipsian's bodyguard. *Also* presumed dead. We'll have to try to capture her and –"

It was Catherine's turn to shake her head. "I know your intent is to save as many souls as you can, which is admirable, but if she's turned, she isn't salvageable. We don't know *what* happens to the soul of a person that has been risen as one of those cretins, but the lore is clear: there is only one solution." She gestured over at the wraith and sighed. "Not all souls can be saved."

"*That's not entirely true,*" Rmaci interrupted. "*There are several. Beheading, destroying the heart with an outgrowth of Nature, bathing one in silver, sunlight... burning, of course, but I would prefer not to entertain that idea, should it be all the same to you both.*" When they looked over at her and started to ask how she knew, she responded with a simple, "*I heard him think it at the Landing after he realized what was going on. Felt important to remember."*

She was right, and Akaran hated to admit it. "Fine. Then if not save her, we can try to prevent her from feeding. Save others."

"Then we must move fast," the Maiden finally decided. "I already have the 4th combing the port and asking questions. We'll give them names and descriptions, as best as we can."

"We can do more than that," he added. "I... figured out a trick back in Toniki. It might help here."

"The 'tricks' you figured out in Toniki directly translated to your downfall and months of suffering. Make sure you pick which method you intend to share carefully," Catherine cautioned.

Warning noted, he reached into his belt and pulled an imprint stone free. "This worked in a way, but now that I can use magic again, it'll work better. I'm going to need a couple of things and a few minutes, but..."

After he relayed his needs to Catherine, she passed them on to the wardkeeper outside. While he went to work – and without asking a single question he didn't want to know the answer to – Rmaci brought up the subject they'd skipped over. *"What of that Quinchecco person? I imagine that you don't trust Anais any more than I do."*

"That's a given," he muttered. "I don't think there's much we can do. We can't be in two places at once. Or three, like the Goddess seems to think we can. Maiden? Send a message with an Adept back to Basion, have him found and taken somewhere safe? The Repository or elsewhere?"

"Given that this woman seems to have an interest in the relics we have stored, putting another object of her interest near the Vault does not compel my thinking to a happy place," the Maiden replied, "though we also can't leave him in the open. Instead of our outpost, we might be safer to move him under the control of the Hunters."

Akaran bit his lip and looked up with deep concern. "I might've had one of their members arrested for attempted murder. Are you sure we can trust *them?"*

"That depends on who they attempted to murder," she answered with a frown.

"Me."

"Ah," she replied, and then added a few heartbeats later, "yet..."

His frown deepened. "Yet what?"

"You have been stirring up quite the hornet's nest in the city," she pointed out. "Is it all that shocking that someone attempted to take your head?"

Rmaci broke down into a fit of unholy laughter in the corner as the priest tried very hard not to be offended by that. "Shocking, well... no, but I mean... still..."

She nodded and rubbed at her cheeks. "Still, I do see your point. However, the Guild is better suited to provide a safe haven for him than nearly anyone else. I'll request a Writ of Protection to be ordered."

"May as well throw in that Writ of Execution," he added. "Elsith is going to be pissed if we don't clue her in on what's going on in the underbelly."

"It'll be done," she agreed as the wardkeeper knocked on the door. The wraith vanished from view as he made his delivery and then just as quickly, made his exit. In addition to Akaran's macabre supplies, the Lover handed over a ruby insignia ring. "I saw this in the ash. Thought you may want to see it, if it belongs to whom I think it does."

"I do," Catherine whispered as her eyes narrowed to cold slits. "This belongs to Lady Sannah Hosheck. She's the Overseer's right-hand." Her lip curled up in disgust. "Some think she's more than that. Or at least, that she uses her hand on him."

Akaran looked up from his efforts. "Why would that be here? You don't think..."

"That monster has found a way to corrupt much in this city," the spy pointed out. *"Would you be surprised if it found a way to gain the ear of the Overseer by turning his lover?"*

"That's a concern we don't have time to consider. If this is hers... if she's the monster that murdered Faldine... I'll have to go through the remains."

"It would be easier merely to find out her recent schedule," the wraith suggested. *"If she's developed an aversion to the sun as of late, you'll know for certain either way."*

Catherine closed her eyes and tried not to bite her tongue. "There were survivors enough, and Sannah is too well-known not to be identified. If she was the one that did this, we'll know," she replied before she noted Akaran's pile with a disgusted snarl. "Corpse-ash from the vampire, a slice of leather, and a knife. For whatever purpose...?"

He took the pile and set them on the table and went to work as quickly as he could. "I'll need all the imprint stones that you can find. You'll want to bless the rest of them yourself. After last night? I don't trust my magic to be strong enough to do more than a couple of these right now." *Which is probably pushing it*, he admitted inwardly. *ALL of this is pushing it.*

"To do what?" she asked again.

He didn't answer, but he let his work speak for him. He first cut a pair of thin slits in the leather, and then he placed the imprint stone and the ash in a small pile. He uttered a quick spell and compressed the ash to the jagged piece of amber-colored stone as hard as he could. After it flashed an angry red, he tucked it into the leather slits – just enough to serve as a makeshift strap.

The next step was to etch the Word for a rune of 'illuminate' around the stone and into the leather. Next, he carved in an extra sigil to bind the spell and the crystal together. "This," he answered once he was finished. "It doesn't look like much, but... it should cause the imprint crystal to glow in the presence of Annix's brood, if they all share the same or similar aura. Even mundanes should be able to use it," he explained as he handed it over.

Catherine looked down at it and ran her fingers over his effort as her jaw dropped. "This is nothing short of brilliant. How did I not hear of this before now?"

"I had it in my report..."

"Your report also detailed an exploration into Tundrala, a glimpse into Frosel, and how we nearly lost Waschali Province due to a wayward mage and his inability to manage, how did you say it? 'Abyssian piss water flowing into a bucket,' – does that sound right?"

He opted against dignifying the remark with a response and simply looked out the window. "We're going to run out of time before we want to. If we're going to make a move and bring Faldine's killers to judgment, we gotta do it now."

The Maiden nodded and handed the makeshift tracking rune back to him. "I suppose you're going to recommend once again that the wraith join our efforts."

"She can move faster than us, she can walk through walls, and she can view the world between worlds," he replied. "We'd be idiots to not take advantage of her."

"*I've had quite enough of people who decide to take advantage of me,*" Rmaci retorted from the corner. "*Though – yes. I'll help. Even if I don't pass whatever test your Goddess has in mind for me, vampires are not exactly welcome in the pit. I may earn credit if I aid you in culling a few.*"

"Hedging your bets?" Catherine asked with a smirk.

"*Planning for all potential futures,*" she spat back.

The Maiden cleared her throat. "Then we'll use her – conditionally. Do I even need to say it?"

The spy gave the Templar the foulest look she could plaster across her disfigured face. "*Oh, no. I think we all perfectly understand what that will be. Should I make a mistake, or somehow cross you, you'll make it your life's work to return me to Zell. Or if not Zell – shall I assume you'll attempt to banish me somewhere specific? Covorn's Quiet, maybe? I will be full of anger and rage if you end me prematurely. Or maybe you would prefer that I be sent to the Emberforge to be subjected to fires and flames again for eternity? Or mayhaps you'd be more of a mind to have me condemned to unceasing servitude in Avaritisha's Palace of Delights or possibly Her Fleshpit – and serve your Goddess's Fallen Cousin, She of Lust? Hmm? Is that the gist of your threat?"*

The Maiden didn't rise to the bait. "Damnation is damnation."

"Oh, no, no no no," Rmaci replied grimly. *"Damnation is only the beginning. Let these words ring true even if you don't believe any other I happen to utter: if all of those of lawful bent truly knew the fate of those that die before they can repent or atone for their sins, or if any of the royals of this world knew the true fates of their soldiers, there would never be another man hung nor another war fought,"* she replied coldly. *"Remember that, if nothing else."*

Except, Akaran had to admit a few minutes later, that wasn't true.

Men of law were about to do much worse than send someone to the gallows. As he gathered up more of the dead vampire's ashes and embers, all he could do was repeat the names of the next two souls he was about to personally see damned to a fate as foul as Rmaci's had been. *Don't have a choice in the matter. Has to be done.*

Or at least, that's what he kept telling himself.

IX. CAST A WIDE NET
Late afternoon of Madis, the 8th of Firstgrow, 513 QR

The waiting wasn't the hardest part, but it certainly felt like it. It had taken precious time to prepare what Catherine decided to call 'tracemarkers' to hand out to the Guard – the literal handful of them that they'd been able to scrounge up. More were on their way down from Basion, but so too were more wardkeepers and exorcists. News of Faldine's death would not sit well with the rest of the Order, which would no doubt serve to galvanize Catherine's men into action.

"What I'm about to tell you will be hard to stomach, and harder to believe," Catherine had proclaimed to a gathering of Order of Light locurats, oucurats (pronounced as 'oh, you-curats,' Akaran had explained to Rmaci), members of the 4th, and members of the 2nd Naval Armada. She was right on both points, and it was probably a blessing in disguise that there were only seven different jackasses from the Stara branch of things. They had the most questions, partook in the most outrageous shouts of disbelief, and otherwise demonstrated why the Lovers rarely got along with representatives of the rest of the Pantheon proper.

They'd had an argument before leaving the *Narwhal* about how much to even say. Admitting that there was a vampire (let alone two) loose in the port would put a lot of focus on the Order, but covering it up would run a substantial risk of scandal if the hunt went south. The Maiden had decided (with Akaran's 'full and unconditional support' brought about by a threat of revoking his status) that the best way to approach it was to only hint at the nature of the beast without naming them directly.

In retrospect, it was probably the only reason that Cableture didn't burn down. It might've improved things if it had. The exorcist had stopped here first on his way to Medias Manor, but neither he nor Badin had any desire to stay long after a week of sea-borne travel. As a naval port went, it was one – the 2nd had no interest in building the small town up any more than it had to be to support the Queen's Navy.

However, the 2nd Naval Armada *was* a naval *armada*, and Cableture still managed to claim nearly a third as many citizens as who lived in Basion directly – and six-thousand people (or so) wasn't a number to sneeze at regardless of where you lived in the Kingdom. Of those, nearly a quarter served *in* the military, and the remaining served to *support* the military. It actually helped to mobilize the locals.

And, as an added bonus, it cut down on the number of places that the vampires were likely to hide. "We have a few things in our favor, though they grow fewer by each drip of a candle's wax – so I will be brief."

That was *almost* a lie, but she tried to keep it short.

"While we have cause to believe that these cretins are hiding for now, once the sun sets, they'll be free to move. Make no mistake, the Order is not hunting humans; we are hunting monsters. We have been at work to unearth a plot of necromancy and demon-worship, and those that dabble with the dark have brought help to aid them in their dark deeds."

That was so much a lie that Rmaci tried to choke on her tongue. She honestly looked sad when she realized she couldn't. "*I think I've said what happens to liars in the next world once before…*" she mused just within Akaran's hearing.

He ignored her even as the Maiden continued. "Yet these monsters are not pit-dwelling demons or flame-blistered abominations that should not walk the world as you and I," she said as the wraith made foul gestures at her just beyond her line of sight (and out of sight of the crowd). "They appear as human, yet assuredly are not. We fear they may have taken human form, and even human identity; be it they started as devils, or have been mimicked to appear as people we may have once known: a man named Ettaquis, and a woman who once honorably served in Basion. Her name is Raechil Lamar, or at least, that is the name that the demon masquerading in her flesh claims to have."

"I'm so glad Seline isn't here for this part," he sighed under his breath. "If Raechil has any other family, their name just got destroyed."

"*Don't complain too loudly, oh vaunted one. One thing that my countrymen respect about yours is your firm stance against those that consort with the dead,*" she said with a mocking smile. "*Of course that also means that given your current entanglements? Even if they didn't hang you for serving Niasmis, they surely could for having this conversation with me.*"

That was harder to ignore than not, but for the sake of sanity, he tried.

Catherine went on to describe their appearance before she added a firm, "If they are seen, do not approach. Send word to any that bear the sigil of Love or those that walk under the auspices of the Order of Light. If you fight, and only if you must, engage with fire if you can. If you cannot, aim for the eyes and neck. Either way, engage with a scream – as many as you can! – so that we can rush to aid."

"*Yes, don't fight them – run. Should you not run – scream. Should you have need to scream, set a building on fire. Even if we don't find them, the smoke signals will be worth enough,*" the spy mocked.

"Did I mention I am so *fisking* glad you're out of my head?" Akaran growled over at her. "Why aren't you hunting them down already?"

Rmaci pointed a blistered finger at the Maiden and spat in disgust. "*If you think I trust her not to drop my name into this pot of half-truths and instructions to murder, you are more deserving of your stay in that asylum than I gave you credit for,*" she retorted.

While he couldn't really argue that, Catherine continued with her grand speech. The next bit of it was better news than the rest. "We have come to understand the nature of the monsters we seek. They cannot stomach the sun, for it is pure and they are unclean. They cannot walk into a home without invitation, for like all corruption of the soul, they too must be accepted willingly."

"*Bull and shit,*" the wraith snapped. "*Corruption can be inflicted as well as coerced. Coerced just allows it to take root easier.*"

"They will likely hide where few men are, or places where men are not typical to go – tunnels, or cellars. Warehouses unused, homes abandoned. Like rats or the lowliest of roaches, they will have gone to ground. But I promise you, I assure you, with the Love of the Goddess at my back, with Her love for all mankind, I give my oath and word that we shall hunt these rats, we shall find them, and we shall claim vengeance for those they have taken from us."

Akaran clenched his hands around the hilt of his sword and grit his teeth tight against each other. "And I so swear I will bring pain to their sire."

"*You bring all the pain to their sire you wish,*" the wraith remarked behind him as her lips turned into an angry snarl of her own. "*As long as you promise that I have my own turn with the one that set the Landing ablaze.*"

He couldn't promise that. He promised he'd try.

But she wasn't the first in line for that particular glory.

***

"You're drunk."

"I am... not," Seline replied after she thought about it. "I am... well. I am not drunk. Does it matter what I am? I'm here."

"Oh, you're here alright," Henderschott replied as he ran his fingers through his ash-blonde hair. The 'here' in question wasn't his usual office. It was hardly an office at all, but more just, 'a place next to the gatehouse where he liked to go to yell at people.' There had been no shortage of people to yell *at* over the last hour, mostly in colorful phrases and ways to get them to, "Hurry the fisk up and get your asses down to the fisking port you cock-sucking sons of dog-fisking whores!"

That concept, even without the phrasing – or the phrasing, even without the concept – had been a steady roll of the tongue since that pain in the ass from the Repository had sent word-by-mage back up the canyon for *how* bad the attack had been. To say that she had excessive, personal offense to be left holding the bag (and the hand of her friend) down in Cableture was to understate the entire exercise. She was pissed, and she'd made it a stated goal to piss on him in turn.

Of course, his own anger at not being told the full state of the strike hadn't done anything for his mood either. Neither of which, as it turned out, boded well for neither the Lovers nor the 4th. The healer's arrival, in whatever state she claimed to be in, was just icing on the tart. "I'm here, and *you're* here, so what's the problem?" she slurred.

"Let's see. The last time we were in a room together with just the two of us, you told me that if I ever wanted my dick sucked again that I'd be brighter if I found a rabid goose and –"

"Yeah yeah, that's in the past. What matters is the *now*," Seline replied as she grabbed him by his tunic and smiled.

Henderschott, to his credit, carefully moved her hands from his shirt and set them at her side before he stepped as far back from her as he possibly could. "Look. Normally I'd love to have a screaming session with you, but I'm lying and I really don't," he replied slowly. "You're drunk, and neither one of us want anything to do with the other."

"That's not true," she said with a pout and a sigh. "I want something from you."

"If you had to get drunk first to get it, I don't want to give it."

"I didn't get drunk to talk to you," she replied. "I got drunk because of that half-blind asshole."

The Lieutenant-Commander rolled his eyes almost to the back of his head. "I'd heard there was something going on between you two. So let me reiterate: if you had to get drunk for *him*, then I *absolutely* do not want *anything* to do with you. I'll find someone and have you escorted back to the Manor where –"

Seline shook her head hard and then grabbed the wall to keep from falling over. "Nooope! Not the Manor. I'm fired. I think. She fired me last night but then acted like I was supposed to stay there this morning. Bloody all if I know; but I'm not going back."

"Fired?" Henderschott asked as his eyes went wide. "Whatever in the world would you have done to get *fired* from there? You eat drink and sleep that place. Sometimes for days on end."

She growled under her breath and tried to straighten her tan dress in vain. "That bastard priest. Hender, I swear, I don't want to know. You don't. You just don't."

"Don't want to know… what?"

"All of it. Any of it. Absolutely all of it. I don't want to know. That's why I'm here. So you can help me with that. I need your help. I need *you*," she implored. "There. You've wanted to hear those words for how long now?"

That comment was not worthy of a response, dignified or other. The question was though, and he crossed his arms as his eyes slowly narrowed. "Aside from drying out, what is it you need, Seline? I'm really, truly, busy and I don't have time to ask you a thousand questions."

She took a deep breath and idly fingered the mouth of the wineskin at her side. "I got fired from the Manor, I got drafted by the Maiden-Templar, I'm on a first-name basis with the man that runs the Fleetfinger's Guild, and I watched that damned priest do something last night that I don't wanna talk about or think about or deal about and now I want to *go*."

"Go where? And what do you mean, *drafted*?"

"I don't know and I don't care," she shot back. "Just… go. I want to *go*. Help me sell my house and get me *elsewhere*."

"You still gotta explain the 'drafted' part," he pointed out. "I can't do anything, and I'm *not* going to try to do anything, until you tell me how much trouble I'll be in if I go do it."

Seline took another deep breath and looked out the door at a cadre of the 4th as they marched out the gate. "She made me sign a document and told me I'd be a medicannia in the 4th now. I think the 4th. Either the 4th or the Lovers proper. I hope the 4th."

The soldier couldn't hide his shock if he'd tried. "What… possible… reason would you have had… to agree to *that*?"

She refused to meet his glare and casually played with the end of her ponytail. "To um… well. See there's this patient, and I thought she was crazy, and she is, but not just crazy, she's being stalked by a vampire and I wanted to go help her and to help her I needed to learn more and now I know more and now I want to leave."

"A… vampire," he said as his jaw went slack. "Of all of the creatures and myths you could've come up with to get out of working for them, you decided to go with 'vampire,' is that right?" he marveled. When she nodded her head rather daintily, he clutched at the side of his head and the new headache that blossomed there of its own free will. "How stupid do you think I am?"

"That's a very dangerous question," she flippantly retorted, "and I should know. I seem... I seem to keep asking that kind."

"I think the only person that's lost their mind is *you*."

"Nope, not just her," another voice interrupted as the speaker walked into the antechamber. "If what I just heard is true, she ain't lying."

Henderschott turned to face him. "Specialist-Major. You're supposed to be my bodyguard. Where in the *pit* have you been for the last hour?"

"Guardin' a body, just not yours," he answered as he reached down and scratched at his crotch. "Erine says hi, and no, I ain't telling you where I found her."

"Oh Gods," the Lieutenant clutched as he grabbed the side of his head again. "I can't. I can't deal with either one of you. The Maiden is absolutely furious and she's taking it out on my ass right now. I *don't* have time for half-sane tales and drunken women."

"I'm not drunk!" Seline protested.

"And she ain't giving you bullshit tales," Badin added. "Erine made it clear: the Lovers probably won't tell you what's really going on, so I should."

Henderschott crossed his arms and took a deep breath. "Explain," he ordered and then quickly added, "briefly. Very briefly."

The battlemage – to his credit – did. He managed to explain everything that the Eclipsian had told him (everything from the infestation of vampires to Donta's death and more) in under five minutes. By the time he was finished, the 4th's commanding officer looked like he wanted to jump off a cliff.

Seline went on to clarify and add a few comments here and there as well. "I don't know what kind of magic he claims to use but I'm telling you Hender, it isn't safe, and I don't wanna be around it. He almost destroyed the Manor last night and you don't know how grateful I am that he got sent down to the port," she told him before she leaned in closer. "Whatever magic bullshit he did made me channel an... ang... a Godde... you know what? I don't know. Some *very powerful* voice and it *made me do things*."

Badin blinked and straightened up. "He's got his powers back?"

"Sure does," she answered as she unhooked her wineskin and took another drawl from it, "and after caring for his ass the last while, I don't want any part of it."

"And he's at the port?"

"That's what I said."

The mage took a deep breath and quickly ran through all the ways that *everything* could be bad. "Lieutenant-Commander?"

"About to ask me for permission to go after him?"

"Yeap."

His boss took a matching breath and nodded. "You know what? Sure. I don't have a damn clue what's going on, and I think I'm okay with that. I think I'd be more okay if I trusted his handler, but since I don't trust you or Catherine, I'm *sending* her," he said as he pointed at the drunken girl.

She choked on her wine and sprayed down the wall with a mouthful of it. "EXCUSE ME? That is not what I asked! I asked –!"

"You asked me to help you get out of a legally binding contract with the Order of Love and or the Grand Army of the Dawn. That isn't something that can be thrown away at a whim, and I want eyes on him. I *told you* months ago that I thought he was the most dangerous man in the city and your reaction to seeing him work only proves me right," he snapped. "Let's speak bluntly: you *hate* admitting I'm right and you wouldn't be here if you had any other choice in the matter."

"Yes but... but... asking to get *away* from him doesn't mean *send me after him*! That's... no!" she protested.

"That's the best you're going to get," Henderschott retorted. "Specialist – go and watch whatever they're doing and come back with a report to me," he said as he pointed at Badin, "and you, you monumental pain in my ass, watch after the cripple," he ordered as he pointed over to Seline.

"Why do I get the feeling you're asking both of us to spy on our friend?" Badin asked with a small frown.

"I'm not his friend," the healer countered.

Henderschott gave both of them a withering glare. "I don't care what you are. I don't care how you feel about it. After what you two've told me and have hinted at? I want eyes on him. Period."

Seline sighed in frustration and flung her hands into the air. "Except that still doesn't get me outta the province."

"No, it doesn't. But. Once they find the bastards that attacked the port, I'll pull strings. Can't promise it'll work, but for you, I'll give it a try. *One* try. I need someone I can trust to make sure he doesn't burn the whole damn port down and since you're not inclined to do him favors it works better for me."

"Want me to tell the Adepts to charge the transport it against the Guard or other?" Badin asked while Seline whined something unintelligible and crossed her arms.

He grimaced and rubbed at his eyebrows with the flat of his thumb. "I'm tempted to tell you to go get on a horse and see if she sobers up by the time you get there, but. Given how pissy the Templar is being, I suspect she could use more heavy hands and healers. Go... I don't know. Charge it to their Order, and brag that you know Akaran. Had a couple of my men tell me that he's made all kinds of *friends* with the Annex. Didn't know *why* until now, but that's my life. Now how honest can you tell me Erine is *actually* being with me right now?"

Seline continued to pout while the specialist addressed his boss. "Sir, I'm not going to lie to you. I don't have a clue what Erine has for proof. I don't know what's real or not, but I know what she swears. I'd take it seriously."

"I *am* taking it seriously," the Lieutenant-Commander replied. "I'm sending you – and with a message. Tell the Templar that I know what she's not telling me and I expect to be briefed fully on what threats the city is facing when she gets back. *No bullshit,*" he stressed. "Make sure she gets the point."

As they turned to leave, another voice interjected into the conversation and all of Badin's confidence crumbled in a heap. "Oh, my good man. If that's all you're interested in, you won't have to wait to speak to the Maiden."

"Shit," the mage whispered as he backed up and bowed his head. "I uh... it's a... uh... hello again, been... been a while."

"Ah, Badin! It's good to see you again, my spark-slinging friend! Play with any more boats lately?" Riorik asked with a smile that went ear to ear.

Henderschott either missed the mage's sudden terror, or didn't care. Instead, he lifted his hands and gestured at the walls of the crowded little room. "Does this *look* like my office?" When no response was forthcoming, he turned to the thief and frowned. "Hi. I don't know who you are and I am exceptionally busy. If you'd like to make an appointment or report a crime, then –" he began before Badin shoved his hand in front of the Lieutenant's lips.

"Sir. Do you remember what I said about a man offering to be your friend?"

"Yes?"

"Badin! You're giving away the secrets to my success, are you?" the thief interrupted with a smile that was deadly as it was warm. "Only saying good things about me, I *sincerely* hope."

Seline groaned in disgust. "Oh Gods. You again."

"That is not a way to greet a friend, my dear. Or should I say, 'dear medicannia'?"

"Say goodbye," she muttered as she grabbed Badin by his arm. "Fine, Hender. I'll go. Just... do what I asked? Please?"

"Saying please, that's new," the Lieutenant muttered under his breath.

"Manners are important, after all," the thief added.

The mage, however, just cleared his throat. "We're going. Hopefully, whatever he's doing, he'll do it quick. Good luck, boss," he said as he flicked his eyes over at Riorik, "and Boss."

"Good luck? With what?"

Riorik's smile glinted in the faint light of the room as the mage and healer left for Cableture. Henderschott tried to follow, but he blocked the Lieutenant from leaving. The thief cut him off before the 4th's commanding officer could object. "I think he was suggesting that we should celebrate our newfound friendship," he said before he added, "because we are overdue to begin our working relationship."

"WHAT working relationship?"

***

The sun was setting on Cableture, and the mood from the combined forces under Catherine's control was so dark that it might have well already been midnight. A damn near full day's worth of a manhunt had left the garrison exhausted, hungry, sweaty, and thirsty – and that said nothing about how utterly drained the handful of priests and mages on hand were. What they'd found was surprisingly little, though he still couldn't tell if that was good news or bad.

One thing worth noting was that despite their rough start, the Maiden and the spy ended up with common ground sooner rather than later. Catherine wouldn't admit it, but she secretly found the presence of the wraith – a talkative, open being of suffering – as utterly fascinating. Even in short back and forth quips, the mouthy spirit had given her more information about the underworld than the Maiden had read in a hundred musty tomes.

That, of course, was by design. *"Be useful,"* Rmaci had whispered in Akaran's ear a bit ago. *"People are less likely to kill you if you can tell them things they want to know."*

The other design that they had to plan for was harder. Due to her nature, and the very fact that she existed, she wasn't able to provide as much help as they would've liked. The Staras, to their own credit, took hunting down monsters that could pose as human seriously... at least, they did this time. It was easier to get their attention when eyewitnesses confirmed some of the Maiden's positions.

So while they had to move Rmaci to the edges of the city to try and find evidence that their targets may have exited the port's stronghold, the holy-inclined and the combined army and navy detachment went to work scouring the center of Cableture. What they found was a spectacular pile of 'nearly nothing,' which resulted in more than a few angry grumblings from both the searchers and the search-ees alike. The latter had more than plenty to offer, and Akaran had nearly gotten punched in the face at least twice.

On the upside, they inadvertently disrupted a small smuggling operation. A missing child had been found too, and the young girl had already been packed up and sent back to her family in Basion. It was a victory, even if not the one they wanted. As the sun started to touch the horizon, Akaran stood on top of one of the port's walls and leaned out over the parapet as he desperately wracked his mind for where else to look.

It was a blessing that they didn't find anything overly amiss in the residential areas, and even the 'Naval Commons,' as a random captain had put it, came up clean. Or as clean as the Navy's barracks ever did. The sailors in the Queen's Navy weren't known for being the tidiest lot when onshore (or on the waves, for that matter). In fact, the Commons ended up being the easiest place in the Port to search – once word reached Admiral Maddon of their targets, and why, he was quick to order his underlings to fully comply in any way they could be useful.

The same could not be said of Merchant's Row. Even less could be said of the traders in the so-called Smuggler's Docks – located not that far from the Row – who apparently paid a sizable fee to a few people in the 4th to *not* conduct searches and seizures of their property. The only thing that expedited their hunt (outside threat of the gallows, Rmaci's warnings be damned) was the way that Akaran not-so-casually dropped Riorik's name in a few choice ears.

He was certain he'd pay for that latter.

He was right, of course.

In the meantime, the threat of another Hobbler-owed favor was far from his mind. When the three largest districts turned up nothing, an effort was made to pour through the harbor and work through one warehouse and storeroom after another. It wasn't an easy task. It was an exhausting, frustrating, and tiring one. Every time they cleared a block, they'd run into a new complaint – someone didn't want to open a door, someone didn't want to let the guard in. Someone put up a fight about being searched when they put up too much of a fight about opening their store for a sweep.

As they ran out of places to look, the Maiden caved and ordered men to start pouring through Yittl while others began searching the nearby countryside. There were a couple of small villages and farming communes to the east that might have become makeshift lairs for the bloodsuckers, but he doubted it. That left... almost nowhere. It either meant his tracking idea was completely bullshit (which he didn't think was true) or it meant that Annix and his minions had ways to hide that the Order didn't know how to counter.

Which was even *less* thrilling to consider.

All of which left him in an *exceptionally* dour mood as he stared out over the wall. "*Is it possible they swam away?*" Rmaci asked as she manifested behind him. *"I can't say that everything has been searched, but most has. To be honest with you, I don't understand much of the monsters you seek."*

"I thought you knew everything about the Abyss?"

"As you pointed out, it apparently doesn't like the damned to know as much as it wants us to think we know," she admitted. *"Even said, vampires are not true denizens of the Abyss. They are as unwelcome and unwanted in the rank and file as your Order is in Civa."*

He grunted and spit over the edge of the wall as he leaned against the rampart. "We're not taught much about them. Or at least, I wasn't. They're supposed to be extinct... or gone from Dawnfire's shores, at least."

She walked over to him and hovered in near-silence. She'd taken it upon herself to manifest a ratty robe over her shoulders – the best she could do, she claimed – just in case someone saw her and got the wrong idea about who she was working for. *"So then you don't know if they can swim or not."*

Akaran rubbed at the stubble on his chin and flexed his knee. The Maiden had been right; even with her efforts to patch it up with spellwork, it still hurt. If he didn't feel so pissed off, he'd have found a new cane to lean on. "From our experience in hunting Defiled, most species them don't like getting in the water. Well, physical Defiled, at least. Damned if I know if vampires need to breathe but walking corpses don't. Either way, get a body waterlogged enough and they float without control or end up being chewed up by the fish."

"I suppose most demons prefer warmer climates than a watery lair... Zell excluded, of course," she mused. *"Though I do suppose I see your point. The damned aren't known for having all the physical limitations of the living, but..."*

"But all the stamina in the world doesn't matter if you're too muddled to remember how to swim, or too monstrous to be able to do it. Can't imagine that getting stuck in the mud and eaten by crabs is a fun way to live out your afterlife."

"No," she agreed with a shudder, *"no, I assure you, it is not. The Brineblood's realm is that of an unfathomably deep lake, and you do not want to know what crawls on the bottom,"* she offered with a shudder. *"Though that doesn't answer the question about these particular killers, does it?"*

He sighed and shook his head. "I can't imagine that they'd be hiding out there," the priest replied as he gestured at the ocean. "They'd have to go really low to hide from the sun unless they found some kind of wreckage in the mud. Or if they buried themselves in it, I guess. If they were desperate enough, sure, anything's possible."

Rmaci flicked a chunk of ice out towards the bay and watched as it melted into the ether. *"The brutality they exhibited do not leave me to think that they are desperate for anything. Cocky, yes. Desperate, no."*

"Exactly my thinking too," Akaran admitted. "I can't think of anywhere else they could be hiding. The longer it takes to find them... if Annix has started to breed for the fun of it, we have a really big problem."

"What of the ships of the line?"

"What, the Armada?" he asked as he looked out over the waves. The 2nd Naval Armada was comprised of over two hundred ships – though the vast majority were out on patrol across the Alenic Ocean. There were only twenty currently in the waters off of the immediate shore, and seven of any notable size docked in the port. There were another fifteen merchant vessels and a handful of fishing trawler docked along the beaches of the small, u-shaped harbor.

She nodded and gestured her arms out wide. *"I know you've had people look under the boardwalk and piers, but have any of the ships themselves...?"*

Akaran pursed his lips and sucked in air. "The merchant ships, the trawlers, yes. Anything that was docked at port overnight, yes. Thankfully the Commander down here had the foresight to halt any departures after the murders were announced."

"But you don't know if they can swim."

"I... I don't," he answered slowly as he let his gaze travel out towards the middle of the harbor and the ships anchored there. "Catherine would, but she's busy."

"Busy? What could be more important than this?"

He shrugged. "She didn't say. Just that she'd been begged to go to the Office of Oceanic Divinations. Told me to keep my eye open and let her know if I figured anything out."

The wraith made a non-committal 'ah' noise and let it slide. *"You know... in my time serving the Empire, I was made aware of a method that the captains of your Navy would use to check the status of ships when they were too far away to easily yell for. Your people would merely send up a burning arrow. They'd burn blue if all was safe, or red if there was distress. Of course, a system of flags as well, but it's easier to drag an arrow into a flame and fire it than it is to hoist the colors."*

"Do they now?" the exorcist asked as his eye narrowed. "Don't suppose you found out if merchants did the same thing?"

"Well of course," she replied, *"of all the faults of the Queen's Navy, redundancy and messaging is not one of them."*

"I don't even want to know what you had to do to find that out, but..." he mused slowly, "...but what exactly would have to be done to have that signal sent?"

She hovered closer to him and mimed firing a bow into the sky.

"Whatever captain was concerned about the state of the fleet would order one of his men to fire into the air. Three blue for 'all is safe, confirm the same yourselves' or two red for, 'we have seen an enemy.' They'd fire one red with a bundle of cannon-powder attached if they had an emergent threat. The sound alone would gain attention. They call it the 'Lights of Dawn's Waves,' which honestly, makes perfect sense."

"I see," he replied slowly as he thought it through. "You wouldn't suggest that it's time to see some fire, would you?"

"I have seen enough flame to serve my interest eternal," she grunted, *"though you may be right. I don't feel comfortable approaching those ships on my own — if there's a nervous priest or bored mage there, I might not enjoy the trip."*

"No," he admitted, "you probably wouldn't. So let's go see what the Navy's up to while we still have time..."

***

"Ah, Maiden-Templar! I'm so glad you come," the squirrelly old man with ratty gray hair and an unkempt beard exclaimed as he greeted her with open arms. "Welcome, welcome!"

Catherine didn't think she'd been offered much of a choice, though she was happy to get away from the search, even if only for a few minutes. She'd also never had cause to step inside the Office of Oceanic Divinations before, and she had to admit that it was almost breathtaking on the inside. It was a tall tower situated on one of the highest points of land in the Port, and the main entry was two flights of steps up from the street.

Almost the full entirely of the first floor was filled by a massive pool of water that only allowed a few walkways along the side and a catwalk that bridged over it on all four borders. Except the pool wasn't decorative — it only took her a minute to realize that she was looking at a reconstruction, of sorts, of the entire southern coast. It was far more than she expected to see in this dingy-on-the-outside tower, and was more than enough to give the Order cartographers a run for their money.

"The pleasure is mine...?" she offered by way of introduction to the odd little man.

"Divinator Todstrum Matthecalics, at your service," the short wizard answered with an extravagant bow that would've been impressive if he was about a foot taller and a few years younger. As it was, it was almost comical to watch his robe flutter out and all manner of silver chains sewn into his sleeves and belt nearly scatter across the floor. "Most people call Tod, though, it's easier to pronounce."

She looked down at his oddly eager face and immediately decided he wasn't entirely to be trusted. "I… I see. Very well then… Tod. You have to know that I'm busy today…"

"Oh, I do. Very busy, very active. Already had your folks through here once. That… that was part of why I wanted to see you, assure you and all that, we didn't know about that. Or the writ. Or anything of that nature," he said in a rush as he turned around and marched up to the closest catwalk. When she didn't follow, he eagerly waved her on.

Against her best judgment, she followed. "Writ? What are you talking about?"

"Oh! Oh they didn't tell you yet?" he asked as his brown eyes went wide in surprise. "I fully expected them to. Well. I apologize either way. We didn't know that there was an interest in her from the Overseer, or we would've turned her away. I do, I do hope you understand that – we, ah, we're a place of research, and of learning Sometimes research is expensive."

Catherine slowly crossed her arms and stood perfectly still as small waves crashed against the faux shoreline under the catwalk. "Divinator, explain what you mean. Clearly."

The poor man flinched at the way she enunciated 'clearly,' but before he could answer, another man shouted out from off to the side, "He means he's sorry he took rent money from that Lovic prat you want."

Tod shot the other mage a dirty look as the Maiden clenched her fists. "You provided aid and comfort to an enemy of the Crown?"

"Yes, but, well. At the time we didn't know she *was* an enemy of the Crown. We only knew she was a woman with a great deal of coin and a willingness to provide some to aid our very very expensive very time-consuming research," he explained in a rush. "I told the other men everything I knew, so that's not why I asked you here. No, I'm afraid, different matter entirely."

His nervous cadence and excited aura was enough to make her want to shake him by his shoulders, but she had the sudden fear that his head might pop off if she did. So instead, she walked closer and towered over him. "I look forward to reading the report," she returned with just a hint of menace in her voice. "Now that you've already admitted to aiding and abetting, how can I help you, *Tod*?"

"Yes, *Tod*, how do you plan on helping the Maiden?" Headmaster-Adept Gorosoch intoned from a bridge overhead. "I apologize, Maiden-Templar, for his ramblings. I'm the one that had him summon you."

"Headmaster," she replied with a slight bow of her head. "It must be critical for you to be involved."

"I've had a few dealings with one of your underlings lately, and once I heard about the Divinators… lapse in judgment… I felt it necessary to take a personal interest. It seems a confluence of fates has brought me here when many other moving pieces in the body politic have also arrived."

She wrinkled her nose. "I've about had it with *confluences of fate*, if it is all the same."

The Headmaster chuckled and casually floated down beside Todstrum and placed a hand on the mage's shoulder. "Yet they do not wait for us, as about to be demonstrated. Now – *good* Divinator, perhaps now would be an ideal time to discuss what you've learned."

That did not help what was left of Tod's nerves in the least. He swallowed so hard you could hear it in the room overhead, but nevertheless, he tried his best to explain. "Oh, well, you see. How much is it that you know about what our Office does? The role we play in... well, the role we play in everything?"

He didn't strike her as a 'role in everything,' type of man, but he was earnest about it. "You... track the weather, announce the tides? That's the bulk of what you do, isn't it?"

"The bulk but not the entirety. As difficult as those tasks are, we have others we have to attend to. As a matter of course, of course," he explained without explaining anything. "It is beneficial to understand the tides and trails of ether across the oceans, too. Every sailor that tilts his hat to Aqualla, or one to the Hircanton, or to Whoever, well. They will attest that the high seas are no place to run afoul of errant magical eddies."

"Fancy way of sayin' that they like to catch foul luck by foul women an' not foul things they can't see," the other wizard called out.

Tod nervously tugged at one of the chains along the neck of his robe and made a rude gesture towards the other man. "Ignore him. My assistant has been in an uncouth mood since one of his projects got accidentally upended earlier by one of the soldier types."

"I don't care about his mood, and I'm in a hurry," Catherine interrupted. "Why did you call for me?"

"Well, you see, it's because... okay. Now you have to understand that most magic that flows across the sea is very benign. The true magic doesn't get invoked until you're deep beneath the waves and into Aqualla's realm. Lots of all that and such – true, no mistake, no shortage of air sprites and the occasional elemental being of the sky that flitters in or about but nothing big. Nothing ever big. Not on the surface, only the bottom." The Divinator looked down at the map of the coast and pointed to a singular dark stream moving in from deeper in the ocean. "Until... until now."

"Until now?" she asked as she leaned in and looked at the swirl. The more she focused on it, the more she realized that it was just a formless mass of shadows that was slowly working its way to the coastline. "What is it?"

"That... well. That we don't know," Tod admitted with a shrug. "We know that it isn't in line with the Laws of Normality, and it's skirting the Guidelines of Metaphysical Entanglements, though as the name suggests those really are more *guidelines* than they are *rules*, so some skirting isn't too uncommon. What's more worrisome is the aura this puts off isn't very old – it's only existed a scant matter of months, if that, and, well. Where it's headed."

"Where is it headed?" she asked even as a sinking feeling developed deep in her gut.

"Well... it's *there*," he said with a pointed finger, "and we're *here*," he added as he pointed at a small walled area on the coastline. "While it's impossible to be sure either way because since we don't know what it is we don't know what it's going to do, it does seem to be... well. And I know that you've already have all manner of chaos to deal with and we wouldn't bother you normally but given the earlier... you know. The *thing* we didn't know we did, I wanted... you know..."

The Maiden pursed her lips as she looked down at the blotch. "You wanted to make sure you told me now in case it turned out to be something that'd you'd get blamed for later."

The water-wizard nodded his head. "Or other ways to say that but more or less, yes. Truly, Lady, I don't know what this is. I have been in this office for neigh-on forty years, and hardly ever missed a day. In all that time, I never have seen such a mass before. If it gets closer to the coast, I could tell you. Of course, if it gets much closer to the coast, you could tell me and I wouldn't have to pretend that I know what that might possibly be," he said as he looked up from the tank and into her blazing golden-green eyes apologetically.

"Oiy! Tell 'er about the fish-talker!"

Catherine paused and tilted her head to the side. "Fish... talker?"

Tod shifted nervously. "I uh... well, afraid he's had to leave. Splitting headache, nausea. The thing... the thing is. We do employ a man who has the gift to speak in tongues of seaborne creatures. I truthfully think he's quite mad but there are others here in this institution that think he's truly a mage above us all."

His short, bearded, and grumpy assistant stormed up the catwalk and dressed down the Divinator with an irritated look in his eye and a frumpy look to the rest of him. "Not more above us than we are above the water," he scolded. "Listen, Maiden? Before he ran off scurrying back to his house, he said that a few of the more talkative fish he knows – and yeah, Lady, I know, that sounds absolutely mad as all pits – said it saw Dawnfire colors on a strange ship at sea."

"Fish... recognize... the colors of the Dawnfire flag?" she asked slowly, as each word rolled off of her tongue and fell on their ears like slabs of granite.

"Well, no. Fish don't recognize much more than each other and things that wanna eat 'em, but they do see colors. In a way. Our man, he's learned to tell what they mean into what we mean. Don't ask 'em to read a name nor any of that, but he *was* able to get them to describe the shape of the letters on the hull."

"How did... you know, no. Please, forget that I asked either of you how any of that happened. You have your magic, I have mine, and I have long-since learned at times, it is better not to ask."

"Oh but you might wanna ask," Tod's assistant replied. "Part of our job is to help the navy find ships they lost. Navy lost a ship. This ship? Sounds awful like it. He thinks the lettering on it calls it the *Huibutten*. Not a name I recognize."

The color drained from her cheeks as she turned back down to the faux coastline, ocean, and all. "It isn't *Huibutten*," she muttered under her breath. "Did that son of a bitch have to be right about *everything*?"

"You have the same tone with that curse as my wife does," Telburn interjected. She'd almost forgot he was standing there. "Akaran, I assume?"

"He has made far too much of a name for himself lately than I am in any way comfortable with," she remarked with an irritated sigh. "Yes, him. I've decided to give him a little rope."

"To see if he'll hang himself, or others?"

She gave the Divinator a very threatening, very withering glare. "Both might be an improvement. We're hunting a problem."

"I see. So then, he's at the docks? I assume you're headed there next?"

"Your man just intimated that we may have some sort of wild darkness approaching the harbor. You think I should be elsewhere?"

Telburn flicked his tongue against his teeth and stroked at his uncharacteristically-present beard. "I think if you're going, I will join you. He's been a very... distressing... subject to study."

She blanched at the way he said 'study' and gave him an askance glance out of her green eyes. "If he's that disturbing, why study him at all?"

"Education is not always comforting, but ignorance is rarely rewarding."

As they left, off to the side, and somewhere below her feet, a distinct voice was almost heard to say, "*[You cannot say warning wasn't offered.]*"

Todstrum just told himself it was his nerves.

Repeatedly.

***

Rmaci declined to follow Akaran further than the boardwalk, and that

211

was just as well. At his order, three arrows – burning blue as the midday sky – lanced into the air. It must have caught the navy by surprise, because their responses took it a lot longer than the spy had suggested they would. However, they did do as she had thought they would and the ships started shooting up matching indicators of 'All's well!' with burning lances of their own. The seven Navy ships at port put up their flares, and it was slowly echoed up and down the miles-long harbor and coastline all the way out to the horizon.

The Lights of Dawn's Waves made for an impressive show.

Except for one ship that didn't send up an arrow at all.

They waited, but while the other thirty-odd ships in the bay each announced their safety, all eyes went to the *Q.R.W. Shatterstorm* as it floated along in utter silence. Akaran described the situation with such vitriol and foulness that it impressed a few sailors standing nearby, but before he could finish swearing, the *Q.R.W. Houndshorn* pulled up her anchor and set herself on course for the *Storm*.

It was another long third of a candlemark before the captain of the *Houndshorn* drew up close enough to check on her sister ship – though, wisely, with all of her cannons turned to it. The cannons themselves were still an oddity for him to see in person; the concept of using burn-dust to hurl chunks of rounded iron out of what looked like glorified cooking pots had only caught on with the navy at the height of the Privateer Wars.

The Queen had made it clear that the walls of her castles would never be decorated with such wastes of steel because, "That is what the Crown has mages for," and other such dismissive remarks. This was the first time he'd seen so many in any given place, and the exorcist wasn't entirely sure if he didn't agree with the Queen on this particular topic or not.

Still, he wagered they had their place. Right now, their best place was to be aimed at the *legata*-class cruiser that still hadn't sent up any kind of signal. *Legatas* varied in size – from a small, ten-man skiff to an armored fifty-man patrol boat. The *Houndshorn* was on the larger end of that scale, but the *Shatterstorm* was maybe half of her size.

When the captain of the *Houndshorn* sent up a single red-flamed arrow and ordered her crew to disengage, the size of the *Shatterstorm* didn't matter as much as the question of how the priest could board it.

***

It turned out, that was a problem with a ready solution. In the space of the time it took him to order someone to get him on board, the captain of a ratty fishing trawler and an equally unpronounceable name offered to let him borrow his ship. When the priest asked why, the answer came in

Queen's Common so garbled that it was almost impossible to understand. Thankfully, a nearby soldier explained it simply:

"His favorite girl worked at the *Spike*. She's dead, he's pissed. You kill the goatsucks that do it, you'll never be hungry whenever you're here at port."

It didn't take long to realize – though it added on what limited time he had left to strike – that the trawler was so shoddy, small, and outright nerve-wracking to stand up in that he wisely opted for a different course of action – even if it took longer. He let the owner of the small fishing ship take him into the harbor to meet up with the *Houndshorn* – and promptly jumped onto the rope ladder offered to him.

All of this took time. A lot of it. And with the rope slick, his hands covered in sea spray, and the stress of the day adding to it? His knee felt like it was going to break all over again – magical healing be damned.

By the time he made it onto the *Houndshorn*'s deck, the sun was already halfway below the horizon. "Don't know who you are, don't know what kind of monsters has the port so upset, and I don't particularly give a shark's shit-eatin' grin," the captain said by way of introduction, "and I ain't thrilled with an Oo-lo standing here on my ship." Before the priest could retort, the sunkissed commanding officer pointed a calloused finger towards the *Shatterstorm* and added, "Except my barrelman saw a whole lotta blood on the '*storm*'s deck and not a single face peering out the windows."

Akaran looked over at the other ship and cursed vehemently enough that it earned a moment of respect from the captain. The *Houndshorn* had moved a good hundred yards away from the smaller vessel, but the priest assumed that the poor sod sitting up in the barrel lashed to the main-mast could see what was going on – if anything. "I have to go kill some things over there," he said after a brief thought, "but I'd like to make sure that what I'm after is actually there. With permission, may I use magic on deck?"

Normally, nobody in the Order would bother asking permission to use a spell or not. However, the Queen (or at least, *a* Queen) had instituted a very specific rule about the use of magic on the open waves, (or at least, the Navy). The rule was summed up as, 'If you don't ask first the crew has full legal right to throw you off the boat.' That, and it was good manners – and considering his planned second request? "Granted, but if it makes the cannon-powder so much as sparkle, I'm throwing you onto Aqualla's harpoon."

Not an unreasonable threat, all things considered.

"Illuminate," he whispered under his breath as he stretched his left hand up in the air over his head. A faint pulse of white light emanated from his palm, and he felt more than saw a faint pulse – no, two pulses – throb from the ship in question. A third throb pulled his hand back to the open ocean, but it was faint enough that he gave it no heed. *Damn wild magic,* he muttered inwardly. *Bloody oceans are a haven for it.*

"Shiny," the captain quipped. "What'd it do?"

"Not as much as I'd like," he muttered. "I'm going to need to climb on the bitch."

"Don't we all boy, don't we all," the captain gruffly chortled. "We'll get you close, but you ain't gettin' any of my boys to go with you – you understand?"

Akaran faltered but gave a curt nod. He didn't really *want* anyone else with him... but he also didn't want to go alone. His knee felt stiff and his whole leg throbbed from the overuse it'd had today, and he was busy doing his absolute best to hide the fact that his hands were shaking. Months without magic? Months without *walking* right? He'd overdone it today, *just* like the Templar had warned.

Just because he got it back didn't mean that it was doing him any favors.

But it didn't matter.

"Here's the deal," he explained as he kept his gaze locked on the other vessel. "Get me close, get a plank across it. Soon as I'm on, pull your ship back. If the sun goes under the horizon before you see my face again?" he asked as he clenched his fist tight on the hilt of his sword. "Fling every barrel of pitch you have in your stores on that thing and turn it into the biggest bonfire that you've ever seen."

"There's men servin' the Queen on that vessel, boy. A few I know. You asking me to burn them out on just your word?"

"There *were* men serving on it, Captain," he replied as oarsmen started to honor his wishes. "You don't want to know what's on it now."

***

Back on shore, similar thoughts were being echoed by his otherworldly assistant. Her cloak hung loosely off of her shoulders but the hood couldn't quite hide the ember glint in her eyes. *"I swear to whomever I am allowed to swear to right now, if you get killed before I get to move on, I am going to hunt you down..."*

"You can move on now, if you'd like," a new arrival interrupted her vocal musings on the far edge of the ramparts – and far away from anyone else. "Though, as none of us are sure of our final destinations, I imagine you are less sure than most. Yet I still won't stop you." The shade tensed up and prepared to jump off of the ramparts and into the ether when the figure put up a small light in the air and let it drift off over the edge of the wall. "No need to rush. Stay – talk with me. You'd be better off with me nearby, I believe."

"*Why is that, hmm?*"

"I know what you are."

She turned to the voice slowly. "*Oh do you now?*"

"I do. For many reasons; though, not the least of which is the one most glaring, should one pay attention to that."

It was one of those damned Oo-lo's, though she had to correct herself and remind herself (again) that technically, she was one of them, too if her bargain with Akaran was going to be honored. "*I went to great pains to cover what I am. This cloak takes more effort to be made visible across my burnt flesh than you would know.*"

"The cloak is the reason," the arrival said after they wetted their fingertip and traced it in the air. "The wind blows strongly up here, and the fabric doesn't so much as move. The rest is simple to deduce, Rmaci."

She uttered the exorcist's favorite phrase and patted at the blasted illusion in vain before she gave up and let it hang down as lifeless as her corpse was, wherever it was. "*I pray that I have not made so many other glaring mistakes as that…?*"

Karaj nodded and meticulously drew a faintly glowing rune in the air in front of their chest. "I am the aide to the Maiden-Templar. Do you think you would have been allowed in the same building as her without my permission?"

"*You weren't in the* Spike," the spy countered as she turned to face him directly. "*I looked for people like you.*"

"I wasn't speaking of the taberna. You made for interesting study whenever your former host was in the Repository," Catherine's assistant replied. "Don't bother asking; she didn't, and he doesn't, know that I knew. The boy had to be judged on his merits. You were one of them."

If she could've sucked in air, she would've. She'd heard that tone of voice before. Felt the kind of aura that Karaj was exuding from every fiber. That aura around someone when you *knew* that they were judging you and *knew* that they could crush you under their boot if they even *thought* about it. "*So what have you judged about his, and I suppose I should ask, mine?*"

"That you shouldn't be as concerned for what he's facing as you should for what he's going to. You can feel it – can't you? It's near. The air leading it is poisoned. The air at its back is grateful it has moved on."

Rmaci nodded slowly. "*I had hoped that if I broke from it, it would be forever lost at sea.*"

"Broke from it?" Karaj asked. "It poisoned your death. It is part of you. You can no more break free from it than I can break free from food, or sleep."

Every word the aide said made Rmaci cringe and she felt like she was shrinking under their gaze. *"Then what happens when it is destroyed?"*

Catherine's assistant didn't say anything for the longest time. As the *Houndshorn* prepared to dock against the *Shatterstorm*, they waited for the exorcist to make his move. "Many things, I imagine. Possibly things I cannot. It has to be destroyed, of course; so I would concern yourself less with the 'after' and more the 'when' and the 'how.' If tasked to bring the core of specter to heel, will you make the attempt?"

For the first time since she'd broken free of the Abyss's immediate chains, the wraith was afraid. Silent, fearful, almost trembling, she watched as a gangplank was extended from one of the Navy's warships down to the other. *"If it... if it keeps me from going back... there. Yes. I will."*

"That is a promise that not even an aide as such as myself can offer," Karaj admitted truthfully. "Yet I would imagine that your path out of the grave may be easier if you have filled it with others that should be dead."

"I've seen many to an end," she whispered, *"though you'll forgive me if I am none too eager to release the souls that have been consumed to their fates below. You could say that I have learned the error of my ways."*

"You have learned the *consequences* of your ways," the Lover debated, "not the error. Unlike some – I will not say many, or none – unlike some of those you brought low, that creature that corrupted your passing has corrupted the passing of others. Their fates have been ordained. They have been trapped in magic not of their own making, cursed by souls long gone. Mayhaps the madness that consumes them be a portion of their own penance, and maybe their suffering has made their sins less heavy. Or perhaps not," Karaj added before she could interrupt. "Perhaps their madness itself has been ordained – and none of us, not you, not I, not the exorcist nor the Maiden – will ever know."

She did her best to sigh and hung her head low. *"That's a great many words for 'kill them all and let the Gods do as They will,' you know."*

"The Gods will do as They will regardless of what you or I or any of the other players on the field do. We cannot stop Them, but we can carry out Their wishes – or confront Their injustices. Their hands in our realm may not be mortal, but they are not without obligation to adhere to simple rules."

"Rules I am aware I am in violation of," Rmaci replied wistfully. *"Rules I am in no hurry to brush against further."*

"A truth. However, were our lives according to our own schedules, I imagine *you* would not have wished to die until a ripe old age with grandchildren tending to your House, or tending to whatever rewards the Empress would have granted you had you returned to Civa alive."

She shook her head and shrank even harder. *"Illiya never saw fit to bless me with child. I served the Empire as I did because it was thought I could not; a childless woman has few uses, even in a land ruled by women as ours."*

"Mayhaps for the best. Children and spies do not always work to the benefit of either party," the Lover agreed as the wind picked up and made their cloak flutter in the breeze. "Said regardless; you have a task before you and you are aware of it. Go and see it done, so that more souls can rest tonight who spent the morning in anguish."

"Except for the anguish that awaits them in other places," she countered.

"Except for, yes. Except that we both know that a beast such as that consumes the damned, the divine, and all those in-between. You know that more than anyone else walking this world of their own volition, and more than anyone else walking otherwise."

Rmaci blinked and let the cloak around her body fade into nothingness as she prepared to follow suit. The source of so many of Akaran's nightmares was out there. It was waiting. It was calling. *"I do. Then may I ask a boon?"*

"You may ask, but I give no promise on offering."

"If your Goddess truly listens to you, or I, or that idiot man-child, ask Her this: grant that no pain be felt by those soon to be Heavenward for the suffering they are soon to endure."

"To them only?"

"The ones that aren't beholden to the Pantheon?" Rmaci asked with an unpleasant smirk. *"I'm sure this will only feel as if it were practice for what's to come."*

Karaj matched her smirk with one of their own, and when the wraith faded away, just laughed.

X. DOWN WITH THE SHIP
Early Evening of Madis, the 8ᵗʰ of Firstgrow, 513 QR

"You look a bit nervous boy," the captain quipped. Akaran had learned his name was Radise, though if that was his first or last was anyone's guess. "Thought your ilk was all brave at fightin' off monsters."

"You can train for a task and still not like doing it," the exorcist countered. "Many a brave man have gone into dark holes and never come out. That ship looks as dark as it gets... suppose it has to be, but still."

"Ships don't *have* to be dark, ya know. Plenty of scuttles there on the sides; ain't fault of mine it's locked up."

Akaran pursed his lips and nodded. "No, I agree. Pity we can't rip them open. The things on that boat don't like the sunlight."

"How bad don't they like it?"

"Well. If the old lore is true?" he half-mused and half-asked. "Then a good dose of the sun will fry 'em both."

Radise stepped closer to the edge of the deck and peered down. The *Houndshorn* was almost within range for the exorcist to disembark. "Both? Interestin'. I mean, I suppose we can open them up, but boy – you certain that nobody on her is alive?"

The exorcist nodded. "Or close enough to it that death would be a blessing."

"That is not close enough for me."

"Eight people are dead, including a paladin of Niasmis, because of what's down there. In there. They aren't the 'take prisoners' type. I don't feel anything living in there, and what I do feel, you don't want to know about."

That was partially a lie. He didn't feel anything alive in the *Shatterstorm*, but mainly? That wasn't an ability he was blessed with. He could tell that death reeked into the ether as the ship listlessly bobbed away in the waves, and that was as close as he could get. With all the blood on the deck, it was a given that they'd at least *been* there, even if they still weren't.

He didn't know which he would have preferred to be true.

Either way, the captain bought it. "Then... then, boy, there may be an option. You need the bowels of the ship opened up?"

"Really would help. They can't get loose, and I can't afford to be wrong about what they are. I *have* to get down there to deal with them."

"Well. Then, as you say," the captain replied with a frustrated sigh as he ran his hand through his long gray hair. "CANNONEERS – FORE AFT STARBOARD! LOAD 'EM SMALLBALL AND SWEEP THE DECKS!"

The *lungs* the man had on him were downright *impressive*. Even as the sailors responded immediately with assorted, 'Sir yes sir!' and 'Aye, captain!' up and down the line, Akaran tried to stop his ears from ringing. "Cannons? We can't sink her. I have to get on it."

Radise grunted and grabbed the priest by his shoulder. "Oh, she'll stay afloat. That I promise. *You* get your head on and get ready. They ain't gonna like what we're gonna do."

Before the exorcist could even ask, twin cries of, "CANNON – FORE STARBOARD – BE SMALLBALLED," and "CANNON AFT STARBOARD – BE SMALLBALLED," went out.

The captain pushed Akaran back away from the rails and did the same before he covered his eyes with his hand. The younger man decided that maybe, just maybe, he'd do the same even if he didn't understand why. "Ain't always the best of ideas to fire this close, ya see, but..."

"Fire?"

"Oh, and boy? Your folks'll be paying for the damages to that ship. You tell us to break it, sure. You got rank to do that. But it ain't coming outta my pay."

Akaran's went stark white. "Wait. I can't authorize the cost of a warship! Are you nu–!"

His objections went unheeded. "CANNONS – SWEEP 'ER CLEAN!" Radise shouted out the top of his lungs.

A shout that was met with the loudest thundering *bang* that the priest had ever heard in his life. Both cannons went off almost at the same exact time and the results were nothing short of spectacular. The *Shatterstorm* lived up to her name as two massive blasts full bundled balls of iron – each ball no larger than a child's fist – shredded her deck. Wood exploded, the mast buckled, and railings snapped off and flew into the water. Chunks of the side hull were perforated and long boards fell away as deck planks collapsed inwardly.

When it was over and done, the *Houndshorn* had peeled the fore and aft decks open like an over-ripened piece of citrus. What was left of the sun's light streamed down into the smoking, dust-filled holes. All Akaran could do was stare at the wreckage with his mouth agape.

Captain Radise, however, stood there with a big grin on his face and his fists on his hip, elbows out, as he displayed himself and the deep-reds of the Queen's Navy uniform for all the harbor to see. "Now. You. Go get to doin' your job while I go explain to my crew why I just ordered us to open fire on one of our own."

"I uh... just..." the priest tried to say as he looked down at the floating hulk a scant thirty yards away.

"Just what?"

"I want one," he whispered. "That... was... *amazing*! I didn't feel *anything* in the ether! You don't use any kind of mage charge for that? That's all... that's *mundane*?!" Akaran marveled as he looked up at the captain with his eye as large as a saucer. "Do... do they travel easily? How... how heavy? I *want* one."

"Bahahahah!" the older man laughed with a shit-eating grin all over his face. "Look here boys! We got a landman that's never seen a cannon before!"

"But... *can I have one*? Please?"

"Argue that up with the Queen, boy, her rules and all that. Get your shit. You're going on board in less time than it'll take for you to say your prayers," Radise warned. "Getting close enough to get you on then we're gettin' out of the way, like you said."

Akaran struggled really, *really* hard to put the idea of carting one of those magnificent iron machines with him on his travels out of his mind. "Yeah. Yeah, time... time to work."

Time to work indeed.

***

There was an argument about 'how' the priest was going to board the ship. He had expected them to make him swing over on a rope – an idea that was quickly shot down as, "Some bullshit that minstrels sing about when they're trying to bed the Queen's dog." Which, truthfully, was slightly paraphrased and borderline seditious.

Another idea was to drop him into a rowboat and let him cross the distance and perform a long climb up her side on his own. That was also discounted fairly quickly as the priest quietly wrapped a rope around his leg to hold his knee steady. Catherine's skills as a Templar or not, there was only so much that the medical corps in the Order could do – and he wasn't entirely sure he trusted her to the extent she claimed. Someone else came up with an idea to stuff him in a barrel and chuck it overboard, but that idea was completely ignored.

Instead, they opted to drop a rope ladder over the side and let him grab onto some loose rigging that the cannon-fire had dropped onto the deck and down along the side of the *Shatterstorm*. It was equal parts the best and the worst idea anyone could have come up with. It was also the only idea. By the time he reached the bottom of the ladder, he realized how much he hated it.

The deckmen above were under strict orders to put an arrow into the neck of anything that tried to jump off or out of the *Storm*. Or for spearmen to stab, hook, and pin any new arrivals down. Thankfully, neither group were needed. That was because the sunlight had done its trick – and the priest could see clearly into the *Storm*'s side. The light was enough to keep the vamps at bay, though it wouldn't last for much longer.

It also let him see inside, both to his relief and his chagrin. It was a bloody mess, but it wasn't – couldn't – have been entirely from the cannons. He saw bodies, and they weren't moving. He saw at least one severed head; but the neck it had been attached to *wasn't* laying in a pool of blood.

The vampires wouldn't be hungry. They'd be at full strength.

All it did was make him be absolutely certain that the rigging was entirely exposed by the light, even with the larger ship covering it with shadow. Once he was safely on the wrecked deck, he waved the *Houndshorn* back at the same time as he steadied himself with another prayer. This time, it was less for guidance and more for steadfastness.

Or at least, good aim.

The old lore didn't talk much about vampires. The new lore blatantly expressed that they should only be handled by, 'true-blessed fists of the Goddess,' which effectively meant that exorcists had no right trying to pick a fight on their own with one. Let alone two. Still, ever since his discovery at the Landing, he'd made a special point to carry a couple of extra tools with him at any given time.

The first was a wardstone carved and blessed with the essence of the Goddess. It hung from a loose rope around his neck. If they tried to bite high, it might serve to repel them. Hopefully. Even if briefly. The other was nowhere near as nice, and a flash of silver glinted in the fading light as he slipped the knife out from under his tabard.

He steadied himself and lobbed a cast of, "Luminoso – Corsinar!" into the closest gash on the deck. Holy light flooded up from under the splintered wreckage, and he counted himself lucky that the *Houndshorn*'s first mate had served on a boat similar to the *Shatterstorm* before. That, and grateful that he had told him where to look for the stairs down – and which end of the ship would have them.

A few minutes later, and this was going to be over – either with his head on a platter or their ash in a bag. The sun was almost gone, and luminoso wouldn't have the same effect on the bloodsuckers at the burning star overhead would. When he slowly slipped down the stairs, he wished he had more of both.

The magelight was enough to illuminate most of the nooks and crannies of the hold, but between the crew bunks and crates of supplies, there were plenty of places he *couldn't* see until he was right on top of them. Those places had more bad than good, and the debris he walked on helped keep the floor from being too slick with blood.

It did nothing for the stench.

The *Shatterstorm* should have held fifteen to twenty men. It was not going to be fun to check the bodies and make sure the roster's count was accurate. He didn't put it past them to try to infect a few and pitch them overboard – though he had no idea if that would even work. The lore said it took three days for a fully-drained corpse to reanimate, and that it had to be buried in defiled ground before the curse would turn it into one of the fanged fiskers.

Unfortunately, that was the old lore.

It didn't say a damn thing about vampires that could disassociate from their shadows. Either Annix was some kind of new breed, or he was older than the old lore. Neither of those options worked well for his peace of mind, and it was worse when he considered the implications for what that might mean for the potential brood. Nor did those options help when a wave hit the ship...

...and caused a head to roll across the floor.

"You know, normally I'd offer a chance of repentance," he called out as he looked around the hold. He walked slowly and with great care as he swept his eye back and forth as he moved. The tip of his knife trained wherever he turned his head as he held it at his side and held his right hand close to his chest with a softly glowing light emanating out of his palm. He couldn't swing half as well with his left, but he had a feeling that his blade wasn't going to be much use down here. "Except I'm not sure you can offer it."

Nothing answered him. He hoped nothing would. Fresh broodlings had a level of intelligence on the scale as a goblin – could understand simple words, use simple tools, could fight. It took weeks before a new spawn could talk well enough to blend into a crowd, and months before they could master the ability to hide in plain sight.

If the shadows talked, it meant that they were older.

Older would mean wiser.

Wiser would mean he'd be dead. Again. Probably for the last time.

He let his eyes travel down the darkness and counted the bodies that dumped on top of crates and others that had carelessly been dropped to the floor. As he passed one, his magelight reflected off of the bloody cheek and open, shiny, dead eyes from a body that laid haphazardly across a crate. He was two footsteps past it when he realized the blood wasn't red and the glint off of the eyes hadn't been white.

As a general rule, silver didn't make for a good weapon. The metal was easy to bend and easier to break. Silver against steel? It might last a few minutes if it didn't take a hard hit. Silver against flesh? It wasn't the best material to hold an edge. Silver against the blue-blooded freak that jumped off of the crate and went for his neck?

When his knife made contact against its cheek, its flesh sizzled like it had been thrown onto burning coal. It recoiled away with hot steam rolling away from the wound as it skidded back into the crates against the wall. There wasn't much to this one – it had short, wheat-colored hair, a lanky body, and commoner's clothes. Yellowed, almost jaundiced eyes glared at him as it exposed a pair of short, sharp fangs and hissed like a cat.

Akaran thrust his right hand out and shouted a singular Word that hammered the vampire like it had been hit with a full-body punch. "**EXPEL!**"

He assumed this was Ettaquis, whomever that was supposed to be.

But in this instant, it didn't matter.

The creature staggered and doubled over as its flesh blackened and split open with glowing orange cracks. It wasn't enough to kill it, but the sight of the beast catching fire made the priest flash back to the first time Rmaci had manifested in his dreams, and the brief lack of concentration cost him with a painful strike across his cheek that split skin and nearly took his eye.

The second vampire followed the raking slap with an attempt to claw open his chest with its – no, *her* – other hand. His tabard ripped and his chainmail screeched as her sharper-than-steel nails raked down the metal rings. He caught her by her throat and pushed her back with his glowing fist. Akaran faltered a second time when he saw who he was fighting.

She was pretty, with soft brown hair and skin that was paler than it'd been when they'd first met. Unlike her sister, there hadn't been a violent bone in her body. Or at least, while she'd been alive.

While she'd been *human*. "Rae… Raechil?"

It was one thing to be told she'd been turned.

The former healer from Medias Manor, the sister to Erine's missing bodyguard, and now-enthralled minion to Annix replied with a wordless hiss. Even in the limited light, there was no mistaking who she was. Or what she'd become.

It was another to see her up close and personal.

As he looked into her sickly yellow eyes, the other vampire recovered from the spell and charged the priest a second time. Akaran had to drop the woman and let the weight of his other attacker lift him up and slam him into the side wall. The impact stole his breath, but even as the vampire clutched his sides and sunk claws through his mail and into his ribs, he started to stab his silver knife into the damned thing's back.

Each shallow strike caused the vampire to scream and buckle as the blade ripped through skin and bent against bone. It let go and pushed away in agony, although the priest wasn't done yet. "**Luminoso – CORSINAR!**" left his lips and his right hand to blind Raechil and force her to scurry back into the thinning shadows of the hold while he advanced on the other creature.

As she staggered, he willed his chains into existence and flung them like a whip at the blistering, burning vampire as it tried to pat at its wounds in vain. They were different this time, to his horror. They were still silvery, still metallic, and still chains. But for the first time in his life, they were coated with a thin sheen of ice and had jagged slivers of cold ether decorating the links.

While he tried to wrap his mind around that, the chains wrapped around Ettaquis's legs and tangled him up. When the priest pulled back sharply, the phantom links wrenched the ratty-haired vampire's legs up into the air and dropped the monster onto his back. "**EXPEL!**" rolled off of his lips and through the etheric metal.

This time, when the spell hit, it burned across the vampire's legs – and caused the chains to sheer through them. The creature screamed in pain as it lost both of its legs from mid-shin down. Its feet arced into the air and started to disintegrate in a cloud of violent black and red ash embers. They hit the floor and exploded like a dropped bag of used charcoal.

It was going to take more than that to kill it, but for a moment, he'd evened the odds. Raechil recovered faster than he expected. She was mid-leap by the time he turned to her, but he caught her with his knife firmly in her ribs and almost in her heart. The former healer screamed and clutched at the bubbling wound as bright blue blood splashed out of the gash. As she landed, she crumpled forward.

As she fell, the blade snapped cleanly in half. She howled in agony and clutched his thigh. She came within an inch of ruining his knee all over again, but the rope along his leg tore apart before she could sink her claw-like fingernails into his flesh. Raechil lurched back and Akaran barely caught himself before he lost his balance on a slick patch of bloody boards; when he recovered, he planted his boot against her chin and cracked her teeth so hard that he heard a few of them shatter from the blow.

Raechil howled in pain louder than her companion; the sound absolutely deafening and horrifying. For one brief moment, he had a choice – capture her or kill her. He *knew* there wasn't any way to save her – and he couldn't bear to see her used as an example by the Order. The other one would have to do.

Akaran willed both of his hands to glow with a brilliant lavender light, and bent down to grab her head with the intent of purifying her from the outside in. He screamed when the other vampire lunged across the hold's floor and clipped the back of his left leg, which knocked him down hard on his back. As the world spun from the impact, the creature flipped around and tried to slash his stomach open.

It managed to split his mail and leave a gash, but the metal *thankfully* saved him from being disemboweled. The light hadn't faded from his hands, and he caught his assailant by the jaw and barked one final Word of, "**PURGE**!" that arced out of his palm and erupted out the back of its head.

Blinding white light erupted out of its mouth and eyes as it was lifted up off of the ground. Bit of brains, bits of bone, and bits of burning embers sprayed out of the back of its skull and all over the ceiling. The rest of the body ignited from the inside and short flames cut through its clothes. Akaran managed to push it off of his legs before the vampire burned up into a heap of black ash, bone shards, and orange sparks.

Raechil continued to howl in pain as she rolled onto her back and ripped her chest bloody in an attempt to try and rip the chunk of broken silver lodged deep in her chest. He couldn't let her, and he couldn't let the burning pain in his gut distract him more than it was. As she dug at the gash, he settled on a quick plan to stop her.

His heart recoiled as his mind justified his choice. He grabbed a loose sword and took a note from Riorik's handbook. The blade arced through the air in a pair of carefully-aimed blows that left her disabled, broken, and screaming.

You can't pull a blade free if you don't have hands.

He had no idea how to knock a vampire unconscious, or if you even could, so he decided to drive the steel blade through her collarbone and out the other side. He leaned in on it and *shoved* until the blade slid through her chest and buried itself into the wood below. She was still screaming when he limped up onto the *Shatterstorm*'s deck and willed a flare of light into the air.

Without hands, she couldn't get the silver loose. Nor could she get free from being nailed to the hull. It was over for her – and her panic meant she knew it.

He collapsed in exhaustion and pain as they flung grappling hooks over onto her deck. A few minutes later, and the *Houndshorn* joined with another vessel that did the same. As the sun vanished below the horizon, they pulled the beleaguered ship into port, although nobody knew it was the last time the ship would return to the docks.

* * *

The Alenic Ocean was not an easy place to hide. Sure, it had size going for it – it was an ocean – but until you traveled the better part of three weeks south, you didn't encounter so much as a few very errant islands. There was absolutely nothing even close to Cableture that would let you hide, minus a pair of inlets that trailed deeper into the Kingdom.

Except those inlets were literally days away from the port.

The pull she felt in the waters was nowhere near that far.

One thing about being dead: darkness couldn't hide secrets from her. The night sky was bright and clear, with the twin moons shining down and reflecting in the calm waters. Nothing looked out of place. There was water. There were waves. Some of the waves had small pieces of ocean debris on them, but nothing that was enough to make her think she was looking at the wreckage of a lost ship.

But as the Port disappeared over the horizon, and the lights of the warships in the bay vanished from sight, she could hear the screams. They were different now. Rmaci assumed it was because she had been cut off from it.

Then she realized that was wrong. The feeling of the wraith's presence was the same. It had that same dark inky feeling to it as she had shared in Akaran's body. It had that same sinking, twisting feeling that made her chilled and burnt skin feel somehow colder. It made her feel hollow. It had to be here. She knew it. She could hear it.

She looked until she found it. Once she found it, she screamed. She screamed and she flew back to Cableture like the Abyss was on her phantom heels.

It was.

* * *

Getting the *Shatterstorm*'s hulk back to the port wasn't an easy task. The Q. R. W. *Devaal* – another *legata*-class cruiser – had thrown additional grappling hooks to try and drag the beleaguered ship back to the welcoming arms of the city. Akaran, honestly, wasn't in much better shape. He'd warned off anyone offering aid from crossing over – there would be a lot of questions he'd have to answer if they did. None of them were best done in the presence of what would be shocked sailors and horrified doctors, he was sure.

Raechil's screaming didn't help him convince them to stay on their ships. If anyone had planned on giving him a hero's welcome when he returned, her cries surely slaughtered that idea as certainly as she had taken the *Storm*'s crew. The bodies were another problem. They'd need to be burned, and almost anywhere else in the world, he'd have done it while waiting for assistance.

That seemed like a truly bad idea with the burn-dust and cannon-powder stowed below-deck. Plus, it was a ship. Ships didn't always last long when they caught fire. He wasn't in the mood to find out if the *Shatterstorm* would be an exception to the rule. He also couldn't risk Raechil getting destroyed, though that was slim comfort as he listened to her screaming for a very long, very slow hour.

Not that the gash in his stomach did him any favors, either.

It wasn't as deep as he feared, but this was going to go onto a *litany* of complaints he planned to draw up once he got back to base. Any base. At this point, it didn't matter where. If he was going to have to fight more of these damn things, he wanted better armor issued from the Order. If not armor, then a better weapon. He still had that enchanted pick from Toniki packed away somewhere – and *that* had a way of leaving a mark on the damned.

Or maybe someone could do something to firm up a silver blade of some kind so it wouldn't bend if you stabbed anything other than flesh. Silver would break if you looked at it funny. Of course, the fact that it did was probably one of the main reasons she'd stayed down after he stabbed her with it. Down, but not out, and between her screams and the furious thrashing, it made it hard to check the bodies she'd left behind.

She and her companion had killed at least sixteen, and he presumed that would've been the full crew. If they'd tossed anyone over, the bodies would've been seen by now if they weren't weighted down. *Not my problem*, he finally had to tell himself as he laid the last one out with as much respect and dignity as he could give it.

His problem started as soon as the *Storm* docked and Catherine made her way on board. She'd picked up Seline at some point along the way, and the young healer had absolutely no desire to follow on board along with her. However, the healer – against her better judgment – wouldn't let him out of her sight until she gave him a once over.

Which turned into a twice over.

Which turned into a screaming fit when she saw the blood seeping out from the gash in his chainmail. The argument would've gone on longer if Catherine hadn't walked back onto the deck and ordered him back into the hold. He flat refused to let Seline follow, and neither of them complained.

"I can't believe you actually caught one."

"One caught, one killed. Didn't get the other one's name," he replied as he quietly stepped over and walked through the wreckage and around the bodies. "They aren't talkative. Assume it's Ettaquis, if Rmaci overhead his name right. We'll never know for sure. Any luck figuring out who he's supposed to be?"

"Word is he's a courier for Anais," she replied, "and the rest is just as well," she admitted. "We don't need them *talking* while we drag them into detention."

"About what I thought," Akaran agreed with a sigh. "It's bad enough I know her. Well, *knew* her."

Catherine looked at him in surprise. "I'm... I am impressed you did that much damage to someone you know. Most wouldn't."

"It wasn't like I was given much of a choice in the matter, was I?" he protested. "Look around. For that matter, look at *me*. Don't ask me if I'm happy about it, pits, don't ask me if I'm *okay* with it. But."

She nodded and sighed, understanding his point. "But indeed. We aren't always tasked with the easy choices," the Templar agreed. "Then tell me — you are sure that this is the woman you mentioned?"

Akaran walked over to the vampire and pulled her hair away from her face. He'd shoved a leather strap into her mouth to try to muffle some of her cries, but she'd mostly chewn through it. "Yes. Erine was convinced that Annix had captured both of them. I hoped... well. Doesn't matter what I hoped."

"No, I suppose it does not."

She knelt down and started to carefully examine the woman. Her right hand started to glow a soft pale pink as she brushed her naked fingers across Raechil's cheek and down her neck where she found a matching pair of dented scars on her skin. "The good news is that the old lore seemed to be about right. Expel didn't kill them, but it hurt 'em. Purge took out the other one. Had some success with luminoso and the bonds." He shook his head and stepped away from the ruined vampire.

He refused to think of her as a woman any more than necessary. She wasn't a woman, she wasn't a friend, she wasn't someone that had helped him get dressed or brought him food when he couldn't get out of bed. She was a humanoid demon that had murdered the better part of twenty people in almost twelve hours.

"Well. I'm going to let you in on a little secret," she admitted. "*You* weren't supposed to catch them."

"What's that supposed to mean?"

"I mean that you were to find me and I would put them both down. You only know the old lore because the old lore is all you're supposed to know," she said as she looked up and over at him. "I understand that won't settle well, but you're only an exorcist. This is outside of your purview. You should know that much. We don't intentionally task your rank on them for a reason."

Akaran blinked and almost nervously squeezed at the wound on his gut. "I don't think I like the implications of that statement, Maiden. What do you mean the old lore is the only lore... and that you don't task exorcists to hunt them?"

She refused to meet his gaze and answered simply as she stood up and stared down at the writhing beast at her feet. "I mean that vampires aren't as long gone as most people think. You're aware of the Second Crusade, but are you aware of the *concerns* they have in the Golden Empire?"

"The Golden Empire of Matheia? The whole place is a jungle full of things that don't like people. From everything I've heard, I feel like I should be grateful that the Alenic separates us. What of it?"

"A jungle with an infestation," she clarified. "It isn't severe enough to warrant an intrusion by the Order to burn it out, but what you refer to as the 'old lore' is ultimately updated almost every season. We call it the old lore because if the Queen or her minions knew how prevalent these damned things are, we'd be out of house and home."

"Are you telling me that the Kingdom is infested?" he asked with a hushed whisper.

Catherine shook her head and her coal-brown tendrils of hair fell down off of her shoulders. "No. Nothing of the sort. Vampires rarely try to cross the ocean; the trip is not easy for them. It's simply that if the nobility knew the struggles Matheia endures? It would not end well. For them or us or both, I am not sure."

"Or the Queen," he grunted. "The Golden Empire doesn't fisk around when they get threatened."

"Considering that they are the home of both the Guild of Hunters and the Blackstone Trading Company alike? As one-and-the-same as they are? No, they assuredly do not, as you put it, *fisk around*. They hunt the damned things constantly, though they've never managed to purge the continent." She looked down at the gash in Raechil's chest and pursed her lips. "I'll assume of the vast number of complaints vying for which one comes off of your tongue first, you'd like a better sword that cuts these?"

"Yes, I would," he grunted as he crossed his arms, "and no more fisking secrets."

The Maiden-Templar gave him a smoldering smirk. "As you will come to learn, if you grow into it, the Lovers exist on a mountain of secrets. Both for our safety, and the safety of those we care for."

He bit back the first obscenity that came to mind and settled for a direct challenge. "*Fine.* Then maybe if you're holding anything back on how to fight these shits, would you mind telling me sooner than later?"

"I had to make sure they were truly before I told you. I gave that poor girl outside more information about what's going on than I really should have as it is," she lamented, "though I won't make that mistake again. Her argument was convincing."

"She has that kind of way about her," he reluctantly agreed. "So what happens to her?" he asked as he pointed down at Raechil. "Do we go ahead and cull her or...?"

"I could only wish," Catherine replied after a moment. "We'll need to get her back to the Repository. Old *or* new lore aside, we'll have to study her. There are methods we can use to learn more about her sire and hopefully track anyone else he's spawned. I don't think I trust the security from the waystation here at port to hold her while we do it."

"Yeah. I can't possibly imagine that Annix will be any kind of thrilled that he's lost two of his minions and we've abducted a third. He'll make a move for her, though what kind..." he replied as he let the idea trail off.

"Murder or rescue. Either way, blood will be spilled."

"Exactly. You're not going to like this but we're going to need to let the Guild know, too."

Catherine gave him an askance look. "Oh, I already had words with them. Writs were issued, under mutually-agreed seals in the event you were proven to be correct."

"Was I right about the size of the bounty?"

She refused to look up at him even as her tone took an edge. "The blame for that *expenditure* will fall on *you*, so you are aware. I would advise that you do not speak to the Caretaker of Coin back at the Repository if you value your face... and do not let him near your food, if you desire to keep it in your stomach."

He blanched but otherwise stayed silent.

The Templar looked down at the vampire and uttered a brief, "Dammit," that for some reason, took him by surprise, and earned a tired little giggle from his lips. "Bind her stumps behind her back and bag her head. The world doesn't need to know what we've caught and I daresay that if we roll a barrel full of vampire out of here, that it would raise more questions and concerns than any of us want to deal with. While you do that, I'll get an escort ready. We'll move her to the waystation and bind her with wards there before we move her north."

"It'd be too much to ask that we can get what we need from her here, and banish her before the sun rises?"

"The Navy is going to want their men back, and they're not inclined to wait. They only stayed back because of the screaming," she answered, "and I've no desire to stay in this... gore-soaked hulk... longer than I must. The smell is..."

It was entirely, utterly, and completely impossible to argue her point. "Maiden? Don't ask me to help with whatever has to happen to her. I know. She's not Raechil anymore. She's not human. She doesn't have the same... considerations... as we do. We as people."

She nodded in understanding. "Except you knew her, and have no desire to see what must be done."

"With no offense? I've spent the last four months coping with a woman I knew being tortured in my head and I had a front-row seat when some of those atrocities were carried out. I'd prefer not to have a hand in doing it to this one and earning new nightmares. They may argue with the old ones."

"Request granted, but only because we have others that can do the job. Do not expect that to be the case every time."

Grateful and filled with dread at the same time, he bowed his head in acceptance. "Should I even ask what you have in mind? Or is that 'new lore' only?"

She looked down at the struggling thing at her feet and pursed her lips slowly. "If you don't want to watch, then you don't want to know. Ask me again once we learn her truths." Catherine looked around the hold and sniffed deeply as she made a disgusted look. "Both of which happen after we leave."

"Yes, Maiden."

"Akaran?"

He stopped rummaging for an empty (and clean-ish) sack. "Maiden?"

"I know we discussed it earlier, and I had decided against leaving you here, but, I had another warning of a coming darkness on the waves while you played sailor. I pray this was it, but I just had an Adept and an Aquallan tell me very differently. I'm leaving you in Cableture with a squad of wardkeepers while we learn what we can about this Annix creature. We'll assess the next step after, and go to hunt – on the oceans or in the streets, whichever seems more prudent."

"Shit. Daringol. The *Hullbreaker*. It really exists?"

Catherine wavered and finally replied, "Seems to. It *must* be is put in its place and *left* there. Old history should *not* be an event that occurs once a season as far as both I and the Order are concerned – nor should exorcisms. I fear your past is not done haunting you. If that's the case, I expect it to be sent to memory *for good*. Do you understand?"

That was the kind of promised threat that didn't leave any room for argument. His mind immediately went to the visions that Rmaci had shown him of the ship of the dead and all the warnings he'd given everyone else about it. He wasn't entirely sure he liked the idea of someone turning that warning around on *him*, but nobody asked. He accepted the order in silence, and worked to bind Raechil's arms and head as best as he could while Catherine gave him one other instruction. "I just want this to be over. I want back in Basion, and I want find this son of a bitch."

"You'll have another son of a bitch to find first," she quipped. "I understand you know him – Headmaster-Adept Telburn? We don't… get along. He's somewhere on the docks, if he stayed where I asked him. If he wants to be helpful, he can help bind this creature for transport. I'm sure I'm about to have my hands full with Admiral Maddon about *this*," she said with a tired gesture at all of the laid out corpses and the ruined ship before she cautiously worked her way out and started to engage in the local politics that needed to be addressed.

One threat was enough.

He didn't need the navy to blame him for the dead.

The Navy ended up being the least of his concerns. The vampire did not give up her struggles as he tied her up, though her lack of blood and the silver in her chest had finally started to slow her down. If she'd been anyone else, almost anyone else at all, he might've tried to see what would have happened if he had opened up one of her arteries to bleed her out faster. It wouldn't (or shouldn't) kill her, but it might make it easier to transport her.

He just couldn't bring himself to do it when he looked into her yellowed, sickly eyes. What he could do was make sure that the ropes around her elbows were so tight that she couldn't move her arms at all, and he added a second rope around the mouth of the sack that he tied around her neck (and another around her wrists to keep the questions to a minimum). That still didn't solve the locomotion problem.

The Bonds of Love did, though they only served to give him enough strength to haul her up and onto the deck. Once he got her up there, he was greeted by a pair of wardkeepers who did not exactly look thrilled to be on call. They looked less thrilled to have to place runes on her to help pacify her struggles – and much less thrilled to have to pick her up and carry her.

Not that it lasted long. Or even as long as it was supposed to.

The Navy, as expected, rushed on board the moment that the priests were down the gangplank and safely on the docks. Their screams and shouts and the ensuring argument when a sailor rushed down the plank and ordered everyone to stop until he had an explanation that satisfied him took a few minutes. They didn't listen to Catherine, and didn't appreciate the attitude that Akaran took. She stepped in before he could get punched in the jaw – and left him face-to-face with one of the last people he expected to see.

"Badin!"

"Hey, my friend. I'd say it's good to see you again, but… you look like shit," the specialist replied.

"I hurt."

"You're a walking infection waiting to happen," Seline scolded from behind the mage. "I'm not stitching that up. Someone else can do it."

Akaran blanched and reflexively covered the gut wound. "It doesn't need stitches."

She gave him a blistering look. "It doesn't need be hanging out in the open either, but there you go walking around with it for the world to see. I thought chainmail was supposed to *protect* people."

"Now now," Badin chastised, "I'm sure the other asshole had a big sword."

"Claws," the exorcist corrected. "Many claws. Listen, I'm so glad you're here but I gotta talk to Seline," he replied before he tried to get a word in edgewise with the healer. "I didn't tell you something earlier. I need to. You won't like it, and I'm sorry."

"I don't like anything you tell me," she groused. "It's taken you this long to figure that out?"

On the gangplank, the argument continued between some captain or other and a few furious, almost brawling sailors. They'd blocked the way for the wardkeepers to get their captive down the gangplank – and they weren't listening to Catherine's orders.

"It can wait," Badin interrupted. "What's this bullshit about you working for Riorik? Have you lost your damn mind? The whole damn prison is pissed about it."

"*With*, not *for*," Akaran countered. "Some stuff had to get done. How'd you get out of the dungeon?"

The mage gave him a shrug. "Some heads blew up. Turns out they don't think I can throw lightning bolts into a castle from inside a dank hole in the ground."

It was a hard point to put up an argument against. "I'm sorry I couldn't do more to get you out. I am. Things here have been beyond insane. It's... I can't even tell you where I think I should start."

"You're alive, I hear you can do magic again, there's monsters I don't want to know about all over the city, and you're on the warpath. Does that more or less explain the situation?"

"Well, yes," he had to reluctantly admit. "There's a lot more to it but first, Seline, I really do need to talk to you."

"Then talk," she huffed as she crossed her arms over her dress.

He didn't get the chance.

As it should've been expected, one of the Queen's finest made the worst decision possible. That was to be expected by the navy, and expected more often when at port than at sea. Still, nobody saw it coming.

One of the sailors came up from the slaughter-filled hold and charged into the middle of the wardkeepers and arguing commanding officers. Without thought nor care, he grabbed the bag covering Raechil's face and wrenched it away. She howled and spun, and blue blood splattered from her covered stumps as that bag fell away.

The sailor saw a wide-eyed, bloodied, inhuman murderer.

Seline saw someone she'd almost considered a sister.

Akaran saw Raechil realize she was a few feet from escape. He willed his chains to manifest while people shouted in surprise, and lashed out at her. One of the strands caught Raechil by her left leg, but not fast enough to keep her from diving into the water. She sank, and he pulled back. She briefly bobbled to the surface but snapped the ropes around her waist and screeched at the crowd.

He did the only thing he could think to do – and he'd wonder later if he did it to stop her from escaping, or did it to save her from the torments Catherine had planned. He dove into the surf off of the dock after her and tweaked his knee as he landed in the chest-high water. The exorcist forced her down under the waves with both hands on her head, and called out the same Word that had exterminated her companion.

Raechil dissolved in a flash of light.

A blast of water erupted around him and divine light illuminated the entire shoreline. The effect caused the edge of the beach to glow for a handful of wonderful heartbeats. The wonder ended when Rmaci manifested on the docks, naked and horrifically maimed for all the world to see.

A scream of, *"NO!"* left her lips at him was full of all the terror her unholy form could muster.

Some of the sailors thought she was the ghost of the woman he'd just killed. For a heartbeat, Catherine did too. The wraith howled in frustration and gave no thought nor care to who saw her or how. All she did, all she could do, was condemn him in every language she knew.

The Maiden's left hand flared to life with purple ether and she gripped the wraith and squeezed her mouth shut as the magic she channeled let her interact with the dead woman for at least a moment. "Mind your tongue or be banished from this realm!" she thundered as she added, "If I don't have to banish you *now* to calm these idiots down!"

"*Please!*" the wraith pleaded. "*Do it! Send me off – please!*"

The desperation in her voice shut the Lover down cold. "What?"

Rmaci grabbed at Catherine's other hand and placed it where her heart had once between and *pushed* it into her chest. "*Banish me. Exorcise me. Whatever it is you people do to things like me do it now, please, I beg of you!*"

"Maiden? Rmaci? What's going on up there? Someone talk to me!" Akaran called out from below.

"*There is no time for talking! You just told it where you are! Get out of the water — get out of the water and never return!*" she screeched. "*YOU HAVE TO LISTEN TO ME YOU HAVE TO GO!*"

The exorcist painfully waded through the water and tried to get back to the beach. "I'm weighed down with armor, what's left of my knee is killing me, I'm getting out of here as fast as I can. What's wrong with you, other than the obvious?"

"*WHAT IS IT YOU KEPT SAYING?! It likes WHAT?*"

"It? What *it?*"

"*DARINGOL!*" she screamed as she disappeared from Catherine's grip and reappeared floating in the air beside him. "*WHAT DOES IT LIKE?*"

Akaran blinked slowly. "Warmth? But we're at sea...? There's no...?"

Badin simply stood on the dock beside Seline and watched the exchange go back and forth. The healer stared in shock while he slowly crossed his arms and covered his mouth with an idle hand. "I... I understand I'm late to this party, but do you know... just... out of curiosity... what all this fuss is about? Or what... what happened to her skin?"

Seline didn't answer.

She couldn't — there wasn't enough time.

"*THERE ARE ANIMALS IN THE OCEAN YOU FISKING BULL-LICKING PISS-DRINKING IDIOT!*"

His face twisted in a slow 'o' shape.

The realization was too late. *He* was too late.

A wall of water swelled up in the bay directly behind the *Shatterstorm*. Before anyone could react, the legata-class cruiser was *lifted* effortlessly up on top of a wall of water. Her hull split in two and all the debris inside tumbled into the waiting ocean below. A ghastly shape under the ocean lifted the ship a good twenty feet in the air before it disintegrated into heaps of wreckage.

The wall fell apart as a new ship appeared to take the *Storm*'s place. It was a hulking, heaving mass of rotted wood, a devastated hull, and sails that were little more than fluttering strips of waterlogged cloth. The sailors on board — if you could call them that — were anchored to the decomposing planks and watched with lifeless eyes as their vessel arrived in the port city.

But the horror wasn't the crew.

It was the ship. It was what had wrapped around it. What had tried to take it into the depths. What had tried to consume the abomination. What had tried, and failed, and had been consumed in turn.

It was the yeshal. The squids that the local fishermen loved so much. The delicacy sold on every street corner in the city. The salty, stringy, purple-headed, cephalopod that lived all over the area. Only it wasn't. Daringol *liked* animals. It found one that liked it.

It had found one out in the ocean that it could keep.

It was the biggest yeshal anyone had ever heard of outside of myth.

The squid had tried to pull the *Hullbreaker* under. That much had worked. The yeshal had tried to rip it to shreds. That part hadn't. Daringol, however, was only delighted to find a new shell and new warmth to migrate into. It couldn't break away from the ship after the yeshal had died – but it was able to claim it anyway.

Daringol hadn't taken only the squid. It hadn't taken only the crew. It had done more than claim them both. It had done the impossible. It had taken a plant. A plant that was long dead, long gone, and long turned to lumber.

As his mind slowly let him come to terms with what he was staring at, the immutable truth came to mind and understanding right away: the spirit that had dogged his steps, that had infected his leg, that had terrorized a mountainside? The damned thing that he was certain he had banished to perdition months ago? The nightmare he'd had almost every day – the one he'd warned those closest to him to run if they heard of a sighting?

Now all of the people he cared about in the city were right here.

And now Daringol had a new pet, a new core, and a new ship.

Except it didn't just have those things. It *was* those things.

Something cracked in the back of his mind and he dropped to his knees in the debris-filled water as he accepted his fate. Without question or hope to stand against it, the only thing he knew for certain was one single, horrible, damning thought. His sanity cracked even harder as he dropped his spells and his hands to his side and began to laugh.

The *Hullbreaker* had arrived.

XI. INSANITY'S RECKONING
Late Evening of Madis, the 8ᵗʰ of Firstgrow, 513 QR

"WHAT THE SHIT IS THAT?" Badin screamed at the top of his lungs.

Nobody answered. Nobody had *time* to answer. The *Hullbreaker* pushed aside the floating wreckage of the *Shatterstorm* as parts of its hull began to *unravel* like a tapestry. Rotted boards mixed with elongated tentacles and etheric tendrils peeled away from the edges of the ship. The monstrous horror swung a length of her hulk around and shattered the next-closest vessel with ease.

As sailors fell into the water in an attempt to run from their sinking ship, a wave of tentacles poured both into the harbor and into the corpses from the *Shatterstorm*. Bodies began to animate as the people on the beach and boardwalk alike scrambled for safety — and tried to come to terms with what they were witnessing. All of them, except for one.

Akaran simply stared and laughed.

Catherine managed to react first, and the Maiden-Templar was quick with an invocation that *somehow* managed to give backbones where most had disappeared. Rationally disappeared, but disappeared nonetheless — and her spell slowed the retreat of the dock's sudden defenders. "I do not know nor do I care what it is! It is an abomination! WE STAND AND FIGHT!"

"*It is Daringol!*" Rmaci screamed at the Templar. "*Should you value your souls, run!*"

Similar responses abounded, but the Maiden grabbed the wraith again and pulled the spirit with her off of the pier — by force of will exerted on the ether around the wraith itself. "He told me that it's just a wraith! *That is no wraith!*"

"*I happened to be present when some of those conversations were had and I am absolutely certain he cautioned you that it had taken over a ship,*" she spat back. "*Neither matters now. It is* here, *and we need to be* elsewhere."

"We cannot, we *will not*, abandon the harbor to a demon," Catherine scolded as they dove into a warehouse with sailors and wardkeepers alike – none of which had any idea what to make of the Maiden arguing with another *creature*. By the time that the Lover had them calmed down, more chaos had erupted outside. "You have *much* to answer for."

"*Oh, blame the dead woman* later. *You have other things to worry about right now than me!*"

"Blaming the creature that was born of it," Catherine snapped back as she addressed the assembled throng. "WARDKEEPERS! We DO NOT allow it to pass the dock!" she shouted as another group engaged the beast outside.

Her idea was correct, if not slow. Poisonous, inky fog rolled out of the ship and attempted to smother the handful of sailors and dockmen left within close range of the decrepit vessel. Telburn reacted swiftly in the face of the monstrosity and established a defensive shield that blocked the first wave of malicious energy that radiated off of the beast. Notably, he defended Akaran – who looked up at the unblinking, rotted eye of the giant squid and...

...and did nothing more than giggle brokenly from his knees. The pain in his leg didn't register. The screams didn't. Nothing registered.

Nothing but the inky, fathomless void in the dead squid's eye.

The world shut down around him even as Badin landed in the water, grabbed his shoulder, and tried to get him to move. He didn't budge. He couldn't. All he could see was the shadow that had swallowed him months ago. A lifetime ago. A lifetime of seeing the void creep up over him, a lifetime's worth of watching it swallow him whole again and again, night after night, even before Rmaci had intruded in his dreams.

Nights that were filled with memories. Nights that were filled with the fleeting shapes of hundreds of faces caught in the wraith. Nights that were filled with their grasping hands and desperate claws. Nights that he'd never forget.

So he stared. So he laughed.

He broke on the inside.

"I can't get him to move!" Badin screamed up at the Headmaster.

Before Telburn could respond, the spy appeared next to him and put her hand on – and then into – the back of his head. "*His mind has... oh this is a poor time for that,*" she uttered as her cloudy eyes turned slate black.

The battlemage twisted around and brought a hand full of sparks directly to her face as he recoiled in horror from her blistered, burnt, and frozen visage. "With him or against him?"

"*If I say friend, will you promise not to electrocute us all?*"

"If you aren't trying to kill us, yes, if not, no."

She wrapped her arms around Akaran's neck and gave him a futile pull. Catherine could get a grip on *her* but she couldn't on anyone else and honestly, it wasn't the least bit fair. "*I like you*," she quipped. "*We have to move him quickly – Daringol is here for one thing, and it's him.*"

Badin whipped his eyes back around at the twisting, floating ship of the damned as it began to disgorge its crew. "That's… but he destroyed it. It's back?"

"*Does it look like it's gone?*" she snapped. "*Hurry!*"

To her surprise, he didn't argue the point. He grabbed the exorcist and *pulled* as hard as he could until he had Akaran's dead weight tucked in the relatively-safe-but-honestly-not underside of the pier. "What am I supposed to do now?"

Rmaci looked out at the bay and the hulking vessel just yards away from where they stood. "*Keep him alive. In the shadow of the ship, his presence may be masked. Or may be easier found. Either way, the ship has a crew – and they will come. You know the beast?*"

"I know it doesn't like being blasted by lightning."

"*Few things do,*" she admitted. "*Do what you can to protect the idiot.*"

He pulled a knife from his belt and flipped it around with the blade pointed down as sparks began to crackle off of the tip and edges. "What are you going to do?"

"*Try to save us all,*" she whispered as she dove inside Akaran's body – and went straight to his turbulent mind, "*or at least just me.*"

***

The Dawnfire Navy was known for many things. Cowardice was not one of them. While the soldiers dockside ran for cover, few of them ran away entirely. It was a credit to their training, if nothing else. Instead, they did as men with cannons and bows often did: they attempted to repel the interloper.

Thundering blasts of cannon-fire punctuated the chaos in the harbor. Each sharp crack of iron balls as they left their steel sheathes behind and the explosions from black powder bombs that roared from their barrels answered every scream and crash from the beast in the bay. Clouds of smoke lit up with bright flashes of light with every boom. The *Houndshorn* lead the charge, and as cannons unleashed thundering doom, archers across the bay picked their targets and let arrows fly.

Daringol made sure they had plenty to pick from.

Though if it was bothered in the least by the heavy balls of iron and thin shafts of wood that penetrated its hide, it didn't seem to show it. Not everything was a failure, however, and there were brief glimmers of hope. Order Wardkeepers and the Maiden-Templar herself hunkered down on the docks and took the fight to the monster with all of the courage she could encourage them to muster – and her instructions were swift.

They had to be.

The *Hullbreaker* disgorged a ship full of rotted dead that had become one with writhing tentacles and the wraith's essence. Each one was a soul, lost and twisted, controlled and confused by the wraith. That was the nature of a nesting wraith – to corrupt, to grow, to spread, to claim other souls for itself. They were a twisted result of the broken world they all lived in, but the nightmare that made up Daringol's core was ruined even beyond that.

It should have been destroyed when Akaran tore it to shreds in Toniki.

While the wardkeepers on the docks couldn't do much about the *Hullbreaker* itself, the multitude of animated corpses it spat out were just that: animates. Animates were a task that the Order excelled in. Like Akaran before her, Catherine made it a point to announce their weakness:

Aim for their heads, or damn them with a spell.

It wouldn't solve the problem of the ship.

But destroying her crew might buy them some time.

***

He wasn't cognizant of what was going on. Not in the least. He was in his own world. Except it wasn't *his* world. She'd liked being in his world. It was pleasant. This place wasn't.

It was dark. *Empty*. A cold wind whipped around her as she stepped foot inside Akaran's mind, and it buffeted against her burnt and frozen flesh like a gale storm. Even worse, she could feel it. She felt it, and the burnt embers across her flesh billowed into short-lived flames that erupted in the cracks of her exposed flesh. The ice in her veins shrank in the face of the empty void.

It howled all around her. It howled around him, too, as he knelt in the center of the inky emptiness. Or presumably the center. A place like this didn't have edges or boundaries. It existed because it *existed*. It didn't matter what the rules of physics or metaphysics were. It existed because his mind had decided it needed it to exist.

And because he'd seen it before.

The blank look on his face said it all. He rocked back and forth as he stared down at a pile of broken glass in his hands. Each piece of glass had a different reflection in it. Some were of him standing with his weapon aloft in the face of the spirit that had wanted to swallow him. Others were glimpses of the inside of the conglomeration of souls itself. Yet more were faces she didn't recognize – doubtlessly some of Daringol's other victims.

Ones that hadn't been so lucky to escape like he had. Ones that he sent screaming into the void like *she* had. Others that he'd only seen in their mutual dreams; faces that were on the beach right this second seeking warmth, seeking control, seeking to spread. Faces that wanted to absorb as much light and warmth and magic as it could find because that's what it was *made* to do.

It had found a font of both the exorcist, and he'd only given it pain.

"You can't stay in here forever," she challenged from across the empty.

He didn't reply.

"You CAN'T, Akaran. This isn't you. This isn't what you do."

He continued to sit in broken silence as the pieces of glass shifted around in his fingers.

The spy stepped in front of him and pulled at his scalp until he looked up at her with an empty, haunted eye. *"People are going to die if you don't leave here. People you like. People I couldn't give much of a shit about, but people I know you do."*

"They're dead already," he whispered. "Once they see it there's no going back. You'll always see it. They'll always see it. I'll always see it. Us. We will. You and me. We won't be rid of it."

Rmaci crossed her arms and gave him a deeply disapproving glare. *"Not to lecture, but we certainly will if you take that attitude about it. It's going to absorb you as soon as it can draw a bead on you. You understand that, right? You think what happened to me is bad? I only suffered a connection."*

He flicked a piece of the mirror out of his palms and let it bounce on the pitch-black floor. "This one knows what bad is," he flatly replied. "And this one, and this one," he added as he flicked two more pieces free.

She ran her hands down her grotesque side and sneered. *"Oh, woe. They lost their minds in a living nightmare. What do you think happened to the ones that you vanquished?"*

"Lost their minds too."

"With a few notable exceptions, the Abyss prefers that its residents retain a touch of sanity. Makes it all the more fun," she countered as she made the word drip with venom. *"You think they all fell?"*

"I hope not," he said with a tired sigh. "We banish from this world because they do not belong here. We don't know what happens. We know, but we don't *know*. I didn't know. Until I met you," he added as he looked up at her again.

Rmaci blinked and stepped back from him. *"Oh. Oh don't you dare put this on* me," she growled. *"Your calling is to literally send the souls of the damned back to perdition! It's called* perdition *because people that go there don't exactly get to eat cake – and when they do, they don't want it!"*

"They poison the cake?"

"Of course they poison the cake you daft twat, what do you think they do?"

He rocked back and forth a little harder. "I don't know. Never… never thought about it. I can't know. I… I knew it was coming. I knew. I know. Of course I knew. I kept warning people. The mirror says I did."

"The mirror says you did, I said you did, so what's the problem? Get off your ass and go cut it. Burn it. I don't know. Whatever it is you do – go do it."

Akaran shuddered and let a small trickle of glass fall to the ground and shook his head. "If I knew, I'd be ready for it. I can't be ready for it. I can't. I can't be ready for something I see annihilate me *every day*. I see it swallow me whole every day so why aren't I ready to be swallowed whole now?"

"By definition that makes you the one man who's capable of dealing with it," the spy deftly pointed out. *"You make it sound like I don't know what you're feeling. I lived this every moment of eternity after I died! You don't think I know?"*

"But it's different," he quietly countered. "You were judged."

"Yes. I was. By you," Rmaci charged through clenched teeth and with more pent-up rage than he knew she possessed. *"By the Divine. By the Beings you serve. It wasn't fair. They didn't care. You didn't care. So you didn't care about me then, you don't care about the people in the harbor now, but you need to wake up and make it choke on you while there's still time to do something – time, I may add, which you do not have a lot left of."*

***

Seline ran. She had promised him she'd run if the *Hullbreaker* made landfall. It was the one and only thing she could do. She started running when she watched that bastard murder Raechil in the bay. *No,* she corrected, *that wasn't Raechil. Couldn't have been. Looked like her but wasn't.*

It couldn't have been Raechil, but it was. He couldn't have murdered her with magic, but he did. She couldn't have been responsible for the murders at the *Narwhal*, but she was. None of it made any sense.

Except it did. She hated that it did.

She heard the *Hullbreaker* smash through the port and gave it only a moment's worth of attention. She remembered – clearly – what and how he had warned her about the ship in his nightmares. She wasn't so dumb that she couldn't put two and two together, and even if he was a murderer, she wasn't going to ignore his warning.

So she ran. And she kept running. She kept running until she ran out of breath, and kept running for another block after that. Other people were running, too, but she made a point to go down whatever empty streets she could find. Sure, it meant that she got lost, but what was the worst that could happen? She'd be further away from the port, she'd be further away from him, and she'd be further away from those that wished her harm.

When she finally slowed down to catch her breath, she ducked inside someone's house and quietly closed the door. She panted and ran trembling hands through her hair as she tried to make sense of what she'd seen. Any of what she'd seen. *Vampires. If that's what that was, they turn people. So it wasn't Raechil. It was a vampire. Something that wore her face. But if something wore her face, it could wear other faces.*

Her runner's flush paled almost instantly. *They could be anyone.*

The door banged open and a newcomer made her presence known immediately. "Do forgive me for interrupting, but I had to assume that if one person found a safe place to hide, I could too."

Seline lunged for a nearby knife and pointed it at the stranger as her hands shook from both the effort and raw terror. "Whatever you want, I don't have it. Just go. Go now."

The woman – an older one with carefully tucked gray hair – rolled her eyes at the healer. "Dear, I want nothing more than out of this accursed city. I think most of us do at this point. You'll forgive me if I decide to risk your knife versus being caught out in the open with that... thing."

"Not buying it," the medicannia retorted. "I ran down side streets. Ducked in alleys. You wouldn't have seen me coming here unless you were following me."

"Paranoia? Is that a trait that has been adopted by the locals of this accursed region as a quality pastime?" the intruder questioned with a droll sigh. "Even if I did, you wear a smock of the Order of Love. I assume that means you're capable of defending yourself even if I did – and that you'd likely be one of the safest people to follow."

"So you did follow me," the healer charged.

"Oh, come now. If I admit that I *happened* to see you running in the vague direction of the port's exit and that I *happened* to notice your colors that maybe following an Oo-lo'er may be better for my personal safety?" she pressed. "Now if you don't mind, would you be kind enough to lower that sad excuse for a cleaver and speak to me like a grown woman?"

Seline snorted and lowered the knife a little. "Safety. Not a damn inch of it to be had around here."

The intruder nodded her head and tracked a wrinkle in the top of her hand. "Safety, and youth. I remember when I had more of the former, and looked as if I had much more of the latter. If only recent events hadn't been so taxing."

"You could say that again," the medicannia grumbled. "All I want to do is get as far from this area as I possibly can."

"Instructions and orders from your superiors, or other?"

Seline gave her a dirty look and sat down on the closest stool she could find in the shabby little hut of a house. "Does it matter?"

"Always, and that answer means it's more for matters of personal protection rather than intensive instruction," the woman replied with a casual flick of her hand. "Reasoning I can certainly understand and reasoning that I have a great deal of personal experience with."

"Unless your reasons for hiding are involve a violent and half-blind sociopath, I don't think they're the same."

The older woman's eyes narrowed and she straightened up slightly. "Sociopath? Yes. Though half-blind? How few men are there that walk with both open."

"Doesn't matter," Seline replied. "Done with him. Done with him, his Order, his people. Just *done*," she swore as she ripped the Order-issued tabard off of her dress and tossed it in a corner. "I'm not even going to bother going back to my dormasil. I'm just going to vanish."

"Vanishing without a trace is a good way to have your absence be noticed, though I do admit that this town has no shortage of the missing. But, no, girl, we can't have that."

The healer spat into her pile of Order garbs and glared hateful daggers at it. "Oh yes we can. Yes I can. Whatever *we* shit you're thinking, don't. I've had enough of being ordered about by women my senior as of late," she retorted before adding a snide, "with all respect required, of course."

The gray-haired woman smiled and wrinkles erupted all along her eyes. "There does come a time in one's life when one must forge their own path, that's true. Though..."

The way she let the word hang made Seline perk up almost against her own will. "Though...?"

"Well, I don't claim to know you, but I do have knowledge for what it truly takes for a woman to think so little of her peers. I suspect that the one thing you were never taught is to respect yourself as much as they demand you respect them."

That statement cut like a blade against bone. "Let's just say that my instructions the last few years has been to stand for myself before my patients, and not stand before my superiors."

"Then I am afraid that life has many a lesson yet to teach you, but... mayhaps we can reach an arrangement. We both want the same thing: out."

"The whole damn *port* wants out," Seline retorted. "What makes you any different?"

"The same thing that makes you different – we don't wish to be out of harm's way *here*, but harm's way *entirely*. A promise that neither of us have hope for until after we can put Basion and Cableture to our backs along with the wind."

The healer looked down at the knife and then up at the stranger. She suddenly looked... pure. Almost *created*. As if she wasn't just someone that had found her way to nobility, but someone that had been *designed* for it. "I'm still trying to catch my breath, so... I'm listening. Talk quick."

She was right, of course. She had been built for it. The woman had been designed for just that. "Madeline Hummadalt," she replied with a smile. It was the first chance she'd had to use her old name since she'd been resurrected and granted the name Anais Lovic so many years ago.

She'd taken the name 'Lady' all on her own.

It was time to remind the world *how*.

***

Any semblance of calm the docks had was the direct result of Catherine and her men. The docks had calm. The harbor did not. The first wave of Daringol's minions were met with desperate violence – though the creature had only spawned a handful.

As they watched, more corpses started to pull themselves away from the rot-covered wreckage. The *Savage Shine* had put a hole through and through her center, and the Maiden could see a gaping hole full of writhing tentacles and stumbling *things* that were trying to claw their way out of the wreckage. When the beast shuddered and shifted, she had a brief glimpse of the massive *Crownship* miles away from the bay. It was Admiral Maddon's command vessel – the *Queen's Dragon* – and it was dead-set on cruising into the battle.

If it got to the port before they were all dead, the weapons on her hull would be enough to turn the tides; she was sure of it. That hope was tenuous at best, although a few more shots dulled the movements within and sparked a small fire that the wraith lashed at in an attempt to extinguish the blaze. It was a temporary reprieve, and Catherine knew it.

The rest of the 2nd Naval Armada wasn't going to wait. Their cannon-shells and arrows were whittling away at the physical form that the beast had adopted – even though most of those efforts appeared to be going to waste. For each wooden plank that was annihilated and for each decrepit limb of the giant yeshal that was wiped out of existence, phantom boards and phantom tentacles took their place.

She just prayed that they would keep going while she looked for an opening. Catherine had her eye on one, but every time she directed someone to fling a spell or an arrow at it, the monstrosity deflected it or sacrificed part of itself to protect the lone figure that was effectively rooted to the deck at the helm. Even when the helm itself disintegrated, what she presumed had once been the captain of the ship stood tall in a rotted, red-and-gold cloak and ruined uniform.

She didn't see the softly-shining figure appear behind him. She didn't see the gleaming woman step out of the captain's cabin or touch him on his shoulder. She didn't see the etheric, radiant woman lean in and whisper in his ear. She wasn't supposed to, so she didn't. She wouldn't have been able to comprehend her beauty even if she could.

"[*Captain Taes. I know who you are, and I know your Master. I know what he wants,*]" the avatar cautioned. "[*If he listens through your ears or sees through your eyes, let Me be clear.*]"

The captain didn't flinch. He couldn't move, even though the wraith holding him upright cringed away from the too-warm energy that seeped into the air around her. He couldn't speak, but his exhausted, pained eyes darted down to the side to try to see Her hand.

"[*If you come for My king, you best not miss.*]"

***

"I told them."

"*Life is riddled with I-told-you-so's,*" Rmaci retorted. "*The afterlife is full of more of them. Blame is not a concept alien to the dead.*"

He looked down at the shattered memories as they started to turn to sand in his hand. "I can't fix this."

Rmaci knelt down in front of him. The gale had softened and the embers under her skin were dying down. They'd left her more burnt than she'd started, and she hurt worse than she was going to admit. "*This is as much my fault as yours,*" she replied with a wistful sigh. "*Though in my defense, none of this has gone to plan. My unwanted departure from life aside, I expected to be on that ship and I expected to rule it from the inside out. Instead, I'd much rather run from it, but I'm not. It isn't my fault that it's here. Or that it was created.*"

"Then why accept blame?"

"*Because people are dying while you're hiding. You're hiding because I took my grief out on you. I didn't know I'd done this much damage,*" she admitted before she added, "*though I suppose it's wrong to be impressed with myself about it.*"

He looked down at a single piece of glass left in his hand. It showed a scene that wasn't from Toniki. It didn't have anyone she recognized in it at first, before she caught sight of... a younger version of him. A boy, in a room of mirrors. Maybe seven, eight years old. Maybe a little older. "Did you? Did you do the damage? I can't remember."

She watched as a figure approached him in the memory, and watched a gang of men approach his younger self and hold him down. She watched as the one in the lead slipped a pair of tongs from his black and gold belt and bent down over his face. The memory cracked and fell apart as the tongs reached for his eyes. "*What... when was that? Who were those men?*" she asked as she looked up at his face and focused on his empty eye.

"I don't know." He touched his face and blinked slowly at her. "I don't know who I am. I don't know why I'm here. And I don't know what to do about that," he said as he slowly waved his hand at a force in the darkness. At the hungering void beyond.

"*There's only one thing you can do,*" Rmaci whispered. "*You can't let it spread. You can't risk it. You hide and others are being swallowed by it. Their souls are being consumed. They'll be eaten, just like you, except they won't be able to get free. Not like you did. Not like I did. So you have one thing to do.*"

The sand on the black floor turned white, and then solidified into a sword. He picked it up and looked into the blade. The side she saw horrified her though she couldn't quite understand why.

There was a dark-skinned man on the side that faced her; a Sycian, with pale red eyes and a blood cloak. There were runes etched in the air around his head in the language of the damned, and as she saw it, she felt the urge to fall to her knees.

It wasn't a man. Or a demon. It wasn't one of the Fallen. It was worse. The man bore Akaran's surname, but his title... his title made her quake in what was left of her flesh. There were creatures in the pit you crossed. Creatures you didn't. Yet even the Gods Themselves would get tired of you – eventually.

Not him. Not what he was. Not with his title.

He dropped the blade, and she saw the reflection facing up. One of the faces reflected in the blade was half of Akaran's. The other half wasn't. It was radiant. It was female. It was pure. She caught a glimpse of it and realized that *pure* was the wrong word. It was *Love* that reflected in the blade.

"*Who... who is that?*" Rmaci asked slowly. "*Who... who are you to be a messenger to the Divine... and a brother to a Harbinger?*"

The gale whipped around them as Love snarled in rage.

***

Badin's antics under the docks had earned attention, and not all of it was good. "SEASPARK!" he barked as he forced another concussive blast of lightning out of his hands and across the waves. The sailors? He'd come to terms with them. After the first three or four, the shock value of shambling, waterlogged corpses lost some of the impact.

Oh, that wasn't to say that he wasn't going to spend the next week giving up his vow of sobriety once this was over. Or that he wasn't going to spend the rest of his life avoiding seaweed. If he ever saw the ocean again, it would be too damn soon.

The sailors? He could deal with those. The turtle?

The smoking shell that bobbed in the water a handful of feet away? He'd never seen one in person. He had a feeling that they were... pretty? No, wouldn't have been the right word. He'd heard them mentioned before in one story or another. He always assumed they'd be more... pleasant, maybe... under normal circumstances. The turtle was the point that he almost checked out right beside Akaran, and would have if Telburn hadn't dropped down to provide aid.

"I daresay your talents are wasted in the army," the Headmaster said by way of greeting as he lowered himself from the pier and hovered above the water. "Interested in an internship?"

The Major arced another blast of energy into a fresher corpse than the others as it tried to climb to its feet. They'd started to emerge from the wreckage of the *Shatterstorm* a few minutes prior, though that was the first one that had taken notice of the battlemage, who at the same time, only gave passing interest in the Adept. "Oh good. A mage. Do me a big favor and *get us the fisk out of here*," he seethed.

"Us?" he asked as he looked past him and saw Akaran slumped over in the surf. "Oh. *Us*. What happened to him?"

"I don't know. He saw this shit and promptly collapsed." Badin looked down at his friend and took a few steps closer to him. "Headbreak. See it in the army sometimes. You see too much and... well."

Telburn nodded in comprehension, if not understanding. "Considering all the shocks he's been through as of late, I'm not surprised. We all have our limits."

The Specialist flicked a spark off of his fingertips and took a ragged, exhausted breath. "If I thought that a shock would work, I'd blast his ass so hard he'd land back in Gonta."

"Tempting, I admit, but your energies are better off aimed at the monstrosity. Has he said anything?"

"Aside from when a ghost grabbed him and then jumped *into* his face and hasn't come out yet? No, he didn't say anything *then* either and honestly, ya'll are going to owe me one big-assed explanation when this shit is over," Badin replied with a grunt. "I want to make sure that's clear."

"Why do you think I have anything to do with it?"

"You're here."

"That doesn't mean anything."

The Specialist-Major pointed a finger at him before he whipped around and arced a bolt of lighting into a crab-like creature that had pulled itself up on one of the pier's pylons. "Am I *wrong*?"

Telburn looked at the wretched pile of twitching bodies and wrinkled his nose. "Well. Not necessarily, I grant."

"Great, now tell me why I'm not running away in terror because every part of my body wants me to and instead I'm down here. I mean I'd be saving his ass anyways but I honestly feel a bit more confident about it than I should," he ranted as he picked out his next target and prepared another blast.

The Headmaster cleared his throat as he took up a flanking position beside the battlemage. "You'll have to give much credit to the Maiden-Templar, I believe. She mentioned something about an invocation to grant 'the certainty of true love' to those that need it."

"I... I don't think I like that," Badin mused quietly as another corpse reared up in the surf. He sent a spark down at it, but this one was smart. Tendrils shot out from its thighs and made it *bounce* away from the blast – and the Specialist's spell impacted the pylon behind it. "I think I'd prefer being afraid, it would... it would probably keep me alive longer."

Impacted, and obliterated it.

In the hail of splinters and wooden chunks that followed, the concussive force of his spell shook the pier from front to back, and wooden boards and rusty nails finally surrendered to the abuse of the day (and the years before). A chunk of wood fell onto the sand behind them, and a lanky corpse of a man staggered out of the mess before the mages could do anything to stop it.

They didn't need to.

Chains whipped up from the surf and wrapped around its throat. Its head disintegrated in seconds, and a dark shadow full of screaming faces spurted out of the stump before it shattered into pieces of phantom glass. "No," Akaran croaked as he slowly stood up. He flexed his left arms and ice-covered chains fell to his side. He extended his right, and a bolt of mana popped out of the palm of his hand and into the face of another zombie before it could get more than a few steps out of the ocean. "No," he repeated.

Badin would've lied if he said he didn't want to cheer, but the look on the priest's face wasn't anything to be happy about. "So glad you decided to wake up and join us!" he shouted.

The Headmaster started to say something along the same lines before Akaran cut them both off. "I... I refuse."

"Refuse?" Telburn asked cautiously. "Refuse what?"

He looked past the pair of mages and focused squarely on the twisting mass of rotted boards and twitching tentacles at the end of the pier. "I'm done. This is done," he said – though the pair realized he wasn't talking to either of them. "Enough of this."

The priest took a rough, slow step forward – then another, and another. He moved like he was trying to remember how to walk all over again. Telburn reached out to steady him, but Rmaci popped out of his back and shook her head. *"Don't,"* she cautioned, *"don't interfere."*

"No! He's my friend and I am *not* going to let him walk into that thing!" Badin spat back as he tried to grab Akaran's arm. The priest pushed his hand off with force and took another rough step forward. "I didn't stand here getting waterlogged for the last –"

"He saw. He knows," she said like that explained everything.

"In my time dealing with him I am quite sure that the boy doesn't know half as much as he thinks he does, and I am equally certain that I should also thank Catherine for her injection of stability in my veins because my dear, I feel I should be terrified of *you.*"

She gave him a lip-less smile and ran a hand down her burnt, blistered, cracked, and frozen chest. *"Flattery will get you everywhere,"* she said before she opened her arms wide and *pushed* at the ether between the priest and his friends. They stumbled back as she smiled at the tiny little personal victory. It had worked for the Templar *on* her, might as well work *for* her. *"Doesn't change things. He saw. He knows."*

"What did he see?" Telburn asked with his head tilted to the side.

"Our impending doom?" the soldier asked as more corpses started to gravitate towards them.

Rmaci shook her head and stepped away from the priest as he dropped his arms loosely to his sides. More chains erupted down the lengths of his forearms, and both of his hands took on a haunting white sheen. *"The reflection of who he is, and what he is to be."*

Before they could ask, Akaran croaked out a simple request. "Telburn? Lift me," he ordered before he looked at his friend and gave him a cold, fatal smile. "No. Lift us."

***

The wind shifted.

That was the only way the survivors on the dock could explain it. Daringol had broken down the first line of defense minutes before when a wardkeeper had caught a small chunk of cannon-shot in the face. When she went down, the barrier the Lovers had placed along the shore collapsed in a cascading effect along with her lifeless, bloody head.

The *arin-goliath* had found more bodies. Lots more bodies. As it siphoned errant magic and fed on the energy of spells in the air all around it, it had found more than a few shipwrecks in the bottom of the harbor – and the dead men trapped inside. They surged to life and pulled themselves from the watery depths to lay siege to the Armada.

Catherine had protected the docks.

She couldn't protect the ships.

Daringol knew its prey was here. It had to be. It felt it. It knew it. It knew that the man that had tortured and tormented and hunted it in the mountains around Toniki was *here* and it wasn't going to stop until it found him. As it raged along the shoreline, the men it killed and consumed were soon raised and recruited into its shell.

It was a plague of souls. The plague that the Man of the Red Death had aimed at the port. The one he had Rishnobia warn Anais about. The plague he expected to lumber up the coast and give her a distraction to work around to reach her goals – to reach his goals.

Given another few short minutes, he'd get his wish.

But the wind shifted.

The Maiden watched in surprise as a pillar of beach sand and debris lifted up into the air from under the broken pier. She saw two people standing on it, but couldn't quite make them out. It wasn't much of a surprise when Telburn appeared out of a mage-gate beside her. "Buy him time."

"Buy him...?" she asked as she realized who it was. "What is he doing?"

"He does his nature – as you do yours. You are a shield. He is not."

"That doesn't answer my question."

"Nor did he answer mine," the Headmaster admitted. "Though you and I are going to have a very long talk about that man when this is done; who he is, what he is, what he does. Since he was restored, there is more than one aura in his essence, and I want to know more about what your people have unleashed on the world."

Catherine swallowed nervously as the living corpses retreated all at once and *every* tentacle and *every* zombie and *every* damned soul in the harbor turned their collective attention to the figures on the column. "Headmaster? You and me both."

***

The Templar's spell could only do so much.

If all eyes hadn't been on him then and there, Badin might've pissed his pants. He thought about it anyway; he was already wet, and he could dive back into the bay after and clean off and nobody would notice. Erine would never know that his courage faltered and he liked it that way. He honestly didn't give a shit if Akaran could tell or not. "Oh… okay. So. We're standing… on a platform. We're up," he nervously exclaimed as he watched the rolling, rotted squid's eye focus on them. "Now… now what?"

The exorcist took a very deep and ragged breath as he bent down and fished a sword from the detritus at their feet. "Now… now I'm going to get its attention, and you're going to destroy it."

"How?"

"Remember how you told me all about Gonta?"

Badin had to stop himself from covering his mouth with his electrically-charged hand as Akaran's intent dawned on him. "Yes but… oh. Oh I don't like this idea."

"Do you have a better one?"

"No?"

Chains slid off of Akaran's arms and wrapped around his legs as he steadied himself on the pillar. "Don't die."

The battlemage took a nervous breath and sized up the monstrosity before them as two very long sucker-covered tentacles unraveled from the edges of the *Hullbreaker*. They had long rotted away to little more than chunks of flesh and muscle held together by shimmering black magic. "Is that a request or an order?"

"Which gets you to do it?"

Badin swallowed hard and braced himself. "You are going to owe me so much rum. I hope you understand that."

The exorcist didn't answer. Instead, he spun a ball of twirling light on his fingertip. It wasn't much. It was barely the size of an apple; just a small, spinning, purple blob of energy. He whispered a pair of small Words, and the ball arced into the air and went straight into the squid's unblinking eye.

It was a message, and its point was simple.

Daringol heard it clearly.

"Come get me, you bitch," he hissed.

The wraith swung one of its animated tentacles down right for Akaran's head. He didn't move to dodge. He didn't move to try and stop it. He planted his feet and they sunk into the sand as he caught the tentacle with both hands and *squeezed*. Phantom tendrils spun away from the decomposing rot and wrapped around his neck.

In that moment, he saw the gaping void all over again. It flashed in his sight and the world went black. The tendrils squeezed and lunged into his soul. They dove into his mouth. Filled his ears. Stuffed his nose. Suffocated him.

Even as they did, his chains blossomed away from his legs and wrapped themselves around the tentacle almost all of their own volition. Daringol had done this once before. Akaran hadn't been ready for it then. He was ready for it now. He was ready.

Even if the wraith had forgotten how it had ended the first time.

***

In the dark, in the void, among all the shadows and the faces, the hungering soul opened all of its mouths. They collapsed around the priest. Hands dug into him. Claws ripped at his spirit and mental flesh. His soul cracked, his will staggered. The pressure built around him as Daringol did everything it could to consume him. As it focused all of its rage, all of its madness, all of its suffering into one singular point in the world.

It tried.

In the dark, in the bottom of his soul, in his mind, Akaran called out.

"*Niasmis*! *Goddess – help me!*"

***

Blood splattered from his lips as the tip of the squid's limb raked across his face. He staggered under the physical force of the attack as much as the spiritual, but through clenched teeth, he croaked out a word. For once, it wasn't a spell.

"Now," he whispered around the choking inky ether.

Badin took a breath and thrust his knife into the center of the phantom chains and clenched his hands tight around the hilt with all his might. "Thundercall," he whispered, and then at the top of his lungs, the mage screamed it again. "THUNDERCALL!"

***

In the dark, the wraith swelled.

The wraith crackled with yellow energy.

The dark lit up.

***

A searing bolt of lightning crashed into the priest. It struck his chains and charged through him and into the tentacles wrapped around him. Badin was blown back from the force of the impact and only stopped himself from falling off of the giant sandbar by luck alone. Electricity and magic coursed down the tentacle and slammed into the haunted ship with a force greater than anything the cannons could offer.

***

On the deck of the *Hullbreaker*, the avatar removed Her hand from the captain's shoulder and stepped away. The corpse shook and the ship cracked around his feet. She faded from view with a smile, but not before the Goddess passed an edict of Her own.

"[*You missed.*]"

***

The winds shifted. The pillar started to crumble. Daringol's tentacles began to dissolve before he could even say the words. The shreds of toxic magic boiled out of his mouth in a thick black steam as he found the air to speak so loud that *everyone* in the harbor could hear it.

Two spells. Two sentences. Six words.

One judgment.

"**WE CONDEMN**," he called out.

The wardkeepers and the templar felt a wave of power pulse out from the pillar as the sand disintegrated and both the priest and the battlemage began to tumble into the surf below...

...but not before he finished the spell.

"**WE PURIFY – AND EXPUNGE!**"

Catherine would wonder for weeks what, exactly, he meant by 'we.'

Daringol would be offered no such time.

Months of pent-up rage, months of pent-up terror, months of magic that had built up around him that was supposed to be *in* him channeled through his arms along the disruption Badin had forced open and it *ripped* into the wraith.

The ship imploded in a flash of brilliant purple, white, and black light. The corpses it had animated seized up, crumpled, and the spirits that had used them as their shells shattered into etheric shards that vanished as suddenly as they appeared. An ocean swell surged up from the burning wreckage as it collapsed into the ocean. What was left of the *Hullbreaker* sank into the bay as the ship of the enshrouded disintegrated in the aftermath of the exorcism.

Below the pier, a dead woman cheered. She cheered as the burning cracks on her skin healed and the embers that deformed her flesh were extinguished. She cheered, and she fell to her knees and called out her gratitude to the Goddess she'd seen in the depths of Akaran's mind.

Badin swam free of the wreckage and caught himself on a still-standing pylon as he struggled to remember how to breathe again. Chainmail *did not* make for swimming attire, and he'd swear until the day he died (and beyond) that he felt someone drag his ass to shore. That thought was cemented when he saw a glimmering figure stand over the vaguely-conscious body of his friend.

He'd swear just as vehemently that he heard the shimmering beauty speak to the exorcist as She stroked his cheek tenderly and lovingly. "[*Good. Now – I want My auramancer back. Go. Go and do unto others as they have done unto Mine.*]"

XII. SURVIVING A LIE
Morning of Lithdis, the 9th of Firstgrow, 513 QR

Like most mornings anymore, it didn't matter where you went: the morning was nothing but misery. Port Cableture was a nightmare of the wounded, the cursed, the burnt, and the burning. The entire city had turned into a massive disinformation campaign overnight, entirely orchestrated by the Maiden-Templar to try to do damage control. It wasn't working (well), but she was giving it her best.

While she worked to convince anyone that saw the battle that they hadn't actually seen a demon raiding the shoreline, Basion wasn't much better off. That wasn't to say that the shock of the attack wasn't felt − it was − or that the rumors that a paladin had been murdered weren't putting everyone on edge − they were. Riots had erupted at the mere *mention* of the battle in the port, with a quarter of the city assuming that the Odinals had walked warships into the bay from the mountains in an attempt to sink the Armada.

How the ships had floated down the mountains and through the woods was a question for the scholars, of course. And the cocasa addicts. And a few people that fit both descriptions.

The rest of the city was mindlessly restless from demonstrations against... everything. 'Everything' was the only answer that fit the bill. People were upset over the wedding. People were upset over the refugees that had been all but forgotten by Akaran and the others that had pledged to offer them assistance on some level. People were upset over a rumor that the Granalchi Academy had somehow summoned an ice demon, while others claimed it was an icy angel.

Either way, people were upset over it.

People were upset over the murder of Kee Tessamirch, though the people that knew him weren't as much. People were really angry about how his mercenary troupe had taken to roughing up anyone that they thought *might* have been involved, which included any off-duty member of the 4th. Those people were being blamed for the murder of Enth-Blade Parl, and the disappearance of one of his bodyguards.

There were all kinds of rumors about what was happening to her. The Odinals had made it damn clear that if she wasn't returned intact, the proposition of wedded bliss was going to turn into un-wedded warfare. There were other issues at play, too. The Woodmason's Guild wasn't at all happy that their leader was about to be marched into the town square with a noose on his neck — blamed rightly or wrongly for organizing a fight that had left a guard dead and an Odinal diplomat injured.

It wasn't helping matters that an exorcist — not Akaran, surprisingly — had been sent to watch over it. A decent chunk of the city had no trust for the Lovers to begin with and the tolerance they had was only wearing thinner by the candlemark. The instructions Henderschott had received were simply, "We have enough problems to not want to risk another wraith rising from an angry hanged man," whatever that was supposed to mean.

He didn't know. Didn't care. Didn't want to ask.

He felt better for it.

He didn't feel better about the meeting he'd attended after the execution at dawnbreak. He'd been summed right to Overseer Hannock's office, which was less an office and more of an attempt to pretend he was royalty. It was easy to see where the city's taxes were going — though the Lieutenant-Commander had wondered for a very long time if they weren't getting padded by a few under-the-table deals. It would be improper to suggest such a thing without evidence, of course.

Evidence that, if he had, he would've gleefully handed over to the often-drunk but unpleasantly-sober Paverilak Tyreening, the Betrothed to the provincial Maiden, Sanlian Esterveen. With all the talk of 'wedding this' and 'groomsman that' lately, he had to remind himself that 'Betrothed' did not necessarily mean 'married.' Rather, it was a title that conferred a portion of the Maiden's power and rank to someone else so they may engage in business instead.

It was a subtle reminder to the rest of the Kingdom that men may have their uses but *women* held the power. It also let the Ladies have someone on-call capable of dealing with obstinate outsiders that might not see it in the same way. That, and it gave the citizenry something to talk about when they saw one or the other with a new *companion*.

The business in question being, 'the paperwork and bureaucracy of running one of the Queen's Provinces.' It was reasonably well-known that Sanlian had absolutely no taste to tolerate men in her presence in general, let alone one that reeked of cheap rum more than not. She took great delight in sending him to any place in the Province that she wasn't and where she didn't want to be.

Which made his threat of her arrival all the more damning. "You must both understand. Word has reached the Maiden of *everything* and she is growing less and less pleased with the recent antics around Basion."

"Letters you sent or letters someone sent under you?" Henderschott quipped from the doorway as he crossed his arms.

"Does it matter? I promise you she's headed to Cableture after the disaster down there. If she comes up here, we're all fisked."

Hannock opened his small mouth and made an irritating whine that cut through the Lieutenant's ears. "We? *We* are not at fault. I have no control over a murder in that damnable asylum! I have no control over the port! I have no control –"

"You have no control, end of declaration," Paverilak spat back with his jaundice-yellow eyes brimming with fury. "If you have no control, then I have no control. If I have no control, then the city has no control. Did you forget your duty to the Crown?"

The Overseer huffed and snarled in his general direction as his unwelcome guest stormed over to a gauze-shrouded window and peered down into the city proper. "It is my duty to provide for the people of Basion. It not my duty to provide for outsiders and interlopers. It is not my duty to deal with... low-born water-folk from the southern side of the province. That is *your* job, isn't it?"

"No, Overseer. Your job is to provide care for the Queen's citizens regardless of where they came from. They are here. In your city. That makes them *your* concern."

"Not without registrations of residence, they are not!" Hannock spat back. "The ones that have signed the necessary documentation as provided by the City Charter are being integrated into the –"

"Have your people ordered to record them into the city's rolls *faster*," the Betrothed shot back. "Right now, they are the least of your worries. We have *bodies* turning up *every damn night* and you aren't doing shit about it!"

The Overseer puffed up. "I will have you know that the refugees are more important than a few random deaths. I assigned my personal attache to work with them. You've met her – Sannah?"

"The attache that couldn't be bothered to show up for this meeting?" Paverilak snapped. "Your trust in your underlings is misplaced everywhere you put it."

The pudgy man with an oval face pointed over at Henderschott, who, to this point, had done a great job of pretending he was part of the wall. "I assume she is doing as she was told. Regardless – criminal activity is *his* concern."

The Lieutenant cleared his throat and casually drummed his fingers on his dagger hilt. "Not to pass blame, but I've made it clear that the Garrison's standpoint is that lawbreaking won't be tolerated. Didn't we just have an argument with the woodmasons earlier over that?"

"The woodmasons are not responsible for the murders and execution of the heir to the Tessamirch family," Paverilak countered. "Though I sense that you are somehow about to make the argument that it isn't *your* problem, either?"

"Yeah, actually..." he started before a withering glare from the Betrothed made him raise his hands in mock-defeat. "I received a missive from the Lovers this morning. They're invoking Articles of Involvement. The Garrison is to hand over everything we have on almost a dozen investigations to a Paladin they're putting in charge. Spidous, maybe. I don't know."

It was impossible to tell who had the more disgusted look on their face – Hannock or Paverilak. "What interest could those Harlot-worshipping fools have in random murders?" the Overseer demanded.

Henderschott thought long and hard about telling them everything he'd heard as of late. He really thought about washing his hands of it and walking away. If Seline could try to make it work, he could too. Except... "I've had several informants advise me that it would be best for the safety of the Kingdom to not argue the point. If nothing else, the fact that the public at large believes that one of our battlemages was responsible for Kee's death would allow for an outside investigation to placate tensions from the Odinals."

"That is a great deal many words for, 'I don't think it's my problem,' isn't it? The Oo-los are distrusted. Despised. It is only by the grace of the Queen that they're allowed to darken this city to begin with. If you think they'll *lower* tensions, well. Then simply put: you're mad." Paverilak countered. "It seems neither of you have any interest in holding up to any kind or measure of accountability."

"Oh, I've got plenty of that," the Lieutenant complained. "I mentioned informants. I'd like you to meet one of them. My advice? Be on your best behavior, or you won't like the end result."

"Do you now? You have someone willing to put a name to that threat?" the nobleman asked with a snide sneer as Henderschott opened the door to the Overseer's office.

Riorik stepped inside and cleared his throat as he adjusted his garish burnt-orange vest. "I certainly have cause for a name. Overseer, Betrothed. It's a pleasure. Thank you, Lieutenant-Commander. May I suggest that you extradite yourself from this conversation?"

"Suggest?" he asked. "No. You don't need to," Henderschott replied as he started to leave the room.

"I have *not* excused you, solider!" Paverilak thundered. "You will stay and explain yourself before –"

"I will *leave* so I don't have to *arrest* you all when your conversation is over," the guard replied with a disgusted snort before he added a simple order to the thief with a low growl, "and don't kill them."

The Guildboss chuckled deep in his throat. "My good man. I'd never kill people of such high esteem," he said as he smiled at the city's speakers. "Not on the first meeting, at least."

The Overseer attempted to show some semblance of a backbone all the sudden and dropped his hands to his tabletop with a meaty thud. "Did you just threaten me? Do you know who I am?"

"I do, actually," Riorik replied calmly. "I am not impressed. Nor, should my understanding be complete, is anyone else. You are a blowhard who thinks far too much of yourself for accomplishments of so little nature be considered inherently useful – though your title does carry some measure of weight."

"I trust that you will not engage me in the same tone," Paverilak intoned. "Especially given that you don't seem to have a name."

"Oh I have a name – I just haven't been so inclined to offer it," the thief replied smoothly as he pulled up a chair and folded his hands on his lip. The edge of a curved, serrated dagger glinted in the sunlight enough to get their attention. Weapons weren't permitted in the Overseer's estate, and this man had strolled in with one without being stopped? "Though given how the situation outside is deteriorating, I will *humbly* ask for your permissions to dispense with the typical niceties."

"Who are you?" Hannock grumbled as he looked around or something defend himself with.

"Someone who is going to offer to provide enhanced security over the next few days, or weeks. Someone capable of ensuring that Sanlian won't have any major interest to pay attention to the mass chaos unfolding in your quaint little town – or the deals you've been hiding behind the scenes."

"Are you accusing me of improper dealings? I will have you arrested for slander of the Crown."

Riorik cleared his throat and raised his index finger with a smile. "Except you aren't the Crown. You are chartered by the Blackstone Trading Company to run the city *for* the Crown, though there is a very distinct difference between the two. Nor do you even rank as their Merchant-Master, whom I've already come to terms with. As a member of the BeaST, you naturally have other dealings at the Crown's expense, though I understand that there's an agreement not to speak of them openly."

The Betrothed turned away from the window and straightened up with a sharp inhalation of his breath. "If you think insulting the Overseer in his office will gain you any interest from me," he began, "you are entirely correct. What do you want?"

While Hannock offered a blustered attempt to defend his honor, the thief cut to the chase. "The Fleetfinger's Guild has recently undergone a change in management. My need for a calm city and a safe wedding has become of utmost importance – and we will ensure that the riots in town decrease in severity. Otherwise, I make no promises for what ensuing events will entail or how they may affect your position of rank."

The Overseer pushed himself up from his chair with both of his hands flat on his desk. "You dare to brazenly storm into my office and admit to working with the guild of thieves? And attempt to extort me? ME?!"

"Yes, you. I thought I already clarified that I knew who you were? I didn't mistakenly walk into this office; not with the bribes I had to spend," Riorik replied dismissively. "Though I think you misunderstand – I *am* the Guild of Thieves for this city. There is no extortion here; accept our help and decrease tensions, or reject it, and we do nothing as it grows out of control. And it will."

"You say that with more surety than I feel comfortable with," Paverilak replied as his eyes narrowed into slits. "What point do you have?"

"My point is simple," the thief explained. "The lower class of this city had an understanding with you both – the poorest of the poor would leave, and they would hide in the Landing until the celebrations completed. In turn, they would have the land granted and be given aid to develop it. The Landing has been destroyed, and regardless of the actual source of blame, most of them no longer feel that either of you can be trusted."

Hannock grunted and slumped back into his seat. "Let them. They mooch on what glory this city has to offer."

The master-thief gave him a faint little smile. "They are the ones that empty your chamberpots and deliver the food that fills your bellies. If you think that you have issues now, continue to disregard their interests."

"Cut to the chase," the other man interrupted. "Grumblings from the lower class is nothing new. I sense there's more."

"Oh there's much more," Riorik admitted, "though this offer is not as straightforward as you may wish. I'm not asking to have control over the city or any such; I don't need to ask for what I already have. I'm asking for a seat at the table – but I don't make such an offer without a gift," he said as he handed over a scroll.

Maiden Sanlian's man took it and looked through it. "A signed confession of...? Oh," he said as the question trailed off. "This is troubling.

From an Adept?"

The thief nodded, and his chestnut brown hair bounced along with the gesture. "Yes. One by the name of Ishtva. He had dealings with someone he shouldn't, which has turned him into a person of value enough that you can leverage the Granalchi into cutting you a deal on their own magical defenses. Use it to cut back on the extent that they have their hands in your pockets."

"What, *exactly*, defines a seat at the table, as you ask?"

"Paverilak You can't possibly tell me you're considering...!?"

"You would be wise to be past the point of mere consideration," Riorik countered. "The ask is simple: one-tenth of the crowns collected in taxes between now and the end of the wedding in twenty-one days. You will also allow agents of my choice to sit in any further trade negotiations you have with the Odinals for the next year," he answered as he opened his hands wide. "In return, before you balk at the cost, I will make assurances that the recent actions agitation in the city due to usual concerns and more... shall we say, *human* interests... are halved. At the least."

The Betrothed stood in silence, though his hands clenched at the parchment so hard it tore a portion of the scroll. "I am not as daft as others would think of me," he started as he slowly walked around the Overseer's desk. "A promise of concern of *human* interests from you, and a caution of Articles of Involvement from the Oo-lo's? You aren't telling us something."

Riorik chuckled. "Oh, good sir. I'm not telling you a lot. Mostly intentional, though not disrespectfully. In a matter of hours, if not *minutes*, I am positive that one of my favorite friends in the world is going to make a request to his superiors that you won't like. It *will* be granted. You will like it less when it is."

"You speak in riddles," Hannock interrupted. "I don't have time for that."

"You will make the time," the thief demanded in no uncertain terms. "Once his request is granted, this city is going to be turned upside down and everything in the shadows is going to be spilled out into the streets. I guarantee you that all manner of cockroach and worse will be pulled into the streets and I am reasonably certain that you will have interests exposed that you *won't* approve of having exposed. Work with me, and we can mitigate some of those losses. Don't? Well. They aren't called 'losses' because they are enjoyable."

"I can have you hung for these threats. The executioner doesn't have to stop at just one man today."

"No," Riorik agreed before he let his tone take on as much ice as the mages had channeled into their courtyard days ago, "he doesn't. Nor does he have full ownership of that particular market."

Cold, almost deathly silence reigned before either of them spoke up again. "I assume that your roaches will be allowed to skitter away peacefully, is that it?" Paverilak asked.

The thief nodded. "Some. Others... how is it his people put it? Oh yes. Some will be condemned – the ones that should not see the light of day."

***

Sleep had been restless, painful, and uneasy. When morning arrived, it was almost a blessing. When *food* arrived, Akaran had never been more grateful for salted fish and hard tack in his life. Turned out the trawler captain had been true to his word, even though it felt like a lifetime ago that he'd offered to take care of the priest's meals. Not just the trawler captain, either – he'd been handed off to the Port Cableture waystation for the Order, and the caretaker had, well, taken care to make sure that he was well-provided for.

Provisions that included bandages. Many bandages, many compresses, and some kind of sticky sweet salve that was a mix of honey and... other things. They'd been able to field-treat some of his wounds, though the gash in his stomach had taken on a foul smell and inflammation around the edges. The concern, he was told, was that he had overdone quite possibly *everything* relating to the use of magic on and around him and that he'd be better off having the wound treated topically at night and to treated extensively by a physician in the morning.

Which meant no magic. Again. Just to be 'safe.'

A physician that, in less than a candlemark, would rip him a new asshole for the injury before he'd pull out a sewing needle, a sharp knife, and a jar of alcohol that was so concentrated that it might cause his liver to fail simply by looking at it. He would then go and rip the field medic that had treated him a second one. That part would be done with Akaran's blessing, and suggestions for additional profanities and obscenities to call the man for waiting to treat it for so long.

It was part of why he slept like shit, but he couldn't blame it all on the wound. Part of it was worry – Seline hadn't been seen since the attack, and he was terrified that they'd pull her body out of the water. The burns along his arms and across his chest were another; it turned out that you shouldn't necessarily channel lightning if you're wearing iron and steel.

The field medic had remarked that it was a, "Fisking miracle you didn't have your heart burned out," among other choice words. Badin was also a bit impressed by the simple fact he wasn't dead. Although he was so busy nursing a cracked shoulder that he didn't give a shit about the priest's blisters and pinked flesh.

That injury was being treated by the army, and much like the priest, he was on hold from additional magical treatments. He'd overheard an Isamiael-ordained healer tell the mage, "Until we are satisfied that the etheric taint from the Harlot-worshiping sociopath has had a chance to dissipate from you, you get a sling. Lucky you aren't being thrown in a wheelbarrow to go up to the Pyre." He assumed the medic didn't have the courage to tell it to Badin's face, though he could've been wrong.

That would've been reasonably acceptable on the surface, had a note not been pushed under Akaran's door before he woke up that read, rather succinctly, *"Don't break my toys,"* signed simply, *"E."* It was rarely a good sign to start your day with a threat from the priestess of night, although he understood her point. It wasn't the only point, but he'd had a conversation with another person bearing an even stronger threat.

"Catherine will be along to see you shortly, but before she arrives, she needs to make sure you understand the gravity of the situation from yesterday – and how important it is to claim the discussion before it can get out of hand," the waystation's caretaker had began after she delivered his meal.

The 'truth' about yesterday was simple. He was told, and in absolutely no uncertain terms, that it was *the* story that the Order was going to stick to. That it was the story *he* was going to stick to. That if he was asked by anyone other than the Maiden, her Paladin-Commander, or anyone else short the Holy General, that this was *the only* story that was to be repeated.

Contrary to popular belief, the city had not been attacked by a demon last night. Rather, it was a 'brazen assault' by an unnamed privateer with a magical bent that allowed him to use illusions and other spells to suggest the presence of demons to terrify the ports he struck. The murders at *Narwhal's Spike* had been a direct predecessor to his assault on the port with the intent to murder one of the Queen's most stalwart defenders – Paladin Faldine Golanstav – to prevent his magic from being detected before it was too late.

The Navy fought valiantly and battlemages from the Queen's army, as well as members of the Orders of Stara and Love had fought off the interlopers before they could succeed in ransacking the port. Unfortunately, many men gave their lives to the cause. A parade would be held in their honor, and plans would soon be underway to rebuild the *Hullbreaker* and the *Shatterstorm* both as larger, greater warships. A third vessel, some transport skiff named the *Servitude*, would be honored with a plaque somewhere.

Further, it is believed that the assault at the *Narwhal* had been carried out by 'enhanced humans,' who were no doubt some kind of experiment from the shores of Sycio. The desert dwellers were the only ones capable of crewing a ship and sending an assault force of questionable humanity. It would tie into the recent apprehension of a pair of Sycian natives in Basion in days prior.

An investigation would be had at length.

The responsible parties would eventually be brought to justice.

Even if they weren't responsible.

Ultimately it didn't matter. None of the politics were going to be Akaran's problem. He found that out soon after he was told the story. He was there, everyone knew that. The Order couldn't hide his involvement even if they wanted. He was there, and he was both blamed for, and celebrated over, the destruction of the *Hullbreaker* – even though it had been taken over by magically-enhanced pirates.

Apparently the ship had been turned into a bomb, of sorts. His efforts to defeat the mage aboard caused an uncontrollable reaction. Destroying it where he did saved the navy from losing any more boats. It also let the privateer get away (though he wasn't sure *how*).

The official story didn't endear him to the Admiralty, but the navy grunts – the ones who didn't give a solid shit what the *official* story was – had taken a shine to him. They'd helped fish him out of the water, and they'd spent the rest night fishing bodies of their friends free too. Friends that were horribly disfigured. Friends that were horribly mutilated. Friends that they'd had to cut down themselves.

Not a demon their collective asses. He'd run his mouth a bit about it while they got him to safety, he heard. Not that he remembered, but that was what they said. Letting Daringol plunge into his heart and then letting a battlemage fry them both with a bolt of lightning had the effect of causing a brief bit of temporary confusion.

Imagine that.

He was confused. He was disoriented. The blast shook him around and left him stunned. *That's* why he was ranting about a demon. Just the half-conscious exclamations of a brain-rattled priest.

Confusion aside, it didn't let him escape a lecture. "I can't even decide where to begin with you," Catherine said with a sigh as she slipped into his room. It was one of three rest areas in the waystation, and was ultimately fairly spartan. They weren't designed to hold a guest for more than an evening at a time, and only one person per room. "I think I should thank you. I think I should reward you. At the same time..."

"At the same time, eleven additional people are dead, three warships are in the bottom of the Alenic, and the Admiralty is about to erupt like a volcano?"

"Fourteen," she corrected, "and yes. I'm not sure if I should blame you for any of that but…"

He nodded and rubbed his aching temples. "Daringol was my job. I failed it."

"Can't say you've failed it *now*," the Maiden retorted. "If there is anything left of it at all it isn't for a lack of effort. Effort, which I may add, was… I can't. I can't explain how I feel about it. What were you thinking?"

Akaran rubbed at his neck. "Which part? The vampires or…?"

She shook her head tiredly. "You know what? No. There's no point in even trying. I don't know if anyone could've known what was coming but I can't blame you for sinking a ship that wasn't even a real ship anymore."

"Oh it was real enough," he grumbled. "I'm… I'm never eating yeshal again. Or… or maybe fish at all."

"You or anyone else. I have seen some utterly *foul* things before in my life but that… You're aware there's a carcass floating in the bay, yes? I have wardkeepers trying to pull it to shore. They *all* hate you. The carcass? It has to be burnt. Oh, and the Navy won't touch it."

"I thought it was an illusion?"

She let the bitterness in his voice slide. "It turns out the illusion was amplified by a sea-creature caught and held against its will. It also smells so foul that there is no amount of soap in the Kingdom that I think I will be able to remove it from my skin."

The priest shuddered. "Is that what I…" he started to ask before an absolutely *murderous* glare cut into him, "…thought I caught a whiff of last night?"

"I'm *quite* sure it was," she retorted firmly. "*Illusions* aside, you just exorcised the largest *arin-goliath* that has been recorded in a century. In public. In the middle of the 2nd Naval Armada's base of operations. After hunting and killing two *entirely different* damned creatures." Catherine took a long breath and steadied herself against the doorframe. "In addition to the unstable ether you channeled at the Manor that caused statues to move while you exiled a possessed shadow."

"You make it sound like that's a bad thing."

"I make it sound like I don't know what to do with you," she snapped back. "In very large part because I am not entirely sure what in the fisk you are."

That was the one statement he didn't expect to hear from the Maiden, and his jaw dropped open in shock. "Excuse me? What?"

"Can't say you're not an exorcist, because… well. Obviously. Can't say that you aren't a follower of Love, because Her essence hasn't quit flowing around you since you got your magic back. You swing a sword too hard to take the title of Brother and be relegated to using defensive or curative magics. You are far too young to be considered for advancement to paladin

– yet if I assume you're human, then you can't be an Avatar. Or angelic. And frankly, I've heard you curse too much to think of the latter."

"You… *assume*… I'm human?" he asked slowly. "I uh… for what it's worth, I think I am too?"

"I think you are a powder-keg with legs," Catherine grunted. "A bomb waiting to go off. An inferno that's looking for kindling. I think you're a danger to yourself and others. For the sake of the Goddess, you had a battlemage *infuse you with a lightning bolt* after *you willingly drew the arin-goliath back into your soul*! You understand how absolutely *insane* that is, don't you?"

"Well I mean –"

"And you were standing in water! *In the actual ocean.*"

"I was standing on a sandbar," he countered.

She lifted her hands and squeezed the air like she was trying to choke him. "It was close enough! That was the singularly most *reckless* attempt at a banishment I have ever seen *in my life*!" she shouted with a strangled cry. "If that had gone wrong what possibly could've happened?"

Akaran sighed and rubbed at one of the compresses on his left arm. "Then you'd have known not to try to do anything else like it. I don't think it would've been easy but that thing was going to be destroyed no matter what I did. I tried to end it fast before anyone else got hurt."

"I should thank you for that, and I would, if I wasn't so damn *mad* at you," she retorted. "I reiterate – you are an *absolute* danger to yourself and others around you."

He didn't try to argue. It wouldn't help, and he was pretty sure his hopes at staying in the Order were fading by the moment. "So what happens next? What are you going to do with me?"

The Templar dropped her hand to her belt and unhooked a pocket. She dug around for a minute and pulled out his sigil of rank and a second necklace. "I am keeping this," she replied as she flashed the Order icon at him.

His stomach dropped. "But… Maiden. Please. I didn't do anything wrong."

"You didn't do anything *right*, either," she countered as she flung the other necklace into his lap. His eye went wide as he looked down at the gold chain with a silver coin embossed with a split-faced woman. One side of the icon was smiling; the other was not. "Yet if I am going to keep the Admiralty out of your ass, you need *that*. You've had it since *before* you arrived at Cableture, you simply *lost it* so you weren't able to show it off."

"I… you're giving me… after chewing my head off? I… I don't understand?"

"It's *provisional*. By edict of the First Exorcist, you are too damn young to be considered for it – so you *won't* get access to the full arsenal you'd be otherwise due. But you can wave it at people and pull rank, which you might need to do. As far as if I trust you with it? No. Not just no, but *in no way shape or form* do I trust you with it." She glared at him and sighed in frustration. "But, again, if I'm going to keep you out of irons, you're going to need it."

He didn't look away from the sigil and he ran his thumb over the face of it again, and again, and again. "Five years, and three seasons; the earliest anyone's received it."

"As it is said: 'Be among the people and live in the dark so you know what it is you lead; for to wield Her sword is to pave the way,' if you remember correctly."

Akaran nodded slowly. "Five years full and one act worthy of ascendancy," he replied as he slipped the lien cord that was looped through a hole in the top around his neck. "That's the requirement, 'Before the rank of paladin shall be granted,' so the writings proclaim."

"Not that anyone outside of our particular Order cares a shit either way for the writings of the First, but they do tend to a give a shit about the weight that sigil carries. Now you can leave the port without having to answer any of Maddon's questions."

The way she said that made it seem that his exit was implied to be sooner rather than later. "I told you what happened. There's not much more to add."

She shrugged. "Me, yes. Did you really think you could *blow up two of the ships of the line* and leave a giant carcass in the Harbor without Maddon and his captains demanding that I strip you of rank, title, clothes, and some skin before I deliver you to them?" she asked with a huff and a snort of disgust. "Because if you did..."

"You're promoting me so I can run away?"

"I'm *provisionally appointing you* to the rank of Paladin so that you can deal with other matters."

He looked a little crestfallen. "I'm being promoted so I can run."

"Yes. That, and... it is impossible to say that you aren't channeling the Goddess. You are, very clearly. A few years from now, and what you did in the harbor would have counted even if the mess at the Manor hadn't already." As he perked up and the idea started to go to his head, she quickly turned around and took the wind out of his sails. "I need you unencumbered by the body politic and the suffocation offered by certain individuals in Basion that hold rank over your former title."

The exorcist-turned-paladin flicked his tongue across his teeth. "You want to be certain that if I tell the 4th to burn down a building, they'll burn it without running to you to see if I have permission first."

Catherine flashed him a steely-eyed glare. "I want you to be able to throw the Betrothed in it without argument if you're given cause. I'm going to be tied up cleaning up this mess, and I don't trust Elsith to purge the city on her own."

"Are you sure you want me up there instead of down here? Daringol was my mistake. Not yours. I have experience with it."

"You have too much experience with it," the Maiden countered. "It's entered your body on more than one occasion. While I am certain it is destroyed *now,* I don't want to risk any further uncontrolled reactions should you interact with *any* residual aura or essence that may still be floating about. Nor can we ignore the supposed source of the monsters that brought us down to the Port to begin with."

Akaran lightly tugged at the sigil and nodded slowly. "Fair. Though, and do forgive me for assuming ulterior motives, but..."

"...but you don't think that I'm just trying to save your ass from an inquiry? You're right. I'm sending you to the city with an upgrade in position after I finished accusing you of being the most reckless, hazardous, and possibly foolish exorcist I've ever met and you doubt that's the only reason?"

"Not in so many words, but yeah."

The Maiden-Templar pursed her lips. "These are uncertain times and you are a loose, and I'm assume, Goddess-blessed *cannon.* You have shown a tenacity that I am not entirely comfortable with, yet one that unarguably yields results. You will have handlers, of course, but you've already done much of the work to hunt these bastards down. We'd be starting over fresh if I didn't. I don't think we have that much time to waste."

"I don't think we have any time to waste."

"No, we don't. There is going to be a brief delay – you'll be going back to Basion by cart, rather than by mage. Telburn has informed me that your aura is too chaotic after last night for him to feel comfortable putting his people at risk opening a portal."

Akaran frowned and almost started to pout. "But I don't *like* going by cart up the canyon. It'll take the better part of the damn day."

"A damn day that you won't be tearing open the wound on your stomach or aggravating the burns on your arms," she countered. "Ideally a day you won't be tapping into the ether. Your soul needs to rest as much as your body does, despite your insistence on pushing it. There's another reason, too, of course."

"What?"

"I don't dare pull a mage away from the coastline right now," Catherine admitted begrudgingly. "That wraith infested one ship. I need to make sure there aren't any others."

That horrible thought sent a chill down his spine. "Do we have any idea why it came here? Was it... all of it... because of me?"

"I don't know," she admitted. "You're the one that saw it coming. Your pet wraith is the one that told you that she was attached to it. It's natural for *arin-goliaths* to seek out parts of themselves when they've been pulled away from their cores. It could be that it came for you. It could be that it was attracted by something that the Office of Divination did. Or whatever core it had. Maybe a reference or an anchor to the port. I don't know. I'm going to rip the sea-mages in the *Ood* a new asshole after I finish with yours."

"Shit," he whispered. "Then this is my fault, isn't it?"

She reached over and grabbed his hand in a tight, firm grip and shook it roughly. "Don't. Don't go down that hole. If it hadn't come *here* it would have gone *elsewhere*. If it had gone *elsewhere*, it's likely it would have spread. Here? We met it with the full force of the temple and the Armada. Some other, piss-pot of a harbor? There'd be more dead than this."

Akaran shook his head. "Men died last night. Men died because it came here for me."

She glanced over her shoulder and out the door. "The men that died last night died fighting for their Kingdom, their Gods, and their families. They died, and that wraith was destroyed. If it had docked anywhere else, the lives it took *then* and *there* would have been wasted."

"I should've pulled it away from the port. I knew it was coming. I could've done... I don't know. I... I should have done something else. Anything else."

"Maybe. Maybe not. Did you know it was this close?"

"No. I didn't. I had a feeling but... feelings and knowledge..."

"Did your wraith? Did you not share a warning that would have prevented it from making landfall here?"

He took a deep breath and ran his fingers across the fuzz on the top of his head. "I knew it was getting close. I didn't know it was... that. I didn't know that it was going to land last night. Then the attack at the *Spike* and..."

"Akaran, I have read every single one of your reports," Catherine replied after thinking his remarks through. "While I didn't believe you were right about the ship, I couldn't imagine anything myself other than what you yourself expected. A ship crewed by the damned, spotted off coast, and kept at bay by the Royal Wizards until it could be disposed of."

"Instead we got a giant dead squid that taught an entire ship how to swim," he grunted darkly.

"Exactly." The Maiden took a deep breath. "The Sisters saw an event that was to unfold, and I am certain this was it. I fear that because of what they said."

The exorcist bristled and pulled his hand free. "What did they say? Don't tell me they found a way to make it worse…?"

"The Sisters don't *make* things, they *see* things," the Maiden corrected. "In short? They referenced a plurality of men – two, three, or more, we don't know – called the 'Kings of One Eye.' They are to decide 'The Fate of Shadows,' after a battle against a ship." She pointed at his patch and looked nervously glum as she did. "I would prefer us not to be in the land of the blind, but an argument could be made that we have not been as all-seeing as we would wish in recent times."

"That's… Maiden. I have no idea. None. None about any of it. I'm just me. I'm just a guy with a sword and a limp and…" he tried to explain before she waved her hand and cut him off.

Catherine stood up and sighed. "We aren't asked if we want to serve. We're told. The Sisters were told something that I don't like the implications of. The Order informed me. Now I'm informing you. Take it to heart – you've already done a whole lot of damage. Good or bad, I honestly don't know."

She left after the remark, and the surgeon came in a moment later. While the medic worked, all Akaran could think of was the first time he'd seen who he came to realize had to be Annix. All he could do was remember the hateful look he had.

In his one good eye.

***

"So then," Anais began, "I do appreciate your hospitality, my good man. Except we both know you aren't a good man. Now you find yourself a lost man, trapped between circumstances you can't control. People you don't have interest in have taken an interest in you."

Overseer Hannock wasn't exactly fat, but he was a large man, and the floorboards of his office creaked as he lumbered out from behind his desk to face her directly. "You don't lead by being good."

"Oh, history would agree with you. It's true nobody has ever taken power without stacking bodies, and the ways that good and ill define themselves allow for some things to be judged appropriate," she countered before she placed a wrinkled fingertip on his chest. "Of course we both know which side of that you're on."

"You have no proof."

"I don't need much. A few whispers here and there; a suggestion for someone to look into one dealing or another. Or maybe a suggestion to look in your basement."

"Nobody will find anything if they look. There's nothing *to* find."

She chortled softly and walked past him with a smile. "Of course they won't. What of the men you have empty it though? I mean you could do a wonderful job of obscuring identities, of course. Or you could miss one. Or they could be seen. Are you as certain your men will keep their lips closed in the face of overwhelming interest by exterior parties?"

Hannock's face darkened and he clenched his pudgy fists tight. "I heard you made hard deals. I also heard you were younger."

Anais flinched and ran her hands across the wrinkles on her face and sighed wistfully. "Yes, well. It's quite amazing how stress can age a person. Stress I would like to relieve."

"You're trying to relieve your stress by compounding mine."

"Quite the contrary," she countered. "I'm relieving my stress by putting you on notice that your actions haven't been as ignored as you'd wish. Now, an argument could be made that I am holding that against you – not an unreasonable one – but a different argument could be made that I am offering to help you. If I know about your hobbies, I can help you find better places to entertain yourself with them that won't draw as much attention."

The Overseer growled low in his throat. "What, exactly, do you want?"

"Safety. Freedom. Life," the broker explained with another wistful sigh. "Things that all people want and wish for, I suppose. Except to find those – two of those – I need access to someone. Ideally in a darkened alley with only one exit." She paused and glanced over at him. "The opposite of the kind you prefer, of course."

"You stormed into my office and you can't get 'access' to someone?" he grunted. "Must be a powerful person."

"He is. Just not in the way you are," Anais admitted. "I need the Tidesinger. I understand he has no intention of leaving the city until after the last of the refugees are settled."

Hannock blinked. "Quinchecco? All this for one of those swimming fiskers? With all the effort you put in to get to me I expected you to demand Paverilak or Esterveen."

She shook her head in mild disgust. "I have had my fill enough of drunks and women with authority to last me a literal eternity. No, no. I need the Aquallan."

"Then go get him."

"I am. How I choose to get him isn't important. This is simply the most expedient way. I would think, of all people, you'd understand the value of both *indirect encounters* and *rapid acquisitions*."

Hannock bristled up but sagged a little in defeat. "How in the pits do you think I'm supposed to arrange that?"

"I don't know, nor do I care. Only that you do it. I need it within days.

Three, at most."

He just laughed at her. "You expect me to arrange a meeting with the Tidesinger, in private, in a place that you can get in and out of without being seen, in three days?"

"Yes. I do. You will."

She said it with such finality that he quit laughing. As he slowly set his hands down on his desk and leaned forward, he studied her face carefully. "If I do this, you go away. You're out of my city, and out of my hair. For good."

"That's the entire point of that particular meeting," Anais deftly returned, "and I shall do you one better – I'll save the lives of anyone you send to silence me before or after by promising you that you won't have to. Once I have my conversation with Quinchecco, I offer my word and a blood pact to say that I will never return again."

"A blood pact, huh?"

"Huh indeed," Anais replied as she drew a simple knife from inside her robe and as he watched, slit the palm of her hand open. Darkened blood seeped from it as she extended it to his. "I'll even sweeten the deal – blondes are your preference, aren't they?"

A shadow crossed over his face as he hesitantly accepted her hand. He had no reason to wonder why she bled, though others in the city would. One woman didn't need to. Anais smiled as she shook and they repeated a sacred vow that would ensure suffering on either party that broke it.

A vow that would only hurt the people that bled.

Elsewhere in the city, in a room beneath the streets, Seline held a bandage with a shaky hand to a bloody scratch on her neck. Tears rolled down her cheeks as she tugged at the iron shackle that had her leg bolted to the floor.

She'd wanted to get away from Akaran.

She'd gotten her wish.

***

"You have a habit of making friends," Karaj said to wake the exorcist up. The surgeon that had visited him an hour ago had done a wonderful job in cleaning out the gash across his stomach, and the belistand he'd offered had done a wonderful job of putting the priest back to sleep. "The medic hasn't quit complaining about you since he left the waystation – well done, I must say."

Akaran rubbed his eyes and shifted a little. The doctor hadn't just worked over his stomach; he'd gone to town on the burns and a few other scratches he hadn't really noticed. He hadn't hurt that much before... but now? "Caretaker," he said with a tired nod in greeting, "what can I do for you?"

"From you, that is a very open question with very dangerous implications," they replied. They were carrying a book that looked oddly familiar, and Catherine's assistant handed it over without fanfare. "I am afraid to say that your life has opened up to a series of complications."

"Complications? What's that supposed to mean?"

"That you will have a task after dealing with the infestation in the city. You've already wanted to work on it; though how the Goddess seems to want you involved sooner than later," Karaj answered. "I know that explains little, but here is the truth: you're going to hunt someone. You need to know about them."

Akaran's face darkened as he looked down at the book. "I remember this. I tried to read it in the Repository before..." he said, as he let it trail off.

The caretaker nodded. "Oh, I'm aware. You must forgive me – there's little I can say. Seals of Order, and all that. If Catherine knew that I was talking to you about this, we would both be in trouble."

"Then why are you? And who am I going to go hunt?"

Karaj took a long, deep breath and opened their hands wide. "His name is Nastavol. He is an enemy of the Order – an enemy of the world. You know him from elsewhere."

The color in his face drained away. "Toniki. He's the one that tried to blind Mariah. Killed Galagrin. Some others of the 13th. His name just came up in Cableture – Anais works for him, if Rmaci is right."

"Rmaci, you say? Interesting. Yet, he's done far worse than that," the aide replied firmly. "That tome. Read it. Study it. Learn it. There are things in this world that are worse than demons, and he is one such of those."

"Worse than a demon?" Akaran asked as he ran his hand over the tome. "Aside from the Fallen, I didn't think that was possible."

"It shouldn't be, and therein is the problem," the caretaker cautioned. "It isn't just Toniki. His name has been circulated in the darkest of depths from Civa to Dawnfire to Ogibus and Sycio. You are not to repeat it, of course; the only people in this city that hold rank enough to even know it are myself and the Maiden-Templar. Were there another way? You wouldn't know at all."

The exorcist looked up from the musty pages and tilted his head slightly to the side. "Then why tell me? I have my hands full right now with everything else."

"Because he's going to come for you. It won't be when you expect it. It won't be when you want it. There's no way to set a trap. There's no way to flip his interests, whatever they may be. He is too crafty, too sly, and too well connected with the worlds beyond for such trivial attempts at capture."

Akaran blinked slowly. "Come for me? Why? I mean yeah — I want this bastard dead for what he did to Mariah. He plucked out her eye and I take that personally. But I want to kill a lot of things that don't know it yet."

"Because there is blood between you," Karaj replied, "and after the events of the last day, I expect that you'll come to spill more of it than anyone would give you credit for," they said as they left the room without any kind of further explanation at all.

***

Akaran didn't put the book down until a wardkeeper came to escort him to a caravan headed to Basion. "Hmm. 'The Fall of A'twol'?" the keeper asked as he caught a glimpse of it. "Oh. I remember that name. City in Sycio? Used to be? Got... it got leveled, didn't it? Does that have anything to do with the attack those sand-sucking fools launched on us last night?"

For once?

He had no reply.

EPILOGUE
Evening of Lithdis, 9ᵗʰ of Firstgrow, 513 QR

The day brought travel and alliances. The night brought planning. Whispers in the dark; words in shadows. The final set of pieces had been on the board, and the players were almost in position. The next moves would set the showdowns.

There were many conflicts soon to come to a head.

This night? There was no madness. No chaos. The moves people made in the dark were the only rational recourse for each soul involved in the future of the city. The ones that had put themselves in the path of the Divine and the actors of both Fallen and Risen – and the actors who held no allegiance to any.

In the tannery by the Overflow, Annix, Sherril, and their newest minion couldn't care less about the losses they'd suffered in Cableture. It had cost the Lovers a paladin, and Anais would eventually stick her head up sooner rather than later. When she did, they'd bite it off. Parl's warmaiden was better suited to do the job than a healer or attache or courier, after all.

But first they'd draw out the exorcist that had destroyed his shadow. Annix hadn't suffered pain of that magnitude for years, decades – maybe centuries. He had felt pain, and he had lost many of his carefully-set plans. Someone would answer for that.

The man held hooded, bloody, and unconscious in the pile of skins in the corner would be that answer. Sherril had tossed him there without thought or care; it didn't matter to her in the least. It mattered to Annix. It would matter to the city.

Her Meister stormed over to the beaten man and ripped the sack off of his head. He moved without shadow, as if the torchlight no longer cared of his existence and moved through him as if he had no substance. With the pain the exorcist had inflicted? It was a guess if it would ever return.

Annix looked down at the muscular, handsome man and spat bile at his face. "If I can't have my new bride, Dawnfire will not have its wedding."

"They'll lash out for this," Sherril warned. "I don't think you understand how angry this will make the city."

"The city? The city will be delighted. The guards? The Overseer? The Lovers? They'll be embarrassed." Annix reached down and tilted the man's head up and smiled. "The Odinals? Well then."

"Will… kill… you…" the half-conscious midlander groaned through bloodied, swollen lips. "You don't… know who I am…"

The vampire just laughed. "Oh I do. I do. Malik Odinal, son of Nemok Odinal, of Clan Odinal. You would've been the husband to an uninteresting bitch – and now?"

Malik kicked in his bonds and tried to struggle free. "I'll kill… kill you…"

"Death is an inconvenience," Annix snapped, "what comes after? That is much more entertaining."

***

The already dead had a meeting of their own.

The Man of the Red Death stood along the edge of Yittl Canyon. He'd spent a few hours watching the exorcist make his way back into the city. He wasn't alone; his favored acolyte hovered beside him. Another figure stood in the dark, and it blended in so perfectly with the landscape it might've been the very dark itself.

"[Don't trust her/she schemes against,]" Rishnobia warned.

"Of course she does. I would not have recruited her if she did not."

"[Want her to move against you/do you not have enough grief?]"

The dusky-skinned man shook his head and slowly pulled the red hood off of his close-cut dark hair and smiled slowly. "The effort it takes to summon forth one such as her is not minuscule. The effort it takes to ensure she remembered where she came from? To remember, and not lose her sense of self? I have no patience for those of weak wills. She will attempt to survive at any cost. I would expect no less."

Rishnobia chittered nervously. "[My Lord/My Master? Then how can we trust/how can you task her?]"

"Because she will do all in her power to avoid a return. She will bargain. She will deal. She will seek to undercut me." The Sycian smiled as he slid his hands behind his back. "In the process, she will do as I ask, even if she does to do against me."

"[But Master/My Master! What if she turns/what if she speaks? She knows much/about much known! She could expose us/expose you to them!]"

Nastavol turned to his minion and nodded once. "You underestimate our opposition. They already know. They do not know what they know – but they know. They are fools in many ways. They are not fools eager to repeat history."

The demon tried to calm itself down, but all it managed to do was convince half of its fur to flatten. The harder it tried, the more it looked like an angry cat with a multitude of red eyes. "[When they react/if they know? It will be violent/it will be final.]"

"Violent? Yes," the Man of the Red Death admitted. "Final? Nothing is final, Rishnobia, until *I* decree it so. Am I not correct, Maelphistiphan?"

The shadow billowed out in a cloud of bones, dust, and darkness before it fell in upon itself and the cloak from the Hunter's guild that the cloud had obscured. His assassin didn't offer a word in agreement or argument. It allowed a skull to appear under its hood.

And it twisted the bones into a smile.

***

Rmaci smiled, too.

The burns were gone. The ice had faded to a dull sheen across her side. She didn't hurt. She didn't ache. She didn't feel the pull of the underworld. She felt at peace. She felt at peace, and she hid on a beach well out of sight of the port.

The wraith couldn't frolic in the waves. She couldn't roll around in the sand. She couldn't dive into the water and swim. She couldn't do more than sit and smile and rock softly back and forth. She didn't know what exactly had changed. She just knew it had.

"You did an admirable job," a voice called out from the night. "You showed him the way forward. You helped him see."

Rmaci spun around and landed on all fours as she turned to Erine. She wasn't alone, either – the freak from the harbor was with her. "*Eclipsian. I thought you had forgotten about me.*"

"No, nor could I ever," the priestess replied. "I am pleased that you have exceeded all my expectations."

The spy gestured down at her body as she started to relax again. "*Is this... is this my reward? Am I forgiven?*"

"Of more murders than I can count?" Erine asked with a shrug. "I do not know if there *is* forgiveness for that." Before the wraith could demand her meaning, she went on. "Though you have proven your worth. That alone, at times, may earn a reprieve."

"*A reprieve would be a wonder. I dare now ask if the same thought will be given to my former host. His mind... there is much in there he doesn't* know. He doesn't understand," she replied slowly. "*Things that I am not sure I wish to. Places. People. Bloodlines.*"

The Lover steeled their body and looked at Rmaci with such intensity that she swore they were looking into her soul. "Some things that are broken should not be put together."

"*I think someone tried,*" she countered, "*and were I still an ally to Civa, I think my superiors would be very interested in if I could find out more. As it stands, I would assume that recent events in his sanity have shaken some of the chains off of things that some would rather stay hidden. Just... so you know.*"

"But you do," Karaj charged as Erine tilted her head to the side. "You spent enough time in his head. You know."

The spy faltered and watched as a sheen of ice blossomed across her stomach. "*I know that there is more to him than there should be. That he has allegiances that have been buried. That his eye was no accident. That there is interest beyond yours in him; interest that was there as a child.*"

With a cough, the priestess cleared her throat as the pair stared at each other in a test of wills. "He is a violent soul in adulthood. Violence in his dreams. Such things are learned at a young age even if one can't remember them."

"*Are you so sure he can't? Or have others made a goal in ensuring he won't? A man of red eyes and dusky skin, perhaps?*" she asked as she slowly slid back across the beach and away from the pair. "*A man with a blood-red robe?*"

Karaj frowned. "You know him, don't you?"

Rmaci unconsciously put her weight – phantom as it was – on her back foot. "*I... I do not know what he is. Either of them. Just that his mind is fractured, and was broken long before I or the arin ever took hold.*"

That wasn't enough of an answer. Karaj took a step forward. "Except you *do*. The Abyss knows, so you know, don't you?"

She blanched and narrowed her eyes into slits. "*I don't know what you mean,*" she replied as the accusation made her remember things that she'd learned below. Things she didn't want to know. Things Akaran wouldn't want to know. Things he'd *need* to know.

Things the Order didn't want him to know.

"Of course you do," the Lover countered. "You know his lineage. You know his blood. After all your time with him, you know the secret locked in his head. The one he *doesn't* know he knows. Don't you?"

The spy took another step back as the implications started to hit home and the image of the cloaked Sycian started to manifest in the air in front of her at the very thought. "*Even if I knew such a thing, I could not say it. My tongue is bound by the Abyss.*"

"Is it?" the caretaker asked. "You no longer appear as a child of damnation. Do those rules still apply?"

Rmaci's eyes went wide.

She started to speak.

Karaj spoke first. "**EXPUNGE**."

A flash of light billowed around the Lover's hands and slammed into her body from head to toe. The Word simply ripped the spy into shreds. When the flash of light and blast of heated air subsided, the wraith was gone.

Erine sighed and hung her head. "A secret so dangerous that you'd annihilate her?" the priestess asked as she stepped away from Karaj with a frown. "I think I should be thankful that I didn't hear it."

"As you should be," the Lover replied coldly.

After a moment of deathly silence, she spoke up again. "I had greater hopes for that one. Do you think she'll make it to the realms above?"

"I don't know," the caretaker admitted. "It is not for me to assume."

The Eclipsian sighed again and offered a bow to the departed spirit. "Then I shall offer a prayer to Lethandria and –" she began to say before the words trailed off into nothingness.

The words, and her life.

Karaj pulled the knife out of the Eclipsian's back as she slumped into the surf. "I do apologize, Night-Mother," Karaj whispered as she died silently on the sands, "but until I know the extent to which his locks have been picked, I can't risk you inside his dreams either."

***

Each move guaranteed finality.

Each move promised an end.

Songs would be sung of the days to come. Bards would recite the events again and again. Tavern guests would cheer. Courts of nobility would offer coin to hear it played again and again. The madness of the days, weeks, and months past – and the hours yet to come?

The reckoning – the *reckonings* – would ring true for years to come.

But not just as a story. It would be a song. It would be a dirge.

It would be the requiem to their insanity.

End:
Insanity's Reckoning
Book III of the Auramancer's Exorcism

Hey there! Thank you for making it to the end of Reckoning. As we prepare to sing for the saints and cry for the condemned, do you mind leaving a review? I hate to ask, but to authors like me, reviews matter.

They let us know what we got right, what we got wrong, and they even play a role in what advertising agencies and book stores will carry us.

To make it easier for e-readers, the link is below.

Thank you! These really do matter, and they really do have a direct impact on if this book can be called a success (financially or otherwise).

https://www.amazon.com/gp/product/B091NBDPVV

Now that the big marketing ask is out of the way...

Dead men won't tell the end of this tale.

They'll sing it.

Next:
Insanity's Requiem
Book IV – and final – of the Auramancer's Exorcism

THE COMPENDIUM OF THE DAMNED, THE DIVINE, AND ALL THINGS IN-BETWEEN

Admiral Theodin Maddon
Admiral Maddon oversees the 2ⁿᵈ Naval Armada out of Port Cableture, though he hates to be on land any longer than absolutely necessary. As such, he tends to spend his time serving on the Queen's Dragon, *a* Crownship-*class warship.*

Alrediah (port city, southern Dawnfire)
A port city of impressive stature, despite being in the middle of the coast that nobody cares about. Nestled firmly in the bottom-end of Thatchell province, and pinned between Waschali and Kettering both, it's a midpoint and waystation for travelers going across the southern shore at best, even if the people that live there think they're the most important location east of Basion City (which they aren't).

Allohoc
A Metora-class frigate in the Dawnfire Navy.

Basion City Granalchi Annex
The home base of operations, education, commerce, and all-things study for the Granalchi Adepts in Basion City and most of Kettering Province as a whole.

Bonchin
Unlike the port city of Alrediah or Cableture, Port Bonchin knows exactly what it is: a cargo terminal. It doesn't proclaim to be anything more, or anything less, and the Overseer for the port is a dyed-in-the-wool believer of

the might of the Blackstone Trading Company and 'Commerce Over All.' (Which may well make it the most dangerous port along the southern side of the Kingdom.)

Brothers of Love
In the Order of Love, the title 'Brother' is both a general honorific and an established rank. These are the men that have taken on the responsibility to train, teach, and educate the more militant branch of the Order in all things magic and general combat.

Celestine 'Cel' Navarshi
The owner of the Drunken Imperial, *a tavern in Lower Naradol.*

Central Indexiary
Located in the bottom of the Repository of Miral, the Central Indexiary is a semi-sentient golem that was created with the ability to remember (and regurgitate the location) of every report ever filed in the depths of the entire complex.

Chacos
A magical foci for a very difficult — and powerful — type of reanimation. The creation of a chacos requires murder and ritualistic sacrifice of the worst sort. The ability to summon one requires understanding of Necrosia to such a mastery as to put the summoner on a pedestal higher than a Headmaster Adept of the Granalchi Academy, if not close to the Dean itself.

Coldstone Shard
An interesting relic of an exorcism-gone-wrong in the village of Toniki in 512 QR. It is believed to be a physical manifestation of the Upper Elemental Plane of Ice itself. The bulk of the main stone has been put under lock and key by order of the Crown itself. Or at least, so says the official report.

Crownship-class
Crownship-*class warships are a true behemoth of the open ocean. Capable of carrying a massive crew of between seventy and ninety brave souls, the arrival of a* Crownship *in a naval engagement signifies that the Queen is done with your shit.*

Dormasil/dormosul/dormahul
In rural Dawnfire, most people are able to live in a house, a barracks, or in or a boarding hall in a small village, even if that house is little more than a ramshackle tent. In urban areas, 'dormosul' are low-rent housing complexes

that can be afforded by semi-skilled laborers. They are a step above 'dormahuls,' which are little more than long halls with beds and a roof. Dormosuls offer individual rooms – or two or three rooms in one – called 'dormasils' that are capable of housing individuals or small-to-medium-sized families.

Elementalists
Mages (typically Granalchi) that focus on using magic of a specific element, such as fire, ice, water, stone, light, air, or darkness.

Eos'eno
An elemental-kin entity, born of a twisted magical experiment and a broken heart. She was a staunch ally to Akaran in the Battles of Coldstone's Summit, despite being entirely inhuman.

Episturine
Guardians of the Upper Elemental Plane of Ice. Until recently, their very existence was speculative at best.

Exorcist's Forgiveness
The Exorcists of the Order of Love are – and even encouraged! – allowed to offer the chance of salvation to the damned, the defiled, and the pit-born. It cannot be forced, and must be accepted whole-of-heart before the soul in question has a chance to seek redemption. It is not a promise that sins will be washed away, but it is a path for those that seek redemption. A difficult path, but a path. The Forgiveness starts the damned on their journey, which then turns to the Otherworldly Walk – the actual acts on the path to righteousness itself. It should be noted that both the Forgiveness and the Walk are a rarity, though they are treated with reverence in the Order.

Granalchi Summoning Grounds
An open, typically flat field located at every Granalchi Annex. Not all magic is safe to be practiced indoors.

Guidelines of Metaphysical Entanglements
A loose collection of suggestions, ideas, and theories that pretend to be 'rules' that govern how magic 'works' in the world. These are an offshoot of the Laws of Normality, and are often said to be the 'Suggestions of the Weird.'

Hall of Sea's Song
A temple devoted to the God of the Seas, Aqualla.

Hannock Bridge
The main bridge leading from beyond the Basion City gate and into the city proper.

Headmaster-Adept
A mage of great learning and understanding who has been placed in charge of a Granalchi Annex. The depths of learning and understanding are typically directly proportional to the size of the city that the Annex is serving at any given location.

Inquiry of Order
The Order of Love, can, at its discretion, open an Inquiry into a public event, figure, or criminal activity should they see fit in order to root out potential corruption or Abyssian influences. The vast majority of the Kingdom hates it when they announce their attention, and most think it's a way for the Order to muddle in affairs that they have no business being involved in.

Kols/Mols
The Knights of Love are magic-less (or magical-minimal) warriors in service to the Goddess. While She may not have blessed them with the ability to channel ether, She did see fit to grant them the ability to use a sword. The Messengers of Love, however, carry out Her will with pen, quill, magic, words, and often, violence. Mols are also known as Paladins of the Goddess of Love and share equal rank as the Knights.

Laws of Normality
The rules of the non-magical, natural world.

Ledel of Narwhal's Spike
The owner of a dingy, dirty, and often foul-smelling tavern in Port Cableture.

Lights of Dawn's Waves
An alert system used by the Grand Navy of the Dawn when ships are too far apart to easily signal at each other. An arrow shot into the sky would burn blue if all was safe, or red if there was a case of distress. A green arrow was to warn of magic on the seas, and was the last thing any sailor wanted to see.

Madder-root
A red root ground up and used to dye fabric a dull red color.

Mattanics
Practitioners of the 5th School of Magic who specialize in conjuration, teleportation, and physical manipulation of physical matter with magic.

Office of the Dean-Adept
The building – and the organization – that directly runs the entirety of the Granalchi Academy. It's located in Ogibus Bay,

Ogibus Bay
A collection of three large (and several small) islands south of Dawnfire and north of the Golden Empire of Matheia. They are a pirate haven, a merchant's dream, a mage's delight, and the centralized trade hub for commerce between Dawnfire, Sycio, Matheia, Atheia, and more.

Oldek
Located in Waschali Province, Oldek is another port city – but calling it a 'city' is a stretch of the word.

Orboria
In 512 QR, a demon named Makolichi attacked the not-quite-a-port-city of Gonta in Weschali Province. In the immediate fallout, a plot to smuggle a magical weapon (which was more of a 'spiritually-toxic bomb' than anything else) was discovered on board the Q. R. W. Orboria... after it had left the port. In an effort to stop it, Specialist-Major Badin called down a bolt of lightning that blew the mast in half. The Navy has not yet forgiven him for that, even as the events were chronicled in the tome appropriately named, 'Slag Harbor – an Unfortunate Interruption in the Snowflakes Trilogy,' which is a very odd name for a report...

Para-psiphonic
Mages and magic capable of siphoning magic from one point and transferring it to another.

Practionia
A building/office/home/other where a doctor, medic, medicannia, surgeon, or other such healer practices their craft.

(The) Provinces of Dawnfire
The Kingdom of Dawnfire is broken up between seven distinct provincial regions across it's oblong territory that stretches from coast to coast, with the Alenic Ocean to the immediate south. Imaii Province sits on the western shore, with Imaii to it's immediate south and Lowmarsh to the north-east.

Lowmarsh stretches under a wide section of the northern border, interrupted only by first Thatchell (the only province to stretch the entire length of the Kingdom) and then Waschali. Kettering Province sits nestled between both Thatchell and Lowmarsh. The Royal Capital Province of Mulvette abuts the west side of Kettering, and the south side of Imaii. Umaii Province – the smallest provincial region – covers a particularly foul section of the south-western coast that the Queen doesn't want to be directly responsible for.

Queen's Law of Contracts
The laws dictating how arrangements between individuals, Guilds, merchants, Divine Orders, and everyone else are handled. The Queen's Rule of Law is heavily based out of these fundamental structures.

Ralafon
Formerly a Civan spymaster. He had oversight of Civan activities in the south-eastern region of Dawnfire, including Gonta, Toniki, and more. He came to a relatively abrupt end that didn't end fast enough for his personal comfort at the hands of Riorik, the Hobbler, in late 512 QR.

The Graveyard
The Graveyard is a myth – because if it was real, it would be horrifying. Said to be ruled by Rear Admiral Xavier Roschell, it is an armada of sunken ships, damned sailors, and worse that openly sails the seas of both this world, and the Worlds Beyond.

The Precipice
The next to last stop. The end before the end. This is the realm where the Warden of the Abyss holds sway. It is a place where the dead are judged, the condemned are sentenced, and worse. There are only two ways to leave this region: you either fall to the Abyss, or you are granted passage to the Fields of Ash; a realm free of pain and suffering, but devoid of joy, laughter, or hope.

The Three
The three Archangels of Niasmis – Miral, the Guardian, Samia, the Passionate, and Li'Orla, the Grand Messenger. It is said that from time to time, Miral and Samia will manifest directly in the world to carry out Niasmis's will... or will choose an avatar to act in Their stead.

Tundrala
The Upper Elemental Plane of Ice, ruled by Istalla, the Queen of Ice.

Upper Adjunct Lexcanna Jealions
The former High Priestess/Upper Adjunct of the Temple of Stara in Basion City. She was murdered in early 512 QR, at first presumably by Specialist-Major Badin… but he's since been cleared of wrongdoing. Her true murderer has yet to be publicly named.

Usaic
An ice-elementalist from the Toniki area in Dawnfire. His efforts to create the Coldstone unleashed untold and unimaginable chaotic evil on the world, and has resulted in the deaths and suffering of dozens, if not hundreds, of people since.

Vahail
A Hall of Sea's Song located west of Port Cableture. It, and the village of Mardux, were flooded in a disaster in early 513 QR. It's believed that the flood was caused by an act of terrorism, though in truth, it was done to prevent the act in question.

Wardkeepers
In the Order of Love, Wardkeepers are defensive magic specialists. The bulk of the magical forces the Order trains fall under this category – ones that protect Love by offering, or creating, safe havens. They can fight, but the blade is not their calling. Wardkeepers are taught healing magic and medical skills as a matter of normalcy, and only receive passing training with weapons or offensive magics.

Watersculpt
Watersculpts are a mix of hydromancers and priests. They mix the elemental nature of water with the joy of creation held by Aqualla to create tools, artwork, and modifications to water – usually done by manipulating song. Their works never last, but they can be powerful (and beautiful) while they are maintained.

Will of Love
The nature, the essence, and the desire of the Goddess of Love Herself.

Yittl Canyon
A long canyon that doubles as farmland, grazeland, and more that leads from Basion City down to Port Cableture. A river runs through it, though not wide enough for a ship… and ships don't go up-mountain, regardless. It floods frequently, and some portions of it are too rocky, clay-covered, and

steep to be inhabited.

THE MAGE'S HANDBOOK OF SPELLS, INVOCATIONS, AND OTHER FLASHY EFFECTS

Order of Love Spells and Invocations
These spells and invocations are used by the Order of Love, and only the Order of Love.

"Know the damned; know thy writhing; know they move."
Spoken in Lythrivol, the language of the damned in the Abyss, this invocation is designed to grant the caster knowledge of a Defiled entity or object's nature and its originating plane of creation or corruption. It doesn't always work, unfortunately.

"Speak Truth and Be Judged."
An invocation often used by Templars or higher rank in the Wardkeeper branch of the Order, this forces a person to speak the truth of a situation as they know it and believe it to be. They can still be wrong, but it is the truth as they understand it.

Order of Love Words
These Words are used to invoke instant effects against a target of the caster's chosing, and are used extensively by Order of Love Paladins, Templars, and Exorcists.

Illuminate
Forces light to coalesce around anything with a dark aura, giving away location – if not necessarily type or intent.

Unmask

Unmask exposes the true nature of a spell, supernatural object/creature, enchantment, or magic-imbued item to the priest that utters the Word. It can be used to quickly identify the general nature of a being or magic, though is typically used to expose magic rather than a third-party spell cast upon physical (or metaphysical) entity.

Eberandia
Forces an entity, object, or other to completely reveal its true nature – regardless of Divine, Neutral, or Fallen affiliation. Similar to Unmask, Eberandia strips away protections granted on or generated by a physical or metaphysical entity rather than a spell or magical effect.

Luminoso/Luminoso-Corsair
Luminoso creates a circle of light around the spellcaster, but invoking the God of Air in addition to the Goddess of Light allows for the light to be projected on a target object or general location at a distance, rather than centered on the caster. Recently, a horrifying rumor suggests that an exorcist of Love invoked the Gods of Hate and Fear both with this Word, not only causing light to erupt, but also to terrify the monster he was hunting...

Invocation: Deadcall
"Oh lost, oh dead, oh soul away from here; my request cannot be denied, my demand cannot be muted, my call cannot be ignored. I command and speak that you speak without command, that you speak with service, and that above all, you speak with truth. You are granted no permissions, no movement, no life, but what is needed to answer that which I ask."

This invocation is part of a larger spell that requires no less than six candles made from spoiled fat, an essence sacrifice, and other consumables of varying quantities, as well as moderate proficiency in Necrosia. It doesn't reanimate a corpse (and specifically prevents it), but it does allow for the body to serve as a window to allow a soul to communicate through from the other side.

Invocation: Hydromancy Manipulation and Manifestation
Hydromancy Invocation
"Essence of Water! Ether born of pregnant clouds and the expanse off-of shores! I summon, I call, I demand! Set thyself into a form I can touch, set yourself into the shell I demand!"

This invocation calls on the material essence of water to be manipulated by magical forces. It is not an invocation asking the God of Water for assistance, rather, an invocation to force magic to respond by the caster's will.

Invocation: Defense of Stone
Stonehewn Invocation
"Invicitum, Invictium, ena'tur, rosad; Ena'tur Manastond, Heknas eh Therond, hesuv tia lodam ches vich kor-kall prothal! Hesuv tia lodam!"

"Invincible, Invincible, eternal soul; Eternal Stone of Power, Inverse of Ether, secure and bury that which has wandered far. Secure and bury!"

This invocation is a request for a defensive ward from the God of Stone and the Unders to bury, control, and seal an object or magic that may do the caster harm.

THE SAGA OF THE DEAD MEN WALKING

Year 512 of the Queen's Rule
The Snowflakes Trilogy
Book I: Snowflakes in Summer
Freshly minted by the Order of Love, a young exorcist is sent to the edge of the Kingdom of Dawnfire to deal with a 'small, simple haunting.' Between a winter that won't end, a girl that doesn't belong, and people being eaten in the woods, only one thing is for sure: he's over his head, and utterly out of luck.

Book II: Dead Men in Winter
As the search for the Coldstone continues, new allies enter the fray in the mountains around Toniki, and in the streets of the City of Mud. But new blood only means new bodies, and Makolichi seeks to provide those in excess...

Book III: Favorite Things
It's time for Usaic's Tower to ascend. Truths will be revealed, blood shall be spilled, and suffering shall become legendary. But it's not just the living who should fear the Coldstone being set loose. For though the dead will rise, the damned had best be ready for Who comes next...

Year 513 of the Queen's Rule
The Auramancer's Exorcism
Book I: Insanity's Respite
Beaten, broken, and battered, Akaran is sent to the Safest City in the Kingdom to recover from his battle against Makolichi, Daringol, Rmucl, and the rest. What he expects is peace and time to heal. What he finds instead is that insanity knows no bounds and offers no respite...

Book II: Insanity's Rapture
In life, the woman in his dreams had been a spy – a murderess, a liar, a fraud, and a thief. Sentenced to burn for her crimes, her screams have haunted his sleep since the moment she was set aflame. As both the city and Akaran's mind descend into chaos, only insanity offers rapture.

Book III: Insanity's Reckoning (May 2021)
The most dangerous man in the city is about to get his magic back – and he's got a murder on his mind. As he prepares to hunt a sadistic vampire, his past is about to come back to haunt him in a way he never could have imagined.

Book IV: Insanity's Requiem (Summer 2021)
It's time for the madness to end, but the insane have no desire to find peace –

and peace will only come when Basion City is turned into an open grave.

Origins of the Dead Men Walking
Year 510 of the Queen's Rule
Blind shot (Release date: TBA)
A self-professed Merchant of Secrets enlists the help of the Northern Hunter's Guild to trek to the Cursed Continent of Agromah to recover a relic lost to time. In this land of the dead, what chance does a blind man have against a demon king?

Year 512 of the Queen's Rule
Slag Harbor (An Interruption in the Snowflakes Trilogy)
After battling Makolichi in Gonta – and before facing him down for the final time in Toniki – Akaran decides to leave Private Galagrin behind in the City of Mud to make sure that nothing got missed in his sweep. What he finds is more than just stray shiriak; it's an answer to an unasked question...

Year 513 of the Queen's Rule
Lady Claw I: Claw Unsheathed
Who's to blame when a young girl is accused of murder? Did she do it, or did her father? And when she's cornered and the claws come out... does it matter?

Year 516 of the Queen's Rule
Fearmonger
Years after Toniki, a grizzled Akaran serves as a peacekeeper to the Queen – and nothing wants the peace to be kept.

Year 517 of the Queen's Rule
Blindsided
Stannoth and Elrok couldn't be any more different. Trained mercenaries in the Hunter's Guild, they absolutely hate each other – but they don't have a choice but to work together.

WELCOME TO A WORLD WHERE GOOD THINGS HAPPEN TO BAD PEOPLE,
AND THE GOOD PEOPLE ARE QUESTIONABLE…
…AT BEST.

Good things come to those who wait, but I'm impatient as the fires in the Abyss are hot (or cold, depending on Frosel). I'm working on the next book as fast as I can (I promise!) and I've got some stuff for you.

Please be sure to follow me on social media to find out where I'm going, what I'm doing, how I'm doing it, and the occasional stupid meme just to laugh. Plus, get some random business insights on the self-published side of the coin AND see what I'm doing when I dress up for charity purposes, too!

There's a newsletter you can sign up for!

You can expect free stories, character information, special promotions, extra information about the World of the Saga, and more! Be sure to visit and subscribe (it'd mean a lot to me if you did)!

Amazon.com:
https://www.amazon.com/author/sdmw

Facebook.com:
https://www.facebook.com/sagadmw

Website:
http://www.sagadmw.com

Twitter:
https://www.twitter.com/sagadmw

Instagram:
https://www.twitter.com/sagadmw

Dead Men Emailing Newsletter
http://www.sagadmw.com/email.html

ALSO!
Please don't forget to leave a review. Your opinion on the story (and the series!) MATTERS. Loved it or hated it, thought it was amazing or thought it was garbage, your feedback helps me be a better author and helps me provide the best experience that I can for not just you, but other readers in the future. Let me know on any media platform – just be sure to tag me if you can, but a review anywhere is awesome!

www.ingramcontent.com/pod-product-compliance
Lightning Source LLC
Chambersburg PA
CBHW060951120726
47910CB00002B/592